FREE TO LIVE

TRACEY JERALD

xoxo,
Tracey
Jerald

FREE TO LIVE

Copyright © 2019 by Tracey Jerald

ISBN: 978-1-7330861-0-3 (eBook)

ISBN: 978-1-7330861-1-0 (Paperback)

Editor: One Love Editing (http://oneloveediting.com)

Proof Edits: Holly Malgeri (https://www.facebook.com/HollysRedHotReviews/)

Cover Design: Amy Queau – QDesign (https://www.qcoverdesign.com)

To Mrs. P. and Mrs. V.

One of you encouraged my love of reading; the other my love of history.
And both of you just simply loved me.
Without each of you in my life, I don't know if I'd be the same woman I am today.
From the bottom of my heart, thank you.

THE LEGEND OF AMARYLLIS

There are variations regarding the legend of how amaryllis flowers came to be. Generally, the tale is told like this:

Amaryllis, a shy nymph, fell deeply in love with Alteo, a shepherd with great strength and beauty, but her love was not returned. He was too obsessed with his gardens to pay much attention to her.

Amaryllis hoped to win Alteo over by giving him the one thing he wanted most, a flower so unique it had never existed in the world before. She sought advice from the oracle Delphi and carefully followed his instructions. She dressed in white, and for thirty nights, appeared on Alteo's doorstep, piercing her heart with a golden arrow.

When Alteo finally opened his eyes to what was before him, he saw only a striking crimson flower that sprung from the blood of Amaryllis's heart.

It's not surprising the amaryllis has come to be the symbol of pride, determination, and radiant beauty. What's also not surprising is somehow, someway, we all bleed a little bit while we're falling in love.

PROLOGUE

HOLLY

Death.

I'm not afraid of it. Not anymore.

Not after the life I've been forced to endure.

I never realized how much my mother sheltered me when I was little until she wasn't there any longer. Now, I miss her occasional lucidness. It's hard to admit that I don't fault her for being so high in order to take all those random bastards into her bed.

She did it for me.

And she did it to protect me from him.

From the earliest moment I could comprehend, my mother warned me over and over about respecting my father's gun. It wasn't a toy like the kids at school might have to play with. He used it for something else; I didn't want to know what.

All it took was the sound of it firing and my mother's accompanying screams waking me from a dead slumber when I was around four? Five? My father yelling, "Now git, you varmint! You'll get your money when I have it, not a second more." I shiver in fear as I heard him repeatedly slap my mother, loud cracks that could be heard reverberating throughout the thin walls of our shoddy trailer that even in her drug-induced haze, she still tries to make a home for me.

Curled in the farthest corner of my room, I wet myself in fear, drenching my hole-ridden blanket. But I'm not ever to leave my room no matter the reason after six at night. All it took was the one time for Papa's hands to crack across my face, slamming me into the wall, to teach me that lesson. Helpless, tears course down my face as I listen to his brutality and her screams until I drift off, still frightened but too exhausted to stay awake any more. My heart and mind collapsed from the stress of blocking out the sounds coming from my parents' room.

The next morning, Mama didn't come out of her room. Papa said to get my own breakfast while he went out on the porch for some smokes and to make a few calls. Soon, I was picked up for school by his sister.

By the time I left, Mama still hadn't woken up. No matter what, she always waved from the window. I stood by Aunt Sheilia's car waiting until she impatiently snapped, "Let's go, brat." I know something is wrong, but I also know better than to ask.

By the time I get home, a strange woman is in the room kissing Papa. My lips began to tremble, and a funny feeling crawls up in my belly. I hate her on sight. "Papa?" My fingers tangle up in each other anxiously.

"Noelle, come here," my father barks sharply. I scramble across the room to do as he demands. "This is Maria. She lives here now. You will listen to everything she says as if I ordered it. Is that clear?"

The woman next to him offers me a bitter smile but doesn't say a word.

"Where's..." I stop myself from asking.

My father reaches out and grabs my thin arm. Even as he jerks it, I know the pressure he applied would leave bruises. It wasn't the first time. "Your mother is gone, Noelle. Maria will be staying with us from now on. Do you understand?"

My head lowers, I nod. My red hair flops forward in braids from the day before. Because Mama often asked me to take care of her since she had so many cuts and bruises on her arms, her legs, and face, it was a labor of love for her to braid my hair. I left them in for days before my head began to itch so badly I'd have to wash my hair.

Sparing a glance at the cold, dark-haired woman in front of me, I wondered who was going to do my braids? Who was going to make me banana pudding on my birthday? This woman? My lips began to tremble before I firmed them up. Papa released me with a jerk.

I slowly backed away before his voice lashed out as hard as a slap. "Noelle?"

I freeze in place.

"Your other rules still apply. In your bedroom by six; don't come out before seven in the mornin' no matter the reason. Ya hear?"

"Yes Papa," I whisper. Turning, I run to my room and slam the door to the dark laughter behind me before the first tear falls.

Mama's gone. She wasn't coming back, and there wasn't any way to get to her.

How was I going to survive?

~

"TOMORROW, I'M TELLIN' ya, Ria. That bitch has got to earn her keep around here. You were younger than she was when you started spreadin' those legs to take your first man."

A dark laugh accompanies my stepmother's words. "It'll be nice to not have to be the one doin' all the work 'round here. She might be needin' some trainin' though."

"Did you have any trainin'?" my father demands.

"No, but if you're tryin' to keep the police chief happy. After all, he's wanted her for a long time..." The police chief? Oh, God. Desperation starts to seep into my soul. And what kind of training do they mean?

"Boyd can do whatever he wants to do in whatever hole he wants so long as I get paid and he looks the other way," my father says stoutly. "You'll just have to fix 'er up if she can't take it."

"That's fine, baby. I don't want your best customer complainin' is all. I'm just used to how rough he can get," she purrs.

"Don't care if Noelle's bleedin' or not. That girl's cost me good money over the years. She takes Boyd as her first customer tomorrow night or I'll find some other way to deal with her," my father tells Maria.

"Fine," she agrees.

"I'll go let him know." There're footsteps before the front door opens and closes.

It's eight p.m. I have less than twenty-four hours to figure out how to escape. Obviously, I can't go to the police, who were my last hope. Shouldn't I be able to go to them? But I guess a girl like me isn't worthy of being saved.

Or loved.

Footsteps approaching my door taunt me. I scuttle to the corner in fear. "Better enjoy your last night of sleep, little girl. It all ends tomorrow." As she walks back down the corner, Maria's vicious laugh comes through the door.

I wish I could feel pain so I could feel fear, but I've lived with both for so long, I'm numb. I'm numb to everything.

Even life.

Reaching up, I feel the braid in my hair and it hits me. Like my Mama, I can be free. I can escape.

Permanently.

There's nothing I can do tonight, but tomorrow. I look out the window and see the moon reflect over the swamp in the back of the trailer.

I'll never see the moon rise from this room again.

I SNEAK home during the middle of the school day knowing my father will be passed out drunk or high, Maria the same. All I need to do is get my hands on his .22. The gun is always kept loaded. A warning and a blessing.

At least right now it is.

As I expected, he's on the couch in the family room. I mentally gag at the irony—some family. I slip into their room; Maria lies on top of the bed still naked from taking another man for my father. Some man's cum is drying on the inside of her thighs. I slow my movements; the beat of my heart evens out. I carefully open his nightstand, and it lies on top for me, the flat, matte metal.

Lifting his gun, I'm surprised it weighs more in my hands than I guessed it would. Ruthlessly, I push that thought out of my mind. It doesn't matter what it feels like in my hands.

Soon I'll feel nothing.

One shot will do.

Then all the fear, all my torment, will be over.

I close the drawer harder than I intended. My eyes fly over to the bed, but Maria is still out. The breath rushes out of me. Resolutely, I walk through the still-open door of their bedroom. I pass the couch where my father lies with one leg hanging off, years of waste showing in his gaunt face and in the gut that hangs over his pants even in slumber. If it weren't for my thick red hair, I'd wonder if my poor mother wasn't knocked up by some john he forced her to take in her short life.

Moving into my bedroom, I wonder if I should leave a note. I have a few people I might call friends at school, but ultimately I'm nothing special. Life will continue to revolve in much the same manner after I'm gone.

It says a lot when I feel no heartache because I know if I live another day, the avalanche of pain will outweigh the nominal amount of pleasure I find in life.

Enough! my mind screams. *Just do it!* Fumbling, I cock the gun the way I've seen my father do before. Heart hammering, I turn it so I'm staring down into the hypnotizing depth of the obsidian barrel.

Nothing and everything waits for me on the other side. I start to squeeze the trigger, but my hand is shoved away.

God, why can't I just escape this nightmare? I turn and Maria's furious eyes meet mine.

"You think it's that easy to escape?" Her bitter laugh is loud and bounces off the walls of my small room. "There is no out. Just accept this is your life."

I don't want life. I just want death. I jerk the gun back and try to take aim at my head again.

There's a hard struggle between us before the gun goes off. The scent after the chamber ejects is almost identical to the moment when a wood match has been blown out—acrid, bitter. It taints the air around it before it dissipates into the air, leaving behind a flickering flame.

I look down, expecting to see my own blood. But it's not mine.

It's Maria's.

The burn in my chest is equal to the one I feel in my eyes, hot and unrelenting.

YEARS LATER, I don't regret pulling the trigger. I know I would do it again, live through what I had to after, if it would lead me to where I am right now.

Alive.

Living as Holly Freeman.

1

HOLLY

People spend so much time primping for pictures by brushing their hair, adding more makeup, arranging themselves, when in reality a perfect photo has nothing to do with any of that. It has to do with the expression on their face. That moment I capture their joy, their tears, the bittersweet longing, and their laughter. Sometimes, I manage to get it all in one shot if I time it just right.

All it takes is one perfect shot to change a life.

It's not just my job to look through a lens to take pictures that will be printed or shared digitally; it's a need that burns inside of me. I want people always to have a connection to that pivotal moment when I need to press my finger down on the shutter. That somehow, I'll be able to transport them back to that instant where their feelings are on display.

I use my skills with a camera to give people a gateway to talk about their memories.

It's a beautiful feeling to know I've captured something timeless. I have this eternal hope the moments I hand over will somehow help each couple to make it to their first anniversary, their fifth, their fiftieth. And when they pull out their photo album, they may not remember my name, but perhaps will remember how they felt in that nanosecond when their lips brushed or when their eyes met.

Using a critical eye, I make a copy of the photo I'm editing in my home office. There's a longing on the groom's face I know the bride will melt over. He'd just finished swinging her out and back during their first dance. Instead of capturing her right hand with his left, he reached for her left and brought it to his lips.

Zooming in, there's a combination of shock, awe, and such a deep hunger in his gaze as his lips touch his new wife's fingers gently above the ring he slid on just a few hours earlier. I smile in satisfaction. These are the shots I strive for when I have my camera in my hand. It's not about taking a pretty picture, it's capturing real ones. Art should make you have an emotion. It should evoke something in your senses, whether that's beauty or pain. It shouldn't be passive. My photos are about making sure I twist the soul of the person viewing them.

Saving the file in both color and black and white, I smirk to myself. I wonder how many times over the lifetime of their marriage this image will stop a fight in its tracks or bring a new life into the world. Because if a man ever looked at me this way... I fan myself. Damn.

Uploading the files to my cloud drive at Amaryllis Events, my family's wedding- and event-planning business, I stretch. Hearing the small cracks up and down my spine, I realize I've been at the computer for way too long. I need a break.

I push away from my desk in my open loft area and make my way toward the stairs around the massive stone fireplace that dominates both the first and second floors of the home I built years ago. Before descending, I pause, admiring the space I created for myself, the smallest house on the property my siblings and I all live on. When we bought the farm almost thirteen years ago, the deal Ali struck with the town of Collyer was that we would build our homes on the foundations that already existed. Even though my foundation is by no means small, I turned a large part of it into an outdoor patio. Since it's just me, I don't need a huge house to maintain. Three bedrooms and a loft are more than ample space.

My oldest sister, Cassidy, looked at the plans I drew up with our contractor in consternation. "Don't you want something bigger for when you have a family, Holly?"

Even though I knew back then I was too tainted by what I had done to entertain the idea of a husband and children, I calmed her objections. "Look, Cass, the side wall has nothing major running through it. If I ever have the need to add on, I'll be able to simply by giving up the patio space. For now, this is perfect."

So even as my brother and sisters began to build their dream homes, which accommodate their now expanding families, I created my rustic retreat which is absolutely stunning. As I glide down the stairs, bright light filters in through the cathedral-style windows, bouncing off the numerous frames gracing every available surface. Of course, I decorated every available space in the pictures I've taken from the first time I was ever given a camera.

I've found there's no better way than to comfort myself than with the people I love who have accepted me for who and what I am.

There are photos of my family from the time we briefly lived in a run-down trailer in Charleston and from when we first moved to Collyer, bunking down in the building that now exclusively holds the office of Amaryllis Events. There are photos of me, Ali, and Corinna at college together in our tiny apartment, learning not only about our chosen courses but how to live again as people after what we survived together. As I wander through my memories on my way toward the kitchen, my eye lands on a picture I managed to capture of Phil tossing Corinna into Candlewood Lake—the very day he met his husband, Jason. Picking it up, I shake my head. It's so long ago now, it's incredible how we've all come so far. Setting the frame back down, I reach for the next one, taken at Phil and Jason's wedding day about eight years ago. They were both so handsome, so in love. They still are. I smile looking at the rest of my sisters and me crowded around them. We all look so young, I muse. And yet so scared of the unknown.

Putting it back, my fingers glance over a frame of Cassidy and Caleb dancing so intimately on their wedding day; one of his hands is wrapped around her neck, pulling her close, the other pressed against her stomach. Moments earlier, she had just told him she was pregnant. There wasn't a dry eye in any of the photos I took, including my own.

Next is an image of Ali proposing to Keene right before their wedding at Daniela Trattoria in New York City. She's sitting in Keene's lap, and her dazzling smile is only overshadowed by the love radiating from Keene's darkly handsome face. I managed to capture him sliding her engagement ring on her finger. They'd both gone to the restaurant that night with the same idea: to make sure neither of them could ever run from the other ever again. It was to all of our delight when Ali took things one step further and told Keene she'd arranged for them to get married that night.

Grinning, I look down at the picture of the box being tossed midair by Colby from center stage of the Brendan Blake concert as he proposed to Corinna. Having survived long years where they were both in love with each other and refused to admit it, Colby went big in his proposal. My lips tilt as I stare down at the enraptured look on Corinna's face. I guess proposing to the woman you love in front of 21,000 people in Madison Square Garden certainly qualifies as go big or go home.

Their wedding this upcoming summer has been three years in the making. Neither of them has been in any hurry. Privately, Corinna told me that Colby wanted his grandfather, Senator Zachary Hunt from the state of Virginia, to be out of office so it didn't turn into a media circus. While we all appreciate receiving notoriety for the work we do, we treasure our privacy. Zachary, who had already been planning on retiring after his sixth term in the Senate, agreed wholeheartedly. Now, he's looking forward to walking Corinna down the aisle to the grandson he reconciled with after many years of a family misunderstanding.

Finally, I pick up the picture of Em and her fiancé, Jake Madison, I took during the night of her Fashion Week debut over a year ago.

When Em needed time away to find her artist's spirit after ending her engagement to another man, she met and fell in love with Jake, whom we all adore. Now. Their relationship was a beautiful tempest and filled with so much tragedy, it almost didn't make it. I shudder to imagine what Em would be like now if she didn't have the strength she had to forgive and to believe in not only Jake but herself.

Every time I look at those photographs, I'm reminded we're no longer broken. We're no longer frightened. We're no longer in jeopardy of losing our lives to the monsters of our past. As for me, I've accepted I'll never know that true contentment because having my own home and family just isn't for someone with the burdens I carry. But seeing the others happy is enough, I remind myself.

I'm startled from my thoughts when my cell rings in my pocket. Reaching back, I pull it out and catch the display. Ali. "Hey." I put Em's photo down and stride into the kitchen. I had been headed there to get a snack before I went back to work upstairs. "What's going on?"

"Just had a doctor's appointment."

I frown. "Anything wrong?" I demand. Ali's the most in shape of all of us, so my sister antenna goes on immediate alert.

"Nothing for you to worry about," she says breezily. I let out a sigh of relief. Life has been calm for a while. It's been nice settling into a routine of work, family, and no drama.

"Then what's up?" Reaching into my fridge, I snag a bottle of water and a jar of salsa before dumping them on the counter. I immediately begin searching for tortilla chips in my cupboard. Ripping open the bag, I unceremoniously dunk the chip into the jar.

"Can you come into the office early tomorrow? I want to talk with you about staffing the photography department." Ali is our corporate lawyer and chief financial officer.

Even as I'm about to pop the first salsa-laden chip in my mouth, I burst out laughing. "You mean the team of me, myself, and I are having some scheduling issues?" My voice is filled with mirth.

"I know you've tried to teach me about photos being in thirds, but

I don't think you've managed to actually split yourself into thirds, baby," Ali rebukes gently. "You're working way too many hours."

"No more than the rest of you," I remind her, even though I know that's a lie. I'm not married, not engaged, and I'm not dating anyone seriously. I don't see the problem of helping pick up the slack while I give back the best gift I can to the family of my heart.

Time.

"Considering Cass just called me to tell me you were uploading files to the completed cloud file on your day off—which if I hadn't called I suspect you wouldn't have clocked the time—I call shenanigans," Ali retorts.

"You know, the new computer system you installed was supposed to keep an eye on Phil, not on the rest of us," I drawl.

Ali just laughs.

I'm only partially kidding. Our brother, in addition to being a genius with flowers, is responsible for the intake of all new clients. He has a remarkable tendency to overbook all of us and then forget to tell us about his scheduling mishaps. It took years, but Ali finally found a way to put him on an electronic leash. Unfortunately, it also allows her to see when we're all working extra hours except for Corinna, who flatly refuses to have anything more than a telephone in her kitchen for fear of electrocuting herself. But since Ali can track her day-to-day activities based on the food ordering and delivery schedule, she's pretty confident she has us all under control.

Shoving another chip in my mouth, I give in as I chomp around it. "Fine. What time do you want me in the office?"

"Can you be in around 8:30? I have a meeting with Cassidy around 9."

I think. If I get in around eight, then I can snag coffee first. "Deal."

"Perfect. See you in the morning. Love you."

"Love you too, Ali. Kiss Keene and Kalie for me," I instruct her. Kalie is Keene and Ali's three-and-a-half-year-old daughter.

"Always do," she assures me, right before she disconnects.

Shoving another chip in my mouth, I chomp down while I mull over Ali's concern. It's not easy to just bring on a new team member to be a part of our family-owned business. We have interns, but they all eventually leave to move on to other positions. A number of my photography interns have moved into companies that specialize in graphic design, website development, internet startups—things like that. Being a professional photographer is so much more than just taking pictures; it's meeting with clients, being at events, taking the photos, and doing all the touch-ups. Keeping up with the technology trends alone keeps me working well past my scheduled hours.

Would I like to have some more personal time? Sure. Who wouldn't? But what would I do if I had it?

That's both my reward and my punishment. Because even as I'm thrilled for the love my family has found, I know I'll never have it for myself. Instead, I lose myself in my art to experience down to my soul what I will never be able to otherwise: lifelong happiness and a forever kind of love.

After all, who wants a woman with blood staining her hands for eternity?

2

HOLLY

"I really don't know how you're going to handle the amount of new business we're signing for this year unless you hire someone full-time, Holly." Ali shoots me a concerned look. We're in her office before the workday at Amaryllis Events officially begins. Cassidy, Emily, and Corinna are making a quick coffee run while Phil's on the phone with a client who wants to make changes to their flower arrangements. Ali and I have been debating the merits of hiring a full-time photographer for me in addition to the interns I bring on as the job demands it. Lately, it seems like I'm needing their help more and more.

"You know why I haven't." I gnaw at my lower lip. "Every time I audition a new photographer, the families just aren't happy with the photographs."

"I know," she sighs. "I've heard the complaints."

"If I hadn't been there taking photos behind the scenes, we could have taken some serious hits to our reputation with that kind of feedback."

Ali taps her nails against her desk in frustration. "I thought you were crazy putting your own interns through a trial-by-fire like that. And then when I saw some of the photos? They were amateurish. It's like they didn't know what end of the camera was up without you there."

"And let's not mention the situation where..."

Ali visibly shudders. "I still can't believe he took off with the maid of honor during the reception. I mean, seriously? First, he had a girl-friend whom we'd met, and second, he was working. Thank God you were there doing one of your crazy interviews."

I shake my head. "If I wasn't, I guarantee you it wouldn't have been just a breakup scene downstairs we'd have had to endure. I guarantee we would have had the mother of the bride demanding a full refund for not capturing all of the special moments of her daughter's wedding."

"I was happy to defend the termination of his internship, draft your letter indicating why you would not sign off on his coursework, and defend to RIT why we stood behind this even if it meant their not presenting him for graduation."

"And you wonder why it's so hard to find someone to hire?" I scoff.

"I'm just pointing out the fact you're looking at the same situation Cori was a few years ago, sister. Your services are becoming more and more in demand. And not just for weddings. Look at this schedule." Ali spins her monitor around. As much as I want to be blasé about it, I'm a little taken aback by the amount of time my name is popping up on the schedule. "Even if you do the events and bring in someone for the editing, won't that help?"

I tap a finger against my chin. "I'm going to have to do at least that. Jesus. When did I suddenly become so popular?"

She grins. "I took advice from Jenna," she says, naming Emily's future stepdaughter, who is a sophomore at UConn and a marketing savant.

I roll my eyes. "Of course you did."

"Some of our interns," she says haughtily, "don't need to be vetted like they're escapees from the local prison."

"That's because some of our interns are members of our family— or soon will be. While your daughter has shown an incredible interest in photography for being three, I really don't think I can send her out on any of my shoots," I retort.

Ali throws me a dazzling smile. "It's super cute, isn't it?"

I grin back at her. "Totally. Think Keene will get pissed if I give her a camera for her birthday?"

"Meh. He'll be fine. Especially since he'll be too busy wondering if this new baby is a boy or a girl," Ali pats her stomach even as she drops a bomb as casually as if she just told me she bought a new pair of Jimmy Choos.

"What?" I screech at my older sister so loudly, I'm unsurprised when I hear footsteps in the hall.

"I can't believe I'm about to say this and not Cass, but what on earth is wrong with you two? People are working in this building. Namely, me." Phil stands fuming in the door.

I point at a very smug Ali. "I...she..." I can't even form a sentence. I can barely catch my breath.

"Yes?" Phil leans against the jamb. It's not more than a second later before Cassidy, Corinna, and Em all stroll up behind him. Em's sipping her drink, even as she hands Phil his. Cassidy gives me mine. I take a large gulp as I try to gather my bearings, wondering if Ali's going to share with the rest of the family.

"Here." Corinna hands Ali her drink. Ali inhales and is about to take a sip when I yell out, "You can't have that!"

Everyone's heads turn toward me. "Why not?" Cassidy asks curiously.

Ali's laughter bounces off the walls of the room. Standing up with her drink in her hand, she gives me an arrogant smirk that rivals those her husband is notorious for.

"You just got through telling me you're pregnant and you're drinking coffee? I don't think so, sister." I stand up and snatch the cup out of her hands. The room gets eerily quiet for a heartbeat. I turn just in time to see Em's drink come dribbling out of her mouth as she tries to speak. She wipes her mouth on the shoulder of Phil's shirt. Instead of being followed by cursing, he's in shock, whispering, "Ali? Is it true?" Corinna's dancing while trying not to drop her cup.

Cassidy is crying as she shoves her way into the room to throw herself into Ali's embrace, and I realize it's perfect. How Ali told us is just perfect. Instead of accusatory, I'm beaming when I say, "You planned it this way," remembering her phone call yesterday. She had likely just come from the doctor confirming her pregnancy.

My sneaky, brilliant, pregnant sister.

"Of course I did." She's wiping tears which are flowing copiously down her cheeks. She hugs Cass one more time before stepping back. "I didn't get to tell you all the first time I found out I was pregnant, so I wanted to memorize your faces when I knew the second. And I didn't want a damn camera blocking yours," she teases.

I take her ribbing in good spirit because if she told me at any other time, she wouldn't be wrong. I'm so used to having my camera in my hand, it's like an appendage to my body. When we're all together, even if it's just for lunch, my camera is there even for the everyday moments. From work to anger, to hysterical laughter, I've got them all.

And for once, I'm glad I don't have the camera in my hand so I could give my sister her moment just the way she'll always want to remember it.

IN MY OFFICE later that same day after much celebrating and swearing to Ali we won't tell Keene, I lean back in my chair. Just like at my home, the walls are covered in black-and-white photos of my family. Where on earth am I going to find room for pictures of a new baby? There's no question about finding a place in my heart; I already have a new space reserved exclusively for Ali and Keene's little one, a niece or nephew not of my blood but absolutely of my heart and soul.

It's hard to imagine I've been with my siblings longer now than I've been without them. My life after my mother was killed by my father was a blur. When I was young, I hid in my room even when it wasn't time for me to be locked in for the night. I never knew life was any different for any of the other students until one day, Masie—a girl in my class whose name I'll never forget—came to school showing pictures from her family's campout. It wasn't anything extravagant, just a bunch of ratty tents in her backyard. But her family was smiling. Laughing.

And I knew what I had at home was just wrong.

I didn't know until then.

That was when the dreams of leaving began. And that's when my punishments started. After I was old enough to begin dreaming about running away—I think I was nine—I became obsessed with the idea. I tried to squirrel away some of the money I made on the paper route my father forced me to take. Rubbing my hand along my jaw, I remember when he found the small stack of ones—maybe amounting to twenty dollars—and backhanded me across the room.

It was then I realized I could dream of escape through pictures.

The library at school was free, and I checked out every book I could, even ones I wasn't interested in reading. I wanted to live through the images I saw on the pages—just like I did through Masie's pictures. In the hours when I could hear the screaming and the moaning, I'd shove tissues in my ears to focus on the images of the whales beneath the water or the lighthouses on the islands. I'd dream about being able to visit the mountains or swim in a lake, not just smell the wretched swamp behind our trailer. If I could only escape.

I was twelve the next time I tried to leave. I shudder remembering the feel of both Maria and my father's feet kicking me. Screaming, I finally told them where the hundred dollars I'd managed to save from my now two paper routes was hidden. My father spit on my face as he stalked away.

Maria leaned close to my ear and whispered, "This pain is nothing in comparison to what you'll have to endure soon 'nough. Get used to it," before standing.

I crawled into my room and cried silent tears. That night, I knew even the pictures would be unable to save me. Not then at least.

It wouldn't be until years later after Ali, Corinna, and I were rescued that I managed to get my first digital camera. Phil noticed the amount of books I was checking out of the library and returning just as fast. "Jesus, do I have two geniuses on my hands?" he griped.

"No," I said with as much dignity as I could. Ali was an actual genius, a college graduate even though she was barely sixteen years old. "I study the pictures. I'm..." I don't know how to say it. "Absorbed by them? I feel like I find a part of myself in them. Gah! That makes no sense." I was so frustrated I couldn't express myself.

"You need a digital camera."

"We need food and money for the electric bill, Phil," I retorted. "I can't afford the kind of cameras that are mentioned in these magazines."

He made a noncommittal sound. It was less than a week later when a small, dated point-and-click camera with nominal settings ended up on my pillow with a note. "My boss said it works. I'll work some overtime to pay for it. He was going to put it in his yard sale. Now, go take some pictures."

My legs collapsed beneath me as I began to sob. I couldn't even go find Phil to thank him because he was working for free to pay for my gift.

I began to purge out the feelings I had boiling inside of me through a shutter and a viewfinder. I'd wander down the waterfront in Charleston for hours. To me, my pictures were immature and plain. I'd frown in disgust at what I'd see every night on the little back square, but what I didn't realize was I was unearthing my soul one frame at a time.

When Ali wasn't catching me and Corinna up on school lessons so we could be re-enrolled in public school when we moved to Connecticut, I'd be wandering or at the library looking up photography. I absorbed the knowledge like a sponge. I learned about aperture, burst mode, and exposure. I began to offer to mow lawns for our neighbors so I could save money for a used computer to convert my files into JPGs and maybe learn how to edit them. And then one day I finally put together why all my pictures looked so light—my camera was exposing too much light. I began to play with the ISO function and a whole new world opened up to me.

My siblings gave me a family, but Phil opened up the world.

Tipping back in my chair, memories of my first real camera come to mind. I saved up enough to buy a beautiful Nikon by the time I enrolled at UConn. I turn my head to the side and smile. It sits on a shelf near my desk. It still works beautifully. Its gleaming black case is still dusted carefully every week with a special cloth. I only take it with me for special occasions.

But right next to it is the point-and-click that Phil bought for me.

They say that pictures are a window to your soul. For me, they're what saved mine. The path I traveled, the images burned in my brain from the life I left before, are there for eternity.

It's been seventeen years since I pulled that trigger. It's been a little less time than that since Ali, Corinna, and I were recovered from one of the most extensive human trafficking operations across the United States. Just shy of sixteen and a half years since I was formally absolved of killing Maria by the benevolence of the South Carolina District Attorney and many others. Shortly after that, as we were being sheltered for protection in a battered women and children's shelter, we met Phil, Cassidy, and Em, all of whom had been through their own traumas yet had formed their own little family to survive. Sixteen years ago—the very minute I could do it legally as an employed emancipated minor—I left South Carolina and my life as Noelle Greene behind and became Holly Freeman, a quiet young woman who had an interest in photography and business.

I studied hard in the first few years we were in Connecticut to have a strong GPA so I could go to UConn with my sisters; Ali vying to go to its law school while Corinna and I were trying to enter as undergrads. The days we received our acceptance letters were some of the best of our lives, bar none.

Due to what we had endured, Phil petitioned UConn to let us all live together off campus. When they first protested because Corinna and I were freshmen, he drove up to the school with his then boyfriend—now husband—Dr. Jason Ross. Hours later, they came back pleased to announce we would all be living in a tiny off-campus apartment they secured the lease on. Nothing was ever mentioned about what they did, but I strongly suspect my now brother-in-law had a few words to say to the housing authority about our recent trauma.

When Ali demanded to know what happened, Jason skewered her with a look. Phil murmured, "Nothing. Just let it drop." So we did. And for the next three years, Ali, Corinna, and I lived in relative harmony. It was a little lonely for me and Corinna after Ali moved back to Collyer, but we only had a year to go until our own graduation day.

Then the real work began.

When we came home on breaks, I began to notice a considerable change in the office. It wasn't just Cassidy who had plans; all of the older siblings had them. Amaryllis Events was busier than ever. There was hardly a down weekend. And things got even hairier when Ali noticed the photographer they were contracting work to was overcharging clients and pocketing the money. She found the disparity because one of the clients scanned a copy of her photography contract over to Ali because she was missing the rights and clearances paperwork and was hoping Ali had a copy of it. The numbers that the client signed off on were 25 percent higher than the contract we had in our files.

We were at war with Ali leading the charge. Not only did we have to prove the photographer was stealing from our clients, but there was no way we were ever going to use him ever again. I clearly remember Cassidy looking at me and saying, "Hols, it's time for you to step up."

And like the others, I did.

The first full wedding I shot was for close to three hundred guests. I was twenty-two years old. While today I might look back and cringe at some of the photos I took because of how my work has matured, each year the couple still comes to me to have their pictures taken.

It was Ava and Matt's wedding.

Every year since their wedding, I've refused to take money from the people who have essentially become extended members of the

Freeman family. And each year, I have to insist they take whatever they would pay me and donate it to their charity of the month at The Coffee Shop.

Because how do you thank people for giving you a chance to live your dream when you don't really deserve it?

After that first assignment, I overcame my final self-doubt I wasn't ready to take my rightful place at Amaryllis Events. I became as driven as the rest of my family to make a success of our business. And over the years, I began to understand life wasn't going to be ripped away from me. I could have this life, this family, and be as happy as I could be.

No one was coming to take it from me. Not anymore.

Leaning forward, I start clicking through my computer. *Enough about the past. No good comes from spending too much time lingering on it. Think about how to visualize your today, Holly.*

And right now, I smile broadly, wondering about how Ali's going to break the news to Keene that she's pregnant again.

3

HOLLY

"Any word on when Ali plans to tell Keene?" I'm on the phone with Corinna as I drive into the center of town two days later.

"No. She and Keene have a parent-teacher conference for Kalie this week she's been ranting about. Something about the teacher is always hitting on Keene in front of her." Corinna's voice, a honeyed Southern drawl, peals with laughter. "Our sister is a barracuda on most days. Pregnant and another woman hitting on her man? This should be interesting for the family dinner."

"You think she'll hold out that long?" I navigate the windy roads of Collyer as I look for a spot near Shimmer, our favorite hair salon.

"I don't know. I mean, it's not Ali I worry about saying anything to Keene..." Corinna's voice trails off.

"I agree. It's Phil."

"Right? Who was it whoever said women can't keep secrets? They obviously have never spent any time with big brother."

I laugh.

"It's true, Hols. I mean, come on. I can't even ask him to come to see the dress we chose for my wedding because you know he'll open his mouth and blab something about it to Colby. If he didn't need to know the color and material for the flowers, I wouldn't have even had Em give him a sample of the material. "

I manage to find a spot near Shimmer. "You are not wrong," I mutter. "Has he asked about it?"

"Asked about it? I swear to God if I am asked by big brother one more time about it..." Corinna leaves off her implied threat of bodily harm. But it gives me an idea.

"So, show him a dress," I say impishly.

"Say what?"

"Show. Him. A. Dress," I repeat. "It doesn't have to be..."

Suddenly, Cori understands. "It doesn't have to be the actual one I'm wearing. Oh, Hols. You're a genius."

"You know, if you find a hideous one, we could make a bet on how badly he reacts to it."

Corinna's howling laughter must have her doubled over as I can hear her pounding the worktable in her kitchen. "Yes," she gasps out. "I've got to get the others in on this."

I slide my sunglasses to the top of my head after I park the car. I mimic Phil's deep voice. "Laura could have designed this." I refer to Cassidy and Caleb's almost-four-year-old daughter.

"It looks like your college toga," Corinna tosses back at me.

"There's no cleavage. You have a rack, for God's sake," I counter.

"Hold on, I'm writing these down." I hear the mad scribbling as I slide out of my car and walk the half a block to Shimmer. "It looks too much like Cassidy's dress," Corinna volleys back.

I stop walking. "I think that one should be interchangeable. Since both Ali and Cass got married ahead of you and everyone knows what Em's wearing for her wedding since she's shown us a million drawings already."

"True. I feel like this should be a bingo board or something where each of us has to buy in."

"The only way that happens is if you put 'Listen, missy, you cannot get married in jeans and a tank' in the center as the free space." Corinna's uncontrollable laughter is ringing in my ear as I walk into Shimmer. "Hey, Gail," I call out.

Gail waves at me before turning back to cut the hair of the cutest little girl I have ever seen outside of my family. With black ringlets and huge blue eyes, the little princess is perched on a booster seat so Gail can reach her more easily. "I'd better let you go, Cori," I murmur.

"'Kay. Give my love to Gail. In the meanwhile, I think I'll float this list to Em and see what she can add."

"Lord have mercy, we're going straight to hell."

"Always knew that. We just have to have spots next to each other," she chirps. "Love you."

"Love you too." I disconnect the call before taking a seat in one of the empty spots next to a middle-aged woman who's avidly watching the little girl with a rapt expression on her face. She touches her own hair as Gail snips and little wisps of the black drop to the floor. "Your daughter?" I ask.

Startled out of her reverie, she seems surprised to find someone sitting next to her. "Oh no! I'm so flattered though. Those days have long past."

Assessing her, I shake my head. "If you are, it's not by much."

The woman beams at me. "You just made my afternoon. Possibly my year."

"I see the same expression on my sisters' faces when Gail cuts their children's hair." When the woman cocks her head, I explain. "It's a mixture of wonder, of delight, and sadness their babies are growing up too fast."

"You know your family very well," she muses. Before she can continue, her attention is diverted when Gail whips the cape off the little girl. "You're all set, Gracie."

"Grandma! Look!" Black curls dance around a cherubic face I want to capture in my viewfinder because it's so easy to see the love these two share. Pure trust is absolutely stunning to witness. Damn, I almost want to reach for my sunglasses to hide my reaction.

"I see, baby. So pretty," the woman coos as she gently runs a hand over the girl's head. That's when the little darling spots me and scoots closer to her grandmother. She whispers shyly, "Hi."

"Hi," I say simply. I've learned with my nieces and nephew that unaffected forthrightness is the best manner.

"Hey, Holly," Gail calls out. "Let me get things cleaned up and I'll be ready for you."

"No rush, Gail," I call back. My attention turns back to the little girl, whose head is now tilted, studying me intently.

"Are you Kalie's Holly?" she asks. I'm so surprised, I almost fall out of my seat. Instead, I nod at the girl's amazed grandmother before I answer.

"You have me at a disadvantage. You know my Kalie?"

Her brows lower to a deep V. "What's a dis-a-pantage?"

I grin. "Disadvantage. It means you have me in an unusual position."

She frowns. "You're in the same position as Grandma." The girl's grandmother chokes on her laughter.

I bite my lower lip to hold in my own mirth. "In this case, it means you know something about me that I don't know about you," I try to explain again.

Her brow clears. "Oh! If you're my Kalie's Aunt Holly, then Kalie's my best friend in Miss Tiffany's class at school. She has lots of family."

"Do you know Kalie's last name, precious?" Because that is precisely what this little girl is.

She nods emphatically. "Mar...Mar..." Her little brow puckers again, and she starts to look upset. I decide to help her out.

"Is it Marshall?" Even though Ali goes by her maiden name, my niece goes by Keene's.

A relieved look crosses her face. "Yes!"

"Then my Kalie and your Kalie are the same people," I declare. Pulling up the photo app on my phone, I scroll to a picture I took the other day of Keene, Ali, and Kalie at dinner.

"Grandma! Look! It's Kalie! Hi, Kalie's Holly!" The little girl bounces on her toes in excitement.

I hold out my hand to the older woman. "Holly Freeman. Ali's one of my older sisters."

She smiles. "Denise Bianco." We shake.

"Denise, I'm ready to check you and Grace out," Gail calls.

"It was a pleasure to meet you, Holly," Denise says warmly. I smile.

"For me as well. Now, just think, Kalie's friend, of what you can tell her at school," I tease her gently. I'm surprised she starts scuffing her shoe on the ground and won't meet my eyes. "What is it, honey?" I ask gently. I scoot forward so I'm at the edge of my seat.

"My daddy's a fireman. He says I'm not allowed to play with fire." Her voice trembles.

I hazard a quick glance up at Denise, whose face is just as bewildered. "Well, that's a good rule to have, honey. He's trying to protect you."

Sad blue eyes meet mine. "But your hair looks like it. And I can't play with fire. Daddy says so."

It takes me a moment to put it together. My hair—naturally a mix of dark orange and red hues—likely does look like the forbidden fire to a little girl who is using careful logic. "Well, I'm pretty certain Grandma will make sure your daddy will be okay with you playing with me if you and I are together when you play with Kalie."

"Grandma?" She tilts her head up. Denise smiles.

"It will be fine, Grace. If it ever comes up, I'll talk with Daddy."

"Okay!" Back to being a happy little girl, she leans in and whispers, "I think your hair is really pwetty."

I whisper back, "I think your hair is pretty too."

Little pink lips part in surprise.

Gail calls out, "Holly? You ready?" just as Denise says, "It's time to go, Gracie."

"Bye, Kalie's Holly!" Grace calls out as she dashes for her grandmother.

Even as I stand up, I call out, "It was nice to meet both of you."

They both wave as they leave Shimmer. Gail stands stationary with her hand over her heart as I move closer. "Such a sad story," she murmurs.

"What is?" I ask.

Shaking her head, she shakes herself loose from her own

thoughts. "So, just a trim today?"

Placing a hand on her arm, I squeeze. "Gail, what am I missing?"

"Let's get you washed up, and then I'll explain."

As Gail uses a wet brush on my long hair, she tells me about how Grace lost her mother when she was just an infant. "There was a car accident at the mall. She was hit. Fortunately, Grace was in her car seat already..."

But Gail's given me enough information to jog my memory. Bianco. Grace. Accident. "Jason was there," I whisper. "He tried to save the mother." I lift horrified eyes to her.

Gail gasps.

"It was at Christmas," I recall. Shaking my wet head, I continue. "The father was just destroyed."

"Joe's got a great family, Holly. They've really helped him, especially with Grace. He lives for that little girl."

"I know Jason's wondered how he's been over the years." For all Collyer has a small-town feel, it's relatively large. And between Jason working in New York and our work events, if we have any free time, it's usually spent catching up as a family.

Gail shakes her head. "I can't really say one way or another. I just get little snippets from Denise. But with what he went through, I can't say he's better. I know Grace helps though."

Knowing that won't satisfy my brother-in-law but that it's better than nothing, my troubled eyes meet Gail's in the mirror. Her hands land on my shoulders and squeeze.

I feel something stir deep inside of me when I think of the little girl who will grow up never entirely understanding what happened to her mother. She may have a heart filled with scars and feel like there's no one there to help her battle them. Fortunately, it appears like she has a robust support system. At least, I hope so. Unlike my father and Maria, I think bitterly.

Curling my nails deep into my palms, I can still feel the blood on my hands from attempting to die. It just wasn't my blood that ended up on me that day. It was hers as she tried to wrestle the gun away from me.

In hindsight, I don't regret pulling the trigger. It was only in the immediate days that followed that I wish I had been able to pull it twice.

But then, I wouldn't be alive. I wouldn't be a Freeman. I wouldn't be Holly.

Slowly, I bow my head as Gail begins to remove the ends of my hair. As each piece falls to the floor, I wonder why God makes the choices to take away the lives of young mothers and leaves me alive to wear the mark of a Freeman.

Suddenly, the bell over the door rings. Gail holds my head in place. "Don't you dare move an inch. You're in the perfect position. I'll be right back."

With all of my hair twisted in knots on my head and what's down covering me, I'm completely unrecognizable except to my family. "Not going anywhere," I call out from a curtain of combed-out wet hair.

"Oh, hey, Joe. Grace and your mother just left about ten minutes ago." Now, I want to spin around so I can get a good look at Joseph Bianco.

"Ah, thanks, Gail. I had a break and thought I might be able to catch them." I frown because although his voice is friendly, it seems distracted. "I didn't mean to interrupt you with a client."

"Not a problem at all. I scheduled an appointment for Grace's next trim with your mom. Is that all right?"

"Sounds good. Thanks again, Gail." It's a moment or two before I hear the bell over the door again and footsteps making their way back over to me.

"Sorry about that, Holly. Let me spray down your ends a bit so they don't split while I'm trimming. Your hair absorbs water so fast, it's crazy." As Gail's spray gun filled with water squirts at my back and gives me the willies, she asks, "How's the family doing?"

Since I can't share the news about Ali, I tell her about how we're planning on a fashion show of horrifying wedding gowns for Phil just so he gets off Corinna's back.

Needless to say, our appointment is much more jovial after that.

4

HOLLY

Two days later, I'm debating how I can escape from the newest hell of my own making. "What do you think about this piece, Holly?" Stopping in front of a colored pencil drawing, my date, Seth, tilts his head. "I hope the subject matter doesn't disturb you?" He actually clucks his tongue like a chicken before catching himself.

I want to go screeching from the exhibit room, but some might take offense because the art isn't the problem. It's not the art that's boring me to pieces.

It's my date.

The Aldrich Contemporary Art Museum in Ridgefield has an incredible display which has been borrowed from local penitentiaries, private collections, and from the permanent collection of the Prison Arts Program that focuses on the behavioral change of art of current and past inmates. I saw the exhibit soon after it opened and was floored by the emotion that gripped my heart. From pencils and ballpoint pens, from more dynamic works that used cut paper, food wrappings, and even grooming products, the emotions evoked draw me in as if I was looking through my camera.

These inmates—past or present—who did these pieces of art

were all searching for what I do each time I lift up my camera: the illusion of life and freedom.

"I should have known someone with your refined sensibilities would likely not appreciate where this art originated from," Seth mutters. He reaches for my hand to do that annoying arm tuck, and I yank it away.

"And where is that exactly?"

"Well..." He lowers his voice slightly. "These individuals are the dredges of society..." When I step forward to get in his space, his voice trails off.

"Dredges?" I whisper, still cognizant of the other patrons of the museum. "These men and women are paying for whatever wrongs they did. They didn't have to put their souls on display. They were brave enough to do so."

"Brave?" A little sneer slips out before his bland mask drops back into place. "I bet they weren't so brave when they got caught." I hear a gasp behind me.

I don't stop to think about the consequences before my temper gets the best of me.

"Yes, brave. The crimes they committed were wrong, and these people paid their punishment to society. A punishment, might I add, that our system agreed is right and just."

"Our system is failing." His voice rises along with mine.

"Then figure out a way to fix it. But do not stand there and berate people who dared to open up their souls after being reformed or while being reformed and judge them. Then it isn't the system that failed; it's you." Around me, people begin to applaud. "I have no problem with looking at the thought-provoking, intriguing art that is in front of me. What I can't stand is someone who refuses to open his mind and realize people are individuals, and perhaps he should read some of the stories beneath the art so he understands why some of these people did what they did." Stomping over to the next picture, I throw my hair over my shoulder. "I'll find my own way home."

"I think it's best if you do." His face is a mottled red. Glancing around at the people who are now openly staring at us, Seth steps quickly towards the door.

Once he's left the area, a small burst of applause breaks out.

I smile before turning back to the picture in front of me. It so perfectly captures the feelings I had living in the run-down house between the time my mother died and before I was taken—it's brilliant. "I wish it was for sale," I murmur quietly.

"I know what you mean," a warm voice comes from behind me. Spinning around, I find the smiling face of the visitor experience manager who I had been introduced to when I first went to the Aldrich many years ago.

Holding out my hand, I ask drolly, "Am I being ejected?"

"Quite the opposite." A light of amusement lights Jasmine's eyes. "Dare I even ask what made you say yes to that odious man?"

"Not all of us are fortunate enough to find love through our work, Jaz," I murmur in deference to the patrons wandering around us. "Some of us occasionally have to swipe right to get a date."

She lets out a low laugh. "I'm always so amused by your constant inability to see yourself as others see you."

I tense without even realizing it. "And how's that?"

"Absolutely lovely. Witty. Pure class. The right man is going to walk through the door one day, Holly. And you are going to have no idea what hit you."

I roll my eyes. "I'll believe that when I start believing Prince Charming might exist."

"And when will that be?"

"When someone makes me believe the Tooth Fairy, Santa, the Easter Bunny, *and* Prince Charming might exist again," I answer bluntly.

Jasmine's laughter causes her beautiful braids to cascade down over her shoulders. A warm hand lands on my arm. "Girl, then you have plenty of catching up to do. The rest of us were dreaming about Prince Charming since we were like six and realized boys were good for something other than spitballs."

I lean forward and whisper, "Wait, they're still not good for that? There goes our fun with Phil."

Jasmine slaps a hand over her mouth to hold in her chuckles. "You're killing me."

I wink.

"Do you need a ride back to Collyer?"

"Nah, I'm going to enjoy my afternoon off. I figure I'll stop off and grab lunch at Genoa. Then I'll call the office for a ride home. Seth drove us here, even though I wanted to just meet him. Next time, I'll listen to my instincts."

Jasmine just shakes her head at me. "If you go to Genoa and don't bring your family back some, they might call your date back and make him take you out again as punishment."

Knowing she is not wrong—my family's obsession with the small Italian eatery is known far and wide—I decide, "Maybe I'll head there and see if they want me to pick up takeout for dinner."

"Good call. Listen, I get a break in a few minutes. Walk around and then I'll drop you off at Genoa and grab myself some Starbucks on the way back. There's no need to be ruining those cute-as-hell shoes," Jasmine looks down at the pumpkin-colored heels I'm wearing with my jeans.

"Are you sure?" A glare is my only response. "Okay. Just come grab me when you're ready."

Jasmine flashes a quick smile at me before she goes over to greet some of the other patrons. And I again lose myself in the drawing in front of me.

It really is a damn shame I can't buy it.

"I appreciate the ride, Jaz." Tugging on a knit cap out of my bag, I quickly tuck my hair beneath it. Even though it's late March, the temperature has turned as temperamental as my date. Where it was warm when the day started, it's downright frosty now, and it's barely two. I'm grateful I decided to wear my peacoat so I don't freeze. Flipping up the collar, I burrow down into it.

"My pleasure, babe. Hey, do me a favor? Tell Ali to call me? We're going to have a new exhibit coming up in a few months, and the director wants to get on the schedule."

I pull out my iPhone, type a quick note, and set a reminder. "Done." And score. I just found a pair of gloves too. I quickly put those on.

"Now you're starting to act like Cassidy being all organized and whatnot," Jasmine teases. Since the Aldrich has used Amaryllis for several events, Jasmine and I have worked together quite a bit. I take her teasing in stride.

"Hush your mouth." I stick out my tongue.

"Better stick that in before it falls off!" With a toot of her horn, Jasmine turns the wheel and heads back through the parking lot toward Main Street, Ridgefield.

I walk with my head down along the elevated platform that houses the tiny delicatessen and rabidly inhale the scents leading me to my Italian demise. Since I sent a text in the family chat earlier offering to pick up dinner, my phone has done nothing but explode. Fortunately, Jason agreed to pick me up on his way back from his shift at NYU, so this ended up being a win all the way around.

I'm reaching for the door handle to Genoa when I'm thrown back a step by a bunch of men dressed in long-sleeve, light blue shirts and dark blue pants, who all come out laughing. Firemen. Surreptitiously from under my woolen cover, and not without a great deal of appreciation, I check out how well their pants mold their forms. As much as I have an appreciation for a good-looking man, I have a greater appreciation for what they do. And how the hell they're not freezing right now doing it. "God bless those who protect us," I murmur as I walk backward into Genoa and slam right into a hard chest. "Oomph!" I stumble forward. Almost tripping on my heels, I'm caught around the waist by strong arms.

"Are you all right?" a deep voice asks me. Twisting my head, I meet a pair of dark blue eyes so incongruous with the rugged Italian features they're set in, I almost gasp out loud. The light blue of his shirt just highlights the differences, making my fingers itch for my camera.

"Yes," I choke out. I'm sure my face is bright red.

"Are you sure?" I get a quick head-to-toe glance that sends my nerves dancing. "Nothing twisted?"

I shake my head. Right now, I'm grateful for the pseudo-disguise I have on. It seems this particular firefighter hasn't recognized me being a Freeman. "I'm okay," I say softly.

His brow lowers. I tilt my head even as I pull my collar closer around my neck. Seriously, where did this weather front come in from? "Is there a problem?"

He shakes his head. "Nothing. You just seem familiar, that's all." His lips twitch in a what passes for a smile—one that doesn't come close to reaching his eyes, devoid of emotion—before he moves past me to join the rest of his crew. Swinging into the red 4x4 vehicle marked with the insignia of the Collyer Fire Department, I now know I'll be able to bring more than just Genoa to dinner tonight.

The name on the shirt read "Bianco."

This is the adorable girl from the hair salon's father.

After Gail finished filling in the missing gaps during my hair cut, it brought back all the memories of a dark period in my brother-in-law's life. A car wreck destroyed the idyllic life Joseph Bianco, Jr. had three years ago over Christmas. A driver at the Danbury Fair Mall hit his fiancée at high speed. Jason, who had been on the scene, had done everything he could to save the young woman's life. For a long time, Jason lived with being unable to do more, compounded by the guilt Joseph heaped on him, no doubt needing an outlet for his own emotions for not being able to be there for the woman he loved.

Jason's occasionally wondered when he's seen his name in the paper after notable fire rescues if Joseph Bianco had set aside his guilt and moved on. "It's been years. He's a good man who deserves to find happiness."

Unfortunately, I'll be able to tell him I don't think he has.

5

JOSEPH

After a full day at the station and taking massive ribbing from the guys from almost barreling into one of Ridgefield's citizens, the list of things I want to do in order are get home, find a shower where I can wash as much of the firehouse from my skin as I can, and cuddle my beautiful girl. Unfortunately, I'm in the middle of a parent-teacher conference that has less to do with my daughter and everything to do with the number of propositions I'm fending off.

I've never had the calmest of tempers, and right now I'm barely holding on by a thread.

"Ms. Tiffany," I grit out. "Was there anything you wanted to discuss about Grace?"

"Oh, Grace is a lovely child. I think we should get into a much more in-depth conversation about her. Maybe over dinner?' I'm just about to open my mouth to flat-out refuse when I hear a frustrated male voice behind me.

"You understand, Ms. Tiffany, that some of us have been waiting for fifteen minutes past our scheduled conference time for you to do nothing more than hit on the parents of one of your students. Some of us would actually like to get home to our children."

"Makes me glad I rearranged my schedule to come with you, Keene," comes a deeply amused female. "You'd have ripped her a new one on her first attempt. Then we'd have had to find Kalie a new daycare."

I close my eyes in mortification. The Marshalls. Between Grace babbling on about her "best friend" Kalie and my mother saying what a lovely couple they are, I've been curious about them for a while now. So far Grace's playdates with the little girl have all occurred while I've been on schedule at the station so I can have as much time with her as possible, but it looks like I'm about to have a quick meet and greet. Just great.

"Mr. and Mrs. Marshall," Ms. Tiffany stammers. "I didn't realize it had got so late."

"Obviously. And for the twentieth time since Kalie joined your class, it's Mr. Marshall and Ms. Freeman. My wife uses her maiden name. Exclusively."

Freeman? Turning in my chair, I come face-to-face with a knockout blonde with a distinct attitude as bright as her blue eyes. While her features are different, she could easily be Philip Freeman-Ross's sister. How ironic would that be after all this time to meet another member of Jason Ross's extended family? Every month like clockwork, I go to Mary's grave, and there's a fresh bouquet of flowers there, courtesy of Jason Ross's husband.

All because I was a complete dick to a man who deserved nothing but gratitude. It's humbling to realize how amazing some people are down to the core of their souls.

Standing, I turn to the couple and hold out my hand. "Joseph Bianco. Grace's father." By the smiles that light both their faces, I can only assume my past behavior toward their brother-in-law isn't being held against me.

"Ali." The blonde holds out her hand. "And we think Grace is absolutely adorable."

"Keene," I hear Ms. Tiffany sigh.

Ali growls. Keene rolls his eyes. "Calm down, baby. Since our appointment time has already been blown to hell, why don't we just call the administrator tomorrow to find out exactly how Kalie's doing in school versus wasting any more of our time."

"Sounds perfect," Ali agrees. We all begin to make our way toward the door when we hear sputtering behind us.

"Joe, you didn't answer me about getting together about dinner!" Ms. Tiffany calls out. Keene's unmistakable sound of disgust almost makes me laugh. Almost.

Instead, I shake my head. "I thought I made that obvious the first eight or so times you asked. But let me be clear. I'm. Not. Interested."

Her sound of distress infuriates me. I think I'll be taking a page out of Kalie's parents' book and calling the administrator tomorrow. "But, Joe..." her pathetic whine grates.

"Mr. Bianco," I correct, my voice like a blast of sodium bicarbonate. "This entire meeting was a farce."

Ali Freeman applauds next to me.

I shoot her a quick grin which she returns.

"Not that I'm a professional, Mr. Bianco, but every time we see Grace, she's behaving like a well-adapted three-year-old. Full of spirit, smart as a whip, giggling, likes too many sweets—then again, so does Kalie, but I blame that entirely on my sister Cori. Oh, and she loves to dress up," Ali tells me. I let out a relieved sigh. I've tried so hard not to let the overwhelming grief from the loss of her mother touch those innocent blue eyes. It's hard most days—next to impossible on others —but to hear affirmation of her good nature from an outsider's point of view is reassuring that I've somehow managed to do it.

We all mutter tart goodbyes to our children's daycare instructor before we move into the hallway.

"Thank you," I say sincerely. Holding out my hand to Ali and Keene in turn, I continue. "You have no idea what that means to know I'm not completely screwing up with my daughter. I was hoping for that from her teacher, but you overheard how well that went," I conclude in disgust.

A smirk crosses Keene's face. "There's something you should know, Mr. Bianco."

I correct him. "Joe. And what is it?"

A dazzling smile erupts across Ali's. "And we're Keene and Ali. First is, your daughter is absolutely not touched by the things you're worried about." My jaw drops. Ali continues on. "Your mother gave us a heads-up about your situation a long time ago in the event Grace had any problems at our home."

I nod. "My fiancée will be missed," I say quietly.

Ali's smile is sympathetic but restrained. Intuitively, I get this is a woman who understands my need to push past the pain and move on.

I'm finally in a place where the fog has begun to lift about losing the woman I planned on spending the rest of my life with. Every day I wake up trying to believe it's going to be a better day, but other people still grieving Mary's loss feel the need to pull me back into the despair I'm trying to remove Grace and me from. I'm stumbling through, trying to find solid ground when every step I take feels like a sinkhole.

I'll never live a day in this life without thinking of Mary. How could I not? I have a part of her, a part of us, that I will cherish for the rest of my life. But I can't live the rest of my life for her. Otherwise, they might have well have buried me alongside her when they lowered her casket into the ground three years ago.

"What's the second?" I say, pulling myself out of my own thoughts.

"Excuse me?"

"You said 'first.' I assume there's more."

Ali lets out a laugh as she leans into her husband's arms. "See, if I were at the office, Phil would have heard the first part of that sentence and walked out before listening to anything else I had to say."

Keene brushes his lips over his wife's hair. "No comment."

Nailed it. "So, you are related to Phil and Jason?" I ask quietly. The hallway goes static for just a moment before Ali nods.

"I wasn't sure if you realized it. I hope that's not a problem?" she asks worriedly.

"Why would it be an issue?"

"I know your beginning with them wasn't under the best of circumstances..." Her voice trails off.

And it strikes me then that while I may have offered my apologies to Jason and Phil over my appalling behavior, those may not have been replayed to the rest of their family. "I was an unmitigated ass to Jason. I ran into him and Phil about six months after the accident and apologized profusely for my behavior." Leaning up against a wall, I reach out and touch a papier-mâché flower. "Do you know what Phil does each month like clockwork? He has flowers delivered to Mary's grave—Grace's mother. An enormous bouquet. Every time Grace and I go there, these beautiful blooms are highlighting her mother's name."

"Now I know why he pays me out of his pocket for his flower budget being off each month," Ali murmurs. Keene squeezes her.

"I'd love to be able to thank them again. And to give them a chance to see Grace, to show them how she's doing. But I lost the card Jason gave me." I shake my head. There are days it's hard enough to find my daughter matching socks, let alone the card of a doctor who gave it to me at a mall just shy of three years ago, and I couldn't remember what hospital he worked at.

Ali immediately begins rooting inside her purse. "I have one. It's not Jason's, but it might be easier to get a hold of both of them this way." She hands out a black card with a red embossed flower on it. I read Alison Freeman, Chief Financial Officer and Attorney, Amaryllis Events with multiple phone numbers and her email address beneath it. Giving her a look of confusion, she laughs again. "All of our immediate siblings work for our company." She nods at the card. "My oldest sister, Cassidy, handles all of our scheduling, and Phil dances to the tune she sets, or she yells at him—mercilessly."

"I live for those moments," Keene adds dryly. Ali elbows him in the gut. He grunts but doesn't stop smiling.

"If you're looking to schedule time with any of us, Cassidy's the keeper of our lives," Ali concludes. "With all of the weddings and events we have on our docket, it's the only way for us to have any balance between work and home life."

Pulling my wallet from my back pocket, I flip it open to a picture of Grace. I slide the card beneath it. I know I won't lose it then. Before I can snap it shut, Ali grabs at it. I gape at her in shock. Keene just shrugs as if to say *Go with it.*

"You need better pictures of Grace than this, Joe. If not for you, then definitely for your family," Ali says in disgust.

"Ali," Keene says warningly, but she just flaps her hand at him.

"We're spoiled by Holly, Keene. This is why we don't do school pictures. They make all of the kids come out looking like bowl-head Martians." I'd find insult in there, but she is not wrong. Between the trim my parents gave Grace right before the picture and the picture itself? Yeah, Ali Freeman's words are disturbingly accurate.

"Who's Holly?" I ask politely and in an attempt to get my baby Martian back.

"My youngest sister. She's a brilliant photographer," Ali brags with unabashed pride, still not relinquishing my wallet. "She could take pictures of Grace for you that would blow your mind."

"I'm sure she could."

"As much as I don't want to encourage my wife any, she's not wrong." Keene reaches for his own wallet. Flipping it open, he shows me a picture of him and Ali together that says everything in one shot: love, devotion, frustration, laughter, and promise.

That, right there, was what I wanted with Mary. Time has eased my grief somewhat, so it's only a small blade that slides into my chest.

"Here's one she took of Kalie recently." Keene flips the insert over, and there's Kalie Marshall, a perfect miniature of both of her parents. With a huge smile on her face, she's flipped over Keene's broad shoulder, laughing at her mother, who's not far behind. There are flowers caught in her long dark locks that are falling to the ground. There's joy, exasperation, and humor—all of which as a parent I can relate to.

Much more than the stiff little picture I have in my wallet of Grace.

Sister or not, the woman who took this picture is enormously talented. And—unfortunately for me—likely charges fees to match. "Incredible," I murmur.

"It wouldn't be a hardship for Holly to get a few pictures of Grace while she's playing with Kalie..." Ali begins, but I cut her off.

"Thanks, Ali, but I likely can't afford her fees."

Ali frowns, but Keene squeezes her from behind. "Baby, leave it. The offer is open anytime, Joe. Holly'd love it though."

I shake my head. "After everything, I'd think you all would hate me rather than offer to help me."

Before Ali or Keene can respond, Ms. Tiffany storms by. Nose up in the air, and apparently out of joint, she snaps, "This isn't a social hour. We're waiting for you all to leave for the school to close," before stomping in the direction of the office.

Ali narrows her eyes after the woman. "I can't wait to talk to the administrator tomorrow."

I chuckle even as I hold out my hand for my wallet. Ali slaps it back in my hand with some strength. "Part of me wishes I could be a fly on the wall for that conversation. The other part is deathly afraid."

"Go with afraid," Keene says. We all laugh as we make our way to the door.

After we're outside, I shake both of their hands again. "It was a pleasure to meet both of you."

"You as well. And truly, if you need anything, don't hesitate to call," Ali repeats. Keene just nods before they head off in the direction of their car.

Shaking my head, I head in the direction of my Explorer. Now that the farce of a parent-teacher conference is over, I can head home and snuggle with my little girl. Even as I put my car in gear and drive out of the lot, I hear a toot of a horn. Glancing over, I wave at Keene and Ali.

And it was great to meet some more of Grace's friends' parents. Who would have ever thought the Marshalls I have heard so much about are Freemans as well? Collyer does have some hidden connections. And Amaryllis Events is the Freemans' business? I never knew that. Thinking back, I realize they've donated to every charity event related to the police and fire department since they opened their doors twelve, thirteen years ago?

There are times when it's great to be living in a small town.

Still, it's nice to see such a happy family that Grace is around. It's pretty evident to me they've been together a long time and have their shit tight.

Making a left to turn onto the road back toward the outskirts of Collyer, I muse to myself that I'm glad Grace is going to get to have people like that in her life. People who can show her about the stability of a traditional family.

As Ms. Tiffany zooms by illegally over a double line—obviously still angry over my rebuff of her advances—I let out a chuckle as the blue lights come out of nowhere to pull her over.

And then there are times when small towns don't mix with people's noses getting out of joint.

6

JOSEPH

"Daaaaaaaddyyyy!" Tiny little footsteps beat lightly against the hardwood floor of our rambler. Reaching down, I catch my dark-haired hair, blue-eyed miracle in my arms and toss her into the air.

"Hey, beautiful." I kiss her on both cheeks. Grace's giggle soothes out all the physical and emotional aches and pains of any day. "Were you good for Grandma?"

She gives me an adorably indignant look. I'd swear on a stack of Bibles, I used to catch that exact look on Mary's face when she'd get irritated with me. Which, I think ruefully, was fairly often.

I was only twenty-five when Mary died, but I've grown up three lifetimes in the three years since. Gone is the hotheaded Italian who thought nothing could trample his part of the world. Now, I'm first and foremost a daddy whose heart belongs to one woman.

I just have to get her past things like school, best friends, first dates, and puberty—God, help me. All while fielding the advice from every parent in the community, all who feel they can and should dole it out regularly.

Is this my penance for being such an asshole after Mary died? Constant meddling?

It's bad enough I've had the eyes of a community judging how I'm handling my grief, but I refuse to have their eyes continually watching my child. I learned to hide my suffering and to suffocate my pain. And somewhere along the way, something changed. Instead of feeling hopeless, I began to realize I've actually been able to do this. I never wanted to do this alone, but I can.

I'm grateful for every day I have with Grace. I feel like we're growing at the same pace. At first, we couldn't handle the most straightforward tasks on our own; we relied on everyone else for everything. Then we were teetering along, and I began to resent the help and started objecting when people tried to stick their noses in. But since then, we've stabilized. Now, we're off and running. We're— in Grace's case at least—making friends and we're getting by.

It's healthy that more and more days pass when the sorrow isn't what's flooding my heart; it's being pushed out by other emotions— flashes of joy, moments of laughter, and hope for the future.

It's what Mary would have wanted. And, frankly, if the situation were reversed, it's what I would have wished for her.

"Eden called earlier," my mother tells me quietly. "She's demanding to see Grace."

"Not now," I warn her. I nuzzle my way through my daughter's curls and find that perfect baby powder smell. "What did Grandma give you for dinner?"

"Nubbets, pasta, and peas." I grin, both dimples appearing in my cheeks. I love how my girl calls all bite-size chicken bites "nubbets" ever since my father took her to have "nubbets and fries" on a date.

"Did she save any for me?" I ask with mock innocence.

"Daddy, those are mine." A little hand slaps innocently against my cheek. "You can have peas."

I burst into laughter. "Thanks, baby. Let me talk to Grandma for a few minutes, then I'll come to tuck you in."

"Okay! Down please." Grace starts squirming in my arms. I put her gently on the floor, and she tears off in search of her next adventure before she gets told it's time for lights-out.

Taking a few steps forward, I lean down and kiss my mother on the cheek. "Thanks, Ma."

She flaps her hand at me. My lips twitch. I'll be in my fifties, God willing, and I'll still get the hand flap from my mother. "Don't be silly. Like it's any kind of hardship to watch that angel."

I brush a hand over her shoulder as I pass her to head into the kitchen. Just as I suspected, my mother saved me some chicken Alfredo—with a side of peas. "And I appreciate the dinner as well."

"I remember what it was like when your father had to work those hours, sweetheart. Always nice to have a good meal on your first night back at home." Denise Bianco barely looks a day older than she did when my father did work those long shifts. I open my mouth to tell her that, but hers opens first. "Eden is not happy, sweetheart. It was all I could do to prevent her from coming over."

Pulling a Coke from the fridge, I pop the tab. "When Eden and Seth flat-out told me both Grace and I needed to be in intense therapy since we both appeared to no longer be mourning their daughter, I laid down the law. I appreciate their grief, but I refuse to let it touch Grace. God, Ma." I lean back against the refrigerator in exhaustion. "Is my baby not supposed to be happy because..."

"No, sweetheart. I agree they went too far. But Grace is the only piece of Mary they have left. What you don't need is for them to have a scene in the middle of town," my mother points out logically.

I take a pull of my drink. "I also don't need to spend days trying to cheer my daughter up after a visit to them where all they do is show her pictures of Mary and make Grace feel upset because she doesn't remember her. For Christ's sake, Ma, Grace was eight-weeks-old when Mary died. I don't hide pictures of the three of us here. But the last time, she came home sobbing because she 'couldn't remember Mommy.' She asked me if something was wrong with her." Finishing my drink, I crush the can in my hand. "She's not even three and a half years old," I hiss.

"I know, son," my mother soothes. Just then the phone rings.

I bet down to the darkest part of my soul I know who it is. I grab it on the second ring. "Bianco," I bite out.

"What a lovely way you have of greeting people, Joseph. Is that what you're teaching our granddaughter?" Eden's voice snaps at me.

Raising my brow at my mother, I remark casually, "Eden, your ears must have been burning. My mother was just telling me about your call earlier."

Ignoring any underlying sarcasm, she immediately launches into what she wants. "We want to see Grace."

"I'll let you know when she's available."

"You're being ridiculously unfair, Joseph. Then again, I shouldn't be surprised," she comments snidely.

There was never any love lost between Mary's family and me after they found out their precious angel was pregnant. They immediately wanted to know when we would be married. It was much to their dismay when Mary was the one to tell them that she didn't want to get married until she was back to her pre-pregnancy figure. Like I gave a damn. We were already engaged. I'd have married her the day, the hour, the minute she told me she was carrying my child under her heart.

But that wasn't the dream Mary had, and I wanted to give her everything. Instead, she ended up with nothing. That's the bitter pill we've all had to swallow. And then I learned that bitterness can be lingering. In fact, it can grow with the more you learn.

I just won't let Grace ever have to taste it.

"Once I know you and Seth won't send my daughter back to me in tears, we can discuss once again when you can visit your grand-daughter beyond large family events." I hold firm to this decision. Nothing, and I mean nothing, is taking the light out of Grace's eyes. Not a teacher, a friend, a grandparent, nothing. Not if I have anything to say about it.

"So, not only are you cutting our daughter's memory out of her heart and mind, but you're also cutting ours out as well. I shouldn't be surprised, now should I?" Eden immediately slams down the phone, leaving me with no chance to retort.

I'm vibrating with anger. Moments later, I feel gentle fingers pry the phone out of my hand. "Joe, let it go for now," my mother whispers.

"Ma..." I can't even get words out, I'm so infuriated.

"Grace is still waiting to be read a story," I'm reminded gently.

Grace. The only thing that can beat back the angry beast waiting to erupt inside me. "Yeah." I let loose a harsh sigh. "Let me go get my girl down, then I'll heat up some dinner."

"I'll wait until you're done." But I'm already shaking my head.

"You should head out. I don't like the idea of you driving so late."

"Joseph Bianco, I've driven a lot later than this to get you to and from football camps all over this state," she barks. I give her a half-hearted smile.

"Yeah, Ma. But your driving didn't suck as much then." I take the whack on my arm as my due. "Seriously, go home. I'll call you tomorrow."

She comes right into my space and cups my cheek. "You're a good man, Joey. And you're an amazing father."

I shake my head at her. Her grip tightens. "I mean every word."

I lean forward and kiss her on the forehead. "I know you do, Ma. Now go. I have to go read Max and Ruby about twenty times."

"You don't have it memorized already?" she teases gently.

"Bite your tongue. If I did, I'd be reciting it in the car." We both smile.

"Maybe they make it on audiobook," she muses. I look at her in horror.

"You wouldn't dare."

Leaning up to kiss me, she walks to where her coat is thrown over one of my kitchen chairs. "That, my boy, is one of the benefits of being a grandparent. I get to spoil the child without the consequences."

"Grace!" I yell. The little feet come pinging down the hallway. "Come say good night to Grandma before I tell her she can't come back with any presents for the next year."

At Grace's stricken look, I burst into laughter. "Don't worry, darling, I'll just give you gifts at my house," my mother reassures her.

"'Kay! Night, Grandma. Love you! Daddy, want Max and Ruby." Grace gives my mother a kiss before running off toward her room. I scrub my hands down my face.

"And on that note, I'll let myself out. Night, son." My mother flutters her fingers at me.

"Night, Ma." I stand at the window to make sure my mother makes it to her car safely. Once she's inside and backing out of my driveway, I yell, "Grace, which Max and Ruby are we reading?"

"Easter," comes her reply.

"Only if you brushed your teeth," I call back. I hear a mad scramble for the bathroom.

Yeah, we're not doing so poorly on our own. As I pass by the fireplace, I look at a picture of Mary, Grace, and me that my parents took after Grace was born. Mary's looking at us with this look of awe.

"I wonder if you'd still have that look on your face if you could see us now, Mar," I whisper before making my way down the hallway to read Max and Ruby to our little girl.

Tonight it only took five times before she was out for the count.

7

JOSEPH

The next morning, Grace convinces me to take her to the park after breakfast. I want to go to Collyer's town park on the weekend about as much as I want to stab myself willingly in the eye. But if either put a smile on my daughter's face, I'd probably gear up to do it. Just as I am right now.

The colder weather from yesterday hasn't abated, so I make sure Grace is dressed warmly in a dark purple coat and beret and throw on my leather jacket. "Grace," I call out before she can make a mad dash for the car. "Do you have gloves?"

The V that forms between her eyebrows is so completely me, I want to whip out my cell to snap a picture. So much of Grace reminds me of Mary—every delicate feature on her perfect little face down to her light blue eyes. But occasionally, I'll see my mannerisms shine through. The first time my father pointed out how Grace was picking them up, I choked. The absolute last thing my little girl needs is to be a hard-headed, stubborn hothead. She's still developing those qualities, but differently. She'll need determination later in life. Just, God help me, please don't let her have them when she's a teenager.

I figure I have zero chance of that happening.

We drive to the park listening to a *Sesame Street* sing-along which

Grace makes me participate in avidly. If there's one sick, sadistic thing *Sesame Street* ever did to torture parents, it's that they worked with the artists of some pretty great music to rewrite the lyrics of their songs so kids would learn things like letters and numbers. I mean, I used to like Feist. Now, I can't count to four without thinking of monsters crossing the floor no matter which version of the damn song is on.

And forget the Elmo Slide.

If there's one good thing out of all my suffering, I know I have enough footage of Grace bopping along at home to this torment her for with payback the first time she threatens me wanting to go out on a date. I figure I can use this leverage until she moves out of this house or until she has her own child.

After parking the car, she' still singing away. I round the car, unbuckling her from her car seat so we can make our way over to the outdoor cesspool of gossip and germs: the playground. I give myself a mental pep talk. *You can do this.* Maybe all the moms have been zapped to some X-chromosome-only event that you can't attend. Knowing the likelihood is less than a gazillion to one on that happening, I brace myself as we approach the fenced-in toddler area.

Grace breaks away and starts running as fast as she can on her little legs, which is damn fast. "Gracie, wait up!" I holler at her back.

"Kaylieeeeee!" she's shrieking, ignoring me altogether. My footsteps falter. Hell, if Ali Freeman is here, maybe this won't be so horrific. At least there's one mom who won't be trying to hit on me. But when I scan the crowd, I don't recognize Kalie's mother in the bevy of women. Instead, a tall, dark-haired man who I haven't seen in years is walking toward me. He waves in my direction before turning his attention back to his niece, who's also wildly waving at my daughter.

"Grace! Wait a second." Recognizing my serious tone, she pauses. "Do you see that man over there?" I point in Jason Ross's direction. I wait for her to nod. "You listen to me, or you listen to him. That's Kalie's..."

"Un-cle Jason." She stumbles a bit over the word. "She has a bunch of others. I like Phil. He's funny and gives me flowers."

I smooth down her coat. "What do you do with the flowers, baby?" This is the first I'm hearing about this.

Impatience leaking into her voice, she tells me, "I give them to Grandma. Just like Phil tells me to. Can I go see Kalie now?"

I chuckle knowing I'll find out more from Jason than my impatient three-year-old. "Go ahead." She tears off screaming. Wishing I'd stopped by The Coffee Shop on my way here for a decent cup of coffee, I head toward a man who's so tied up in my memories of the past, I don't know how to separate them.

The day Mary was hit by a driver in the Danbury Fair Mall parking lot, Grace was just eight weeks old. Mary had in her head she would find for us the perfect outfits for a family photo. I promised her I'd take her after work, worrying she wouldn't have enough energy between being up all night with Grace and having to care for her since I was on shift, but she insisted she felt fine. She headed to the mall super early, sailed through the stores, and called me on her way to the car. I made her promise to head straight home for a nap. Instead, she never made it there. Jason Ross saw it all happen. An exceptionally talented trauma doctor for NYU's emergency room, he was waiting for her parking spot. After witnessing the entire horrific event, he did everything possible to not only save my fiancée but to ensure my daughter's safety in harsh weather conditions at such a young age. Mary was too far gone to save, but I still have Grace due to the gifts God gave the man I'm walking toward. A man I'd treated as my enemy.

A man who tried everything to save my life then but instead gave me a reason to wake up in the morning now.

I still don't know how to handle the emotions he stirs in me or how to approach him three years later.

"Joe." Jason holds out his hand with a smile.

"Jason." We shake firmly. "It's been too long."

He chuckles. "I know. I thought I was lucky it was my day off, and all the siblings were at a wedding, so I could get my time with Kalie and the twins. Then they told me they wanted to come here." He rolls his eyes.

I chuckle even as I ask, "Twins?"

"My brother-in-law Caleb should be here soon with his two. Keene went to get us coffee. He hates the park."

"He's not alone." We both start laughing.

"I haven't heard from you in a few years. I thought maybe you didn't want to be reminded…" His voice trails off, and guilt settles in hard.

"I swear, Jason. I went to call you one day and couldn't find your card. I figured I washed it along with something that Grace had just thrown up on." Muttering, I tack on, "That's probably why I wanted to call in the first place."

Jason chuckles. We stand there in silence as childish screeches of joy pierce the morning air.

"So, who'd have thought your niece and my daughter? Tied at the hip?" I remark as Kalie grabs Grace's hand and drags her off to the sandbox. I wince thinking of all the places that sand is going to end up, with the coat being the least of my concerns.

This is my actual punishment for everything I did to turn my mother prematurely gray—all things sand and glitter.

"I think it's perfect." Jason brings me out of my thoughts. "Two girls from very unconventional families found something in each other they'll likely cherish for the rest of their lives, providing one or the other doesn't move away."

"Unconventional? I've met Ali and Keene. They seem pretty normal."

A boisterous male laugh behind us has us both turning. "Keene? Normal? That's hysterical. I can't wait to tell Cass." I don't recognize the dark-haired stranger, but Jason obviously does as his lips turn up.

"Caleb, would you give ammunition to your wife just so she can make fun of Keene?"

He doesn't hesitate. "Yes." Looking down at a boy and a girl who are raring to be let loose, he orders, "Stick close to Kalie. Be nice to Grace. Jon, don't do anything to get your sister mad or we won't go for hot chocolate when we're done."

"Dad," the little boy whines. And the man mercilessly continues.

"Laura, don't do anything with Kalie that makes your brother come over and complain to me, otherwise same goes. No hot chocolate."

"Yes, Daddy." Both children blink bright blue eyes up at their father before he sighs.

"Go."

They race off yelling, even as he turns to me. "Caleb Lockwood. Cassidy's husband."

I give Jason a helpless look. Jason laughs. "Cassidy is Ali's older sister. Caleb, did you give Keene your order?"

Caleb answers Jason's question with a question. "Do you really think I can handle taking my two to the park without a shot of caffeine from Ava and Matt?"

At the mention of the owners of The Coffee Shop, my mouth begins to water.

"Then have him get something for Joe. I have a feeling he's going to need it if we're going to give him an abbreviated who's who."

"Too late," I hear Keene say. We turn as one to see him carrying a tray with four cups. "I'm already back. You can just give him Phil's drink, Jace." He begins passing out drinks.

Jason rolls his eyes. "Of course you would say that." He accepts his drink before taking a sip.

"It would be cold by the time you give it to him, anyway." Keene hands me a cup with a *P* on it. "I hope you like lattes made with cream instead of milk. Cassidy is still paying her brother back for something he did, what? Four years ago now?"

Caleb pulls his cup down from his lips and nods. "A little more than that."

I gape at them. "You all hold grudges that long?" And yet, here's Jason amicably drinking coffee with me.

"Don't worry. That's just the how the siblings act towards each other. By the way, Caleb." He holds out a hand.

"Joe Bianco," I mutter. I'm beginning to wonder if it might have been easier to hang out with the crazy moms when all of the men burst into laughter. I realize I spoke out loud. Caleb claps a warm hand on my shoulder.

"Trust us when we say no, Joe, you're better off with us."

Taking a long drink from Phil's coffee, the richness of it almost chokes me. "Phil likes his coffee like this?"

"Phil thinks he's getting a super-skinny latte that only Ava can make magically delicious," Jason explains.

"What he's getting is a Freeman revenge," Keene concludes.

I tip my head toward Jason and ask, "Have I groveled enough? Do I need to do anything else to show my abject remorse for the jackass way I behaved after Mary died?"

The air between us changes, cooling despite the sun warming the brisk March air. As I remember the days after Mary's death and my offensive behavior, I cringe. "I deeply regret what I said, what Mary's family tried to..." Jason steps forward and lays a hand on my shoulder.

"This is where it ends, Joe. Your guilt over emotions you were in no shape to control or contain. Right here, right now." His fingers tighten briefly before letting me go.

I lost so much more than my future; I was stripped of my certainty of self. I was left with as many bruises as I'm sure covered Mary's body. Possibly more. They just weren't visible. By focusing on my daughter, I've fixed the worst of them. It may be possible I'll never be ready to heal them all. I nod, even as I hold my silence.

"Don't know what I'd do if we lost a member of the family," Caleb mutters. My head swings toward him. "Let alone Cass or the kids? No way."

"I do remember what it was like to lose Ali," Keene reminds him. My jaw falls open. "So while I can't emphasize in the same way, I do know what it's like to lash out at people you don't mean to."

Caleb hides a smile. "You do that regularly."

Keene goes to throw him the middle finger, but Jason slaps it down. "Will you please remember where we're at?" he says exasperatedly.

Caleb laughs at Keene's narrow-eyed glare. I grin as Grace comes rushing over. "Daddy, is that hot chocolate?"

I crouch down. "No, but after I think everyone's planning on going to get some. Do you want to go?"

Smacking my lips with a kiss, she goes rushing off. "Kalie! We're getting cocoa too!"

I've been had. In the best of ways.

There are days when my reality comes rushing back, and I'm overwhelmed by the bleakness of it. Today isn't going to be one of those days when I'm surrounded by three men who are laughing hysterically at the way I was just played by my three-year-old. "I have a lifetime of giving in, don't I?" I grouse.

"Welcome to the club." Caleb holds his cup aloft. I shake my head after tapping mine against it. I take a sip. My face twists in disgust.

Everyone chuckles.

Walking over to the trash, I toss the remains of Phil's drink in. "If you all don't mind us following you to The Coffee Shop, I'll wait to get something that doesn't feel like I'm sucking down a pint of coffee-flavored heavy cream."

Caleb mutters, "Not if Jon keeps... Jon! I thought I told you to leave your sister alone!"

"But Daaaaddddd..." Caleb shoves his coffee at Keene before he stalks off.

"So, it's not any easier with boys?" I wonder aloud.

Jason smirks. "Not that I've observed."

Keene glares. "Thanks, brother. That gives me hope for Ali and me if we ever have another baby."

After Caleb rejoins us, we give the kids another thirty minutes before we begin calling out countdown warnings. Fifteen minutes after that, we're all walking back to our vehicles to make our way into the center of Collyer. Parking behind The Coffee Shop, Grace and I head in to grab two tables near the windows. Within a few minutes, Ava is taking orders from the adults for the kids and walking away muttering, "Like I don't know what you all drink?"

An hour after that, just as the kids begin to get fussy, Keene excuses himself to take a call. A few minutes later, he comes back and says, "We're all set. Let's get these monsters to their respective homes before they all melt down."

Jason sighs. "Should I even argue with you over the bill? I was told it was supposed to go on the Amaryllis account."

Keene smirks. "It went on ours instead."

I open my mouth to argue, but Jason just shakes his head. "Don't even bother. Just tip Ava extra if you feel the need to."

Pulling out a ten, I slide it under my cup. "Thank you for a much better trip to the park than I was anticipating."

Ava swirls by our table with to-go cups, depositing them in front of each of us. "Have a good afternoon with the kids, guys."

Caleb stands and kisses her cheek. "Give our best to Matt."

"Will do, honey. Oh, Joe! You need to make sure you bring the boys from the station to eat next month."

I cock my head. "Why's that?"

Keene wraps an arm around her and squeezes. "Because Ava doesn't accept tips. She donates one hundred percent of them to a charity each month. This month it's for Danbury's Pediatric Cancer Research Ward. "Who's it for next month?"

Even as the words come out of my mouth, I know. My gut tightens before she speaks.

"The Collyer Police and Fireman's Victims Association, of course!"

8

HOLLY

I try to blend in as much as possible at weddings. I've done everything from wear a bikini to an anorak to match the attire of the guests. But today's outfit? I glance down at what I was asked to wear. This is a bit much for even me.

I'm dressed like one of the bridesmaids.

Luckily, they chose to go with one of my sister Emily's designs—the Jenna—in a beautiful chocolate brown. So, at least I have a dress I can wear again. But it's March, and I'm freezing my ass off in the delicate cap-sleeved, doupion silk creation. So, as I wander among the two hundred guests at the outdoor ceremony, I feel the need to express, "I'm freezing my ass off," into my earpiece.

Emily mutters back, "But you look great in that dress. It's like someone custom made it for you or something."

"Bite me," I retort before I still, not due to the wind picking up but due to the vision coming into focus through my precious Nikon D850. The maid-of-honor, in a dress identical to mine, glances around quickly before striding up the aisle. Soon, she's running.

Right into the arms of the groom.

"Bastard," I murmur.

"What is it, Hols?" Corinna asks.

"I should work for your men," I whisper before I push the button capturing images that are breaking my heart. Because I know the bride is completely head over heels in love with her groom.

The asshole.

Phil groans, "Not another one." Cassidy sighs, knowing I'll be up in the bridal suite soon with evidence of every bride's worst nightmare: infidelity.

As many times as we help create happily ever after, there are so many it just doesn't work out. Years—hell, months—later, we'll hear something about our clients splitting up. What's worse is the times I get vibes in advance, and I want to tell either the bride or the groom to run before their hearts get broken. I feel like I've let them down by not speaking up, but as Ali has to remind me, my intuition isn't foolproof. They're not hiring us for marital counseling.

Only when I have proof can we go to our clients to let them make a decision on whether they want to continue with their wedding or not. I've been shocked by the number who continued despite the flagrant exposure of their soon-to-be spouse's behavior until one said, "Not all of us marry for love, Ms. Freeman," before she turned to have my sister attach her veil.

Sadly, I've learned masks slowly begin to degenerate the minute a ring is slapped on the finger of their intended.

And once again, the camera never lies.

Shaking my head, I turn around and head toward the bridal suite.

"Well, that went about as crappy as we expected," Em says, handing me a glass of champagne back at Amaryllis Events.

Corinna, having sliced up the top tier of the wedding cake—the only layer left after the bride stormed into the kitchen and nabbed the bottom two before running outside and smashing them in her former fiancé and best friend's faces—begins passing around the pieces. "I thought Tara was super ballsy when she came storming in for the cake," she offers.

"True," Cassidy concedes. "It was after when the screaming started that it went bad."

"God, what a prick." Ali is outraged. Rightfully so. Although my siblings know what happened, they just saw the aftermath; they didn't see the images.

Those images are only burned on the brain of the bride, her parents, and me.

"Where's Phil?" Em asks, looking around.

"He was calling Jason. I think he wanted to give him a heads-up before meeting us in here," Cassidy explains.

"Gotcha," I mumble through a bite of the frosted butterscotch cake. "Jesus, Cori. I want leftovers. I may not have bleach for my eyes, but this will help make the pain a little easier."

Everyone laughs. "I will incur the wrath of my husband and let you take all of the cake without protest," Ali concedes.

"It would be easier if you would just let me teach you how to bake, Ali," Corinna tries once again to convince my sister.

Ali lets out a less than delicate snort. "Like that's ever going to happen."

"I taught Brendan," she argues. When Corinna went on TV with our now family friend, country music star Brendan Blake, they ended up winning the show *Caketastic* against more seasoned chefs, putting Amaryllis Events even more on the map than it already was.

"No," Em corrects. "You were a drill sergeant to Brendan. He readily admitted to Jake he was petrified." Jake, Em's fiancé, is also one of Brendan's best friends.

"What a wuss," she grumbles. "You bark orders at someone to stir faster and to smile…"

We all bust a gut laughing. "Somehow, I think it was more than that despite what they showed on TV," I comment drolly.

Corinna turns golden eyes—eyes practically the same shade as my own—on me. "But Hols, isn't that how you get us all to do it?" Her voice is so full of false innocence, I have to press my lips together hard to smother my grin.

Lifting my camera, I turn it toward Em just as she takes a drink. "Smile, damn you, Em! Smile!" I bark out.

She spews her drink just as Phil pushes his way into the kitchen. As always, timing is everything in our family. Her champagne lands on the sleeve of his coat. "Jesus, Em. I just had this suit dry-cleaned."

Em is laughing too hard to reply. Instead, she just flaps her hand at him. I am clicking away photo after photo. Especially when Phil turns and grabs her by both cheeks and lays a smacking kiss on her forehead. The smile she gives him in return is brighter than the diamond on her finger. Lowering my camera, I take a sip of my own champagne.

Love comes in all forms, but when it's right and beautiful, it doesn't matter if it's between family, friends, or lovers. It lights up my heart, my mind, and my camera with its beauty. It begs me to capture it. Not so it can be stolen, but so it can be pulled out on those days when life's shadows seem to overcome it.

"Sorry I'm late." Phil strolls up to the table where his champagne and cake are waiting.

"How are the kids?" Cassidy and Ali ask at the same time. Looking at each other, they burst out laughing.

"Your men haven't lost or smothered a child yet," Phil reassures them. "In fact, they've been so well behaved, they're presently out for hot chocolate at The Coffee Shop."

The two mothers' jaws fall. "It must be Jason," Cassidy says to Ali.

"No other explanation," Ali agrees.

"Actually, I think they had a bigger impetus to behave than my husband," Phil casually throws out before shoving an enormous bite of cake in his mouth. We all wait impatiently while he chews. "They had a friend with them when I called," he finally tells us when he swallows.

"What? Did Colby get out of work early and show up?" Corinna guesses.

"Or did Jake abandon his studio and show up? I know! Jenna must have come home for the spring break early," Em says excitedly about her future stepdaughter.

"No and no." Phil dashes both of my sister's guesses. With a thoughtful expression, he says, "It was Joseph Bianco and his daughter, Grace."

"He was the man who lost his wife in the car accident who initially blamed Jason," I remind my siblings quietly.

Phil turns to face me. "It was his fiancée, Hols, but yes, while he was in the worst of his grief, he did blame Jason."

I lift the camera back up to my face and zoom in on Phil. There's acceptance and peace on his handsome features. Inside me, the knot that was beginning to form relaxes. "Okay. So, this is a good thing?" My voice communicates something to my sisters, who all relax slightly, Ali more than the others. "I actually met his mother, Denise, and daughter at the salon the other day. You know him, right, Ali?"

"Keene and I have known his daughter for a while. We mostly see her while he's on shift. She's in Kalie's preschool class. It's like having my own set of twins." Everyone bursts out laughing.

"Bet they don't fight as much as mine," Cassidy mutters, stabbing her cake with a fork. That sets off another round of chuckles.

"They're tight," Phil confirms. "According to Jace, they were thick as thieves at The Coffee Shop. He sent some pictures. I don't know which one had more whipped cream on them."

Ali groans.

Phil shrugs. "It's been a while since I've seen Joe. Jace says...he's different."

"Maybe there's someone new in his life?" I suggest. Three years is a long time, I think. But Ali shakes her head.

"No, and let me tell you it's not for lack of offers. That parent-teacher debacle from the other night I told you guys about?" Ali starts.

"He was the other parent there?" Em guesses.

"Yep. It was bad. Well, you know. You heard me rip into the administrator the next day," We all nod. It was not pretty. Ali is our corporate attorney and a barracuda in the courtroom. I almost wanted to sneak down to get pictures of her while she was on a rant, but I didn't want to interrupt her eloquent genius as she explained that hitting on the parents of her students was not part of Miss Tiffany's job description.

Yeesh.

"Seriously, I felt horrible for him. No man should have to put up with that kind of harassment. None of us would have ever tolerated that kind of behavior from a client, and we would have been out of business if we ever behaved that way," Ali concludes in disgust.

Phil sneers. "And she still has her job?"

"Barely. She's apparently been given a warning. I strongly encouraged the administration to contact him for corroboration if they needed to. I sincerely hope they don't have to." She shrugs. "He just wanted to forget about the entire incident and get home to his daughter. It seems like she's his whole world."

Put together with everything Gail said at the salon and the emptiness I saw on Joe Bianco's face at Genoa, Ali appears to have Joe pegged fairly accurately. Even though I don't have the same experience of lost love driving my occasional bouts of emptiness, I appreciate what might drive him to live for only one thing. After all, after everything that happened to me, I channeled all of my soul into the people in this room. I feel a strong compassion for a man I don't know.

And with that, I pick up my camera and begin to twist with the dials to disguise my absorption in the conversation instead of playing with my fingers like I used to do when I was nervous or anxious as a child.

9

JOSEPH

"Joe!" My head snaps toward the office that holds the Collyer Fire Chief where my name has just been shouted out. I'm hanging out in the lounge while men and women around me are taking some downtime. "Get in here!" he bellows.

I shrug as various heads turn toward me. "Listen, it wasn't me," I protest, though in reality, I have no idea what may have happened. I don't think I did anything recently to piss off the chief—who happens to be my dad.

It's both an honor and a burden to follow in your parent's footsteps. While there's a long line of tradition, there's an even longer line of expectation.

"How many times have you said that before, Joe? Did you come out of the womb saying that to him?" taunts Brett Stewart, my best everything since we were in high school.

"I think he only started that since he went through the academy, Stew. Before that he blamed you for everything," my other buddy on the squad, Justin Brady, calls out.

Throwing them both the finger, I slide off the worn couch and quickly make my way toward my father's office.

Knocking on the jamb, I walk in. "Dad? What's happened?"

It wasn't too long ago Brett's teasing would have been entirely spot-on. But the death of someone you love changes you. You either emerge from it changed, or you wither away. I've changed. I'm no longer the complete hotheaded, ask-questions-second, smart-ass I used to be. I have too many responsibilities for that now.

I have Grace.

"Sit down, son," my father says kindly. "We've got a problem with the plans for the 5K."

I make my way to one of the visitor chairs in front of his desk. My father's talking about the joint 5K we run every year with the Collyer Police Department to raise money for living families of fallen brothers and sisters that I was put in charge of this year. After Mary died, they insisted on including her name among those who had been killed, despite my protests. I knew it was an honor they were trying to give to Grace, to my family, to me, but it keeps the wound fresh. It seems everyone wants to do that. Every moment of every fucking day.

Nothing's been easy since I lost Mary. And some parts have been made worse in the last year. The rational side of me that's pored over the accident reports realizes if a freaking ER trauma doctor who happened to be Christmas shopping and at the scene couldn't save the woman I intended to marry from the clutches of death, nothing could.

A lot of things haven't been able to be saved.

"What's the problem?" My voice is controlled, even if I'm a raging inferno inside. I've learned to contain the fiery anger that still burns deep.

"The event-planning company who was supposed to do the work for us." My father hesitates before continuing. "They just backed out."

"What?" To hell with my control. I explode. "How can they do that? We had a contract with them!"

"Apparently they're willing to return all the money we paid them to take this other business, which is what our contract states, Joe. I don't know how we're going to do this unless we run the 5K as planned and trim back the after-party to something at one of the stations and hope people understand." I would be ready to take off his head at the suggestion except I see the defeat on his face.

None of us want this to fall apart. We've faced a wall of flames with these people at our back; their memories deserve the best we can give them. Suddenly, my conversation with Ali Freeman skates through my mind. *We're the very best at what we do, Mr. Bianco. There's not a single member of the Freeman family who doesn't take their responsibilities seriously.*

"Let me make a phone call before we go that route," I suggest.

"You have a miracle in your pocket?" he jokes.

Shaking my head, I move toward the door. "No. I just know someone who might be able to point me in the right direction."

"You've got until tomorrow morning, Joe. Then I'll activate the volunteer committees."

I nod, my mind already on the business card I'd shoved behind Grace's photo last week.

I just hope that there's a chance in hell they can take our business.

"Amaryllis Events, this is Alison. How may I help you?" Her lightly accented voice floats over the line.

"Ms. Freeman." I hesitate, even as I look down at the card she handed to me the other night. "This is Joe Bianco. Our children both attend..."

She interrupts before I can continue. "Of course, Joe. And it's Ali. How can I help you?" Her voice is pleasant and curious.

I clear my throat. "Well, first, I'd like to apologize if my blowing off your offer of your sister's services came off as being rude. It wasn't meant to be taken as personal." I wait for a heartbeat before continuing, but I'm not given a chance as Ali breaks up laughing.

"Joe, if I took everything someone said personally, I'd be out of business and likely have no family members left. Now, how can I help you today? Have you changed your mind?"

I can't help the smile tugging at my lips. Ali Freeman's personality is exactly the same as I remember it: open, bold, and up-front. "In a manner of speaking." I flip the thin cardboard over and over between my fingers. "I need an event planner—quickly as it turns out. I'm calling to inquire about the cost of your services?"

There's silence on the other end of the line. "I didn't realize you were getting married," Ali asks, confused.

I bark out a rough laugh. "Not hardly."

"Then what..." I interrupt her.

"Have you ever heard of the Collyer Police and Fireman's 5K?"

Ali snorts in my ear. "Heard about it? I run it every year. I have a side bet with Keene. I'm going to kick his ass at it."

I pull the phone away from my ear a little before putting it back in place. "Seriously?"

"Oh yeah. Keene thinks just because he can outrun me on distance, he'll...never mind. You were saying?"

"Ali, our event planner just bailed. If I can't find someone to help us on a shoestring budget, the event is going to go to hell. That means the Victims Assistance Fund won't raise money to help the families of our fallen—"

"Give me five minutes," Ali interrupts me and immediately places me on hold.

I let out a deep breath. And inhale another one. Just as I'm about to let that one out, a new voice comes on the line. "Mr. Bianco? This is Cassidy Freeman. I'm the CEO of Amaryllis Events. Do you have time to come in today so we can talk about what you need?"

"Ms. Freeman, I don't want to waste your time if I can't afford your services," I tell her bluntly.

Her warm laughter rings out in my ear. "First, call me Cassidy. We're going to be working together a lot over the next few weeks. And second, you don't understand. Amaryllis Events is going to donate our services."

What? My jaw unhinges. "This is unreal," I whisper.

"No, what happened to you and the police and fire department of

Collyer—people who keep us safe—is unreal. And trust me, we're going to help make this a day you'll never forget."

"I absolutely have time to come in and talk with you after my shift ends at three, but I'd also like to bring in the other members of the planning committee," I blurt out. "I also have to pick my daughter up by six…"

"Joe, if you call the school, I can grab Grace when I pick up Kalie if we run over," Ali offers.

"I'll get Grace but…" I hesitate.

"But what?" Cassidy asks.

Are you all for real? I swear I think the words until Ali and Cassidy both break up laughing. "Oh, God," I moan.

"Come see for yourself," Ali challenges.

A grin breaks out across my face. "I will. Is there anything I can bring?"

Cassidy's responds, "No. I have it all handled."

Ali's laughter can be heard through the line. "She isn't kidding when she says that, Joe. Knowing my sister, it's likely she'll have a twenty-page, single-spaced typed plan…ow, Cass! That hurt!" Their antics have me chuckling.

This all may work out. I let out a massive sigh of relief.

"Let me let you go so I can call the other members of the committee."

"Until three," Cassidy offers.

"We'll see you later." Ali disconnects the call in my ear.

Leaning back in my chair, I hope this works out. While I don't rely upon the Victims Assistance Fund, many do because living in Fairfield County isn't cheap by anyone's stretch of the imagination. Doing so as a single parent is next to impossible.

Even with the small inheritance I received from my maternal grandparents, my salary is stretched paper-thin with the addition of daycare to a budget that includes a mortgage and utilities. Even though Mary was a teacher and her income wasn't enormous either, we would have had a comfortable life together. She had been planning on staying home those first few years with our child so we didn't have this added cost, but like so many other things, that changed when she died.

While my parents were amazing not only in getting me back on a path that didn't have me wishing I could shove my body into the dark earth next to where Mary was buried, I could only rely on them for so long before I had to pull myself from the pain. And while I refused to take money from Victims Assistance, I relied heavily on their counseling services to get me through the worst of the grief that would barely let me hold my daughter without collapsing to my knees. Three years ago, I lashed out at everything and everyone—including Jason—the man who tried to save Mary's life. This 5K is more than a fund-raiser; it's personal gratitude to each and every person who pulled me from the abyss.

Until the night I got the call to come to the hospital about Mary's wreck, I'd led a charmed life. I was the kind of guy who figured out what I wanted, and nothing and no one stopped me from doing it, having it, beating it. It took a long time to realize I didn't just lose most of my heart, I lost all sense of self that night. I often wonder what Mary would think about the man I am now. I'm not always the funny guy with a joke who made her laugh. I used to be a colossal wiseass; I find myself much more empathetic now. I'm a lot more somber than I used to be.

And I'm a lot quicker to admit my faults.

Those who have been along this path with me worry I'm living under her shadow. That's not the case. I'm just no longer the person I used to be. It's as if the fire that used to burn so high was dampened in me. It flickers on occasion, but for the most part, the flames are banked. There's nothing there to kindle them.

Fire needs fuel to burn, and there's nothing to feed mine with. Not anymore.

Through circumstances I wouldn't wish upon anyone, I've changed into a man whose path has one clear direction: raising a beautiful little girl to become an extraordinary woman.

Picking up the phone again, I make a quick phone call to my counterpart over at CPD. Detective Idrissi assures me he and Chief

Drever will meet my father and me at Amaryllis Events at three to see what the Freeman siblings can come up with. Hanging up, I yell out, "Hey, old man! Got an update for you!"

"Better be a good one," I hear yelled back at me.

It is. At least, I hope it will be. Standing, I make my way back into his office. I'm rewarded with a huge smile, a slap on the back, a "Great job, son. Come grab me when you leave," before he throws me out of his office.

I roll my shoulders and head back to the desk I commandeered where I've been reviewing old case files even as I study for the lieutenant's exam. I'm determined to be a better firefighter, a better man, a better father.

All for Grace.

10

JOSEPH

"It's a pleasure to see you again, Joe." Ali Freeman firmly shakes my hand after she takes those of my father, Detective Mike Idrissi, and Chief Pamela Drever. "Please take a seat." We've been escorted into the conference room at Amaryllis Events by a young blonde woman I don't recognize. "Jenna, would you mind telling the others we've gathered?" She nods before disappearing. Ali offers me a quick smile. "That's my sister Emily's future stepdaughter and one of our interns. She's home on a break between semesters at UConn."

"And she's not partying with her friends during her break?" I ask incredulously, thinking back to what I would likely have been doing at young Jenna's age.

I hear a rich laugh behind me. Turning, I expect to find a similar replica of Ali's tall blondeness. Instead, my eyes drop downward to meet the eyes of a petite brunette. "Joe? Cassidy Freeman." Her smile lights up her face even as she holds out her hand. I take it carefully in mine, careful not to crush the delicate bones. "It's a pleasure to meet you. I've heard a lot about you from Phil and Jason."

I wince. What must these people think of me? Before I can get another apology out of my mouth, a hand drops on my shoulder. My head turns, and I meet Phil Freeman-Ross's smiling eyes. "All good things, Joe," he says quietly. "Jason says hello."

Jesus, I can barely swallow past the lump in my throat. Despite running into Jason the other day, I can hardly comprehend how the two men I attacked so wrongly can forgive me when I can barely forgive myself. I nod, even as I hold out my hand. "Good to see you, Phil."

His lips quirk in a half smile even as he grips my hand tightly. "You too." Turning toward Cassidy, he asks, "Where's everyone else? We've got a lot of ground to cover." Phil sounds authoritative, but I can tell who's really in charge when Cassidy rolls her eyes.

Trying to hide my laugh behind a cough, I fail when Ali hears her brother and chimes in, "Please, Phil. The only reason you're on time anywhere is that that I finally have you on an electronic leash. Cori's bringing up snacks; Holly and Em are helping."

My father and Chief Drever simultaneously groan aloud. "Corinna's baking?" My father, the man who swears off most desserts, is practically drooling like a St. Bernard puppy.

Ali pats his arm gently. "It's okay, Chief. She also made a box for you to take home to your wife."

"Actually, I made enough for everyone to take some home tonight." A voice that sounds like rich honey and whose owner has eyes that match strolls into the room. She's carrying a tray of brownies. "Hey, y'all," she calls out.

"Hey, Cori," her siblings call back. Phil starts to slide her way, but Cassidy hooks an arm around his stomach. He practically trips over his feet. "What's your problem, Cass?" he gripes.

"Our guests get first dibs, Phillip," she snaps.

"If brownies aren't to your liking, Cori also baked cookies," a willowy blonde calls out. "I'm Emily." She smiles at my father, Chief Drever, and Detective Idrissi first before throwing a smile over my way. Spotting Cassidy's arms wrapped around Phil's waist, she directs her comment directly to him. "You have issues. Jason should really find someone to deal with them for you."

"More than just a few, Em. We've always known that," a husky voice drawls from the hallway.

All the occupants of the room, myself included, burst out laughing. But the minute the voice takes shape and walks through the doorway, my laughter disappears as does the oxygen in my lungs.

Fire.

Ever since I was a child, I was warned about the most dangerous kind of fire long ago. It lives and breathes, sways and moves. It ignites your every sense until it's tingling.

Fire comes in all forms.

What they didn't train me on was apparently it cascades in silken sheets down the back of a woman. No one warned me a woman's skin could block the sun; her skin is so fair. No one told me firelight would dance in the face of a woman who's merely pushing a cart of coffee into the conference room filled with people or that she'd do it with a camera hanging from her neck like it's an everyday occurrence.

"Hey, everyone." Coming to a stop next to Corinna, she ducks her head to fiddle with a few dials on the camera around her neck.

At that moment, a cloud shifts. Light streams through leaded glass surrounding the conference room windows, illuminating her beauty even further before she lifts her camera to her face.

All I can think is, God, I can't let the fire consume me.

Cassidy beams. "Great, now that Holly's here, we can get started. Why doesn't everyone take a seat?"

Inside, my stomach rolls as I realize this is the last Freeman sister we've been waiting for. But I feel like I'm knocked off my feet by a blast of water from a fire engine when I realize as she moves closer, I've seen that face before. Most recently when I caught her body against mine as our crew barreled into her at Genoa.

I feel like I'm coming out of a long, deep sleep as our eyes meet briefly. She smiles, and my gut clenches, before she turns to say something to Cassidy, who nods in return.

We all move around the table, except Holly. She moves away and straddles the back of an antique sofa, lifting her camera up to obscure her face. I'm almost relieved I won't have to look into her face across the table as we hammer out the details over what is likely going to be long, arduous hours.

I brace myself for the inevitable.

THIRTY MINUTES LATER, I'm shocked, but I'm sure as hell not speechless.

"Hold on." I raise my voice to be heard over the excited chattering around the table. "This event is less than three weeks away. You're not only saying you can take over the existing plans in place, but you can also amp them up?"

Cassidy shrugs. "Sure. And next year, we'll be able to do more if you come to us right from the beginning."

"Next year?" I choke out.

"This was the best I could do with such a limited time frame." Cassidy sounds almost apologetic.

My father jumps in. I think he's in shock as well. "Cassidy, let me reiterate the revised plan. The 5K is not only going to happen, but Emily is going to design a logo and participant event T-shirt for those that preregister."

"Yes, but that's only for those who register at least seven days before the event," Emily cautions. "We'll make ten percent extra to sell on race day for last-minute sign-ups or family members after the race."

My father clears his throat. "Right. Corinna has already worked it out with The Coffee Shop to cosponsor an after-race pancake breakfast—"

And he's cut off by Corinna. "Ava and Matt were thrilled. The Victims Assistance Fund is already their charity of the month anyway."

"That reminds me," Em mutters. "We'll put all the high-level sponsors on the back."

"I'm sure the guys will donate," Ali muses aloud.

"The guys?" Chief Drever asks. The former State Trooper major moved to Collyer when the position opened a few years ago. With more than thirty combined years of experience, she is extremely well respected among the boys and girls in blue.

Cassidy, Ali, and Corinna all exchange a quick look. It's Ali who explains. "Our husbands operate a private investigations agency based in the area. Their team is comprised of primarily former military or law enforcement personnel, so this is something they'd likely be interested in sponsoring. As I told Joe the other night"—she nods at me—"my husband and I are already registered for the race."

"We should all run," Cassidy says. Phil groans.

"Jesus, Phil. It's a little over three miles," Ali says in disgust.

"Y'all know I don't run. Besides, I'll be getting stuff ready with Ava and Matt," Corinna drawls.

My eyes drift to the side to the sister who's remained silent. "What about you?" I don't know why I feel the need to challenge Holly, but I do. Maybe it's because she's been so quiet while her siblings have been enthusiastically plotting away.

The camera her face has been hidden behind is pulled aside. The grin that lights up her face is as massive as the lens she's holding up. "I'll likely be clocking a hell of a lot more than three miles race day."

I'm confused. "Why's that?"

"Because while I have interns who will be taking the majority of the photos at both the start and finish, and I'll bring on a few extra people to take photos at water stations along the course, I'll be everywhere else race day. I'll be on the course with a camera around my neck. I'll be at breakfast after. And Cass hasn't even got to the best part of her plan, yet." She directs the attention back to her sister.

"There's more?" My head's spinning and I'm not entirely sure if it's because the Freemans have managed to pull all of this together in just a few hours or because Holly Freeman has me so knocked off balance.

Cassidy just smiles. "I called the owners of Tide Pool. We're... friendly with them." Cassidy begins to cough loudly at the same time all of her siblings start howling with laughter. "Let's just say they know us well."

My lips twitch. "Why are there alarm bells clanging in my head telling me there's more to this story?"

Ali's voice is droll. "Because you have good instincts?"

Good to know. "Anyway, Cassidy, you were saying?"

Cassidy clears her throat. "The owners of Tide Pool normally don't charge a cover. And the night of the race for any CPD or CFD officer, they won't. For everyone else, there will be. We also got a band to play, and we know someone who will DJ for us once the band's done for the night. If you request a song, you have to donate. There will be a specialty drink called 'Up in Smoke' being made. Any money from any of those things will go toward the Victims Assistance Fund. We reserved a spot in all the local newspapers for the next three weeks. I spoke to the board of education about sending home flyers for sign-ups—they do this cool electronic flyer sign up now—and I also spoke to most of the businesses on Main Street about hanging posters in their windows." She shrugs. "If I had additional time, I could have done more."

I gape at her. "Are you kidding?"

She shakes her head gravely. "That's why I said we need to start earlier next year."

Sweet Jesus. I called Ali like six hours ago. I look across the table at Mike, who gives me a single nod. My head swivels over to Chief Drever, who's beaming. My eyes meet my father's. His face is just as shocked as mine.

Finally, my eyes turn toward Ali. "What do we need to sign?"

All of the Freemans let out a cheer.

I just shake my head at the incredible luck I had. And to think I owe it to a ridiculous parent-teacher conference and a flighty event planner. It might be that intuition Ali said I had earlier, but somehow I just know this is going to be more amazing than any fund-raiser we've ever done before.

"I NEVER EXPECTED anything like this when I called," I tell Ali honestly. We're standing by our cars in the parking lot of Amaryllis Events. We both have to leave soon to get our children.

"Cass wasn't kidding. You should have heard the ideas she had, but she needed an extra month to be able to pull them off."

I shake my head. "This is so much more, Ali."

"It's not enough, Joe. People rely on you all day after day for their lives. This is nothing in return. It's our honor," she counters fiercely.

I suspect something more is driving the Freemans' assistance more than just the fact it's a worthy cause, but I don't have the right to pry. I go to open my mouth when out of the corner of my eye I see Holly racing to her car.

"Later, Ali! I'm late for a client shoot. Nice to meet you, Joe. I'll touch base with you about the photo op this week, so you'll be hearing from me."

"Um, okay?" I call back, confused.

"Cassidy must have caught Holly and handed out more assignments," Ali explains.

"That must mean something in your world because I'm still lost," I tell her honestly.

Ali doesn't bother to hide her mirth. "It will mean something to you soon enough." She pats my arm. "Now let's go get our kids. I suspect you'll be hearing from all of us sooner rather than later."

"Do you have a schedule of when that will be?" I joke.

Ali smiles. "That will likely be in your inbox by the time you make it home. Cassidy's pretty astounding when it comes to organizing...everything."

My smile dies. "I think all of you are, Ali. With the way I behaved, I had no right to make the call today. I just couldn't let anyone down."

She's quiet for a moment. "Joe? If there's any family who understands what trauma can do to a person, it's this one. No one, particularly Jason and Phil, holds the way you behaved against you."

I focus on the line of trees over her shoulder. "I do," I mutter.

"Is the measure of a man his anger? Or is the measure of a man how he behaves when the anger and bitterness pass and he takes steps to recover from what caused that devastation?" Ali asks me softly.

I open my mouth, but she beats me to it. "If it were the first, then the men in our family would all be living a life in purgatory versus the path of righteousness. Think on that a while." She beeps the locks to her car, then opens the door and slides behind the wheel. Lowering the window, she smiles. "See you at the school."

I don't have a chance to respond to any of it before she's backing her car out of its spot.

"I often find it annoying when my sisters are right because they often are." Phil's hand comes down on my shoulder.

"Even about it only being a three-mile run?" I try to lighten the mood because right now, I don't know how much more wisdom I can handle without breaking.

Phil laughs. "I get crap from all of them about working out. What they fail to note is that I do those workouts religiously. I plan on being around for a long time."

I shake my head. "All we can do is bank the memories, Phil. None of us are guaranteed forever."

"It doesn't mean we shouldn't live, Joe." Squeezing my shoulder, Phil casually remarks, "You should come by the farm for dinner. Bring Grace."

Squinting at the other man, I ask dubiously, "Why do I get the feeling you're up to something?"

Phil looks affronted. "Listen, the only time all the family's schedules seem to mesh is over our weekly dinner. It's a good time for you to get to see Jace as well as hang out with people you'll be dealing with a lot over the next three weeks."

Crap. "Sorry, Phil. There have just been so many people who have come at me with good intentions..."

"And it's been a crock of shit trying to hook up the newly eligible single dad?" Phil concludes.

"Yeah."

He waves that away. "Don't worry. Everyone in my family is very taken except for Holly, and I despair of that girl ever settling down." Phil scoffs.

Relaxing, I agree. "I'll take you up on that, then."

"Good, because Cassidy already put it on your schedule."

I bust out laughing. "I'll check it against the schedule at the station."

Phil tosses his keys in the air and deftly catches them. "We'll talk soon. You heading over to get Grace?"

I glance down at my watch. "Yeah." If I don't head out soon, I'll be late, and I refuse to let my baby girl worry. About anything.

"See you."

"Yeah, see you, Phil." I open the locks on my SUV and slide into the seat.

Driving to daycare, I reflect on the miracle of today. I realize I've been living in a world of insanity these last three years. Even if it's one burden removed, somehow I've been sent an army of angels to help me deal. And I know who's been looking out for me.

Catching a glimpse of the rosary hanging from my rearview, I mutter, "Thanks, baby," to my deceased fiancée as I turn into the parking lot to pick up our daughter.

11

HOLLY

Pulling up to the distinguished fire station on the outskirts of downtown Collyer a few days later, I shove my sunglasses to the top of my head. The faded antique brick of the three-story building is a sharp contrast to the bright blue of the late March sky. Sliding out of my vehicle, I stand beside it for a minute squinting at the presence the building makes. Memories trickle to the forefront of my mind of the first moments and days after Corinna, Ali, and I were rescued.

Although it was Charleston Vice and ICE who burst in and snatched Ali off the auction block from the human traffickers, there was a mass of Charleston public servant volunteers who escorted us to safety. I remember being in the back of the fire chief's SUV holding desperately on to Corinna and Ali wrapped in a blanket, seeing the sun for more than the few moments it took for our captors to hose us down before sending us back into the shipping container we were being held captive in.

After it was a race to get us to safety before the press could swarm in with their microphones and cameras. We were victims, but because someone felt it was their right to know, we were hidden for our own safety.

And it was during that time I had to admit my culpability to the death of my stepmother because my father used it as a bargaining chip to get his own sentence reduced. I remember the prosecuting attorney coming to the battered women and children's shelter where we were being kept and questioning me over and over.

"Did you intend to kill your stepmother, Ms. Greene?"

"Why did you have your father's gun in your hands?"

"Where was your father when all of this was happening?"

And my answers caused tears to fall down her face. Because a fifteen-year-old should never have to respond with, "No, I never intended to kill her. I was trying to kill myself since my father intended to sell me to his friends, his enemies, anyone he could make money from." I remember bitterly laughing at the slack-jawed attorney and whispering, "I made a decision I was fully prepared to execute; there was nothing that was going to be worse than repeated rape. Not even death. I was prepared to die the day I pulled that trigger instead of letting my father get paid for my slower demise." As I sat back, my chest heaving, I bit out, "The only reason I'm glad it didn't is that now I can watch my father go down for what he did even if it means I have to serve time for accidentally shooting Maria. But if you think knowing I killed her is an easier burden to carry, then you are so wrong. I have someone's death on my hands. The two girls I just survived Hell with don't know I killed someone to land me next to them. I have yet to share that with them. I'd like a chance to say goodbye because I'll soon be in prison serving time for that. But if you think prison is going to break me after what I just went through, you are so very wrong."

The prosecuting attorney soon excused herself for a phone call. Within moments, she came back more composed, "Noelle, tell me what your plans are?"

"I don't know." I had no idea. I was living minute to minute.

"Let me get back to my office and review the case. I'll be back tomorrow. Can you trust me until then? Please?" My eyes, which had been focused on the center of the table, lifted. "Just give me one day."

I nodded.

"Tonight an officer is going to be sleeping outside your room, but I don't think after tomorrow you're going to need that," she said ambiguously.

At the time, I thought it was because I would soon be taken to the local jail for intake. I never thought it was because I was being issued a pardon from the governor of South Carolina, the prosecuting attorney's cousin.

Days later, I held the paper in my hand blinking rapidly as tears coursed down my face. "I don't understand."

"Find your life, Noelle," the prosecutor whispered. "Live without fear. If there's one thing I'll ever do right in my career, this will be it."

Later when I chose my new name as we became Freemans, it wasn't a leap. I chose Holly after the prosecutor who saved my life by merely giving me one.

I followed her career. When I saw her husband—a local Charleston firefighter—lost his life five years ago rescuing a stranded family on a barrier island during a hurricane, I asked Ali to make a donation in all of our names in his honor. I included a note that said, *You asked me once to trust you and to give you one more day. You worked a miracle at that time. Don't give up on the fact all it takes is one day for a miracle to happen. - Holly Freeman.*

The next time I saw a photo of her, I saw she was heavily pregnant with her deceased husband's child. In the newspaper article, she said, "I never knew I was pregnant when he died. This baby is my miracle. When I was grieving Ed's death, I received a letter reminding me all it takes is one day, and they can happen. The person I received it from touched my heart deeply with her words." I smiled when I read that.

Leaning against my car, I look down at my hands and think maybe just a little more of the stain on them is washing away. It's hard to take in the beauty I've been blessed day after day and not appreciate that somehow it's a gift, that some higher being understands. The life we've been blessed with since those dark days hasn't been simple, but it's been beautiful.

And we've tried to give back as much as we can.

Including donating to every fund-raiser hosted by the team of firefighters that reside in the building in front of me. My head swivels to the left. Not to mention the police in the building next door. We understand firsthand the sacrifices these men and women make to rescue people in need. After all, we were one of them. Even as recently as Cassidy being shot just a few years ago during one of our weddings. I shudder in remembrance at the dark days that followed, when we hovered in the waiting room of Greenwich Hospital wondering if she was going to live or die.

"Every second counts when God's trying to decide whether or not to give you a miracle," I murmur aloud.

"That's profound, Holly." Startled, I turn and find the kind face of Chief Bianco. "Not everyone sees what we do in quite that fashion."

I respond simply, "Then they've never been on the edge of giving up on life when a miracle's stormed through their door."

He continues to hold my eyes. "I find it both disturbing and heart-warming to realize you understand that."

"It's like most pictures, Chief," I tell him honestly. "There are many things I see through the lens that either could hurt or harm people. But if given a chance, I'll focus on something else to find the beauty where I can."

"That's an interesting way of viewing the world."

"That's the way I choose to look at it," I correct him. Turning my back to him, I reach into the back of my car for the camera I'm never without. "I've been called a dreamer." Among other things.

"I wouldn't say that." He chooses his words carefully. "I'd say you're made up of the same things the rest of the people in the world are, you just have a different perspective."

"What's that?" I challenge him.

"We're all made up of broken pieces of those who have come and gone before us. Sometimes, that—" He nods towards my camera. "—can't quite capture the depth of the scars that live within us."

His words make me think he can see the red stains on my skin. Looping my camera around my neck, I shove my hands in my pocket. "True. And sometimes, the camera exposes too much."

"Also true." His eyes drift over my shoulder. "Are you ready for what you're about to be exposed to inside, Holly? I can't promise it's going to be photoworthy today."

Suddenly, the chief's warning begins to make sense. "Something's happened today, hasn't it?"

Joseph Bianco Sr. lets out such a long breath of air, I'm afraid his chest is going to decompress. "Yeah, it did. We were called in to help with a four-car pileup on the border between here and Ridgefield."

"There were casualties." I'm not asking. His whole body is screaming in the agony of failure and loss.

He nods. "And Joe was there. You can't imagine how it kills me every time I have to send my boy to an accident like that. I wonder if I'm doing the right thing as his chief—as his father. Am I ripping open wounds that are starting to scab over?"

I pull a hand from my pocket and reach over to touch his arm. "I suspect that if you tried to pull your son off of those calls, you'd be doing him more of a disservice than you are by sending him."

He tips his head to look down at me. "What makes you say that?"

"Because we're all forged of the things that have tried to break us. And in the end, if we win, we're not only living, we're shoving the Devil back into Hell the way he tried to drag us there." With that, I move away from my car and toward the entrance of the fire station. Tossing my hair over my shoulder, I look back at the chief.

"Now, take me in. Let me show this town what they should be supporting." As I watch Chief Bianco make his way over to me, I can see the pain plainly across his face. But now, I also see something else there.

A tiny bit of hope.

12

HOLLY

I intended to come to the firehouse for informal shots, much like the ones I took at the police department. But unlike the CPD, who knew I was there, I used my instincts and became a ghost in the wake of what I learned happened.

Quietly, I stood at the entrance. Even I was taken aback at the two men and one woman inspecting the hydraulic lines and blades of the tools I knew must have been used to cut victims out of their car this morning. Each one still in their waterproof boots and yellow pants being held up by bright red suspenders, they didn't take the time to change before they finished their job. Automatically, my camera flies to my face as I zoom in on their faces.

Absolute dedication to the mission.

Click.

My throat tightens.

Someone else is over by the ambulance restocking it. My head swings that way, and I zoom in.

Joe.

I feel his father come up behind me even as I depress the shutter, his breath ragged. "These are the moments I'm proud to be sitting in the chair the most." Then he leaves me to open the door to the side. "Come upstairs when you're ready, Holly."

I spend thirty minutes down in the bay absorbing the beautiful pain deep into my soul, click after click. Just as I turn and head upstairs, I feel a burn down the back of my spine. Turning back, I meet Joe's eyes. From across the room, I can feel his pain as if it's nails skating across my skin.

Lowering my camera, I find myself doing something instinctively. Lifting my closed left fist—behind which my amaryllis tattoo lies—I lay it across my chest in a silent tribute he won't understand. But I do. Turning, I head upstairs to find the rest of the department on edge, affected by the day's incident.

Because even though pain and depression could be a toxicity that spreads like a fire, there's something in this building that puts it out even faster than water to a flame.

Family.

And I understand that feeling as I'm blessed with it every day.

I capture it all on my camera before hours later I drop by the chief's office to let him know I have everything I need.

LATER THAT DAY, I'm going through the pictures when Cassidy strolls into my office. "What are you thinking for the photos?"

Leaning forward in my chair, I tap my mouse a few times before the Photoshop file comes up on my giant monitor. When it does, Cassidy's gasp fills me with warm satisfaction. "I think if we get permission from CPD and CFD to use these photos, the Victims Association is going to get a significant boost in their fund-raising," I remark.

Cassidy's fingers try to trace the monitor. I've managed to capture the essence of both our police and fire departments: the fierceness, the pride, the weariness, the desperation, the heart, and the struggle. In one shot, Detective Idrissi has a young girl cradled in his arms as she cries. I happen to know it was because she lost her beloved dog and wanted to put a sign up at the police department. In the next, Chief Drever is running drills and demanding more from her newest officers, not to be a bitch but to keep them alive. A picture of Joe resting his head on his arms against the ambulance is there with his other coworkers slightly blurred in the forefront. One of his father from behind, wearing the weight of chief. Both squad rooms where the people are blurred, but the memorial walls are in clear focus.

Turning my head slightly, I see Cassidy's eyes are watery. "You make magic behind a camera, Hols," she whispers. Standing, she brushes her lips across my head. "Send me the mock-up. I'll get the sign-offs."

Basking in her praise, I export the file to my cloud drive. Sending it via email to my sister, I copy Ali knowing she'll have to attach the rights and clearances paperwork so we can distribute the photos. Before I close the file, I look at it again.

My eyes linger on Joe. My heart hurts when I think of the fact he'll have no one waiting for him tonight other than Grace. But maybe that will be enough, I tell myself firmly as I close the file.

After all, not all of us need someone to get us through the rough parts of life.

Some of us just need to be alive.

13

HOLLY

"I think Phil's going to burst," I mutter to Corinna as we're preparing dinner in the communal kitchen at our family's farm that night. While we all have our own homes, there's a massive structure on our property with a huge great room, kitchen, and workout space that overlooks the lake. We use it frequently for family gatherings, especially now that our family has more than doubled in size in the last few years.

"He's loving the fact he knows something Keene doesn't," Corinna whispers back. "Ali will stab him with her steak knife if he spills the beans though."

"When is she planning on telling him? It's killing me."

"I honestly don't know. It's been two weeks since she told us." Corinna turns a concerned face toward me. "You don't think there's anything wrong, do you? I mean, we weren't there in the early part of her pregnancy with Kalie, Hols."

Shit. I hadn't thought of that. I bite my lower lip and look at Ali anxiously. She must feel our eyes on her because she glances our way. Her cobalt-blue eyes narrow in question. Then her face smooths out. She reaches for her phone at her side, and her thumbs begin moving.

Soon, my hip is buzzing. I drop the knife I was using on the cutting board and pull my phone from my pocket. Corinna reads over my shoulder.

Will the two of you relax? There's nothing wrong. I swear to God, I have a plan on when I'm telling Keene.

I frantically type back. *Is it any time before the baby's born?*

"You tell her, Hols," Corinna mutters as she slides baked donuts into the oven for dessert. My mouth begins to water knowing she'll dust them with two different types of sugar before serving them all warm and delicious.

Ali looks directly at me, raises an eyebrow, and begins typing again. I just wait for her to finish and the incoming text to reach me.

I'm sure I'll have plenty of time to tell him by the time by the time the babies are here, yes.

I choke. Corinna screams. Loudly.

All eyes turn to us. Colby jumps up. "Princess, are you okay?" he demands.

A new text comes in. *Say anything, and I really will take retribution for the hair dye incident.* I burst out laughing remembering how Corinna dyed Ali's hair red because she assumed it was Ali who ate Colby's birthday cake in college, when we found out only a few years ago it was Colby himself. "We're fine, Colby. It was just a spider."

"Two of them, actually," Corinna calls out. "I just got jumpy since I've never seen two."

"Not from there," I correct.

"No, not from there."

Ali cracks up laughing. I beam at Corinna and then turn my wonky smile on Ali. "You two are completely nuts," she declares.

"That's us," Corinna agrees, throwing an arm around my shoulders. She's squeezing me hard. Containing this much joy is next to impossible, but I'm not taking Ali's threat idly.

"God, she better tell him soon," I mutter.

"Now I feel like Phil, and that's just wrong," Corinna announces.

We look at each other and burst out laughing. Corinna picks up a towel to wipe her tears of laughter before handing it to me to do the same.

Fortunately, the doorbell rings. Throwing down the towel, I call to the room at large, "I'll get it."

Jogging for the front door, I look through the peephole to find Joe and Grace Bianco on the other side. "Well, hey! Welcome to the farm. I didn't know you guys were coming to dinner."

Joe looks anxious for a moment. "Did I get the date wrong? Cassidy put something on my schedule…"

I smile before stepping back. "Not at all. It explains the extra place settings. Welcome to the madhouse."

Even as Joe passes by, I see Grace whisper something to him. He closes his eyes briefly before a small smile touches his lips. "Baby, I told you in the car, Miss Holly's hair isn't actually fire. If she lets you, you can touch it."

She ducks her little head into her father's shoulder, and just like that, my heart melts.

Joe looks at me and shrugs.

"Hey, Kalie's Grace," I call to her softly. Her head flies up so fast, she almost clocks her father in the chin. I bite my lip in amusement. "Laura, and Jon are in the big room. Do you want to go see them?"

"Can I, Daddy?" she asks. He plunks her down on her feet and begins removing her hat and coat.

"You sure can, but remember what I said in the car." She nods furiously.

"No running around the table. Say pwease and thank you. Eat slow." Joe rolls his eyes heavenward as his three-year-old parrot begins to repeat literally everything he must have reminded her about good manners.

I swallow hard to keep the laugh in. His deep blue eyes cut over to me in a warning. "That's right, baby. Now, go have fun."

She takes him literally, screeching, "Kaaaaaaalllllliiiiiieeee!"

I wait about two seconds before the laughter bursts out from me. "Grace was adorable the first time I met her. I'm so thrilled to see that hasn't changed."

"She's really excited to be here."

"We're thrilled to have you both with us," I say magnanimously.

"Even though you didn't know we were coming?" I sense vulnerability behind the question.

"Joe, not kidding, Cassidy literally arranges for Caleb's brother and husband to show up. We normally have no idea until they walk through the door."

A smile breaks across his face. "Okay, then I don't feel like we're imposing."

"Not at all," I say warmly. "Now hand over your coats and I'll hang them both up."

Shrugging out of his jacket, Joe looks around. "You all live here?"

"If you mean on the property, then yes. We haven't lived together since we built our individual homes though."

"It's nice you all have that."

I toss him a smile over my shoulder as I hang up his and Grace's coats in the hall. "Thanks, we think so as well."

Joe shakes his head. "You know, you made quite an impression on Grace."

Closing the closet, I raise my brows. "I did?"

"Yeah. I spent half the ride here telling her that your hair wasn't actually going to burn your head off."

I choke as Joe and I make our way into the great room where the kids are dancing amid the adults. "You're kidding me, right?"

"Nope. She was worried 'Kalie's Holly' was going to get hurt."

"Now that I find absolutely precious." Reaching over, I squeeze his bicep. I ignore the feel of it beneath my hands and the fact a small part of me wouldn't mind spending time running my hands over the sinewy muscles. Attributing the feeling as to the fact I'm an artist and I appreciate a well-built man's body, I continue. "If no one has told you lately, you're doing a remarkable job raising her. She's a treasure."

He lets out a deep breath. "Each time I hear it, it's like the first time. So, thank you."

I tighten my fingers once more before I let him go. "Now, what can I get you to drink?"

"I don't drink while I have Grace in the car..." he starts to explain. Instead, I launch into a litany of soft drinks we keep on hand.

"And that's if you don't want us to make you a mocktail or something fancy," I conclude.

"A Coke sounds perfect." He grins. "Water for Grace until dinner."

"Then make yourself at home. And I'll apologize in advance if they let the inmates out of the ward too early this evening." At his confused look, I explain, "My family likes to unwind. Sometimes that involves arguing. Sometimes that involves dancing..."

Corinna adds to my comment as she breezes by with an antipasto platter in her hands. "She's being polite, Joe. She's not adding on that often we dance on tables."

I roll my eyes at my sister at the slack-jawed look on Joe's face. "I was trying not to scare our guest, Corinna, but thank you for doing so," I grit out.

"Meh. No worries." She sends Joe a saucy wink before she plunks the antipasto in the center in the table. Sauntering her way over to her fiancé, she grins at the antics of the kids dancing. Colby leans down and whispers something in her ear that makes her laugh.

I hear the front door open behind me and in rush Phil and Jason. "Sorry we're late!" Phil calls out.

"You didn't miss anything," Em shouts to be heard over the noise.

"Other than it being your turn to cook," Cassidy yells out. Joe blinks at her, likely wondering where my mild-mannered sister disappeared to.

"I was...held up," Phil beings to explain. And we all break out in laughter. Even Jason can't hold back the laughter.

"Babe, I think that worked on them when they were eighteen and we were dating," he tells Phil.

Phil shrugs unapologetically. Then he spots Joe and grins. "Hey, you made it!"

I don't know why, but I jump in front of Joe and throw out my arms. "No. Just no. You are not tormenting our guest to get out of your own colossal..."

"Yes?" Phil purrs.

My eyes dart around the room, and I spy all the children. I can't say what I really want to as loudly as I want to my older brother.

Instead, I lean in and whisper, "If you mess with our guest to save your own ass, I will have you drugged, then brought to a tattoo parlor to have Keene's name tatted on your ass in a color to match his eyes."

Jason begins choking with laughter behind me. "Jesus, Phil. That's so much worse than Cass threatening to cut off all your hair."

"Whose side are you on?" Phil demands of his husband.

"The side of love. Then the side right and sane. Always. Which is how I've survived being married to you," he retorts.

I hear a deep rumble of laughter behind me that I've never heard before. Spinning on my booted heel, I find Joe Bianco's hands braced on his knees as he's doubled over. His head is dropped, and his shoulders are shaking.

Phil comes up behind me and kisses my cheek. "And that's how you help heal a broken man, sister. Good job," he whispers in my ear before he makes his way into the room to greet everyone.

I stand there frozen in place as Joe continues to laugh. When he finally gets it under control, he stands and wipes his fingers under his eyes. "I needed that."

"Yeah?" It's a question because I'm not really sure where to go with this. But Joe hands it to me like the gift it is.

For all of us.

"So many nights after a shittastic day like the one you know I had, there's been nothing and no one there to help take away the pain, Holly." His eyes do a scan of the room where his daughter is dancing with my niece. He smiles falters a little as Cassidy is twirled by Caleb to the strains of Luke Bryan. He chuckles again as he watches Phil get sprayed in the face by Em as she laughs at something he says. Jason merely shakes his head and pulls out a handkerchief. Too bad Jake's at parent-teacher conferences of his own tonight. He'd have been impressed with Em's aim. "For once I'm not sitting around wondering if the only blessing I've got is Grace." Turning, his dark blue eyes meet mine. "I'm beginning to think there might be more I've encountered and just haven't seen, you know?"

I nod, choked up that someone else sees my family that way.

"I'll say thanks in advance for a great dinner." His lips crook up in a half smile before he bravely makes his way into the fray. Quick arm squeezes from Cassidy and Ali, handshakes from most of the others, Joe settles. And even as I make my way over to my camera, I realize I don't need the lens to see the burdens from earlier in the day have already started to lift.

The glimmer of a miracle is shining. I just want to see if I can capture it on camera.

14

JOSEPH

"I can't thank you enough for a wonderful evening." I'm walking out with Holly, carrying an exhausted Grace in my arms.

Holly stops by the hall closets to collect our coats. "It was our pleasure. And I feel you have a much clearer understanding of what we're trying to do for the race, don't you?"

"Completely. And I haven't laughed so hard since..." My voice trails off. *Since Mary died.* But I don't feel like it's a betrayal to think that. I feel like it's another step toward the healing journey I'm supposed to take as Grace and I learn to function in this world without her.

Holly smiles, but her eyes are quiet even as she begins to thread Grace's arms through her little coat. "You're awfully good at that," I note.

"I've had a lot of practice," she murmurs. Pulling the curls away from Grace's forehead, she manages to get her little hat on snugly. "Can you manage your own coat, or do you want to transfer her to me?"

"If you could just help me with the sleeves. I really don't want to wake her."

"Not a problem." Holly steps behind me. Efficiently, she holds my coat out for me to slide my arms into while I shift my baby girl from one arm to another without waking her. "Nice trick, Dad," she teases.

My lips quirk. They've done that a lot tonight. I've also felt a loneliness I never expected to in a room crowded full of people.

Maybe time does take the edge off of the of pain because, for the first time since Mary died, I was able to see the beauty of the relationships before me and not feel envious because I didn't have her at my side. Instead, I was wondering if I was always going to feel alone.

Throughout dinner, I got to let the weight of today's nightmare slide off my shoulders as I observed the banter between the Freeman siblings and their significant others. Even though minor skirmishes erupted, it was funny to see how the family unilaterally goaded both Phil and Keene. I was fortunate to have Holly at my side translating much of what was happening at the table, otherwise, I know I would have been lost. Her occasional sidebar of "Don't worry, Phil just likes riling up Keene as much as possible before seeing if he can explode," along with "I'm so glad I brought my camera," let me know this was usual family antics and not something I should feel concerned with.

There's something unique about the woman before me. Like the rest of her family, she is compassionate and self-confident, but there's something else I can't quite pin down. I shake my head.

"Is there something wrong?" Her eyes, the color of the ancient coins, stare up at me in concern.

"No, thank you for all of your help tonight. It's been the kind of day I didn't expect to end with a smile on my face."

Even as she runs her hand through her long hair and it catches fire in the light of the hall, my breath falters.

How is it possible this woman isn't attached?

The thought runs through my head unbidden, and I immediately feel a sense of betrayal as I hold the manifestation of my love with another woman in my arms. I squeeze Grace harder, and she murmurs a protest.

"Oops, I didn't mean to wake her," Holly whispers. "Do you need help getting her out to your car?"

"No. Don't touch her." My voice comes out harsh. I can tell Holly is taken aback by my words because she retreats into herself, pulling away from Grace and me, the gentle smile dropping from her face.

Damn.

"I didn't mean... I'm sorry. I guess I'll let you get yourself sorted. I'm glad we were able to get things ironed out for the 5K." Her voice has gone from animated to careful.

"Holly..." I try to say something, anything, to explain that I'm a fucked-up mess. That it isn't her, it's me, but I'm not given a chance.

Holly moves to the large oak door and holds it open. "There's no need to explain. I overstepped. You have a little girl to get home." Her voice is perfectly polite, but I'm missing the warmth that was there just a few minutes ago.

The hope it gave me.

Shit.

"Thank you for tonight," I can't say more than that. I can't try to break through, to explain there's just something I don't understand going on. I'm holding my baby in my arms. Now's not the time. Besides, Holly's face is a polite mask that almost makes me wish she had her camera in front of it so I didn't need to see what I did to it because I don't understand my own reactions around her.

"I'll let everyone know. Y'all get home safely." She waits until I cross the threshold before she closes the door gently behind us.

And when she does, the weight of every burden from the day I just had—starting with the accident to the swirling emotions being at the Freeman farm—returns to rest on my chest. Brushing my lips against Grace's cheek, I walk over to my Explorer. After strapping her in, I back out and make my way onto Pine Lane.

Feeling more miserable than when I walked in a few hours earlier.

AFTER GETTING Grace settled for the night, I grab a beer from the fridge and walk up to the mantle over the fireplace where a picture of

Grace in Mary's arms sits in a place of honor. Carefully pulling it down, I stare at her delicate features, so like our daughter's.

And all I feel is an overwhelming sadness.

"You didn't have a chance to live, sweetheart," I murmur to the glass. Lifting the cold bottle to the side of my face, I press it tightly against my skin to help rein in the ache. "You had so much you wanted for us—for Grace. How am I supposed to do it alone?"

Maybe you're not supposed to. The thought whips through my head. "No. I can't. I'm not ready," I growl softly.

A knock at the front door interrupts my thoughts. Carefully placing Mary's picture back on the mantle, I stride over before whomever it is can wake Grace up. Throwing open the door, I come face-to-face with Eden and Seth. Eden's holding a casserole dish, and the look on her face is sad.

It's just terribly sad.

"Joe, we heard what happened today. I..." Her voice warbles. "I know Mary used to make you this when you were feeling low after something at work. Here." She holds out the casserole dish. And as awful as it sounds, the smell of stuffed peppers which used to be comforting is almost noxious to me.

Jesus, what the hell am I supposed to do? With a deep sigh, I step back out of the entryway and allow them to come in.

"Is Grace awake?" Eden asks hopefully.

"She's been down almost an hour, Eden. I hope we can keep our discussion quiet so we don't wake her," I tell Grace's maternal grand-parents firmly.

"Oh." The heartbreak registers on both of their faces, making me feel more like a schmuck for keeping my daughter from them, but I can't let my baby be tainted by the brush of grief. She has to be able to live the life she's meant to with no burdens other than the ones she chooses to take on.

Not even my own.

"Come on back into the kitchen. I'll just put this up." Without waiting for them to follow, I make my way back to the back of the house.

"You're not hungry," Eden surmises as I slide the dish she made directly into the refrigerator. She and Seth take a seat at my kitchen table uninvited. "Was it that bad?"

It was, but I'm not about to share that with her. "Grace and I already ate earlier." There's an awkward silence.

"We drove by earlier and didn't see your car here," Seth tells me. "We assumed you were working late."

"We had other plans for the evening."

"Oh, with your parents, I assume. That would make sense. It was a tough day for your team," Eden concludes. "We could have made enough to have spent time with all of you so we could have seen Grace. It's been so long since we had a family dinner."

I don't know what it is, but suddenly I snap. "You're not my family."

With those words, you'd have thought I suddenly shoved a knife in Eden's chest. Seth wraps his arm around his wife tightly. "What did you say, son?"

"And I'm not your son either," I bite out. "Neither of you wanted me marrying your daughter until she became pregnant with Grace. And damned if you didn't try to do your best to take my girls away from me." Despite the pallor that crosses Eden's face, I keep going. "Do you think I didn't find out how you really felt about me? Do you think I don't know you thought I was a phase she was going through and she'd 'grow out of it'? Do you think I don't know you tried to convince her to leave me after Grace was born?" I whisper.

"Maybe she'd still be alive if she had," Seth mutters.

I slam my hand down hard on my table. "Get out of my house."

Eden begins to cry softly. "Joe, please, we just miss Mary so much."

"And this is how you honor her memory? By systematically destroying any happiness of the people who loved her, including her daughter? Why the hell do you think I'm so determined to keep Grace away? The last time she spent any time alone with you, she was apologizing to me for killing her mother. Since that's something that

not even remotely close to the truth, I wonder where she heard it."
Seth's eyes slide away. That wasn't a hard leap.

Seth's jaw tightens as Eden shoves at him in horror. My stomach
rolls as the pain they've tried to hold in for so long comes spilling out.
But I can't let it affect the life I'm trying to build for Grace. "So, this is
where I'm at. I refuse to let your anger and your sorrow burn out the
light of my daughter."

"It's better than having to bury your daughter," Seth shoots back
as he drags Eden to her feet. "Come on, we're leaving."

"Seth, no. We have to work this out," Eden protests.

Seth drags her through my home, his heartache and anger
leaving a foul trail. As he reaches my front door, he turns. "She could
have had anyone. I don't know why she settled for you."

Neither do I anymore, but for the short time we had together, I'll
eternally be grateful she did. I wait for Seth to throw open the door
and storm out. Eden stands there helplessly. "This wasn't what I
wanted when I..."

I run a hand over my head in frustration. Mary's eyes look back at
me every time I see her mother. "It wasn't what I wanted either, Eden.
But I won't have Grace suffer for whatever resentment you all
continue to harbor toward me."

Her eyes drift from mine to the picture over the mantle. Then she
nods before walking out my door, closing it behind her.

God. This day has turned into one massive clusterfuck. I stalk
back over to the mantle and rest my arms against it. I take comfort
seeing Mary holding our daughter. Her eyes are looking at me with
everything young love should contain—laughter, hope, sweet lust.
Every time they looked at me that way, I was helpless to anything but
what she asked. Whether it was making love under the stars in our
backyard or hanging out in a bar riddled with firemen when she was
barely twenty-one, she'd give me that look and I was done for.

She gave me that look the day she told me she was pregnant with
Grace and wanted to keep the baby. It took me less than five minutes
later to propose even though I didn't have a ring.

"This wasn't the forever we swore we'd have, Mary," I choke out.

"And now, I'm fighting the world for our daughter already. That wasn't supposed to happen until Grace became a teenager and she found boys." A watery laugh escapes. "What do I do now that there are no long nights of staying up late talking like there's no tomorrow? What happened to the bright days laughing at everything and nothing? How am I supposed to teach Grace how to live when I'm afraid to do it myself? How do I go on when I can't forgive myself?"

Putting my head down on the mantle, I wait for some kind of sign, but there won't be one.

There never is.

15

HOLLY

"What's the current numbers so far with the donations?" I'm standing in Ali's office where she has the Victims Association spreadsheets open a week later. Her fingers are flying across the keyboard, entering in numbers. "Now if only I could edit a photo that fast," I mutter.

"It'd be a damn miracle. Then we wouldn't need to hire you an assistant," she agrees. "How's the search for that coming along?"

I roll my eyes. "With the fund-raiser, I haven't even had a chance to place an ad." Ali goes to open her mouth to screech at me. Before she can, I cut her off. "Listen, there's a senior at UConn in Jenna's sorority who's been interning the last few times Jenna's been home. Graphic design major. Excellent work. I'm thinking of making her an offer for full time after graduation."

Ali's fingers pause on the keyboard, "Seriously?"

I hold up my hand over my chest. "Hand to God, Ali. Her mother lives in Fairfield County, and she's not well. She's looking for work locally that offers flexibility. So far nothing's panned out. While we can't pay as much as a larger firm, we can definitely give her flexibility. Also, she works for us for a few years; it looks good on her résumé."

"Plus it gives you time to do a more in-depth search," Ali concludes.

"Yes. Because let's face it, just because we love small-town life doesn't mean that everyone will."

"Have I met her?" My studio is a stream of interns, so the question doesn't surprise me.

I nod. "Meghan Murphy."

Ali's face turns thoughtful. Then she snaps her fingers. "I know who you're talking about. She's also fantastic at software design too. She helped with some of the tweaks on the scheduling software."

My brows reach my hairline in shock. "Really? That wasn't listed on her resume."

Ali snorts. "We'll educate her on proper resume building after we hire her on."

"Nice employee-coaching skills. Are your husband's techniques rubbing off on you?"

"I prefer other things of his to rub off on me."

With a pointed glance at her still-flat stomach, I snicker. "So I've heard. Have you told him yet?"

Ali shakes her head, a small smile on her face.

"Why not? Is there something wrong?" Now, I'm genuinely concerned.

"Not a thing. I'll just say he'll know one way or another by the time we finish the 5K."

"Jesus, you may have to staple Phil's lips shut by then. I'm not sure how much longer big brother can hold out."

The Devil's dancing in Ali's eyes when she smiles. "He's under an NDA. I made him sign one before he left the office the morning I told everyone. If he spills the beans early—even to Jason—he'll forfeit his rights to all profits for the upcoming quarter. He may look like he wants to wet his pants, but he won't say a word." She sits back smugly.

I fall back against the wall behind Ali's desk in shock. "You completely neutered him. Again."

"Of course I did. Otherwise, all of you would still be in the dark until I could tell Keene."

"I'm aware you're a genius, but that? Sheer brilliance." Ali's smile is cocky, but she has every right to be.

"Your idea about showing him Cori's fake wedding gown was up there too."

I polish my nails against my shirt before blowing on them like a gunslinger. "Did we get everyone's bets on how he's going to react?"

"Let me check." Ali flips to a different spreadsheet. "Yep. I got Cassidy's entry last night. We're good for the showing at any time."

"Outstanding." We break into gales of laughter so hard we don't hear the knock on the door. It isn't until we hear a rough male voice ask, "Ali? I can come back if you're busy?" that we regain our composure. Both our heads swing toward her doorway to find Joe standing there. Dressed in a thermal shirt beneath his uniform, he looks uncertain.

And delicious.

I decide to leave my sister to it.

"Send me a text with that number I was asking you about when I first came in," I remind Ali. Her fingers tap her mouse a final time before she gestures me to look over her shoulder. My lips part. I tip my head her way and whisper, "No freaking way."

"Yep. Cass says she expects it to go at least thirty-five percent higher too," Ali says proudly.

Even the fifty-two thousand dollars we've helped the Victims Association raise is nothing to sneeze at. I slide my arm around her shoulder and squeeze hard. "You have a lot to be happy about. This is just one more thing."

"This is something we all get to celebrate, Hols. I'll ping the chat with updates as I confirm them." She squeezes my hand, then lets it go. "Sorry to keep you waiting, Joe. I have some last-minute scheduling to go over with you. Cassidy is meeting with one of our regular clients and asked for me to take the meeting."

"That's not a problem at all..." He steps into the room, clearing the doorway for my escape. His eyes track my movements as I make my way from behind my sister's desk and make a beeline for the door. "This meeting isn't with both of you?"

"I'm just the girl behind the lens. The next time you have to deal with me will be race day," My voice is polite and professional. He flinches. I ignore it.

I was surprised to find how much the way Joe behaved at our family dinner bothered me. It called up some ugly feelings I have about myself. I've had to spend time alone with my lens reminding myself that I am good enough to be around my family. That I am clean enough to touch them. I don't know whether it was his words or his tone, but something there just hit me in the wrong spot—under my heart. So, I'll just keep myself at a distance to avoid any other triggers.

"Have a good meeting." I flick a wave behind my shoulder as I walk out of the room, closing the door behind me.

As much as a small part of my heart might feel the sting, I appreciate the honesty of Joe's reaction the other night. After all I'm a stranger, but something told me when our eyes met across the bay that day at the firehouse I was someone who understood the pain he was in, who would have given a damn. I understand the complicated feelings behind grief, but I could have been an unbiased ear. I could have been a friend.

What I refuse to do is add to the weariness evident in every line of his body.

16

JOSEPH

Holly shuts the door behind her, and I feel a chamber of my spirit close down along with it. I have no way to fight against silence, no words to say to apologize for snapping at her for a perfectly innocent question. Instead, I'm left again with a bunch of unspoken apologies that once again seem inadequate.

Making my way to one of the chairs in Ali's office, I drop into it with a sigh. My head falls forward; my hands are clasped together between my knees.

"It's a hard road you're on, Joe," Ali says quietly.

My words are harsh when I ask her, "What would you know about it, Ms. Freeman? You're surrounded by a family who loves you and a husband who adores you." When she merely stares at me with her intense blue eyes, I realize my mistake and want to crawl into a hole. "Oh, God. I'm so sorry, Ali. So sorry." Scrubbing my hands back and forth over my head, I can't sit still. I stand and begin pacing her office.

"A broken heart is the loneliest thing in the world to protect because you don't know who you can trust it to," she continues. "You don't know who to lean on, who to let in, who to keep out. Especially when people are coming at you with their advice from all sides. All you want to do is curl up in a ball and wish the world away."

My head snaps toward her in shock because that's experience talking. Ali's eyes have taken on a distant look as she focuses somewhere deep inside. "But I learned something the hard way. Something that helped me find the right path."

"What's that?" I whisper.

"By shutting out love in its many forms, I was letting the fear win. And I don't like to lose." Ali takes a deep breath. "Whatever you have to get through, learn to trust a few people with how you're really doing, Joe. They may be the only thing that saves you in the end."

I nod slowly. Ali lets her lips tip up before tidying the stack the papers on her desk. "Anyway, that's not why I called you in today. I wanted..."

I raise a hand to stop her. "Thank you."

Her smile turns quizzical. "We haven't even started," she jokes.

"Not for all of your help, though I sincerely hope you know that all of us at the CPD and CFD will be eternally grateful. But for reminding me I'm not alone."

"Joe, it's hard to be alone in the world. People just choose to be for a time when they need to be. Now? You're finding it difficult to let people back in. Just remember, you're stronger than you think you are. That includes asking for help when you need it."

She's given me so much to think on. Diverting our conversation back to why I came, I ask, "Right. So, about the schedule?"

Ali nods her understanding. Handing me a copy of the fundraising day's itinerary, she begins reviewing all of the items which have checks next to everything Amaryllis Events will be at, stars for the CPD, and double swirls for CFD.

"What do the double swirls mean?" I ask, tongue in cheek.

"Fighting fires? Water?"

"Ahh." I focus back on the schedule. I tap at the paper in my hand. "Is this a special seating for the CFD to get breakfast?"

Ali nods. I ask, "Can we switch the time with CPD? We need to get back to the station and dump our gear."

"Gear?"

I explain. "We run the 5K every year in our full suits, boots, gloves, and hat. Some of us run with our tanks on our back, though we don't use the oxygen."

Ali snaps her fingers. "That's right. I remember thinking y'all were nuts last year. Remember how hot it was?"

I groan. We had an unusually warm heat wave hit. Running in those suits was akin to being deep-fried to be served up with a side of ranch at the finish line.

"Hence why I want to change with CPD. We have got to go back to the station to shower before we show up at The Coffee Shop."

Ali's frantically nodding. "Agree. We don't need to scare the patrons due to the...aroma."

I grin. "Thanks."

"No, thank you. I want to keep my breakfast down," Ali counters.

We finish going over the schedule, and there's little else to change. "I can't believe how efficiently this is being handled. With the other firm—" I can tell by the face she makes she's not impressed over our previous choice. "—I was doing as much work for the event as they were."

Ali opens her mouth to speak but then shuts it. "What?" I challenge her.

"Nothing. Let's just say I'm not surprised. Give me a moment to make these changes and send them to Cass." She turns to her computer. Within minutes, I have a revised schedule in hand with an additional hard copy to drop on my father's desk.

"Not bad, Ali. You know, you guys should do this for a living," I tease. It feels rusty but somehow right.

"Get out of here. I've got work to do. I'm sure I'll run into you at daycare." Standing, we shake hands. I make my way to the door before I pause.

I might regret this, but something is telling me I should do it.

"Ali, is Holly around?"

"Do I look like my sister's keeper?"

With all seriousness, I reply, "Yes."

She winks. "You're right. At least, one of them." She turns to her keyboard and taps in a few keys. "You might be able to catch her. Second door on the right before you hit the stairs."

"Thanks. For everything." I hold her glance for a second longer than necessary before I disappear down the hall to make amends to a woman who did nothing wrong.

Other than being kind.

"Knock knock." My fingers rap on Holly's open door. Her hair whips around before settling on her shoulders in a cloud of reds and golds.

"Something I can help you with? Did Ali forget to go over something? She should still be in her office," Holly goes to stand, but I wave her back in her seat.

"No. I just wanted a moment of your time."

She tilts her head. "For?"

"To say I'm sorry."

"Nothing to apologize for." Holly dismisses my apology verbally, but she won't look at me.

"Holly, I..."

"If you're referring to the other night, it should be me apologizing." She turns to grab a pen. Fiddling with it, she says, "You're obviously a capable man, Joe. My help wasn't needed."

"I'm just so used to doing things on my own..." I try to explain, but she cuts me off again.

"Really, there's no need for explanations." Her lips are turned up in a smile, but it doesn't reach her eyes. "We all have off moments, right? Let's just put it aside and move on."

Can we? The thought flies through my head even as Holly turns back toward her desk and looks at a picture on the screen. Uncapping the pen, she takes quick notes on the pad next to her before she clicks through a few photos. Without turning around, she asks, "Was there something else you need? Unfortunately, I'm swamped trying to get these photos back today."

"Can I have a minute of your time?" Her spine goes ramrod straight. "Please?" I add.

Carefully, she recaps the pen before facing me again. All the animation I saw before I interrupted her and Ali is washed away. Her intake of breath causes her wide-collared V-neck sweater to clutch even tighter to her body. I try not to notice how the black offsets her dramatic coloring and fail miserably. "What is it?" she asks quietly.

"My reactions had nothing to do with you and everything to do with me," I say simply.

Her expression doesn't change. I work up the courage to continue. "I...just don't know how to handle... It's been Grace and I...too many people...after..." I stare down at my boots.

"Joe, you don't need to explain anything." Her voice washes over me like a healing balm, a gift of acceptance without my having to say a word.

"I do because all you were trying to offer was help and... Look, I'm not doing this very well." I lift my head and find Holly staring at me. Only her eyes have shifted. There's a glow to them now there wasn't just a few moments ago.

"I think you're doing fine."

I let out a deep breath. "I just wanted to say thank you for being kind."

She stands and the sweater she's wearing shifts to drape over her hourglass figure. I try not to let my reaction to her natural beauty affect me. "A wise person once told me apologizing to people is worse than running. Ultimately, you'll end up more out of breath due to the number of apologies you have to make."

"Sounds like a smart person."

She surprises me by rushing past me through the door where I'm standing and looks out both ways before stepping back into her office. She's so close I can smell the floral scent of her shampoo. "Shh! We don't tell Phil he's right. Freeman family rule number one. He gets a big head." Her wink does a lot to ease the burning in my gut I've felt since I walked into Ali's office.

I grin. "He deserves an award for growing up with five sisters."

"Yes, yes he does." Quirking her lips in a smile more real than any since I've stepped into her office, she retreats toward her desk. A silence settles between us as a frown pulls her eyebrows back down. She glances down at her notebook, uncaps her pen again, and jots down a few items. I stand there uncertain what to do next.

"I guess I'd better head back to the station." The awkwardness between us hasn't entirely been erased.

Her head snaps up, and her eyes go wide. Honest to God, did she forget I was there? Her cheeks flush in embarrassment. "God, I'm so sorry. I'm trying to clear as much off my plate for a shoot later and..."

"And now you're apologizing for something you don't need to," I say firmly. "Really, Holly, I know I interrupted what you were working on."

"My life revolves around being focused in one way or another." She shrugs helplessly. "I tend to ignore the rest unless it's shoved right under my face."

"Or it's in your shot?"

"Something like that, yeah." She smiles.

"Then don't let me distract you. I'll see you next week?"

Stepping toward me, she informs me with exaggerated mock-hauteur, "My job is to make sure you don't see me. Besides, you'll likely be expounding your energy running."

Why that causes a flare of disappointment, I don't know. "Then I'll see you when I see you."

"Absolutely." Her voice is firm, but at least there's a smile behind it. "Be safe, Joe."

It's a small thing, but her words warm a place in my heart that hasn't been warm since Mary used to whisper, "Take care of my guy," before every shift. Unknowingly, my smile's a little broader when I whisper, "Will do, Holly," before I leave her office, stride down the hall, and head downstairs.

My thoughts drift while I'm studying between calls. I go over my conversation with Holly. It's nice knowing there's someone out there who cares about my safety even if it's in the most superficial of ways. She probably would have said the same thing to Brett or any of the guys in the house, but for just a moment, it made me feel special again.

17

HOLLY

Race day has finally arrived. And while Phil has done nothing but bitch about the fact he's been awake since five, the day itself couldn't be more perfect. Every member of our family and extended family are working. Ali, Phil, and Em are swamped at registration. Jake is spinning up tunes this morning but will be turning over that duty over to Jared, Cassidy's brother-in-law, tonight so Jake can take center stage with some of the students from his school district to play live at Tide Pool.

Caleb, Colby, and Keene are selling T-shirts while Charlie—our family's adopted father figure—and a bunch of the guys from Hudson who are all professionally trained EMTs are going to be mobile on bicycles, patrolling the route. Cassidy's also arranged for the spouses of the CPD and CFD volunteer to either set up, hand out, or break down the water stations along the course.

I'm racing around taking shot after shot. Ali's idea of a prize for craziest running costume has me howling with laughter. Oh my God, is that person wearing a cardboard cutout of a flame emoji? How the hell do they expect to move their legs? Some of the prizes we're going to hand out later are going to be epic, I think to myself, as a couple who are handcuffed together go jogging by to warm up; she's dressed in a police outfit, he as a criminal. Or they're going to inspire some fun later. I'm definitely amused.

There must be at least five hundred people milling around for the start and more waiting to register at the last minute. Even without the pancake breakfast later or tonight's party, today is already an unmitigated success.

"I couldn't agree more," I hear behind me. Cursing myself for speaking aloud, I swiftly turn and almost trip over my own feet in my worn-in running shoes.

Joe grabs me beneath the arms to prevent me from falling. That look—the shock, the awe, the pride, and happiness. I have to have it. Quickly, I lift my camera and snap a close-up. He chuckles. "Can't resist, can you?"

"Not today. Happy?" I don't want to ignore him, but I have a job to do, so I keep my camera up and start to move around in between people. He follows me.

"I don't think that quite covers what I'm feeling. I'm astounded. This is beyond my wildest imagination."

I reply, "That's how it should be."

Even as we edge closer to the start line where all of the CPD and CFD racers are beginning to gather, I ask, "So, on average, how many of you pass out because your egos get in the way of common sense?" At Joe's blank look, I gesture to the full fireman's gear he's wearing. "Running over three miles in that? Likely going full out so you can have bragging rights?" Quickly, I unsnap my water bottle from my waist pack and take a sip.

Joe eyes the rest of the guys at the start line dressed similarly to the way he is before leaning in to murmur, "I've never had a problem with my ego, Holly. It's not finishing first that's important."

My eyes widen. It must be the Freeman brain that Phil's instilled in all of us because that sounded a hell of a lot like flirting. And no way is that possible.

Stepping back, Joe snaps off a salute. "See you on the race course," he says before he jogs over to join his colleagues. I regain my wits long enough to see him heft an oxygen tank on his back and secure it. One of the other guys come up and raps him on his helmet. Joe shakes his head before he does the same.

"Hols, can you hear me?" Em's excited voice comes through my earpiece. With the noise at the start line, I can make her out, barely.

"Yeah."

"Ali's telling Keene at the finish line."

No. Freaking. Way. "Are you serious?" I yell over the cacophony of noise.

"You know that's how she told him about Kalie. So, after they cross the finish line together, she plans on giving him something. She says he'll understand immediately what's happening."

"Damnit, I'm not supposed to be at the finish line until the end of the race," I growl. Em pauses.

"Hold on." There's silence in my ear. Em comes back on. "She said to tell you she doesn't plan on starting until fifteen minutes after the last runner starts. Keene thinks this is because she's working the event. Since they have a bet on who is going to win against one another and not anyone else, it doesn't matter when they start."

"So, what you're telling me is I get to sprint to get to the finish line," I drawl sarcastically. Faster than my marathon-running sister and my brother-in-law who is so in shape, the Army still regrets saying he should ride a desk.

"Pretty much. You'll have about ten minutes to make it before they do."

I growl. Without my camera gear in my backpack, that would be completely doable. With the extra forty pounds on my back, I'm going to feel like I'm running a Spartan Challenge for one.

"I'll make it. Now, go away."

Em laughs in my ear.

Ignoring her, I regain my focus. I switched cameras today to my Nikon D5 DSLR for the race. With the ability to shoot fourteen frames per second and auto refocus, it's the perfect camera for this kind of event. Beyond the fantastic clarity and speed this camera offers me, one of the best parts is during a lull, I can use the built-in Wi-Fi transmitter to upload the photos to our corporate cloud. Right now, I have a zoom lens on my camera. Even though more light can be let into the picture, I need the ability to capture the action from wherever I am at the start. Fortunately, I can adjust the light some-what based on where I'm standing and using the filters I packed in my custom-made backpack.

Swinging the soft leather backpack off my shoulder, I unzip the front and check it for the fiftieth time to make sure I packed my prime lens as well. Once I find a good location, I want the clarity the prime lens will give me. Sighing in relief, I slip it back on. This bag, a gift from my family a few years ago for Christmas, was one of the best presents I ever received. It gives me enough space for more than one camera, as well as multiple lenses and filters.

Just as I secure the straps tight around my chest and waist, I see Chief Drever and Chief Bianco make their way to the stage with Cassidy. Boldly stepping before the start line in front of the police and fireman, I ignore a myriad of wolf whistles and catcalls as I assume they're directed at the combined chiefs' direction. Nothing like the men and women in red and blue giving some grief to one of their own, I think with some amusement. My camera captures the confidence in my sister's stride, the laughter on Chief Drever's face, and the discomfort at being in the spotlight on Chief Bianco's.

"Welcome to the fourth annual Collier Police and Fireman Victims Assistance 5K!" Cassidy calls into the microphone she just turned on.

There's a loud roaring behind me. I discreetly move to the side. I want to be able to take shots of what happens next, but there's a way to do so with respect and honor for the men and women behind me.

"Before we start, we'd like to bring up the Collyer A Capella Choir to sing the national anthem," Cassidy says into the microphone. A small group of boys and girls come out followed by a girl dressed in Collyer's High School dress uniform who is carrying the United States flag.

As I'm looking through my viewfinder, I hear helmets being swept off. Up on stage, Chiefs Bianco and Drever turn and salute. A beau-tiful stillness washes over the crowd as the group begins singing the lead-in. Francis Scott Key's immortal words he originally penned rings out in the morning air to the music combined with the English drinking music "To Anacreon in Heaven" that became our national anthem in 1931.

Chills race up and down my arms. It has nothing to do with the morning coolness and everything to do with the flutter of my heart as I absorb the feeling in my soul as we all stand together to fight for what's good and right. It might not be something as monumental as a war, but the people who are impacted by the death of their loved ones fight this battle every day.

Even Joe.

When I was proofreading the materials about the Victims Assistance Fund earlier this week, I saw Mary's name listed. There was an asterisk next to it with a note that although she was not a member of the CPD or CFD, Victims Assistance was able to provide help to the Bianco family upon her death.

Today is for you too, Joe, I think to myself fiercely, as the whooping that occurs at the end of our national anthem breaks out. I swipe at the tears obscuring my vision.

"Before we turn you all loose on the course, Chiefs Bianco and Drever have a few words. Chiefs?" Cassidy turns the microphone over and steps back.

"We've lost brothers and sisters to the blue line," Chief Drever opens.

"And the red line," Chief Bianco adds.

"You all give everything you have to give," Drever goes on.

"Some of you give everything. That's what we're here for today," Bianco says.

You could hear a pin drop in the crowd.

"Whether it's because our brothers and sisters were taken out on the job or because of the destruction they've had to deal with day after day, it doesn't matter. They're still gone. And we still have to go on without them," Drever says grimly.

"And so do their loved ones. What you're doing today makes the everyday things a little easier. Like doctor bills."

"School clothes."

"College funds."

"Birthday parties."

"And groceries," they conclude together.

Chief Bianco goes on. "I'm proud to walk the line with each and every one of you. I'm proud to call all of you family. This includes our brothers and sisters in blue." He holds out a hand and shakes Chief Drever's.

A huge roar goes up from the crowd. Shouts of "Chief! Chief! Chief!" are heard from the members of the CPD and CFD over the crowd. I capture it all.

Even as I have tears forming in my eyes again.

"So, it's with pleasure we turn the race back over to Cassidy and another team we're proud to stand beside so we can join our own at the start line," Chief Drever concludes warmly.

"We'd like to thank them in advance for everything they've done to make today happen," Chief Bianco leans in to add.

My sister flushes as she takes the mic back. "Thank you both. Let's give one more shout-out to our chiefs and to both the CPD and CFD for doing everything they do to make certain we are safe and secure in and around Collyer!"

The crowd goes wild as the chiefs make their way off the dais.

"Okay, runners. Here's how it's going to work. All CPD and CFD personnel are in front. Because this race is honoring them today, we're giving them a two-minute head start." Cassidy pauses. "That and because they're insane to be on the course in full gear. Can one of you explain that?" Someone goes to call out, but Cassidy waves them off. "Save your breath, Officer Brady. You're going to need it."

Everyone laughs good-naturedly at Justin Brady, one of CFD's extraordinarily good-looking fireman.

"Two minutes after I sound the horn, please allow our wheelchair racers to go next. Then a minute after, our runners. Finally, the last time I sound the horn, all walkers are welcome. Sound good?" Cassidy waits for the cheering to end before saying, "Then CPD and

CFD, you have thirty seconds." She looks at her watch. "Who's ready for the pancake breakfast at The Coffee Shop when this is over?"

The crowd goes wild again.

"I don't know about you, but running sure gets me hungry. I just hope the firemen running in full gear get to shower and change." I burst out laughing at my sister's audacity. "Runners, are you ready?"

The blare of the horn signals their start.

I'm less than five seconds behind them, taking a different path along a trail through the woods so I can get to the 2.1-mile mark and set up before any of our first responders get there.

I ignore the jumbled thoughts vying for space in my head as I time my way to my location so I can be sure to get back in time for the big reveal at the finish line. Because my thoughts about how good Joe Bianco looked this morning can lead to nowhere good.

And I know it.

18

JOSEPH

"How are you doing there, buddy?" Brett pants next to me. Both of us are profusely sweating as we come up on mile two.

"I'm praying to God there's a water stop soon," I gasp. I usually can run five miles easily, but in this gear? In these boots? I'll be lucky if I manage to avoid blisters.

"Didn't you study the race map?" He shoots ahead.

"I can barely remember it," I grumble as I lengthen my stride to keep up.

Our booted feet slap against the concrete as we make our way around the corner. And then we see it like an oasis in the desert.

A water station.

"Race you," I call out, sprinting ahead. I hear Brett's muted "Dick" behind me as I snatch up the first ice-cold water cup. "Thanks," I gasp out.

"You're welcome," a feminine voice says warmly. I nod as I chug the second.

I'm debating whether to get a third to pour over my head when Brett makes his way next to me. "Hey, Em. Thanks."

"Hey, Brett. It's been a while." My head snaps up, and sure

enough, Emily Freeman is smiling at Brett. My eyes narrow as they flit from one to the other.

"Congratulations on your engagement. Lucky guy," he throws out casually.

Emily's face lights up. "We're both lucky, but thanks."

He grabs another water and chugs it. Emily meanwhile turns her attention back to me. "Joe, you want another one?"

"Only if I can pour it over my head," I tell her honestly.

A huge smile crosses her face. She bends and reaches under the table. Coming back up, she hands both me and Brett ice-cold frozen paper towels. "You're a goddess, Em," Brett moans, wiping his face.

Emily just laughs.

Quickly doing the same, I also wipe the back of my neck. "Jesus, that's amazing."

"Be sure to thank Ali. We've had them on hand for most of the races she's run since college," Emily confides.

"I remember her being hugely competitive," Brett recalls.

"She still is. She has a side bet with Keene today," Em tells us, amused. Her eyes scan the horizon behind us. "Better get a move on, guys. You're still in the lead, but looks like some of your comrades are coming up hot."

"Shit," we say simultaneously. Em reaches under the table for a trash can. We dump our dirty cups and towels in it before taking off.

We're a few feet down the road before I ask, "How do you know Emily?"

Brett waits until our boots slap a few times in unison before answering, "I went out with her on a few dates years ago before she started dating some doctor. They got serious, so we ended things."

"Now she's engaged to another guy," I muse.

"You had dinner with them. Did you meet him?" My head whips toward him. He sounds resigned and a little crushed at the same time.

"You had feelings for her," I accuse. I punch him in the arm. Hard. "And you didn't bother to mention this? Jesus, Brett, we've only been friends since we were kids. What the hell?"

"It felt like it was so soon after things happened with Mary. What was I supposed to say? Hey, buddy, sorry you lost your woman, but I might have found one?" He shrugs. Things are quiet as we pant our way through the next few yards. "Besides, as you can see it didn't work out."

"Still." We round a corner, and my eyes light on the sun glinting off a fire sitting on the side of the road. I assure myself the only reason I'm not racing madly to throw myself on top of it is the fact that she'd likely knee me in the nuts for breaking her camera.

"Still," Brett continues. "It was done. Em's happy, and I haven't been sitting home miserable myself," he reminds me.

"True," I concede. Even as we approach Holly, I know she has to be taking a million pictures. I throw off a two-fingered salute in her direction. She lowers her camera away from her stunning face to throw a smile in my direction.

"Smile pretty, boys," her lightly accented voice calls out.

Brett, the asshole, decides at that moment to jump on my back like a kid. Since I have Grace, it's instinctive to grab him beneath his ass and boost him up. Holly hoots and hollers. I give her a show for a few seconds before I drop him and keep running.

"Daddy," Brett calls out plaintively, "I want something to suck on after the race is done."

"I'll give you something," I yell.

Holly almost falls over laughing as we thunder past. Realizing what I said, I curse. Is there a time when I could not act like an ass in front of this woman?

"Wow. You're not being a douche in front of strangers? Did I zap you enough times with water to break you of that bad habit? Did my house training finally work?" Brett's in shock. Ripping my helmet off my head, I run my hand through my hair.

"Not helping," I grit out. Slamming my hat back on, I realize everything, even Brett's labored breathing, has become quiet next to me.

"Seriously, Joe. We've never talked about this because there's always someone else around. Do you want to...? Are you interested in dating again?" Brett asks cautiously.

No. At least not just any woman. In the last three years, I haven't given much thought to hurting another person so long as the protective shell that cocoons me and Grace remains intact, yet every time I see Holly, I feel compelled to smooth out any rough edges I create.

I am, however, becoming fascinated with Holly Freeman. Even as the thought enters my mind, I realize it's true. "Not exactly," I hedge. We pant our way through the next quarter mile in silence. I'm hoping that's the end of it.

I should have known better.

"Listen, you know I loved Mary too, but she would never have wanted you to be without love."

I think before I respond. "There are things I took for granted with her, Brett. I feel like I'm still paying for that. We have a child I will raise and love for the rest of my life. And how do you explain that to someone new? 'Hi. Nice to meet you. I have a child, and I will never apologize for missing things about the woman I used to love'?" Swinging my head toward his, I demand, "I doubt this means I'm fully capable of loving another woman wholly again. Fully? With everything that's in me? Is that the kind of man who should be out on the dating scene?"

Letting out a huge breath that has nothing to do with the fact we're closing in on the 5K mark, he replies, "I don't know, buddy. I just want you to be happy."

I just wish I wasn't so damn lonely. The thought pops into my head even as Brett yells, "Breakfast is on the loser!" right before he sprints toward the finish line.

Since there's no chance I'd ask him to pay for Grace, my parents, and myself, I let him take the glory knowing there's no way he'll lord it over me at the station considering our next closest team member is a good quarter mile back whereas I cross the line ten steps behind him.

I'll always have his back. Just like he's always had mine.

19

HOLLY

Keene and Ali just passed by Em's water station. For two people who are supposed to be in a "race," they're goofing off as if they don't have a care in the world. Part of me wants to scream, "Hurry up!" but I know Ali will murder me if I give anything away.

As soon as they clear the water station, Em takes off. Her relief came about twenty minutes ago to cover any of the walkers who show up behind Keene and Ali. I want to call out that she's just rude, but I refrain.

I have to get this shot.

Ali is running slightly behind Keene, who's wearing his trademark smirk. Instead of leaping in the air like a gazelle like she normally does in front of running photographers, she throws out her left thumb behind Keene's back, making sure it's angled at him, and holds up two fingers downward toward her stomach.

I know the only way I keep myself from falling down on my face laughing is that I have about ten minutes to run a mile back to the finish line. Knowing I'm going to have to sprint, I drop my camera in my backpack and swing it over my shoulders. Taking the few seconds to tighten the straps, I take off.

I'll never love it the way Ali does, but the burn in my legs feels great. I just wish I didn't have the extra forty pounds of camera equipment on my back. Fortunately I'm in good shape, so when my phone rings, I'm only moderately out of breath when I growl, "What?"

"Caleb says you have about five minutes. Are you going to make it?" Cassidy asks worriedly.

"How the hell does he know?" I pant as I put a little bit of churn in my legs.

"He has Charlie tracking Keene's phone, of course."

I want to laugh, I really do, but I just don't have the breath. My brothers-in-law investigations firm does very well for a reason. It surprises me not in the slightest that they have one of their employees—who happens to be an extremely close member of our family—doing something like this for fun.

I spy the finish line ahead. "ETA one minute."

Cassidy lets out a long whistle. "I'm impressed."

"Don't be. When I die later before we get to The Coffee Shop, just remember to take my cameras there...okay. I'm here. Let me get a camera out."

"We see you. We're all hiding around in the crowd. Hey, just a FYI. We have Kalie here. You should get a picture of the shirt she's wearing."

I grin. "I take it she's part of the reveal?"

"Well, Ali did say Keene would know instantly. Oh! I see them!"

"Let me go," I demand instantly.

Cassidy hangs up without saying another word. Sliding my bag to the side where the support holding the finish line banner is, I crouch down—not without some burning in my thighs. "Jesus, Ali. This had better be worth the wait."

Then I see them come into view. They're jogging like it's a normal run, not like they have some big bet riding on the line. Lifting the camera up to my face, I zoom in. Ali's lips move and Keene gives her a narrow-eyed glare.

Suddenly, he takes off in a burst of speed, leaving his wife behind. *Click..*

Ali slows down even further, waiting for him to cross the finish line, an incredibly gentle look on her face. *Click.*

Keene's practically on top of me. I zoom out and capture his confusion before I turn and see Ali holding out her hand just before she walks toward the finish line herself. *Click.*

Kalie moves from the safe haven of Cassidy and Caleb's arms to Ali. She's running with something in her hand. From where I'm crouched, I can hear the clanking medal sound. I zoom in and see the pink and blue ribbons attached to the medals. *Click.*

Oh God. I'm barely holding it together as it is when Kalie yells, "Daddy! I have your prize!"

Keene woodenly moves back toward his wife and daughter. "Alison?"

"Last time you found out, you gave me the most beautiful medal in the world," she calls out, still not crossing the finish line. "So, Kalie, I need you to go put one of these around Daddy's neck."

"Okay!" Kalie skips toward Keene, who's already dropped to his knees. *Click.* "Daddy! Here's your..." She looks back to Ali for help.

"It's a medal, sweetheart," Ali calls to her child as she finally, *finally*, crosses over the finish line. "Isn't it a great picture, babe?" she asks her husband.

Without even looking at it, Keene swoops an arm around Ali, burying his face in the side of her neck. *Click.* Pulling back, I see my badass brother-in-law's eyes are wet. "We're having another baby?"

And that's when Ali does it.

She reaches into the zipper pocket of her running skirt and takes out another medal. "Actually, honey. We're having two."

Keene's jaw hits the ground. *Click.* He swoops Ali up in his arms and begins to spin her around in circles. I feel like my finger hasn't let up off the shutter. Kalie is jumping up and down with joy. "Yay! Yayayayyayay! Two babies!"

Keene gently places his wife back down on her feet. "Are you...is everything all right?" I may capture the worried look on his face by accident, but I'll never share that with them. Since Keene and Cassidy's mother lost a set of twins between them, and he almost lost their mother then, he's extremely sensitive about the dangers of child birth.

"I'm right as rain. The doctor told me so, and I've been talking with your sister..." Ali slaps a hand over her mouth.

Keene's face clouds like a thundercloud. Oh, I'm so getting this on camera. "The family knows?"

Only slightly abashed, Ali puts her arm back around his neck. "I wanted to make telling you special. After everything we went through, this was the best way I could think of."

Keene opens his mouth and closes it a few times before he leans down and whispers something only Ali can hear in her ear. It's obviously perfect as she melts into him before tilting her face up for his kiss.

After I take a few more shots of them, I let the lens wander into the crowd. Capturing pictures of my siblings, who have all emerged from their hiding spots, I snag Cassidy wiping her eyes against Caleb's shirt. Em snuggled into Jake, the rock on her hand glinting in the sun. Phil leaning over the back of Jason's shoulder, his arms wrapped around his husband's flat stomach. Colby with his phone up, which tells me he's streaming this live for Corinna, who's at The Coffee Shop serving up pancakes to the hungry hordes with Ava and Matt. And I realize that once again, we all won.

Just like we did all those years ago in Charleston when we found each other.

20

JOSEPH

Hours later we're squeezed in cheek and jowl into The Coffee Shop. The energy is high but goes electric when Ali and Keene come through the door with their daughter. From my vantage point in the corner booth with my family and Brett, I watch Corinna race out from the kitchen, weaving her way through the people, and jump into her sister and brother-in-law's arms. Keene has two medals around his neck and looks stunned but thrilled.

Leaning over to my father, I ask, "Did Keene win some of the awards today?"

My dad shakes his head. "I have no idea."

Ava then walks up and kisses both of their cheeks and gives Kalie a hug. Kalie jumps up and down, wearing her own set of medals, holding up two fingers. Keene slides a hand protectively over Ali's stomach. "Well, I'll be damned," I say softly.

"What is it, Joe?" my mother asks.

"If I'm reading this right, I think Ali might be pregnant." I barely get the words out of my mouth when Ava comes up to refill our coffee as Keene, Ali, and Kalie find a seat toward the back. Corinna makes her way back to the kitchen with a bounce in her step.

"You are two hundred percent correct, Joe." She beams. "Twins. They run in Keene's family. Corinna only told Matt and me today when she knew we wouldn't be able to blab to Keene."

"That's terrific news," my mother declares with a worried glance in my direction. But surprisingly, hearing about their joy is just great news. It doesn't burn quite the same way it would have a few weeks ago. Ali, Keene, hell, their whole damn family just went beyond the call of duty helping put on events to benefit my fallen brethren. To be honest, their news feels more like a celebration than a reminder of what I wouldn't have.

A future with someone I love.

"Tell them congratulations, Ava." I look around the table. "From all of us."

She scurries away when my father's hand comes down on my shoulder. "You're a good man, son."

I shrug, uncomfortable.

"You are, darling. I don't know what it is, but something's changed recently."

Grace shoves a forkful of pancakes in her mouth before she opens her mouth. Her declaration of "Happy" comes out warbled and with some food dribbling down her face, but no one misses it.

Especially me.

"Was I so unhappy before, baby?" I ask her quietly.

She tilts her head and shrugs. "Happier," she concludes.

"Out of the mouths of babes," my mother murmurs.

"Ma," I start, but my mother waves me off.

"Sweetheart, it's all right if you allow yourself to be happy again."

And therein lies the problem. How can I allow myself to be when the person I asked to be happy with me for eternity is lying beneath the ground?

The bell above The Coffee Shop door rings out. I catch sight of her out of the corner of my eye as she comes in with more of her family. It's hard to miss her gorgeous hair cascading freely down her back.

She doesn't glance our way, but I'd be lying if I didn't admit to tracking her movement toward the back of the cafe where the rest of her family was sitting. Her musical laughter ringing out causes me to clench my hand into a fist under the table. And when she's boosted on the counter and steadied by a muscular man I don't recognize to get a picture of everyone at the pancake breakfast, I want to howl in disappointment.

What does that say about the eternal love I'm supposed to have for my dead fiancée?

21

HOLLY

"This place is a mob scene!" I yell to Em from behind the speakers where I'm presently capturing the insanity at Tide Pool. Jake and the students from his district are up on stage rocking out, their parents all in the audience beaming with pride and ready to sweep them away the minute their set is done. There are first responders from counties all over Connecticut and New York state mingling with the Collyer teams, lifting glasses to the fallen. The Tide Pool manager took the stage earlier to announce that all monies collected tonight are going to the Victims Assistance Fund, not just a percentage. Cassidy jumped up and down in glee.

"It's going to get crazier as the night goes on, sister!" Em shouts back. Jake is wailing away on his sax, and every single female in three counties is trying to get his attention. One goes to unhook her bra under her shirt—presumably to toss it on the small stage—but Em, who's sitting on top of the speaker, catches her eye and flashes her diamond in her direction with a glare.

The woman backs down like Em kicked her hopes and dreams into next eternity. *Click.*

Damn, I'm so glad I have my camera tonight, I think wickedly.

Tapping Em on the shoulder, I tell her, "I'm going to take a lap of the room."

She nods, but she's distracted because Jake has turned his attention to her. His dancing brown eyes don't miss much. My guess is Em's going to enjoy her night immensely for openly staking her claim on her man.

Pushing off, I walk behind the stage and into the fray. Although my neck will be killing me tomorrow, I'm glad I brought both cameras with me so I don't need to worry about switching lenses from my prime to zoom, wasting precious minutes I can be snagging memories out of thin air. I zoom in on a team of patrolmen from CPD lifting pints of Guinness to clink them together with CFD Officer Justin Brady. I capture Brett Stewart laughing so hard with Chief Drever; she's wiping her eyes. I click just in time to see Tide Pool's bartender, Jessica, hand Ali a ginger ale right before Jessica hoists herself onto the bar to smack Keene on the lips. Ali's head is thrown back in laughter. My own curve in a very private smile at the fact my brother-in-law is still wearing the medals Ali slid on his neck earlier to announce her pregnancy after she let him cross the finish line in front of her.

Turning the camera a few degrees, the reflection of a table full of first responders lifting their drinks in a toast is mine just as it belongs to the window I actually take a picture of. I get a full-length one of Chief Bianco as he stands by the door with Cassidy greeting everyone as they come in. There's a weighty burden that lies across his shoulders that has little to do with his command. I nibble my lip as I depress the shutter. More than just about anyone in the room, he understands he could have lost so much more with the accident three years ago.

While I was getting ready for tonight, I thought about Joe and everything he lost. I just hope he eventually finds it within to forgive himself for what he couldn't have prevented. Time doesn't heal all wounds, but the life that comes after can help scrub away the bloody mess left.

My own life is precious even though maybe without love I'm

missing a huge key to my own happiness. I set off a cataclysmic chain of events the day I pulled that trigger. But I also found my salvation. I hope when it comes time for my judgment there's a mercy for what I contemplated—for what I did.

In my mind, the scales are balanced, so I dare not ask for more.

"I thought I taught you not to dwell on things," a familiar male voice murmurs directly in my ear, startling me from my thoughts. I whirl around and find Phil in my space.

"I wasn't..." I protest. He shakes his head, stopping the denial on my lips.

"You're taking photos of people who have been through so many similar emotions to what we've had to endure."

"Really?" I drawl sarcastically.

"Yes really," he bites back. "Pain, loss, desperation. And if you're not seeing that on their faces, what are you seeing through that lens of yours?"

"It's different," I argue.

Phil throws up his hands. "Why are you so damned stubborn about this? Do you think the men and women in this room haven't felt what you have at taking a life? Some part of them is glad—damn glad—they did it, and the other part is suffocated in guilt." He leans in. "Does that sound familiar?"

I'm taken aback by my brother's attack more so because he's right. That's precisely what I feel.

Constantly.

Fiddling with the dials on my camera, I hear Jake announce the band's done for the night and the DJ will be up soon. "Why are we talking about this here?" Why now, is what I really want to ask.

"Because I'm so tired of coming into a roomful of people who care about you and finding you hiding instead of living, Holly. I want to grab that camera out of your hands and smash it so you see what's waiting for you if you just look for once with your own eyes." Phil's stares hard down at my face. "I just want you to be happy, baby."

"Until just a few minutes ago, I thought I was," I whisper before I push past my brother.

Cursing, Phil moves to follow me. "Damnit, Hols,"

I wave him off. I pray the back deck to Tide Pool is open so I can escape for just a few minutes because Phil isn't wrong. I've spent so much time being afraid my happiness is going to disappear if I dare to ask for more than I now need to question whether or not I've been really living.

And I'd really like to do that alone.

I'm TAKING in the chilly March night sky. I know I'm slacking on my job, but after the words my brother flung at me, if I didn't get some air, I was going to vomit in the overheated bar that is smelling particularly ripe with spilled alcohol. I need to get back inside soon, but even in a room full of people that are pushing the limits against the fire code, I feel so alone.

Is it possible to feel such love and such self-loathing at the same time?

You didn't mean to do it, I remind myself. *But you don't regret it*, the other part of me forcefully states.

Of course I don't. I'm alive, and they're not; Maria by my hands and him due to the prison sentence he couldn't endure. So, the battle I've been fighting internally for years rages on.

Life in this world wouldn't have been better if Maria had lived, that's for sure. My father would have forced me into taking a man within twenty-four hours of overhearing him tell my stepmother "She takes Boyd as her first customer tomorrow night or I'll find some other way to deal with her,"

But even through absolution by governors, ministers, and shrinks, I still question the validity of my decision. Because there's never a time it's not in the back of my mind, when I'm not both guilted and freed by what I did. The truth I know is this: I wouldn't be standing here if I didn't pull the trigger, even accidentally. Even if what I did was evil, my intent wasn't toward her. And doesn't intent count for something? It must have, as I was pardoned so I could begin a new life as a free woman.

Shame courses over me, heating my skin, thinking of the words Phil flung at me. His observations aren't wrong, just his reasons. I'm terrified I'm going to somehow taint any love I find with whatever enabled me to think about pulling that trigger on myself.

I'll continue to pay a life sentence as surely as if I were sitting in a cell, only my bars are constructed of guilt and self-flagellation.

I shiver in the cold night air. None of this is going to get resolved tonight; some of it may never get resolved. But I can't let my family—the family that saved what's left of my soul—down. I start to head down the wood deck when I hear a shrill voice ask, "Want some company? You look so lonely out here."

Turning the corner of the building, Joe Bianco's being pushed against the railing by an aggressive blonde. And before I know it, my mouth's opening without hesitation.

"That's because he's been waiting for me."

Strolling over to him slowly so as not to let my cameras jostle too much, I slide my arm around his waist. I whisper, "Go along with it," right before I brush my lips under his firm jaw.

I don't count on when I wade in to save him that I'll be waking up long-dormant parts of myself. Joe's arm tightens around me, curving my body perfectly into his. I can smell the citrusy scent of his cologne.

Damn.

Focusing on the fuming woman in front of me, I smile vaguely; offer my hand, and say, "Holly Freeman."

The nasty scowl that drops onto the woman's face confirms my decision that I made the right choice to help.

22

JOSEPH

I'm nursing a drink while I stand on the deck behind Tide Pool when I hear her grating voice. Is it not enough I have to deal with it each time I pick up Grace from school?

"Hi, Joe."

Internally groaning, I turn, and Tiffany is wearing tight jeans and a revealing top, sauntering up to me. I jerk my head in a nod.

"Want some company? You look so lonely standing out here," she purrs.

I don't know to handle this. I'm about to text someone to get me out of this situation when another voice breaks through the shadows of the night. "That's because he's been waiting for me." And when Holly Freeman appears out of the shadows and into the light, I'm simultaneously grateful and disturbed.

Because her words trigger something in me. *Maybe you have been waiting for her.*

As she slides up next to me and casually slips an arm around my waist, I stiffen. She must feel it but doesn't let go. Instead, she nestles under my shoulder before whispering, "Go along with it," and brushes a soft kiss on the side of my jaw. Turning to face my daughter's teacher, she lets go of the camera she's been holding, despite the strap around her neck. Holding out a hand, she says, "Holly Freeman."

Tiffany is fuming. "Joe and I were trying to have a private conversation..."

Holly laughs at the other woman. "That would be surprising considering this is the first time I've had all night to escape to spend some time alone with him." Holly tips her head and then snaps her fingers. "Now I recognize you! You're my niece's teacher. Kalie Marshall. My sister Alison speaks of you." She pauses for dramatic effect. "Often."

Tiffany takes a step back. "You're related to Ms. Freeman."

My body reacts not only to her nearness but also to her calm efficiency in dealing with this troll. "Hmm, yes. She's fantastic. A barracuda of an attorney, you know?" Turning to me, she gives me a brilliant smile. "I forgot to tell you, Joe, Ali's pregnant again. Keene's beside himself. The whole family is, really."

Sliding my arm around her shoulders, I squeeze her hard. "I heard at the pancake breakfast. It is great news. When did she tell him?"

"After the race today." Holly angles her body slightly toward mine.

I chuckle, because I'm enjoying how naturally this show is playing out. Tiffany, on the other hand, finds nothing about our conversation amusing. In the overhead light above her, I can see her face turning a rather unpleasant shade of mottled red.

Holly grins, and my gut clenches because that smile is so damn appealing. I almost forget it's an act until I hear the stomping of Tiffany's heels as she storms off.

We wait a few moments in silence before Holly whispers, "Is it safe? I swear, she's a freaking piranha."

I burst out laughing. "Yeah, after you started talking about Keene and Ali, she took off. Thanks for the save." I look down into her smiling face. "How did you know I needed it?" I ask curiously.

She shrugs. "I came out to get some air. Very few people know about the back deck. And Ali told us how fun things were at the parent-teacher conference. I listened in to see if you might need an assist."

I squeeze her shoulder. I still haven't let go, though I can't explain why. "So, you're an eavesdropper."

She stiffens in my arms. "Did I misread the situation? Should I go apologize and send her back out?"

"Hell no! I was just joking." I look down at my booted feet. "I guess I'm out of practice."

"Joe?" My head snaps up to hers. "It's okay. Don't beat yourself up about it. I just...see things and try to help where I can."

"I'm glad you did," I tell her. We stand there in silence before I ask, "How much do you know..."

"About what happened to you?"

I let out a deep breath. "Yeah."

She pulls away to lean against the railing. I'm both amazed and disturbed to find I miss the warmth of her next to me. "Enough to understand she"—she nods to where Tiffany was standing—"would have made you uncomfortable."

"She's pretty much the nightmare of most single dads. And a few of the married ones." I reach for my drink and take a sip. I decide to ask a question that's been on my mind. "You don't have any kids?" Even though I didn't notice any of hers at the farm the other night, she could be divorced and sharing custody.

She shakes her head. "Nope. Thirty-two and still single. I have one nephew, two nieces, and a soon-to-be step-niece. And two yet-to-be determineds." I smile at her phrasing of Ali and Keene's future babies.

"Can I ask a personal question?" She raises her eyebrows. I lift a hand. "You can tell me it's none of my business."

"Fire away," she says smoothly.

"Are the men around here idiots, or is your single status by choice?"

She chuckles. "If you were on the date I was the other day, you'd understand better."

I nod sagely. "Idiots." Holly's musical laughter rings out in the night.

"To be fair, I'm also not looking for forever," she concedes. "I want someone I can go out with where there's no pressure to be..." I interrupt her.

"More than friends?"

She nods.

I let out a deep sigh. "That's been the hardest part since I lost Mary," I admit. Her lips tip in empathy, but she doesn't say anything, so I continue. "I want to be able to enjoy some of the things I used to and not feel like..."

"A fifth wheel?" Holly inserts dryly. "Extra baggage with all the happy couples? A permanent target for all the fix-ups?"

"Oh, God. You just became my new best friend. I'm dumping Brett the minute I go back inside." Holly's smile washes over me. Grinning, I add on, "Since he's been my best friend since we were kids, this will devastate him for about point two seconds before he gets another beer and says, 'Whatever.'"

"That reminds me of the night my sisters and I declared we were going to marry each other and become 'sister wives,'" Holly chortles. "In fact—" She tips her head back toward the entrance of Tide Pool. "—it happened right inside while we were sitting on the bar."

I choke on my laugh. "Isn't that illegal in all fifty states?"

"None of us are biologically related; we could have made it work. But after the liquor wore off, Ali kept threatening to disown us, so we gave up the idea."

I throw back my head and laugh so hard, I feel wetness spring to my eyes. I'm wheezing trying to get my breath when I hear her say, "Smile." I know I have a wonky one on my face when the flash on her camera goes off, but I do.

And damned if it doesn't feel right.

I have no idea what tricks this red-haired witch has up her sleeve, but I can't think of a single time in the last three years when I've laughed so much or smiled so hard.

"Holly, let me ask you something?" Her head swings my way, and

I feel a punch in the gut from those golden eyes that I'm so not ready for.

"Sure." Her uncomplicated simplicity makes liking her very easy.

"Keene and Ali mentioned you do photography outside of the wedding stuff." I wait for her nod. "I don't know how much you charge, but I was wondering if you have an opening...maybe I could schedule some time for me and Grace. I know Mother's Day is coming up soon, but my mother does so much to help out with Grace..." My voice trails off when I feel the warmth of her hand on my arm.

"Joe, it won't take more than an hour or two. And that kind of photography is fun for me. Do you have my number or just the office?"

"Whatever Ali gave me on her card."

"Give me your phone," she says, holding out her hand face up. Digging in my pocket, I pull it out and unlock it. Quickly she programs herself in and then dials. A phone rings in the cold night air. Slipping her phone out, she programs my number in. "I figure your schedule is fairly hectic, but if you can, give me a day's notice. Dress Grace in cute, casual clothes. Nothing super fancy. We'll hit the park or something like that."

"How much am I looking at?" I ask warily.

"A couple of cups of coffee and the cost of printing the pictures. I don't charge friends of the family for my services."

"Holly." I drop my head and rub the back of my neck.

"Please. After all the planning for this event? I would like to think we're all friends now, right?" Her voice is firm.

I shake my head back and forth. I feel like a level of mercy is being bestowed upon me I haven't earned, but I'm not foolish enough to let it go. "Thanks, Holly." My voice comes out all husky.

She just smiles, then pauses as the music changes. Her smile gets larger until it illuminates her face. "Uh-oh." A soft laugh escapes her lips.

"What?"

"We're about to be invaded," she says confidently. Not three seconds later, Phil throws the back door open while he shouts, "Get in here, baby girl, it's time to dance!"

Holly fiddles with the dials on one of her cameras a moment before sliding both of them off her neck. "I've been summoned. How handy are you with a camera?"

"If you're asking for me to be able to do more than point and click with your livelihood, then no." I whip my hands around my back as she laughs.

"Man up, Joe. These pictures are going to be priceless." Reaching up, she slides both straps over my neck. "I already changed the settings, so they should come out perfect. I'll check them before Phil drags me off. Just make sure you take a lot of photos. If you press this button here—" Holly grabs my hand and puts my finger on the shutter. "—and hold it, it will take a series of shots. Press and release for one at a time." She starts to walk away.

"Holy crap, you're not kidding!" I chase after her, leaving the rest of my drink on the deck railing.

She shakes her head, which sends her long mane of hair rippling down her back. "Nope. Not at all."

We walk in, and the DJ who's taken over for the band has house music blaring through the speakers. Holly's already swaying her hips back and forth. Phil's impatiently tapping his foot, waiting for his sister. She checks out the lighting around the room before grabbing the camera that's tightly looped around my neck. "Oomph," I choke out.

"Give me just a sec," she yells. Making an adjustment that I'd have no idea how to make, she turns the camera on Phil, who preens. I choke out a laugh. "Just wait till we get on the dance floor." Snapping the shot, she flips over to the viewfinder. Her lips tip up, and she shows me.

Damn. It looks like Phil's standing in a studio. My jaw slightly unhinges. Holly reaches up and pats my cheek. "You'll be just fine. Now you can just point and click." Turning to Phil, who's holding out his hand, she takes hold while he drags her through the gathering crowd.

Muscling my way through, I get close enough to the dance floor to see where all the action is. The DJ has on an extended version of "Shut Up and Dance With Me." How appropriate, I think as I watch the Freeman family dominate the dance floor. I snap a picture of Caleb bending Cassidy backward and then flipping her up. *Click*. Keene has Ali's body molded to his as his face softly stares into the eyes of his wife. *Click*. Colby has Corinna's back to his front. His hands are on her swaying hips as they drop down and back up. *Click*. Em's leg is hitched around a guy whose face I can't see. I presume that's her fiancé *Click*. I turn the camera and freeze. Holy crap. Phil is dropped down on his knees in front of Holly, who has Jason at her back. Somehow, in tandem with the beat, they switch, and Holly's siren's body rocks back and forth on a pair of heeled boots I didn't notice outside to land between both men. She turns until she's facing Jason when she rises back until she's standing. Her body sways between her brother and his husband. I press the shutter repeatedly as Holly laughs up at both men.

Suddenly the music transitions to an old '80s beat easily recognizable from the movie *Footloose*. The siblings are pressed up against each other as Kenny Loggins belts out about fighting his fears and love. The Freemans move in a coordinated dance that ends with Cassidy, Em, and Phil standing while Ali, Corinna, and Holly drop on their knees in front of them. I press the shutter down and hold it while their hands fly doing some complicated hand and finger snapping maneuver before they're all on their feet dancing together in a tight huddle, immune to the wolf whistles that break out around them.

What I realize as I look through Holly's camera is she looks fierce and fearless while she's surrounded by her family. We share more than just a need to be by ourselves in the middle of a crowd, I muse, even as I keep taking pictures, this time around the room of all the admirers of the epic dancing. Our hearts are so tied so closely to those that we love that in the middle of anything being thrown at us, we know they're our reason for hanging on.

23

JOSEPH

When the song ends, Holly dances her way back over to reclaim her cameras. Her eyes are sparkling, her face flushed. "Thanks, Joe. Did you get some good shots?" She immediately goes to flip through them, but I keep her hand from lifting the cameras off my neck.

"I guarantee I did." Her eyes fly up to mine. An arc of something dances between us. Ignoring it, I grab her elbow and lead her over to the bar. "You need a drink."

"Dangerous words to say to us in this place." Already sparkling eyes turn mischievous.

I stop behind a few of my coworkers. "Oh?" My voice is pitched high to be heard over the DJ.

A slow smile crosses her face. "Whatever you order will be fine. Just no tequila. They might throw us out."

I shake my head. When we get to the bar, I yell to Jessica, "Two Belvedere martinis."

"Make mine filthy, Jess," Holly calls out.

Jessica rolls her eyes and yells, "Like I expected any differently from a Freeman, Hols. I'm surprised you're not up on the bar already."

Holly's cheeks turn pink. "That's 'cause Cass planned tonight's events, not Phil," she calls back.

Jessica laughs and turns to make our drinks. I raise my brows and watch Holly turn pinker. "Your face is going to match your hair soon," I remark.

"Shit." She's saved when Jessica slides two drinks in front of us. "Family tab, Jess." Jessica nods before turning toward the next customer.

I go to object when Holly skewers me with a look. "Don't argue. Cass would have my throat if I didn't cover you and Detective Idrissi after midnight. If your dad and Chief Drever were still here, it would be the same. As it is, CFD and CPD haven't been paying a dime."

"Seriously?" She nods. Whoa. "Who do we have to thank for that?"

"Cass is going to make an announcement about it in just a few." Holly takes a sip of her drink. "I'll take my cameras back now."

Carefully, I untangle the expensive equipment from around my neck. Holly casually puts the straps around hers. I notice something ease in her beautiful features. "They're an extension of you, aren't they?" I take a small drink and nod down.

She nods. "I'm nowhere without at least one. Even in the office, I have a camera with me."

I grin. "Sure you don't have a secret fantasy to become a PI?"

She wrinkles her nose. "There have been more times I've ended up in that position unintentionally. So no, thank you."

I'm about to ask her about what she means when the music fades down. Cassidy is up on the stage with the DJ. "Could I ask my family, Officer Bianco, and Detective Idrissi to join me on stage?" Holly begins weaving her way through people who graciously move out of our way. As we get closer to the stage, Holly holds up a camera with one hand. Cassidy shakes her head. "Hols, give it to Keene. We need you up here."

Turning toward me, Holly asks, "Can you hold this a moment?" She passes me her drink.

"Sure." She takes a step back and looks up at the stage. Fiddling with the dials of one of her cameras quickly, she turns and hands it to her brother-in-law, who appears to our left. "Thanks, Keene."

He grins down at her. "No problem. Now get up there. I got you covered."

She winks at him before turning back to me. "Ready?"

I pass her martini back to her. We make it the few steps over to the stage. Squeezing up with the other Freemans, I glance over at Mike. "Any idea what's going on?" I mutter.

He shakes his head. He opens his mouth to speak, but Cassidy starts talking. "Thank you, all, for coming tonight to support Collyer's Police and Fire Departments. There are not enough words to express our gratitude to the men and women who willingly step into harm's way to protect the citizens of our town every day." Cassidy waits while the bar breaks into cheers. "Let me go on, y'all!" she yells into the mic. "Before midnight all of the CPD and CFD have been drinking free courtesy of one of the sponsors of today's event, Hudson Investigations." My eyes drift over to Keene as he's snapping photos. He throws me an arrogant smirk. "The men and women of Hudson are primarily veterans of law enforcement and our armed services. They know well what it means to complete a successful mission. It's a constant battle you endure, a constant war you face. And despite that, you all fought as one today to stand for your fallen. This is their gift to you."

Damn. I feel the knot in the back of my throat. Feeling Mike clap me on the shoulder, I turn to him in time to hear him yell, "Fuck, man, did you know..." I shake my head.

"But Holly just told me you and I are drinking free all night; not just 'til midnight." Mike's eyes widen.

"What?"

"I just found out myself."

"Jesus," he mutters. We both turn our attention back to Cassidy, who isn't done.

"We have some early totals we want to share which is why we asked Officer Bianco and Detective Idrissi to join us on stage. Joe, Mike, can you make your way forward?" Cassidy beams at us.

My stomach turns. *God, please let it be better than last year's total. Just better than eighteen grand.* I slide past Ali, whose dazzling smile gets even more bright if that's even possible. I maneuver past Cori, who's practically bouncing in her Chucks and CPD T-shirt. Suddenly I'm next to Cassidy, who is proudly wearing a CFD T-shirt and form-fitting jeans. Mike's made his way up the other side.

"I know we threw a lot of this together at the last minute. So, I swear right here and right now, we'll do better next year. But I'm so proud that as of ten minutes ago, the current total for the Victims Association is $101,343."

My jaw goes slack, and the mostly empty martini glass starts to fall. It splashes all over my pants before a hand grabs it in midair before it shatters on the floor. "Holy crap." The words are out of my mouth before I can stop them. Cassidy turns around to face me, her feet having just touched back down after being spun in circles by Mike.

"How does that work for a few weeks of planning, Joe?" she jokes.

The whoop I let out is heard through the open mic. As if I give a shit. All that's running through my mind is the fact that Tara's family won't have to cut down on their heat next winter. Kelley can buy her family new school clothes without stressing. And Wendy's family will be able to stay in their home. I give up the battle and let my tears fall into Cassidy Freeman's neck. "Thank you," I say hoarsely in her ear.

"No, Joe. It's all of us who need to thank all of you," Cassidy murmurs. Stepping back, she wipes her own tears. "Just remember, I promised next year is going to be even better."

"I don't know how," I say honestly.

She smiles confidently before tossing a long dark braid down her back. Holding the mic away, she grins. "Just stand back and watch us." Pulling the mic up toward her face, she yells, "Now who came here to dance and celebrate?"

The room goes wild.

"Then let's get those hands up in the air for the CPD and CFD! Remember to drink safely tonight. Numbers for safe transportation are available at the bar. See you on the dance floor. And one more time, let's hear it for the men and women of the Collyer Police and Fire Departments!"

"Cass," Holly yells to her sister over the noise. She's holding a metal bucket in her arms. In fact, all of the Freemans are.

"Sorry! One more thing! If you see myself or any of my siblings around holding one of these buckets"—all the Freemans simultaneously lift up large metal pails—"and you feel like donating more to the Victims Assistance Fund, toss in some spare change, cash, whatever you have to give. They'll be around the rest of the night holding them. Finally, my thanks to my brother-in-law Jake and his band for playing earlier and my brother-in-law Jared, who has been our DJ tonight. Let's give it up to everyone who has had a hand in today's events."

Tajo Cruz's "Dynamite" starts pounding through the speakers as all of the Freeman siblings jump off the stage holding their pails over their heads. I quickly move over to the DJ to shake his hand and mouth, "Thanks." Jared shakes my hand before letting it go. I turn around and my body locks as I take in the scene.

Every person in Tide Pool is on their feet dancing and waving money in the air like it's a flag of honor. The Freemans are dancing, plucking money out of their hands like it's an Italian wedding dance before shaking it with them for a few seconds before moving on.

Helplessly, my eyes follow Holly through the crowd. She's made her way about a third of the way around the room to a booth of women all wearing Hudson Investigation shirts. She's giving them—and the place—quite a show as she's jumped up on the table. There's a line of people on the ground ready to dance with her. Her cameras are on the table behind her, so her hands are empty. But the pail at her feet is filling up. She's laughing as she points at Corinna, who's up on another table across the room filled with guys also wearing Hudson Investigation shirts, I notice.

A guy I don't recognize comes up next to me. Quietly, he hands me an envelope. "Thank you for everything you do to keep my family safe. And tell my sister-in-law she's amazing." He smiles at me.

I squeeze the envelope in my hands. Tightly. "Which Freeman are you related to?"

"Technically? Just Cass. I'm Caleb's brother, Ryan. Jared's my husband." He points at the DJ, who blows him a kiss. Then my scattered brain catches up with me. Caleb and Ryan Lockwood? The brothers who inherited Lockwood Industries? The largest transportation company in the Northeast? And he just handed me an envelope? "Do I even want to know what's in this?" I ask, pitching my voice beneath the music.

"Only if you want to watch Cassidy lose her mind on the dance floor." Ryan smiles. "I'm going to go hide with my husband for a while before I head out. I'm flying out later in the morning to try to broker a deal in Singapore. It was a pleasure to meet you, Officer. We were sorry to miss the last family dinner. Maybe we'll see you at the next one." He holds out his hand.

After I grip his firmly, Ryan starts to move away. I yell out his name. "Ryan?" He pauses. "Why?"

Taking a step back, he murmurs close to my ear, "If you knew what a comfort it is to know they're all finally safe, you'd understand money is the least I can do." Stepping away, he says louder, "Now, go put that check in a bucket, Officer. And enjoy their reaction when it's opened. I certainly plan to."

And he silently disappears behind the table where Jared's sitting.

Jumping off the stage, I head directly toward Holly. I can't explain why, but it's her hands I want to put the check into. Shifting between the dancing bodies, I see Phil pulling dollars and tossing them into his bucket. Bypassing the line of men and women waiting to dance with her, I reach up and hand her the envelope. She stops moving and gives me a quizzical look. I nod at it. After using a nail to unseal it, her jaw drops. She grabs her cell out of her pocket and quickly takes a picture of the check. I scan the room to see all of the Freemans grab their phones. Corinna starts jumping up and down on her table. Phil grabs Jason and kisses him. Ali screams and leans over and kisses Em smack on the lips. Cassidy stands still in the middle of the dance floor for a moment, stunned, before she reaches into her pocket for the microphone.

"We've just had an anonymous benefactor who pushed the Victims Association Fund to over a quarter million dollars!" she ends on a scream. "Thank you! Thank you so much!"

A quarter of a million dollars. My head spinning, I whirl around toward the DJ, but I can't make out Ryan Lockwood's features. I repeatedly swallow, but it doesn't stop the tears burning in my eyes. It might be a business decision for him, but I know how much this money will touch the lives of real people. Snapping off a salute in his direction, I let out a massive yell with both fists in the air. In the middle of it, I'm swarmed by Brett, Mike, and Justin.

"Holy crap. Did that just happen?" Mike chokes out.

"I was handed the check. It sure as hell did." I bang our foreheads together.

"What does this mean?" Justin yells.

"When it's done? We can help everyone. No apologies. Not just right now, but for a while." We're standing right beneath a spotlight as we slap each other's backs and revel in this miracle. Breaking apart, we grin. The room has gone electric. Suddenly, all of the bartenders behind the bar begin ringing all the bells. Spinning around, I wonder why before I burst out laughing.

Brett, Justin, and Mike do too.

Apparently, when the Freemans cut loose, they don't care who's watching. Each of the siblings are dancing on tables, celebrating with their significant others guarding them. Holly's the only one who technically is alone, but I have no plans on moving. I yell to my friends, "Go! I've got her covered." They all grin and take off to find someone to celebrate with.

The line to dance with Holly keeps growing when a behemoth of a man from Hudson Investigations saunters up. "I can cover her if you want to party, Officer." He's much older, but I have no doubt he could take down anyone in the room—let alone the planet—who messed with Holly Freeman. A smile breaks out across his face. "You deserve to cut loose."

I shake my head. "I'm perfectly fine right where I am."

Sharp blue eyes assess me before he reaches out a paw. "Charlie Henderson."

"Joe Bianco."

He bellows out a laugh. "I knew who you were before I walked in the door, son. Take care of our girl. Tap me in if you need assistance."

I wait for half a heartbeat before I ask, "What branch were you, Mr. Henderson?"

He doesn't hesitate in responding. "I was a SEAL, son. And make it Charlie. I have a suspicion we'll be getting to know each other. Eventually." Turning, he heads back across the room to the table of Hudson Investigation guys who are beneath Corinna.

A frigging SEAL. Jesus Christ. No wonder he was confident enough at his age to know he could protect Holly. Glancing up, I see she's lost in the music. Her hands have wrapped themselves around her body as she spins around on her heeled boots. When she turns forward again, her hair fans out around her. I want to sink my hands into the strands to feel if it's as thick as I imagine it is.

It must be the emotion flying through the air. I dismiss the thought as quickly as it comes into my brain. I had my chance at something permanent, and I lost it. But damn, tonight's a night that helps obliterate some of my pain. I never want to let this feeling go.

And for the first time since Mary died, I'm grateful to be doing so with the woman dancing at my side, not wishing it was a woman I'll always love and miss.

Maybe I'm beginning to understand that in fear of losing again, I haven't been living.

Maybe Holly can help me with that.

Just as friends though.

24

HOLLY

A few days later, I'm editing the pictures from the race so I can get them up on our website when my cell phone rings on the desk next to me. I reach for it blindly with one hand while I pick up my coffee with the other. "This is Holly." Quickly taking a swig of the coffee that Cassidy grabbed on a run to The Coffee Shop earlier, I give the caller a chance to identify themselves. There's no response. "Hello? Is anyone there?"

"Holly," his deep voice comes through the line. I plunk my cup down. Ignoring the increase of my speeding heart rate, I reply.

"Hello, Joe. What a lovely surprise."

"I'm glad you called," I toss over my shoulder at him as he, Grace, and I make our way to the gazebo in Collyer's public gardens a few days later. "Your timing—photographically speaking—couldn't have been more perfect."

The spring blossoms are going to make a gorgeous backdrop. When I told Joe over the phone to dress both himself and Grace in plain long-sleeved white tees, there was a long pause before he doubtfully asked, "Are you sure?"

I replied, "Trust me," before I hung up on him.

My instincts were spot-on. The white of their tees contrasted with their dark hair so richly and would make them stand out from the riot of colors of nature's backdrop. Seeing the bush I want to start with up ahead, I resolutely make my way there and then wait for Grace's reaction.

I don't have long.

Grace is delighted by the heart-shaped pink flowers. Her lips form a perfect O before her fingers are tangled in them, pulling them toward her face. Joe is immediately behind her. "Grace, be careful that doesn't hit you in the face, sweetheart." His hands come up to rest on hers. Even on his knees, his face doesn't obscure hers.

Neither do the branches of the bleeding heart that's come into bloom so beautifully. I start snapping away. I get pictures of Grace picking up fallen leaves and draping them precisely over Joe's dark hair before he shakes them off with a growl and starts tickling his little girl. She squeals and darts away; Joe chases after her.

I follow them both.

For about an hour, the two of them play amid the marigolds and violas, and dart in and around the rhododendron bushes. But finally when Grace starts to wind down, plopping in a field of daffodils, I get what I think may be the best shots of the day: Grace is leaning back trustingly against Joe's chest, his arms wrapped around her. Slowly, her eyes start drooping before she's entirely out.

"And I think we're done, Dad," I whisper as I get closer to Joe. Swinging off my backpack, I detach the lens and store it before putting the camera in its specially designed pocket. Unlatching the top, I pull out a thin blanket and hand it to him. Joe looks at me quizzically. I shrug. "Sometimes when I'm filming kids, they go down for the count because they're so wired. I've learned it pays to be prepared."

Carefully shifting Grace so he can wrap her up, he stands with her in his arms. I'd be lying if I didn't admit to my mouth watering a little when I saw the muscles in his arms flex as he lifted Grace high against his chest. "Thanks."

"Hmm?" I make a show of buckling my backpack again while I mentally slap myself for drooling over a family friend like he's nothing but man meat. *For God's sake, Holly, snap out of it. This is a man who's still grieving the love of his life*, I berate myself.

"For the blanket. Even though today was fairly warm, she gets cool when she conks out like this." Joe leans over and kisses his daughter's forehead. My heart melts. There's no other way to describe it.

Adorable.

We make our way back to our vehicles. I quickly slide my backpack into my car while Joe navigates getting his daughter strapped into her car seat. Remembering the last time I offered to help with Grace, I hold my tongue. So, I'm surprised when he calls out, "Hey, Holly?"

"Yes?"

"Do you mind if I keep the blanket and get it back to you?" *Of course, you ninny. He doesn't need your help.*

"Not at all. Just drop it by the office one day this week. I may even have proofs for you to check out by then." Striding over to my driver's-side door, I open it when he calls out, "Or maybe I could give it back to you during dinner one night? Maybe a movie?"

I freeze. There isn't a single hair on my body that's moving.

Leaving the door behind the driver's seat of his Explorer open, he approaches me slowly. "That night, at Tide Pool..." He hesitates.

"Yes?" I don't say more.

"You seemed to have the same opinions I had about finding someone who can be a friend."

I just don't know if it can be you. I nod instead.

He takes a deep breath. "So, let's give it a try."

I open my mouth and then snap it shut. *You can do this. Even if this is the worst form of torture there is, you can do it.* "Joe, if people see us together for the first time at night, there's no way they're not going to make a leap that we're not dating," I declare boldly.

His face takes on a look of consternation. "I didn't think of that. I'm so out of practice with this shit," he mutters.

"Look, come by the mansion. Drop off the blanket, take a look at the photos, and grab a meal with us," I offer.

He appears intrigued. "Go on."

"Then we'll go out to lunch another day. You know, ease our way into it."

"That seems a lot smarter," he agrees.

And safer for my sanity. I just shrug in response.

Two dimples he probably reserves for his daughter light his face. "Sounds like a plan, Ms. Freeman."

"That it does. I'll see you sometime during the week, then." I slide into the driver's seat. Pushing the key into my ignition, I hear a tap against the window. Rolling it down, I turn my head slightly and meet Joe's dark blue eyes head-on.

"Drive safely, Holly," he whispers. Rapping his knuckles against the roof of my car, he moves away so I can back out of my spot.

Rolling up the window, I back up and pull out. In the rearview, he's standing where I left him, arms crossed in the white shirt, looking like temptation and heartbreak wrapped up in a single package.

"Shit. This is not going to go well," I mutter as I turn onto the road to lead me back to the mansion.

And some order and sanity.

25

JOSEPH

"Is it unusual to just be friends with a woman?" I ask my father as he passes me the bowl of antipasto.

His eyebrows shoot straight to his forehead. He and my mother exchange glances. "I would like to think I'm a friend to everyone who works at the house, Joe," he replies carefully. "Whether they're a man or a woman."

My mom stands up to usher Grace out of the room under the pretense of getting the pasta from the kitchen. "I don't mean like that." Stabbing my fork into a bite of cheese, I pop it into my mouth and chew thoughtfully. "I know you were aware of how much I resented working on the Victims Assistance Fund, Pop. It felt like I was constantly being reminded of Mary."

"I know, son. But..." Before he can start to enumerate the many reasons he asked me to work on it, I interrupt him.

"But I think I understand now. There's something about stepping outside your own pain to help others that furthers your own healing."

My father blinks at me. "Honestly, that wasn't what I intended at all, but if that's been one of the outcomes, I couldn't be more pleased."

"I laughed so much recently," I tell him just as my mother approaches the table with Grace. The bowl of spaghetti and meat sauce she's holding clatters to the table.

"What?" she whispers, her voice filled with equal measures of hope and shock.

Reaching over, I pick up my little girl, who's balancing a bowl of freshly grated parmesan in her hands. "And not because this one's dancing around the living room to Elmo," I tease.

"Elmo!" Grace shrieks. Just as her hands are about to fling the cheese everywhere, my mother rescues it.

I grin. "The red furry one appreciates your devout worship, baby."

Grace nods seriously. I brush a kiss on her forehead before I face my parents again. My mother has tears in her eyes. "What is it?"

"I don't care if you told me the person who's giving me back my son has six earrings, multicolored mohawk-shaven hair, and is an arsonist," my mother declares.

"I might draw the line at arson, but what your mother said. Who cares if the person is a woman, Joe? And for that matter, if it grows into something more over time." He shrugs.

I can't mentally even go there yet, but I appreciate their support knowing all they want is the best for Grace and for me. "So, knowing you might hear about me and Holly Freeman sharing a few lunches together won't upset you?" I ask carefully.

"That entire family is welcome at this table," my father says gruffly. I smile knowing there's no more significant honor from my father.

"Their table is bigger, Pop. In fact, it wouldn't surprise me if you get an invitation to join them. When Grace and I were invited over for a meal while we planning the event, their farm table could probably..." My voice drifts off when I catch both my parents staring openly at me.

"It seems to me, my sweet boy, that this friendship started a while ago," my mother says gently.

"Before, it was about planning the event. Now, it's just about Holly and me. There will be talk."

My father leans forward, resting his chin in his hand. "The only two people who I could think of who might object to you living, son, are Eden and Seth. And I don't need to go into why." He gives my daughter, who's too busy trying to stick her fingers into the meat sauce, a pointed look.

Eden and Seth are still so wrapped up in their grief. They feel nothing. I firmly believe no one should have to move on from that kind of pain we all felt until they're ready, but not at Grace's expense. Gently pulling Grace's fingers away from the hot sauce, I bite them in my mouth, setting her to giggling.

Grief doesn't have a deadline, that's for sure. But life does. I don't want the rest of mine to be spent feeling the desperate shards of pain being shoved into my chest when I might be able to enjoy a few moments of happiness with the ability to scar the wounds left behind.

I lift Grace, then put her down. "I don't know about you all, but I'm starving. I can't come into this house and not want to eat."

"Eat!" Grace dances, but suddenly she crosses her legs. A telltale sign.

I laugh. "Come on, sweetheart. Let's go potty before we eat so we don't ruin Grandma's chairs."

"'Kay!" She grabs my hand, and I let her drag me to the hallway bathroom.

Leaning against the jamb, I think about what my mother said and laugh. A six earrings, multicolored mohawked arsonist.

"What's so funny, Daddy?"

"Life is, sweetheart," I tell her honestly. Kneeling down, I help her readjust her clothing. "Now go wash your hands so we can eat."

As she steps on the little stool to do just that, I stand to my full height. Catching my reflection in the mirror, I realize that after all these years, I'm finally taking steps to move forward.

As a man who by choice runs into a wall of flame, taking this step seems both more frightening and more astounding.

"Get a move on, you two! I'm getting hungry out here!" my father bellows.

"Yes, Grandpa!" Grace goes tearing back toward the table. I turn off the light and follow at a more leisurely pace, my soul more settled than it has been in a long time.

26

HOLLY

"So glad you suggested this," I tell Joe as I shove a bite of Frances' macaroni and cheese into my mouth. "I rarely leave the mansion for lunch."

He chuckles. "You all sound worse than we do. Unless we're out on a call, we make the probies cook for us." His face twists in a grimace. "That can be pretty hit or miss."

"We're normally not that bad. If we've just had a family dinner, we bring the leftovers in for the next day. Otherwise, we just congregate with whatever we've brought from home. If we're splurging or it's a special occasion, we'll beg for someone to bring us Genoa."

The groan that passes from Joe's lips causes my lips to turn up. "I take it we're not the only one obsessed with it?"

"I think they funded their expansion due to the CFD," he tells me.

I break out laughing. His eyes twinkle as he shoves a bite of food into his mouth and chews.

"So, what's an average day like for you?" I ask once he's swallowed. "A lot of callouts?"

"Because we're EMTs as well as firemen, I'd say a fair amount. And then we go through a full safety check of all equipment and our vehicles when we're back at the house. That includes stocking supplies, checking to make sure everything is in working order for the next callout, things like that." Joe stabs his fork into his container of pulled pork, takes a bite, and swallows. "Then there's the paperwork."

"Not a lot of downtime to just hang out, then," I surmise.

His face turns thoughtful. "I wouldn't say that. It comes in waves. We do get downtime which we spend it in a lot of ways."

"Like how?" I shove a bite of my own pork into my mouth.

"Well, we could probably beat the pants off any teenager at most online games. In fact—" He leans back in his chair, pulling his uniform shirt tight again his firm chest. I dart my eyes down to my food trying not to notice. "—we help the CPD with some of their cyberbullying cases by hanging out in the online game rooms."

My eyes fly up to meet his. "Seriously?"

He nods. "Yep."

"That's awesome."

"Most of the time it is," he agrees. Then his face breaks into a huge grin. I'm temporarily blinded by those dual dimples. "That is until we have to testify against one of the little punks and we have to create a whole new handle, losing our high score."

I roll my eyes, my enchantment with his handsome features broken over such a guy comment. "Your sacrifice is noted."

He chuckles. "What about you? What's a typical shoot like?"

I snort. I can't help it. "There's nothing typical about any shoot, Joe. That's what makes it almost impossible to hire someone to support me on staff."

Picking up his cornbread, he tears off a chunk. "Give me an example."

I take a drink of my soda while I think about it. "Okay." Leaving out the names of the individuals, I tell him about the wedding that didn't occur the other day where I ended up breaking the bride's heart and we brought the cake back to Amaryllis to devour.

By the time I'm done, Joe's face is outraged.

"And that's not the first time..." I shake my head. "That's not even the fifteenth."

"That's horrible," he declares. I shrug.

"It's a part of the job. Sometimes you see things through a lens you wish you'd never captured, and other times you capture beauty so magnificent you swear there's nothing on earth that's going to top it again in your lifetime." I take a bite of my own cornbread and swallow. "I prefer the second, obviously."

He grins. "Like for example, the pictures of you and Grace?" I shake my head. "Astounding."

His face takes on a cast of vulnerability that hurts so deep inside, I don't think I would take the shot even if I could. "Really?"

I reach for my phone and quickly access the office cloud drive. "These aren't touched up yet," I warn, handing him my phone.

There's silence between us for a few minutes as he taps the screen. It stretches on so long, I begin to fidget in my chair. It isn't until I hear his murmured "I knew you were talented, but I didn't realize you could pluck love and happiness out of thin air" that I begin to breathe again. "These are...there isn't a strong enough of a word."

"Thank you," I say sincerely. "That means the world to me."

I don't think I'm meant to hear his heartbreaking "This was what Mary wanted. Just a beautiful family photo," so I ignore it and focus on eating my lunch. Joe continues to flip through the photos of him and Grace until he comes to the end. "As I said, even though I'm sure you've heard more eloquent compliments, they are spectacular."

"If they're from the heart, each compliment means everything to me," I counter.

"You have to let me pay you," he begins, but I shake my head.

"We have a deal. Coffee from Ava and Matt's and the cost of printing the photos," I say stubbornly.

"Then how about this." He leans forward. "I don't know what your family plans are for Mother's Day, but I'd love if you were to bring the gift by for my mom. She makes a hell of an Italian feast that day. She'd be honored if you joined us."

"We celebrate as a family for brunch, but I couldn't intrude," I protest.

"Holly, we're friends, right?" His hesitancy is my undoing.

"Of course we are." I'm going to give in. I just know it.

"Then join us. It's a huge thing. Mom cooks enough for every off-duty officer at the station. Most of them end up at my parents' house that day."

Realizing it won't just be the two of us, I relax. "Then I'd be honored."

His smile reaches ear to ear until his phone pings with a text. "Crap, I hate to eat and run, but I have to head back to the station." He stands abruptly.

"Don't worry about it." I wave him off as I deliberately stay in my seat. "I'm just going to finish up before I head back to the office. Stay safe."

He reaches down and squeezes my shoulder. "Will do," he says before he strides out the door.

Letting out a slow breath, I text my family that I should be back in the office shortly when Frances herself comes out from the kitchen. Dropping into the seat where Joe sat, Frances gives it to me straight. "If you don't think that half the town isn't going to be speculating on whether or not you're dating that gorgeous Italian, you're deluding yourself."

Gritting my teeth, I get out, "We're just friends, Frances."

Cackling like she just heard that fried catfish was found to be a good source of healthy fat, Frances leans in to tell me, "Honey, a year —no, six months—from now, I want you to come back and tell me that," before she hefts herself from the chair and heads back into the kitchen.

Losing my appetite, which for Frances's Southern cooking is almost as bad as losing it for Genoa's, I leave the rest of my meal uneaten and head out the door so I can edit more photos from the race.

27

JOSEPH

"What's one thing that's different for you now that you're a father?" Holly asks me while we're on the phone.

I think about it for a moment and answer seriously, "Pigtails."

She giggles. It's a great sound. "Seriously, I have a new appreciation when I'm at a store when the package says 'painless' on it. I think that's more for the parents than the kid. Those suckers hurt when they snap in your hand."

"That wasn't exactly what I meant, Joe," Her voice still holds a huge thread of amusement. "I meant, what was a day like for you before you had Grace?"

"Empty." The word pops out of my mouth before I even know it was there. "I was busy, sure, but my life wasn't as fulfilled."

"That's sweet."

I shrug, even though she can't see it. Then I give her the rest as uncomfortable as it is. "Before Grace, before Mary, it was all about the station and the guys. If I wasn't there, I was trading in on the whole firefighter bit."

"Ahh. So you had more groupies than just Tiffany? Maybe I

should have left you to her after all." Her voice is teasing and, much to my relief, without judgment. I begin to relax.

"I don't get it. Half the time we smell, the other half we talk about smelling. Where's the attraction in that?"

Holly's shrieking in laughter on the other end of the phone. "Can't breathe."

I grin. "Ma used to ask her doctor if she had a problem with her nasal passages because they must be burned out from all the stench in our house."

"Joe Bianco, your mama would be so upset if she knew you were telling me that!" Holly admonishes me.

"There were a number of things I did that would have upset my mother far worse," I assure her.

"I'm afraid to ask."

"Be afraid. Be very afraid," I joke.

"So, what you're saying is that you were a handful?"

"I guess as much as any perfect kid could be."

"Please. Let's come back to this planet for a minute." Her sass makes me grin before I answer her seriously.

"I'm the only child of two amazing parents. I was brought up in a house that took no crap and doled out huge amounts of love. I wanted to be like my pop more than I wanted anything else in the world, so it didn't matter how good my throwing arm was or if my grades were perfect."

Her breath catches on the other end of the line, but she doesn't interrupt me.

"I was—am—overprotective about those I love. I have a temper I try to control, but it's a crapshoot. I was a decent date, an okay boyfriend, and then one night I met a woman who rocked my world. I thought we were going to live a dream together. But...in picking up the pieces, I made other people bleed along with me." I whisper the last words. "I still don't know how to live with myself."

"So, what you're saying is that you were a good son, you're a good man, and you lost your mind when something horrible happened."

"I guess so." I shift uncomfortably.

"As much as I hate to say it, it's nice to know you're not perfect. God, you were beginning to worry me."

And this time it's me who bursts out laughing.

Holly spends the next few minutes asking about some of my antics with Brett when I was younger. I tell her about the two of us sneaking into the station to toilet paper the engines on Halloween before his father and mine caught us.

Thinking back, I was more than a handful. Now I'm more glad than ever I decided to get my mother the gift I did for Mother's Day.

"**D**o you know how long it's been since I've been to a movie?" Joe whispers as the lights go dim in the theater. "At least one that doesn't involve princesses or the God of Red Fur?"

I grin in the dark. Joe's and my friendship has blossomed in the last few weeks. We've gone to lunch together around Collyer a dozen times or more. We have a running text chat where he describes his pain of repeated Elmo sightings, so I immediately understand his reference. But I was both saddened and appalled to hear that he hadn't gone to a movie in over three years.

I asked if he wanted to and he said sure, but he had Grace. He felt terrible about infringing on his parents' personal time since they do so much to help. I told him to leave that to me. Ali was thrilled to help. When she found out Joe had Saturday off, she arranged for Grace to come over and play with Kalie so we could sneak off to the AMC 24 in Brookfield. Little did we know that because we left it so late, we'd be stuck with the worst movie in the world.

"Holy crap, this is so bad," Joe mutters.

I giggle because it really is. "The first two were so much better."

Even in the dark, I can feel his eyes on me. "You watched the first two?" he asks incredulously. Since we're the only two in the movie theater, his unmodulated voice disturbs no one.

"Ummm, yeah," I say as if watching a man who's red with horns is an everyday occurrence. "We used to watch all kinds of crap on this dump of a TV we had in our trailer in South Carolina. Then we moved here. We didn't have a lot of money between starting up the business and saving for school. So, we watched movies together. A lot." My voice is nostalgic. "We haven't done that in so long. I kind of miss it."

"I didn't realize you grew up poor," Joe says quietly.

Whether it's because we're in a dark theater or because there's something else to focus on, I give him the truth. "I think the dirt had more money than we did. But we had something better."

"What's that?"

"Each other. None of us would have survived without the other."

"You said none of you are biologically related," Joe asks. I hear him slurp on his drink.

"No. None of us are."

"Does it make it easier or harder?"

I go to open my mouth to speak but close it quickly. "Do you know, in all the years we've been family, no one has ever asked me that? I don't know of any other way, so I can't say for certain. It just is, and it's more beautiful than what any of us had before."

He goes to ask me a question, but I hush him. "Wait, I read this is supposed to be the good part." We both lean forward eagerly only to slump back in our seats. "God, this is worse than *The Mummy* 3 where they replaced Rachel Weisz," I say in disgust.

Joe bursts out laughing.

"It's true! I mean, come on. The sparks between her and Brendan Fraser were off the charts. That movie just shouldn't have been made."

Joe lays his head on the empty seat in front of him, trying to catch his breath.

"It must be a girl thing. My sisters totally get it," I dismiss him and reach for the popcorn.

As he sits back, Joe shoves his hand in there at the same time. Both of our hands, full of greasy movie butter, slide against each other. I feel the sparks all the way through my body, across my now heated skin. My nipples get hard beneath my worn UConn sweatshirt.

Jesus, what is happening to me? Pulling my hand away with a handful of the soggy kernels, I focus on the movie. "Let's watch this for a few and see if anything is redeeming about it."

"Yeah. That's probably a good idea," I hear him mutter.

For the next few minutes, we're in complete silence until I hear the word "fuck" for the eighth line in a row. "Come on, people! You got paid a lot of money to use your vocabulary. And what the hell? How do people get transported in this world? This isn't a *Star Trek* movie, for Christ's sake." At that point, I take another handful from the giant-size tub of popcorn and throw it at the screen.

Joe just chuckles beside me.

"Well, I'm sorry we ended up at such a crappy movie," I declare as we make our way to his Explorer.

"I'm not."

Surprised, I stop in my tracks. "What?"

Hooking an arm over my shoulder, he guides me out of the line of traffic. "That was the most fun I've had..." He freezes.

This time it's me who turns toward him. Laying a hand on his chest, I tilt my head to the side. "Joe?"

He shakes his head.

Intuitively, I know this is something enormous. Hesitantly, I offer, "I'm here for you if you want to talk." I go to move away, but he holds me close.

His voice takes on a faraway cast when he admits, "I promised to love one person forever."

My heart breaks for him. "I know."

"So, what does it say about me when I was just about to tell you I had more fun in that stupid movie than I ever had. Ever," he adds with emphasis. "What does that say about the kind of man I am, Holly?" Pain radiates from every pore of his body into mine.

Since we've become friends, Joe's opened up to me about his lingering emotions for Mary, so I understand how much pain this is causing him. I close my eyes, praying for the right words. "Maybe what it means is that your 'ever' is divided into the life you had with Mary and the life you've had since." He goes to open his mouth, but I gently lay my finger across it. "Sometimes, I get lonely thinking of a person I've never met. I can't even imagine having met them and lost them." Stepping back, I squeeze his arm. "Don't hide your grief, Joe. Not with me."

His eyes drag over my face while my words—I hope—penetrate. He lets out a ragged breath. "I must seem so stupid."

"Did you suddenly turn into a superhuman somewhere along the way? Why don't you get to feel your aches and pains the way the rest of the world does?"

"I don't know. Maybe because I feel like I have to be strong for everyone, especially Grace?"

I shake my head. "You have a right to be a man, Joe, before everything else. And trust me, the pain isn't going to go away. It just dulls to remind you that you can survive anything, even the most horrific nightmares life can throw at you."

Stepping closer he says, "I thought you said you'd never fallen in love."

I nod. "I haven't. That doesn't mean I haven't felt agony." Turning away, I walk the few steps until I reach the passenger side of his SUV. "Come on. If we don't head out now, we'll be late."

I hear the locks beep, and I open the door. Joe climbs in on the other side. Settling myself in the vehicle, I pay careful attention to fastening my seat belt when Joe lays his hand on mine. I lift my head to find his inches from my own.

"This friendship isn't one-sided, Holly. I'm here if you need me." Squeezing my hand, he lets it go before starting the ignition.

Joe, if I told you about my past, there'd be no friendship left, I think sadly. But all I do is settle back in the seat as we listen to Ed Sheeran on our way back to Collyer.

29

HOLLY

"I had a great time at the movie the other night," Joe tells me.

"Me too. We'll have to figure out a time to do it again." I'm sitting on top of my bed rubbing lotion on my arms.

"Absolutely. You can choose next time though. I still can't get over how awful that movie that was."

I laugh at the disgust in Joe's voice. "God, it was the worst thing I've seen next to Phil trying to decorate cupcakes we were shipping out for Brendan Blake's nephew." There's such a long silence, I check to make sure we're still connected by hitting the screen with my elbow. Seeing we're still connected, I wait.

"I kind of don't know where to go with that."

"With what?"

"The fact that you were decorating cupcakes for Brendan Blake's nephew. I mean, he's a huge star." Ah.

"He's also just a guy who has a nephew he adores who was really ill." It was weird for me to consider Brendan a family friend as well at first, but he's a great guy who loves being able to cut loose with those he trusts in his downtime.

"Was?"

"Knock on wood, he's been in remission for a few years." Even I can hear the relief in my own voice.

"Shit. Cancer?"

"Yes."

"How do you all know him?" Through the phone, I hear the clink of the ice cubes of the drink Joe told me he was having earlier.

"Well, Corinna was on Food Network with Brendan a few years ago..."

Joe's incredulous voice comes through the line. "Seriously?"

I laugh. "Yes. And through Brendan, we met his fiancée, Dani—who also happens to be Em's fiancé's cousin."

"Say that to me again when I might have a chance at understanding it. Let's go back to something I might understand. Is it just Phil who sucks at baking?"

"No, we all pretty much do. Most of us can at least cook."

"I'd have thought all of you would be exceptional at it since Corinna would have passed along her tricks."

"It's precisely for that reason we all are awful at it. Why bother when you can just ask for the best? Ali and I were spoiled the worst; we lived with her for years during college. Although—" I lean back against my pillows. "—the only thing Cori can't make as well as any of us is banana pudding."

"Really?"

"Yep."

"You're kidding."

"Every single time. She absolutely hates it because I won't hand over my recipe."

"Huh. Maybe you'll make it for me sometime."

"If you're lucky," I smirk. "So far that recipe has only been eaten by members of this family."

"Damn. Can't I have leftovers? Lick the bowl? Something? I'm willing to do just about anything. I love banana pudding."

Nabbing my phone from the blanket next to me, I'm about to thumb off the call. "Good night, Joe."

"Night, Hols. Now I'll be dreaming of things that are creamy and taste good."

I burst out laughing as I disconnect the call.

30

HOLLY

One of his strong hands slides over my shoulder to capture the tip of my breast even as the other moves over my hip, spreading my legs to penetrate my core with his long fingers. My head tips back against his shoulder as he begins thrusting. I let out an agonized moan.

"I told you, I love all things that taste good..."

Waking with a start, my heart beating out of my chest, I gasp aloud. What the hell was that? Judging from the state of my sheets, obviously last night's sleep wasn't any better than those of the previous few nights. Crossing my legs in my bed, I lean my elbows down and yank my hair away from my face.

I can't see his face in my dream, but I know who I'm dreaming about.

A man who's friend-zoned me so hard, I have no idea when he went from being just that to something more in my mind.

Groaning, I flop back in my bed wondering if I'll be able to get back to sleep when the alarm goes off. Even as I roll over to slap it off, I scream into my pillow.

It's going to be one of those days.

IT's the end of April and wedding season is in full explosion. I'm so desperately grateful I hired Megan on as an assistant and that she's been coming down on weekends, otherwise due to the heavy booking it would be at least four months from the time I took photos to the time they were received.

I'm in the process of heading toward the office from a late-afternoon shoot when my cell rings. Using the hands-free, I answer it. "This is Holly."

"Tell me you haven't had dinner yet." It's Joe. As much as I want to say yes after waking up frustrated by my dreams this morning, you don't lie to your friends.

"Not yet. I'm heading toward the office to drop off some stuff for Megan, and then I was just going to grab something at home."

"Swing by here. My mother made her homemade lasagna for Grace and me." My mouth begins to salivate.

"That does sound a lot better than some hummus and veggies," I agree.

"Seriously? That's what you were going to have?" His disgust is evident.

"I honestly think that's all that's in my fridge that doesn't require cooking."

"Get over here, Hols. We'll fix you up. If you're nice, I'll let you take some home without begging," he teases.

What if I want to beg? flashes through my mind. Instead of giving voice to my thoughts, I simply say, "See you when I can," before disconnecting.

About ten minutes later, I turn off Main Street and pull into my space at Amaryllis Events. Walking into the mansion's beautifully restored front door, I hear my siblings' voices coming from Emily's private design studio. Heading in that direction, I stop in my tracks when I hear Phil's voice.

"Isn't it so cute to see how they're 'just friends'? I want to swoop her up and smack her on the lips at the way she's bringing his heart back to life."

"Forget him. Have you ever seen Holly this animated about any man?" Em's voice is laced with excitement. "I mean she's barely talked about him—which isn't that unusual—but if any of us bring his name up, there's this thing that comes over her face."

Damn me and my red hair, I curse silently. If I wasn't blushing so furiously right now, I'd stomp right in there and give them a piece of my mind.

"Perhaps they are just friends," Corinna's honeyed drawl comes out amid the chattering of voices. "Holly would never withhold something from us."

Thank you, Cori. I relax a little. Easing my way closer to the door, I wait to see what else the rest of my siblings have to think about that.

"I agree with Cori," Ali declares. I relax too soon though because she continues. "And, sadly, I agree with Phil. I just don't think either of them is in a place where they're ready to recognize they're more. And when that time comes, we'll need to be there to support our sister."

"Why do you say that, Ali?" Cassidy's sweet voice asks, concerned.

"Because if we're right, then she's doing everything in her power not to fall. That's how much she's already there. She's become the sole person Joe can talk to about his deepest secrets and all of his pain. And if for some stupid reason he doesn't feel the same way, it's going to wreck her," Ali concludes sadly.

Hearing that, I back away slowly, feeling absolutely nauseous.

Because Ali's right.

I've become such an integral part of Joe's life that when he's fully healed, what happens when he calls to tell me he's going out on a date? When he's fallen in love?

My dream from this morning flashing in my brain, I race up the stairs and make it to my office before I start dry heaving into my trash can.

Footsteps follow me. In between retching, I call out, "Go away!" I try to kick the door closed, but Phil gets to it first.

"Baby, what's wrong? We didn't even hear you come in." His concern is evident as he swiftly makes his way over to me and holds my hair back from my face. With the other, he reaches over to my desk for some tissues.

"I bet you didn't," I hiss, as my stomach begins to settle.

My brother stills, making me wish he could stay this immobile when I'm trying to take his picture. "How much did you overhear?" he asks with no subterfuge.

"There was more after you claiming that Joe and I were so cute in our obtuseness?" Phil's eyes close as I rip the tissues from his hand. "Now, I'd like to be alone."

"Hols," he whispers, pain in his voice. I understand none of them meant to hurt me, but until this very moment, I didn't realize how much my feelings were starting to shift.

"Please, Phillip. For once, just shut your mouth and leave," I beseech him. "Think about how you would have felt if you'd have come upon all of us talking about you like that and understand I just don't want to be around any of you right now."

"Okay," he whispers. He reaches the door and stops. Taking a deep breath, he says, "We're just worried..."

I nod. I get it. Boy, do I get it. But now's not the time for me to dive into the number of ways this could end badly for me.

"I'll just tell the others you're heading home." Phil disappears from view.

Home. That's all I want, I think wearily. I want to curl up with a pair of pajamas and some tea and just...

My phone chimes with an incoming text. Pulling it out of my pocket, I see it's a selfie of Joe and Grace. Behind them, the table is set for three with heaping plates of lasagna at the ready.

This time when I start to vomit, I can feel my tears intermixed with the bile coming up from my stomach.

As I weep quietly in my office, I wonder how the hell I'm going to survive to pay this part of my penance for the past nightmare of my life.

31

JOSEPH

"You made it home okay?" I ask immediately after Holly picks up.

"Yes," she sighs. "Your parents' house is about three miles away from mine. I promised you I'd call as soon as I got in."

"It's been twenty minutes, Hols. I started to get worried."

There's a very long pause. Shit, what if there's someone there? I strain to listen carefully, but I don't hear anything. As much as I can't get Holly out of my head, I don't know how to change what's between us. We had rules in place when we first started out. I don't know if they were because of what happened to me or because...

"I had to pee."

I burst out laughing. That was not what I expected her to say.

"Jesus, Joe. You have a daughter. It's not like..."

"I was just picturing all of these worst-case scenarios," I lie glibly.

"Yeah, well, add that one to your repertoire," she grumbles at me. "Your mother kept giving me enormous glasses of lemonade and talking my ear off about how beautiful the photos were. It was sweet —both the drink and the compliments—but I never had a chance to use the restroom."

"She loved her gift," I tell her for the ninetieth time that night. It's

Mother's Day, and Holly dropped by my parents' house with my mother's gift a few hours ago.

Last week, Holly was a freaking badger asking me if there was a place for a large frame in my parents' home. When I told her I thought there was, she said to find out quick and hung up on me. After calling my pop and being assured there was a spot in their formal dining room for a picture any size Holly wanted to put there, I was stunned speechless today when Holly showed up with a beautifully mounted picture of Grace and me in an elegant silver frame, which was a gift from my father. Also, there was a large box of smaller silver-framed photos all from that day in the botanical garden as well as an album.

When Holly presented the beautifully wrapped presents to my mother, she told her, "Denise, these are from Joe and Grace." She then stood back and watched while my mother's eyes overflowed with tears.

After receiving the longest hug from my mother I think I've received since Mary's funeral, my mother wasn't far from Holly's side. Either she was asking her questions about the specific pictures, about taking pictures professionally, or about working in the wedding business in general. Holly was terrific with her. When Grace wandered over, Holly just scooped her up and began braiding her curls into two perfect french braids, undoing the pigtails I had her hair in. "Daaaaadyyyyy! I got bwaids!"

Holly effortlessly charmed Justin, whose parents were on a trip to Vermont for the weekend, so much that I began to get confused and surly every time she would laugh at his jokes. But what claim do I have? Mary's photo peers down at me from its place on the mantle. I gave my heart to someone who I can no longer have. And Holly's a beautiful woman who's my friend.

And who's made me more at peace with my life than I have been in longer...

"Have you been listening, or am I talking to myself?" she demands, laughing.

"Sorry. I thought I heard Grace," I lie.

"Oh, do you need to go?" Her voice is warm and concerned.

"No, it was nothing."

"Anyway, I was asking if you wanted to grab lunch this week. I'm not sure what your shift is."

"I'm on starting Wednesday for three days straight. What about you?"

"I have events on Friday night, Saturday, Saturday night, and Sunday night."

"Ugh. Big week," I commiserate.

"It's the start of wedding season. They'll all be big weeks. Ali told me I have a couple of graduation photo sessions being thrown in here and there too."

"Lunch for certain Wednesday and Thursday?" I ask hopefully.

"Sounds perfect," she says softly.

There's a lull in the conversation that I don't feel the need to fill. Through the open line, I hear the soft whisper sound of material shifting. My heart begins to pound. "What are you doing?" Instead of strong and steady, it comes out choked even to my own ears.

There's a pause in the sound. "Umm, throwing my sheets in the laundry? Why?"

Because I thought you might be changing and the image was going to drive me mad? "It just got super quiet. I thought I might have leaned on the button to disconnect you."

"Generally that's followed by an obnoxious beeping sound, Joe. At which point, I would hang up and hope you would call or text me back." Her voice is dry.

I burst out laughing. I can't help it. In the few months I've known her, I've laughed more, smiled more, felt more than I have in years. And I don't want to go back to the way I was before. The thought flies into my head so quickly, it almost causes my head to snap back. Is it possible I'm ready to move on? I push off the couch and stand in front of the picture of Mary holding our baby.

"Joe? Are you there? Damn. Maybe I did lose him," Holly mutters in my ear.

I'm beginning to wonder if that's possible. "Hmm?"

"Oh, there you are. I was just asking if you wanted to go to The Coffee Shop Wednesday for lunch?"

"Sounds great." *And maybe between now and then I can figure out how to bring up if you want more from this than just being friends.*

"Then stay safe," she whispers. "And thanks for calling to make sure I was."

"Of course. You too." I disconnect the call.

32

JOSEPH

"Waiting for someone?" I've been nursing a cup of coffee, waiting for Holly to find Eden, and Seth is glaring at me. Sliding off one of the stools that surround the counter at The Coffee Shop, I get to my feet. I haven't heard from them in months, not since I told them to get their act together around my baby girl. Something—judging by the expressions of mixed fury and tragic sorrow on their faces—they still haven't managed to do.

My heart hurts for them, but I lost Mary too. I've been over and over and over it. And I did exactly one thing wrong.

Love her.

And that gave me Grace.

"Eden. Seth," I say politely. I don't know what direction this conversation is going to take, but if it's an opportunity to bring them back into Grace's life, I'll take it. During one of our phone calls, Holly offered to make up photos like the ones she gave to my mother for Mary's parents. When I explained they weren't in Grace's life at the moment, her only comment was "That's tragically sad."

I couldn't agree more.

Our collective loss of Mary is just that: tragic. Her life ended too soon with too many people who loved her that are still mourning her loss. Although I will always love her, the pain of every day is edging away. Time will never take away our love; it's just dulling the edges of the legacy of its ending. I'm finding it easier to remember and share with Grace the laughter and joy. All because someone taught me how to do those things again.

Because she was brave enough to be my friend.

But as for Eden and Seth, I can't fathom what they've been through. The very idea of losing a child—especially now that I have one—is incomprehensible. I want Grace to know them, but not at the cost of polluting her joyous innocence with pain she can't shoulder.

"Where is she?" Eden venomously throws out. Seth steps behind his wife, crossing his arms.

I'm so taken aback, I physically move. In the process, I knock over my mug of coffee. "Who?"

"Your new girlfriend. It's the talk all over town that you're dating some woman. We hear she's even been to the house you bought for our daughter. What are you going to do next? Move her in?" Eden cries piteously. Seth doesn't say anything. Instead, he just continues to glare at me.

Before I can open my mouth, a voice comes from behind me. "This ends right here. Right now." Matt, the owner of The Coffee Shop, ambles forward. "First, I won't stand for my patrons to be harassed."

Seth opens his mouth, not to stop his wife's antics but to enable them. "Then come outside..."

"Stop. Just stop. Do you hear yourselves?" Matt goes on before I have a chance to escort Mary's parents out of the front door. "Mr. and Mrs. Moss, is this honoring your daughter's memory any?"

"It's honoring it better than the way the father of her child is," Eden snaps. "She's barely gone, and he's dating some..."

"Don't," I bite out. "You don't know anything about what is going on. Once again, you're being judgmental based on your own overinflated, self-righteous..."

"I know if it wasn't for you our daughter would still be alive!" Seth thunders.

A quiet settles over the restaurant. Matt moves from around the counter to stand next to me. "Tell me how that is, Seth. Did I force her to go shopping that day? No. I asked her not to. Did I ask her to buy new clothes? No. Tell me what it was I did?" I scream the last in the face of the man who would have been my father-in-law.

"You got her pregnant! She would have never stayed with you! You..."

I hold up my hand to stop his tirade. "And that?" I say thinly. "That right there is why you will never see your granddaughter until you can get past these emotions. Because the only living piece of your daughter will not be tainted by your pain."

"Just wait till you see what we do to your girlfriend," Eden hisses. "I hear she has a business in town. By the time she's done, she'll barely be able to get any work."

They wouldn't do that to people they don't know. But the smug smirks on their faces tells me they not only would but that they likely have already started. I open my mouth to respond, but Matt beats me to it.

"Mr. and Mrs. Moss, I reserve the right to refuse service. At this time, I'd like for you to leave the premises."

"Excuse me?" Seth says haughtily.

"I don't think I need to make myself clearer. If I do, I'll be contacting the CPD." Matt crosses one arm over the other.

"We'll see how long you stay in business as well," Eden declares.

Matt just laughs. "The door is directly behind you."

Without another word, Seth takes hold of Eden's arm and escorts her out. The only sound is the ringing of the bells. My mind can't wrap itself around what just happened.

"Joe." My head whips toward Matt. "Don't let them get to you. Nothing will come of what they said. The Freemans are too well respected in this town. Talk to Holly." Matt ambles off behind the counter.

Talk to Holly? If I do, I could ruin her, I think wildly.

Just like I did Mary.

Pulling out my cell, I do the only thing I can. Scrolling down, I find her number and press Send. "Hey."

"Hey! I was just about to call you. I'm running fifteen minutes late. Can you order?"

"I, uh, can't make it."

"Oh. Did something come up?" The disappointment in her voice is causing my throat to close up.

But it's for the best. Her best.

"Yeah. Can I talk with you later?" I choke out.

"Of course." She pauses. "Joe?"

"Yeah, Hols?" Just saying her name is like a scalding wound on my heart. I'm deliberately lying to her as I stand in the middle of The Coffee Shop. This isn't the man I am. This isn't the friend I want to be.

But it's who I need to become because I need to protect her the best way I know how.

"Stay safe." Then she disconnects the phone. I drop my head under the weight of the pain. And the shame.

"You're not doing her any favors by not talking with her," Matt tells me from behind the counter.

"I'm protecting her this way," I mutter more to myself than Matt.

"That woman can protect herself."

"Can she? She has no idea how awful they can be."

"And you have no clue what she can handle, son. You're too new for that kind of understanding. All I can recommend is to talk to her. Don't throw the best thing in your life away." Matt heads back into the kitchen.

I make my way to the front of The Coffee Shop and walk out the door, letting it crash shut behind me. I was crazy to think I could broach being something more with Holly today.

Eden and Seth were a reminder of that.

33

JOSEPH

Frowning at the phone in my hand, I read Holly's message. *I'm sorry. I can't make dinner. Give Grace a hug for me.*

Something's off. I just can't put my finger on it. I type back, *Everything okay?* I wait a few minutes while I'm relaxing in the lounge of the station when her response causes my phone to vibrate.

Turning it to face me, I read, *Fine. I told you; busy time of the year. Just need to decompress. Besides, we'll see y'all at the party tomorrow?*

My fingers fly back. *Right. Anything we can bring?* The Freemans invited my family to an all-out bash at the farm for all of their clients to kick off the summer season. My mother—who hasn't had her hair done in anything but a trim in longer than I can remember—made a special appointment today for "something special." Even though I've been assured by Holly—and again by Ali—that the dress is spring casual, my mother just glared at me when I suggested wearing jeans.

"Joseph, you will dig out a pair of khakis and a polo or so help me, God, I will go buy them for you," she threatened.

When I came home from work the other day and realized she made good on her threat, I chuckled and gave her a kiss before thanking her profusely since I couldn't find anything to wear. And the only other person who I would have wanted to go shopping with is apparently swamped with work.

Wedding season is seriously no joke for the Freemans, I surmise. Taking a quick drink of soda, I think back to the missed lunches and dinners Holly's had to bail on this past week. Then again, when you have a reputation as strong as theirs, and you get the results they do —Matt wasn't kidding that day—you have to put it above a lot of things.

Including someone who misses you.

I'm surprised when my phone vibrates in my hand. But when I read the words, I choke.

There's going to be plenty of food and drink if you want to bring the woman I saw you with Tuesday.

My eyes widen. Who the hell is she talking about? Another woman? What woman? Is she insane? I'm trying to figure out a response when another text comes in.

Hey, Joe. It was great running into you the other day. Thanks for cheering me up. That's sweet. It's Brett's baby sister, Melissa.

Shit. Melissa. Holly had to have seen me with Brett's sister and completely misunderstood. Melissa's been in love with Justin for as long as she's known him, but despite her attempts to get him to notice her, nothing. She came into The Coffee Shop utterly dejected after going to visit him and her brother at the station. I called her over to my booth while I was waiting for Holly.

She's a wonderful woman with a heart of gold, but Justin just can't get it in his head that it's okay to date one of his best friend's sisters. What did I do? I think frantically. I remember throwing my arm around Mel, snuggling her like I always do and... Groaning, I remember the bell rang above the door. Shit. Before I can even think of how to reply, another text comes in. My heart pounding, I read, *It's fine. You're dating. That's great.*

Great? Her encouragement to be with someone else makes me want to hurl my phone against a wall. My head drops back on the couch in defeat. Is this why she's been distant? Is she clearing a path for me to move on with my life with a phantom someone I neither want nor asked for?

"Joe? What's wrong?" Justin's voice comes from behind me. He's been one of my closest friends for years. I wish he'd wake up and see what's in front of him before it's too late. I scrub my hand down my face. Pot, kettle much? What am I supposed to say? That he's as much of a fool as I am for not seeing what's been in front of him for a while now? That instead of dreaming about my dead fiancée, I'm beginning to dream about a woman with sunlight in her eyes? That every moment I spend with Holly is precious because of who she is, the woman who makes me smile even when I least want to?

"Nothing." Pushing up from the sofa, I shove my phone in my pocket, knowing I have to fix this, somehow, someway. I have to make her understand that there's no one else.

Not even Mary.

34

HOLLY

T o anyone but my family, the smile on my face probably looks like I'm having the time of my life when in reality, I'd prefer to be anywhere but under the twinkling lights of the farm's back patio. Em made sure I at least looked halfway decent. Ali's covered my hands twice so I'll stop worrying them together. Phil's reminded me to stop biting my lip more times than I can count. Cassidy's stood by my side to make random conversation with our clients. And Corinna—bless her heart—she handed me a martini.

Ali was right, I think to myself. I'm a wreck, and it's my own stupid fault for having developed feelings for a man who made it abundantly clear from the beginning he was emotionally unavailable. Taking a sip of the drink in my hand, I think, well, unavailable to me, that is.

I feel a familiar arm slip around me. I lean into the weight of it. "You're supposed to be mingling," I gently admonish my brother.

"I will. I just wanted to let you know there's been more than one set of eyes on you in this dress tonight." He pulls away and looks down at me. "Under these lights, you look like a nymph, my beautiful sister."

I shake my head, setting the loose curls that are in a top knot on my head dancing. "Did Jason slip something in your drink or something?"

He shakes his head. "Come on, Hols. Dance with your ol' brother."

I laugh, truly laugh, for the first time tonight. "Finally admitting you're old?" I tease him just as he swings me into his arms.

"I said 'ol',' Hols. I refuse to admit I'm old," he says haughtily. Clasping my hand against his chest, we begin to sway back and forth. Laying my cheek against his chest, I remember out loud the first time we taught each other how to dance. "It was a YouTube video, remember?" I murmur.

"How could I not?" His lips touch the crown of my head. "I had my feet stepped on more times that night..."

I giggle. "And Cassidy almost lost a toe when you trampled on hers." I let out a soft sigh.

"I hate knowing you've lost your glow, baby."

In the safe confines of Phil's arms, I can admit the truth because it's so tiring to keep it inside. "It only hurts because I was foolish enough to hope. If I'd just stayed on the path I was meant to be on, I'd be fine."

"And you'd never know..." I'll never know what Phil was about to say as we're interrupted on the dance floor. "Hello, Joe."

"Phil." My brother and I pull apart slightly. "I hope you don't mind if I cut in." His question is directed at Phil, but his eyes are searching mine.

I want to look away, but I force myself to nod. "Of course." I smile vapidly at my brother, who's glowering at Joe's back. "We'll talk later."

Angry blue eyes meet mine over the man who's causing so much conflict in my soul. "That we will, baby," he says before he slides to the edge off the dance floor near Cassidy.

All I can pray for is the band we hired for tonight picks up the pace a little. But just as Joe clasps my trembling hand, the strumming of a guitar starts. I recognize the song within the first few notes and decide God is out to kill my soul. Unable to escape, I'm pressed into

Joe's space. His hand burns my skin through the sheer material of my dress. "You look beautiful," he tells me quietly.

"You look nice yourself. You all do. Did your mother do something different with her hair?" I'm babbling.

He doesn't answer me. Pulling me infinitesimally closer as Chris Stapelton's words wash over both of us, he states, "I miss you."

Even as I avoid looking at him, I'm finding it hard to avoid the scent of his powerful body so close to mine. "Same," I reply lightly. *Just keep the conversation going until the end of the song. Then you can escape*, I tell myself.

A light breeze picks up the end of my dress. Dropping my arm from Joe's shoulder, I reach down to hold it in place. When I stand back up, I see sorrow and regret in his eyes. I thought I could do this, but I can't. If I don't break away now, I'm going to be stuck in this cycle of wanting more from this man and unable to move on, even if that's only casual dating for the rest of my life.

I begin to make excuses. "I'm sorry, Joe. Cass's waving at me. I have to go. Duty calls."

He curses, "Damnit, Holly. We need to talk."

My mask in place, I say, "We will. Text me during the week. You, me, and Grace, we'll grab lunch. Promise." Before he can say another word, I wind my way through the dancers to the other side of the dance floor where Phil's got his arm around Cassidy. Approaching them, I whisper, "I don't need a lecture. I need my family."

Cassidy just opens her arms. Phil wraps both of his around me before he guides us both up to the farmhouse.

35

JOSEPH

Every night since the Freemans' party, I've seen nothing in my dreams except Holly. It's a good thing I've got those because that's the only time I've actually seen her.

She looked exquisite lit by the twinkling lights at the party. Her hair—what wasn't caught in a knot on her head—was left in long curls. Her dress was a sheer teal that enhanced her creamy skin. Around her neck was a simple coin necklace that should have been dull in comparison to the light in her eyes but actually outshone it.

Punching the pillow under my head, I roll to the side. I understand why Holly might have misinterpreted what she saw; unless it's related to work, she doesn't know many people in town. But Mel's been as much a part of my life as Brett has since I was a kid, the little sister I never had. I didn't think twice about sharing I'd run into her with Holly, although, in the back of my mind I'd been planning on introducing them since. Now?

Falling back with a loud sigh, I scrub my hands through my hair. The problem is, I don't know if it was—dare I let myself hope—jealousy driving Holly to act this way. Or is she truly that self-serving and giving me space to date?

Closing my eyes in frustration, all I can think about is her light floral scent filling my nose as I held her as close as I dared.

"Shit," I curse roundly.

"Bianco, if you don't plan on sleeping, get the hell out of the bunk room," Justin gripes. "Some of us would like actually to get some sleep in this decade."

Swinging my legs over to the side of my bed, I sit up. "Sorry, buddy," I mutter. Nabbing my phone, I stalk from the bedroom into the connecting lounge.

Pulling up my texts, I check to see if Holly's sent anything. Nothing. Taking a shot, I open up our text string. *I miss you. We need to talk.* Before I can talk myself out of it, I hit Send.

Suddenly, the alarm is going off. "All teams, report to your stations. We have a report of a fire at 14 Old Stonebridge Road. I repeat, all teams, report to your stations."

Men and women come pouring out of the bunk room. Putting my thoughts of Holly aside, I race over to the pole and hook a leg onto it to swing out. Sliding down, I don't hesitate to sprint over to the room where our turnout suits and boots are kept. I step into a pair of pants and boots, and quickly grab the coat. Justin's hot on my heels.

"We're in the bus, bud!" he calls out. Turning, I race for the ambulance and throw the driver's-side door open. Soon, we're following two engines with sirens blaring through the quiet streets of Collyer.

I was given the best advice about preparing for the moments between the call and the arrival. My pop told me, "Leave your fears behind the minute the garage closes behind you, son. Otherwise, that drive is going to be the longest of your life because it might be your last." Long before I became a single dad, I've ridden out of the station with that mentality. Now, knowing I have Grace to go home to, I'm more hard-pressed to ensure I make it out alive.

For just a second, Holly's face flashes into my mind, but I brutally shove it out. I can't allow myself to get distracted by going there. Focus on the victims, the team, and the beast. Get the first two out alive and kill the third.

"You need to get your head out of your ass about Holly," Justin says abruptly.

"What?" I take my eyes briefly off the road to glance at him. His eyes are staring out the front windshield. "We're not doing this now."

"When else? In the middle of the lounge? When you have Grace? This is the only chance I have to tell you I think you need to admit to yourself how you really feel about her and date her before someone else gets in there, you ass!" he exclaims. "What if you run out of time?"

My chest hurts. I know what it feels like to run out of time. And only one person was able to make that pain disappear.

And I'm letting her slip through my fingers.

"We'll talk after we clean up this mess," I promise just as we pull up to the mess on Old Stonebridge. I slam the bus in park, and we both leap out.

Justin meets me around the front of the ambulance. "It's not me you have to discuss it with, buddy. It's Holly. And I'd make the words count. I'm sick of seeing your miserable mug around the station. Besides," he taunts me, "you burn the crap out of dinner when you're in a pissy mood."

Dick, I think with some amusement. I put our conversation to the back of my mind as we stare at the beast consuming the back half of the house for just a moment. Soon, we hear what we've been waiting to hear. "We've got wounded!"

Justin yells back, "Do we need the board?"

"No, just the kit!"

I race around the back and grab the enormous portable medical kit so we can begin treating the victims.

36

JOSEPH

"My dog's still in there!" the woman screams at Justin and me.

Hell. There's no way we'll leave any living being behind if we can possibly get to it. "Where?" Even as I cough in the fresh air, Justin's clasping the front of his jacket up again. I mentally gird myself to enter the inferno.

"The laundry room." Her lips tremble even as tears streak down her face.

"Where is that in relation to the rest of the house?" I demand harshly.

"Upstairs. Near the master bedroom."

"What's the dog's name, ma'am?" Justin asks.

"Champ. Like Longchamp bags? I love them so much," the woman blathers on, but we've already tuned her out. We have seconds—maybe a minute—before the entire house is engulfed in flames. If it weren't for the fact this mansion has multiple access points to the second floor, we'd never be able to make it. Even now, I'm wondering if we should even try.

Almost as one, we slam through the front door this time. The inferno is defying the water being hurled at it from the team outside along the back of the house; making our mission even more dangerous than it was when we were standing with the crazed homeowner.

Our booted feet hit the stairs at the same time.

One.

Two.

Just as I'm about to take the third step, a sharp crack fills the air. I hear Justin scream just before a hand is shoved in the center of my back, plunging me face forward. It takes precious seconds to recover from my fall. Scrambling to my feet, I scream, "*No!*" Justin is buried under mounds of plasterwork that has melted from the ceiling under the scorching heat.

I scramble back down toward him and immediately begin shoving off the heavy plaster. He's not moving, but I can still see his chest moving. "Come on, Brady!" I yell over the roaring of the fiery bitch trying to engulf the house with a demonstration of her power. "Stay with me!" I demand.

A weak woof behind me supports my statement. I close my eyes in disbelief. The dog.

Its head nudges me even as I'm shoving enough plaster aside to lift my coworker, my friend, to safety. Carefully, I scoop up Justin and haul him over my shoulder. I whistle between my teeth, and Champ races ahead toward the open door.

I clear the open doorway, and I hear Brett call out for all CFD to fall back.

Too late for Justin, who I'm racing over to the nearest ambulance. It just happens to be the one we drove in together.

HOURS LATER, it's well past midnight. I don't know why I'm here except I can't go home. I can't deal with my phone ringing off the hook with the empathy, the weak-ass explanations, or the excuses.

Justin was declared legally dead at Greenwich Hospital two hours ago due to a hemorrhaging brain injury from the plaster falling on his head. His parents were brought in to decide what to do next.

I bolted. It was too reminiscent of before where people kept asking me to make decisions on Mary's behalf as her medical power of attorney. I still remember being in a fucking haze of devastation while everyone wanted to plead their case for the necessity of organ donation while Eden and Seth stared at me with horror and accusation in their eyes.

And all I wanted to do was hold my baby girl and sink into death right next to her.

Now, I reek of the stench of fire and death, and I'm about to turn to a woman I desperately care for to help me get through a night where I can't be reminded of any more memories.

Dropping my head to the steering wheel, I debate whether or not I should put the car in gear and turn around when I hear a light tap at the window. I don't even realize I've been silently crying until turning my head to find Holly standing there tips the salt against my lips.

Turning the ignition off, I open the door of the Explorer and just sit there, saying nothing. We haven't said a word to each other in days, and right now I don't know how to start. For long moments I take in her clean, unmade-up face. Something tightly wound inside of me relaxes just seeing her. This is what I needed.

A friend.

She bites her lower lip. My eyes are automatically drawn to it. I reach out a finger to tug it out. "You should stop doing that. It's going to bruise," I say solemnly.

Her hand reaches up to touch my cheek. "I heard what happened on the news. What do you need?"

And this right here sums up how I've come to care about Holly so quickly. Forget about the fact we've been on the outs with each other. She doesn't give me any demands, no arguments or pressure, just openness and giving. Closing my eyes on a wave of pain, I whisper, "I need to forget for a little while."

Her hand squeezes my face gently before it travels down my arm.

When she reaches my wrist, she gives it a tug. "Come on. Let's get you cleaned up. Then I'll help you forget."

Guiding me into her home for the first time, I just hope I don't bring misery to her sanctuary.

IF YOU'D HAVE ASKED me if I would have ever thought I was a bath man, I would have called you a liar. And I would have immediately been wrong.

Soaking in Holly's bathtub with a martini on the floor next to me, I'm in the almost dark. Holly left the light in her water closet on after she filled the tub. She also left me some of Phil's clothes that "He leaves here in the event he decides to crash when Jason has to work overnights," she explained. So not only would I be able to luxuriate in water that's easing the aches from my body and mind, I'm able to do so without smelling like a choice of a floral bath bomb or children's shampoo since Phil keeps a supply of his own toiletries in each of his sisters' homes.

Reaching for the martini, I take a long drink. Absentmindedly, I notice my fingers pruning. I guess it's time to haul my ass out of this tub and give Holly her bedroom back. Placing the drink on the floor, I push myself to my feet. Water sluices down my body. Blindly, I search for the switch to pull for the drain when I start to slip. "Shit," I curse as I catch myself.

"Joe?" Holly's voice comes from outside the door. "Is everything all right?"

Heat floods my cheeks. "Yeah, I was just trying to find the stopper."

"Just step on the drain. It's built in."

Grateful she's not able to call me out on my almost header, I do as she says. The water quickly begins to spin as it circles down the drain. "Pretty damn cool," I mutter as I reach for a towel. I'm more than a little surprised to find it warm. Alcohol making my filter disappear, I yell out, "A heated towel rack? That's sweet."

There's a pause before she calls back, "I'm from the South, Joe. Winters up here aren't my favorite time of the year. I had it added when I built my house."

"I might need to look into one of those." I wait for her comment back as I dry myself off, but there's nothing but silence. Carefully laying the towel on the floor so I don't slip again, I dry my feet. Picking up my drink, I pad naked over to the stack of clothing on the bathroom vanity. I'm pleasantly surprised to find drawstring pajama pants and a thermal pullover shirt. Holly even left me a comb, which I quickly use through my hair. I finish off my drink before I set her bathroom to rights.

Bundling up all of my dirty clothes and the wet towel, I open up the bathroom door. I spy two chairs over by the giant window overlooking a grove of trees. Holly is ensconced in one with her knees pulled up to her chest, her arms wrapped around her legs. Her hair is cascading down her back and side like liquid flame. It reminds me of the fire we fought and sacrificed another brother to tonight. And just like that, the pain of Justin comes flooding back. I lean against the jamb, pressing the fist of my free hand into my chest. Hard.

Having heard the door open, Holly witnesses all of this. Sliding her knees to the side, she pushes herself to her feet and makes her way to me. Her nose twitches slightly as she gets closer, but other than that her expression doesn't change. "Give me all of that," she demands quietly.

Passing off a bundle of wet and smelly clothes shouldn't feel like a burden shared, but it does. I hope my expression conveys my gratitude because when I try to open my mouth, my throat closes up.

Her lips curl in a sad smile. "Hold on to your glass while I toss all this into the wash, then we'll head downstairs. Tonight sounds like a perfect night to raid the liquor and the food."

"Why liquor and food?" I ask, not disagreeing. It sounds fucking perfect.

"Whenever one of our hearts were broken, it's what we'd do for each other. If it works for us, I figure it might work for you."

Closing my eyes, I send up a small prayer for stupid event planners, for teachers who think they're God's gift to men, and to whatever brought the Freemans to Connecticut. Opening them, I murmur, "That sounds perfect, Hols."

The inner glow that lights her eyes sparks one inside me I thought might be dead. I thought I smothered it when I was stupid enough not to give her my honesty. How horrific for me to realize it still blazed on the night Justin was killed in the line of duty?

37

HOLLY

"So, there we were trying to sneak back in—" Joe's wiping tears of laughter from his eyes and takes a sip from another martini; we've drunk so many I've lost count. "—and my father's voice booms down at us, 'I don't want to know! Just get to bed before I have to call Hulk to get your asses in line.'"

I'm wiping my own eyes on my shirtsleeve. Jesus. I can totally picture this. "Who's Hulk?"

"Brett's dad. Worked with my dad for years before he and his wife retired to Florida a couple of years back. He was a fixture at the station my whole life."

"How did he get that nickname?" I ask curiously.

"Because just like Bruce Banner, his eyes would change color when he was pissed. As Brett grew older, we saw that look happen more and more." Both of his dimples appear when he grins. I ignore the fleeting skip of my heartbeat and just shake my head.

"And you were such an angel for your folks, I'm sure?" I reply drolly.

"A paragon. Never a harsh word," he says just as I take a drink.

Fortunately, I don't spit at him as Em would. I manage—just

barely—to aim for the glass. Joe lifts his own and drowns it down in a single guzzle. "Finish up, I'll make the next round."

I shake my head in astonishment. We've about crushed the large bottle of Belvedere I pulled from my liquor cabinet earlier between us. Scattered across my counter are also the remains of Genoa's leftover lasagna, salsa, chips, and a tub of cannoli filling I managed to lift out of the fridge at Amaryllis Events from a cake Cori made the other day. "We're going to be sick as hell tomorrow," I declare, tossing back the rest of my drink before placing the empty glass down with a clink. I vaguely hear Joe shaking up more of the briny goodness that has my mind on a comfortable loop where pain can't intercede. It's a night where I'm choosing to forget that old wounds and new are causing me to bleed.

Tonight, the only thing coming from my pores is vodka.

Joe's already filling my glass before I can tell him I'm ready for my next drink. "If I forget to say this..."

"Say what?"

"Thank you." He reaches over and cups the side of my face. Leaning forward, he presses his forehead against mine. "Later I'll have to face it, but tonight I couldn't."

My hands slide to his wrist. I blink a few times, trying to get him into focus. Why have I never noticed his eyes were this blue before?

"They've always been this color," comes his amused reply.

I frown. "You're not supposed to be answering my thoughts. Those are private."

"They're not private when they come out of your mouth."

"Oh." I pout.

"Besides, it's not like I told you that your hair reminds me of dancing flames or anything embarrassing like that," he says casually. "That's when we'd really need to be concerned."

"True," I concede. "Except..."

"What?" His eyebrows draw down into that cute V I see all the time now in my dreams. I reach out to touch it.

"You kind of just did," I whisper.

"Oh." We're so close, there's no way I can't notice his lashes are a thick fringe. I can see them brush against his cheeks as they dart down. My lips part of their own accord.

"Don't let this be a mistake," we both whisper simultaneously. And even though I know it is, I can't draw my head back to break our physical connection.

Tonight, Joe's been reminded of his own mortality, lost a team member who was a close friend, and is likely reliving the death of his fiancée. He's come to me for comfort, not for confusion. Besides which, we still have so much unresolved between us. I have to keep him in the right place.

But when his fingers slide along my jaw and pull me closer to his descending lips, I'm helpless to do anything. Instead, I whisper, "Don't let this change us."

Right before his lips brush mine, he murmurs, "It won't."

I know it already has.

Then every thought is driven out of my head as he settles his lips more firmly on mine.

His mouth causes my brain to empty in a way the Belvedere couldn't since I heard the news of the fire. My arms slide from his wrists up to his shoulders to find purchase in a world that's suddenly upside-down. I dizzily try to remind myself, *He's only your friend*. But as our tongues dance along one another, slowly chasing the other, I'm more confused than ever.

We break apart, our breath intermingling with one another, and I'm about to take a step back to give us a moment to regain our bearing when he hauls me against his chest and slams his mouth down on mine.

And I'm lost.

My hands thread themselves into his thick black hair. I can feel one of his tangled in mine, the other banded around my waist to hold me against his body. If I'm feasting against his mouth than he is starving against mine. We're devouring each other the same way we've been consuming alcohol all night.

For Joe, it's to dull the pain. For me, it's to calm the fears.

We're taking back life the only way we can.

But as much as I want this, as much as I crave this, it's wrong.

Tears form behind my eyes even as I break the kiss. I'm supposed to be Joe's person. The one person in this world he's opened up to about how he's felt about Mary, about his fears about Grace, and who's supposed to make him feel less alone. As much as he might think he wants this right now, I know better. It's pain and the alcohol driving him.

It's not me.

Turning away, I wrap my arms tightly around myself. Where just a few moments ago we shared hysterical laughter, now there's an oppressive silence as what just happened registers.

I wait for the first blow. I know I don't have to wait long.

"Jesus, Holly." Joe's voice is shaky. "I didn't mean…" I hold up a hand with my back still turned toward him.

"Let's just call this a drunken aberration, okay?" I wish my voice would come out stronger than a whisper, but I can't force it to be.

"No, let me…" he starts again, but I quickly interrupt. It hurts to hear him want to apologize for something I've secretly been wanting since the first time we went to a movie together and our fingers collided against one another in the slippery popcorn at the same time.

It hurts worse because I know I'll never be able to have it again.

"Just head up to bed, Joe. Second door on the left. I'm going to clean up some of this mess so I don't have to face it in the morning." I don't want the reminder of what happened between us when I wake up.

Though he doesn't say anything, I feel him come up behind me. My body stiffens even as my heart melts as his hand passes through my hair. "Thank you."

"There's nothing to thank me for," I reply truthfully, albeit painfully.

"There's more to thank you for than you could possibly understand," With a last brush of his fingers, Joe leaves me standing in the early-morning light of my kitchen.

I wait until I hear the bedroom door close upstairs before I begin cleaning.

And crying.

Hours later, after I fitfully toss and turn in my own bedroom down the hall, I get up to make some coffee. To my surprise, there's a pot already made. Alongside it is a note that says, "It was the least I could do."

Before I pour myself the first cup, I walk over to the window and glance out.

Joe's Explorer is no longer in my driveway.

Letting out a sigh, I turn away from the promising spring day, knowing it's already gone to hell. Right along with my hopes and dreams.

38

HOLLY

A few days later, I'm in my office touching up some photos. I've only got a few more pixels to finish, and I want to get this done. I need to get out of here tonight before I murder someone—namely Phil, who thinks it's his goddamn right to know everything about my life.

It's bad enough we had Justin's funeral today. As if a sea of black uniforms and the flag draped over his casket wasn't heartbreaking enough, I had to witness a petite blonde throw herself into Joe's arms when the ceremony was over just as I was working up my courage up to offer my condolences since we've barely communicated since the night we kissed. I froze when I realized it was the same woman who was with him at The Coffee Shop. I didn't recognize her at first until he wrapped his arms around her and steered her away, her long blonde hair draping over his arm much like it did when I saw them. My heart aching and calling myself three kinds of a fool, I detoured and offered them instead to Chief Bianco and his wife on behalf of all of the Freemans. Once I made my way back over to my family, we left just as we arrived—together.

In Em's Rover—the only car large enough to hold all of us—Phil immediately turned toward me and began his interrogation. "I thought I saw his car outside your house the day after the fire."

"Let it go, Phil," Em gritted out. She was driving, otherwise, I think she might have punched him.

"This is complete bullshit," he growled.

"No, what's bullshit is we just laid someone we know in the ground, and this is what you want to talk about?" I snapped.

Abashed, Phil turned around to shut up.

As soon as we reached the mansion, I hopped out of the car and raced inside. Sprinting up the grand staircase to my office, I slammed and locked the door before I burst into tears.

My cell immediately started ringing. Without glancing at the display, I just knew it was Joe calling. I wish I could have been stronger and answered, but I just couldn't. I helped him move on from his grief, but who was going to help me move on from mine?

I thought the loss of my life the first time hurt when I was fifteen, and I knew I would never be able to earn love. I was wrong. It hurt worse when the possibility was put in front of me and then taken away.

So instead, I reached into my purse and flicked the switch to Silent. I pulled up photos from a wedding I shot last week. With a quick email to Megan to let her know I was going to work on this particular file, I got to work.

Hours later, I'm blurry-eyed and not just from having stared at the computer for so long. It will take time, but I'll make it through this. Sitting back, I stretch, feeling the pain in my back and neck. They temporarily erase the one that's taken residence in my heart. My lashes flutter shut, the thickness of them trapping the tears against my cheek.

"I know I don't have the right to ask for anything; I've been given so much after what I've done. But can you please help the pain stop? Just help me," I whisper to anyone listening. "I just need to go back to the way it was before I knew I wasn't enough."

And quietly in my office, I let go of the torrent of tears I've been holding in since I realized I had feelings, let alone knowing they never had a chance at being returned. I cried for a good man who lost his life trying to rescue another being. And damned if I don't cry for a young mother who lost hers too soon because if she were still alive, I'd never be feeling this pain to begin with.

39

JOSEPH

"Joe, could you come in here for a minute?" My father calls me into his office. Before I can respond, he turns and walks away.

Brett goes to open his mouth, but I hold up a hand. "Don't okay? Just don't." I've lost the capacity for laughter somewhere between Justin's death, kissing Holly, and realizing she walked away after the funeral without getting a chance to talk with her. Fuck, nothing's gone right between us since that day I ran into Eden and Seth. I should have listened to Matt. I should have talked to Holly and let her in. I don't know why I didn't except for a misplaced pride and lingering heartache of the things I've still never dealt with.

Standing at Justin's graveside, I was assaulted by memories. My friend. My brother. My partner. The wisdom he gave me right before he saved me echoes through my mind and my heart.

But how in the hell do I fix this mess?

If it wasn't for Grace, I know a smile wouldn't have crossed my face in the last eight days. Because that's how long it's been since I stayed at Holly's. That's the night I completely fucked up everything by giving in to the urge to kiss her.

That's the night I lost her.

The pain is different than when I lost Mary, but God, does it hurt.

It hurts so much, I don't know how I'm putting one foot in front of the other to make my way into my father's office.

Crossing over the threshold, he quietly asks, "Close the door, son." Realizing this isn't a discussion between a chief and his employee, but a father to his son chat, my shoulders slump a bit before I do as he asks.

Dropping into one of his visitor chairs, I look out the window down toward Main Street. If I try hard, I can make out the rooftop where Amaryllis Events is housed. I tried to call and text her so many times. If she'd just let me explain, maybe I could find a way for us to go back to...something.

"Tell me what's wrong, Joey," my pops says softly. "I haven't seen you like this since..."

I let out a bitter laugh. "Since Mary died? It's entirely different, but tell that to my heart. Right now, it feels an awful lot like it." Not having Holly to talk with every day is reopening the void in my chest that's been sealed for so long with laughter, warmth, and love.

"I know Justin's loss must bring a lot of it back," my father starts. I blink.

"Justin hurts, Pop, God, does it hurt." My head drops to my knees. "He saved my life by pushing me forward."

"I know, son."

"I have so much guilt eating away at me."

My father stills. "Why?"

"Because..." I shove to my feet and stand in front of the window. "I screwed up, Pop," I admit. "I let Eden and Seth get to me."

Starting back at the altercation at The Coffee Shop, I explain how I was confronted by Mary's parents. On top of that, I've been dealing with how Holly's been forcing space between us. I tell my father about how I'm almost certain Holly misinterpreting seeing me with Melissa started all of this confusion. I bow my head when I whisper, "I miss her. I've barely been able to get through to her. She agrees to plans and then at the last minute, something comes up and she cancels. Except the night Justin died I went to her and she...she let me in. She was there for me all the way—better than before. Then I fucked it all up all over again." Wearily, I run my hand through my hair and meet my father's eyes.

"What did you do?" he asks quietly.

"I..."

"Joe." His voice holds a note of warning that lets me know just like when I was a little kid I'm not about to escape his question.

"I...I kissed her. And ever since, I can't get close enough to make things right."

My father falls back in his chair, an incredulous look on his face. "I can't believe this."

"I was going to go to her after the funeral, but then Melissa was so distraught over Justin, which I get. She's been in love with him for years. But Holly left with her family before I could get to her, and now she won't even answer my calls...I..."

"I don't know how I raised a son to be so completely blind and stupid," my father states abruptly, shoving to his feet.

I'm taken aback by the vehemence in his tone. "They're not..."

"If you finish that sentence with 'her problem,' I might smack you upside the head just like I used to do as a little kid. Son, wake up and realize what everyone else has. You're falling for Holly Freeman. For Christ's sake, that's why Eden and Seth attacked you. And Holly's doing the same. That's why she's pulling back. She cares about you enough to not stand in the way of your happiness even though she's somehow managed to heal you."

I absorb the impact of my father's words. Falling back, I stumble back to the chair again. "But, she said she was single by choice," I manage to get out.

"Probably because none of the other ass clowns she was dating before ever managed to get to her. Somehow—and right now I have no idea how that's possible—you did."

"Pop—" My voice is broken. "She won't talk to me. I can't even get through to explain."

His fist comes down hard on his desk. "When you were training to take down a wall of flame, did you give up?"

Listlessly, I shake my head no.

"When Mary died, I know you wanted to give in. Did you? Did you walk out on your family? On Grace?"

"Hell no," I spit at him.

"Then why would you give up before you even try to fight for Holly? You find her, you make her listen, and then you hold on as tight as you can to her for as long as you have the chance. You never —I mean never—give up on someone you can't go a day without."

"A day? Try an hour; maybe a minute."

"Then you're more of a fool than I thought. Now get the hell out of my office." He begins to fiddle with papers on his desk.

I stand up, but before I leave, I ask, "Pop?"

He lifts his head.

"What do I do if she still wants to walk away?" I voice my biggest fear aloud.

He lets out a huge sigh and comes around the desk. Clasping me on the shoulder, he mutters, "Stop worrying about what's going to go wrong, son. That's no way to live. There's going to be pain and heart-break; we both know that. But to live, you have to find joy in life. For you, that's our family, Grace, and now Holly. You have to focus on everything that makes the world beautiful so when you have those nights where the dark is only lit up by the monster, you have the strength to fight the bitch back."

I nod, unable to speak.

"You're allowed doubt, but never give up. I'm just sorry to say, it looks like you gave up on your woman at absolutely the wrong time."

I close my eyes on his words of wisdom that cause a shaft of pain through my already battered heart.

"Thanks, Pop," I choke out before I open the door.

I need to call someone who might be able to help me like she did once before.

"Mr. Bianco, what a surprise. What can I help you with today?" Ali's voice comes through the line. Only this time, it's as cold as an iceberg.

I wince. I bought this and everything else the Freemans are ready to throw at me. "Ali, if I could talk with you for just a moment…"

"I'm afraid I don't have much time. Is there a question about next year's 5K? "

"Ali…"

"We really won't start planning for that until the fall."

"If you just give me a chance to explain…"

"Contracts will be sent over in late August."

Finally, my temper snaps. "You have no idea what I feel for her!" There's finally silence on the other end of the line. "None," I whisper.

"You hurt her. No one gets to do that," Ali says in a voice so deathly quiet I know if I was standing right in front of her, I'd be bleeding.

"I was trying…I didn't think…There were things I was trying to work through so I didn't hurt her," The words come out as a jumbled mess.

"In other words, you didn't give her a chance to think for herself," Ali concludes brutally. "Why is it all of you stupid men think we need protection? That after all we've been through, that we're not strong enough to handle a little adversity?"

All they've been through? I want to probe more, but I have more pressing concerns. "I need to see her. I have to explain."

"Joe." I let out the breath I didn't realize I was holding. "She's closed up to even us. She won't talk about what happened. All I know is she's hurting. I don't know whether seeing you will help or hurt her even more."

"Ali, just let me know where she'll be and let me take it from there," I beg.

There's a heavy sigh on the other end of the line. "We're leaving at five to head into the city. All of us are going. Holly's staying an extra few minutes to lock up. That's all I'll give you." The phone clatters in my ear.

I have until then to come up with a plan.

I just hope it's enough.

∼

I WONDER if Ali sent me here to get a taste of my own medicine.

As Holly steps through the mansion doors wearing a rose-colored, knee-length dress that's hugging every inch of her perfect figure, my heart skips a beat. The color brings out the creaminess to all of her beautiful skin on display. I'm sliding out of my SUV to approach her when a Honda Pilot pulls just past the steps. A blond man in a suit I vaguely recognize jumps out of the car with a smile on his face. "Hols? You ready?"

She nods. "Just a minute. I just have to lock up." She teases him gently, "I know you don't want to be late tonight of all nights."

"Might pose to be a bit of a problem for my plans," he jokes back.

Witnessing her sweet being directed toward another man makes me want to give up already. I know if I walk away she'll find a way back to the smiles and the laughter she gave me so I could heal. The rest of me—the part of me that she guided into the light from never-ending darkness—can't. I'm too damn selfish to let her go.

Slamming the door, I startle both of them as I stalk my way toward the front porch that wraps around Amaryllis Events. "Someone you know, Hols?" The man steps protectively toward her.

Even as she steps to the side, the small bit of laughter disappears from her face as she watches my approach. "Give me two minutes? I promise we'll be on the road in time." She reaches out and squeezes his arm.

"I can..."

She shakes her head. "It's okay. Just wait in the car for me," she says softly.

Giving me an assessing once-over, he nods. "Hols, we need to talk," I start. She holds up her hand.

"It's really not a good time right now, Joe. As you can see, we're in a bit of a hurry." Her voice is polite but flat.

"Please."

She shakes her head and starts to make her way toward the stairs. "Everything's fine. I'm just going through a few...things. We do have to catch up though. I haven't had the chance to tell you how happy I am you found someone." I might have believed her if it wasn't for the fact her eyes are completely dead.

God, was my father right? Were we both looking right at each other and not seeing?

I leap down the steps and land directly in front of her. "She's not what you think, and I suspect neither is he." I jerk my thumb behind me to the man spinning his key fob impatiently. "Promise me—right here, right now—that you'll meet with me tomorrow. I don't care where."

"Joe, I appreciate this. You're being sweet. I get that, but..." She tries to move past me, but I grab her hand.

"You're everything." She freezes. Haunted eyes lift to meet mine. I want to shout in relief there's finally something else there besides a polite blankness. More than that, I want to kiss her, but I can't. I figure I have about thirty seconds before the Neanderthal picks her up and carries her to the car. "I have no idea how that's possible after I had it all and lost it once. Tell me how not to be afraid of having it all ripped from me a second time."

"Joe," she whispers, her voice trembling.

"Holly, we have to go. We're going to be late picking up Jenna." Her eyes dart over to the man. She nods.

"Don't leave me empty again, Hols," I beseech her. "Just promise me a chance to make it right."

She shakes her head back and forth. My heart is in ashes at her feet. "I see." I begin to back away. Until her trembling voice resurrects me.

"I have a wedding tomorrow. I don't know when I'll be done."

Not caring if the man's late, who Jenna is, or anything else, I surge into Holly with a force so strong, I lift her off her delicately sandaled feet. "Thank you." My voice is so hoarse from unshed tears, I almost don't recognize it.

"I have to go," she repeats. "Joe, we really have to go."

Slowly, I lower her back to the ground. Looking over my shoulder, I know my time is up. "Who is he?"

"That's Jake, Em's fiancé. We're picking up his daughter at Grand Central for a family thing in the city."

Oh. "Sorry," I call over.

He snorts. "No, you're not. Hols, if you're not in this car in point two seconds, you can drive in on your own. I have a college boyfriend to torment."

Before she can say it, I guide her to the passenger-side door. "Go. We'll talk tomorrow."

Without another word, she slides into the seat. "Okay, I'm ready." I close her door reluctantly.

Jake slams his door shut, and within seconds they're out on Main Street. Standing there, I realize for the first time in years, I'm not scared about what the next day's going to bring.

I'm excited for it.

40

HOLLY

I'm terrified as I pull into Joe's driveway the next night.

Although he tried to find a babysitter so we could talk, his mother's come down with a bug that she doesn't want to pass along to Grace. So, despite my offering to postpone our conversation for a later time, his growled "If you think I'm the only Bianco who's missed you, then you're very wrong" convinced me I should hightail it over there.

Earlier today, I also received a phone call from Brett and his extremely nervous sister, Melissa—the blonde I saw him with. She assured me Joe would give me a full explanation later, but that he was like another older brother to her. She didn't feel right about my going in without understanding there wasn't actually anything between them—ever.

I find myself even more confused. I was prepared for him to tell me he had found someone just like his deceased fiancée. Now, I don't know what to think other than the fact the man who stood in front of me last night doesn't just want to be friends.

But what he wants to be, I have no idea.

Ali pulled me aside after dinner last night to let me know she was there if I needed a shoulder to cry on. "You've been doing this by yourself for too long, Hols. This is one of the many privileges of being your sister," she said, right before she hugged the hell out of me, smearing my camera lens in the process.

I almost lost it crying then.

Pulling up next to his Explorer, I try to find something to focus on to calm me before I walk up the front stairs. I've been living on a diet of sadness and pain during the last few weeks, and I'm beginning to feel it. I guess it's better to know the answers than not to. Sliding myself out of my car, I grab my camera bag—more out of habit than anything—and an old UConn sweatshirt from the back seat. I'm halfway up the slate stairs built into the grass when the door flies open.

And there they are, waiting for me. If I was foolish enough to think I deserved it, I could easily imagine coming home from a day at the office and finding them there. Squaring my shoulders, I trudge forward.

Joe swings the door open when I'm just a few feet away. "Hey," I greet them both.

Then he does something he's never done before. Leaning down, he brushes his lips against my cheek. "Hey. How was work?"

Stupefied, I stare up at him when suddenly I feel a wet kiss on the other side of my cheek. "Hi, my Holly."

My Holly. Not Kalie's Holly. Mine. I can't stop the tears from building behind my eyes, but I can damn sure try to prevent them from falling.

Joe sets Grace down and says, "Why don't you go play until dinner, baby? Holly and I have a few things to talk about?"

"Okay!" She gives my legs a squeeze before racing off to her bedroom.

Dropping an arm around my shoulders, he guides me into the kitchen through the family room. It's not the first time I've been to Joe's in the months we've been friends, but it feels like it all over again. I spot the picture of Mary on the mantle and desperately send her a mental *Help me! What the hell is going on here?* But of course, she doesn't answer.

"So, after he called you and left you utterly confused, Brett called me. Is Coke okay? I don't want to drink with Grace around." Joe reaches into the fridge to offer me a red-and-white can.

"Sure." I look for a place to drop my stuff since Joe's already set the table.

"Shoot. You take this; give me that." He hands me an unopened can of soda. I'm so anxious, I drop it to the floor while Joe heads back into the living room with my things. Deciding to let it sit for a moment, I place it on the counter.

When he comes back and finds I haven't opened my drink, he demands, "What's wrong?"

"Nothing." I'm just overwhelmed and petrified right now is all, but Joe spies my drink and doesn't take it that way.

"Holly, I didn't invite you here to torture and torment you." He makes quick work going over to my drink. "I invited you here…"

"No, Joe! Wait!" But it's too late. He's already popped the top and soda sprays everywhere. It's on both of our shirts, in his face and hands, and on the counter. "I tried…" But the giggle escapes. His beautiful blue eyes narrow at me. I bite my lip, but another laugh comes out.

He steps closer. I snicker. The look on his face is pure outrage, but it's not like I shook the soda. I try to explain, "That's why it was on the counter—to settle."

"Uh-huh." He still advances. I bite my lip to keep the laughter in because it really is funny when his eyes shift from outraged to seductive.

Holy crap. My back hits the wall. I'm surprised and a little disappointed, to be honest, when Joe doesn't come into my space farther than to tug at my lower lip.

"I thought I told you to stop doing that. You really are going to hurt yourself." I suck in a breath so hard, it's audible.

"You remember?" I would have thought there was no way he remembered anything about that night.

Anything.

Bracing his arm to the left of me, he leans in slightly. "Hols, I've drunk with the best—and the worst—of them. That night with you didn't even rate against some of the drinking they made me do as a probie. Think frat-boy drinking and amp it up by a factor of ten with running drills and climbing stairs with hoses added in for fun. Not only do I remember every single minute of that night, but I've also been kicking myself in the ass wondering if you've hated me for it."

I shake my head. "I thought it only happened because you were drunk," I whisper.

The fingers of his other hand play with the fine hair at my temple. "Before this goes any further, let's talk, okay?"

I nod.

Dropping his fingers, he tugs at my hand. "Come on. I'll get you a clean shirt to wear while I throw that one in the wash."

Soon, Joe and I are ensconced on the sofa in his living room while Grace is happily chattering with Elmo. I'm wearing one of Joe's CFD T-shirts, and it looks like a mini dress. Until I slipped it on, I never realized quite how broad his chest really is. Or at least I never admitted it.

"It's always been hard for me to talk about Mary," Joe starts. I'm pulled out of my thoughts, and I swivel around so I'm facing him. "I loved her, Holly. I'm never going to deny that or denounce it. She was beautiful and sweet. I'll miss her every day for the rest of my life." His eyes drift over to where the picture of Mary and Grace sit on the mantel. "But it's different now than it was when I first met you. You helped me keep moving forward somehow. And I'm grateful for that."

Gratitude? Oh, God. Do I really want to hear this? I keep my face expressionless as he continues.

"I realized my feelings for you started to change the day Mary's parents attacked me about you at The Coffee Shop," Joe states matter-of-factly.

"Excuse me?" I don't even try to keep that in. Both things in that statement are shocking.

His lips tip up slightly. "Which part of that are you asking about?"

"Both, but talk to me about Mary's parents. I don't even know them. Do I?"

He shakes his head, "Not that I'm aware of. And that's only part of what infuriated me so badly. You have no idea of the stuff they said about Grace; about you."

Oh my God. I jump up out of my chair. "Are you kidding me? What is wrong with those people?"

Joe nods at me. "I know. But just the threat sent me into a tailspin, Hols. I went back to the station freaking out."

"Why didn't you tell me?" I ask. I'm not judging, I just want to know.

He barks out a rough laugh. "Why didn't you talk to me about Melissa?"

I flush. "Is that her name? I guess because she seemed like more," I say bravely when all I want to do is cry.

"Hols..." he starts with an apology in his voice, but I plow on.

"It wasn't my place to ask if you were finally moving on with that part of your life."

"Except I wasn't."

"That's what it looked like," I whisper.

He grips my jaw and forces me to look at him. "It wasn't."

I'm trembling at his touch. It physically pains me to pull away. "We're supposed to be friends. You came to me about Justin," I whisper. Pain whips across his face. "But I had no idea of what was happening with your in-laws," I conclude.

"They're not my in-laws," he bites out.

"Close enough," I shoot back.

"No. And maybe that's why I didn't say anything." Shoving himself from the chair, he starts pacing back and forth in front of me. "Do you realize what it's like to realize you love someone and that you'll never be good enough for them?"

"I have a fair idea," I say softly, but Joe doesn't hear me, lost in his own confession. He stops in front of the picture of Mary. Lovingly he traces a finger around the edge immersed in a love so strong, death can't break it. I feel the same painful burn I always do whenever I watch him do that, knowing what I feel for him will never be enough.

I will never be enough.

"Eden and Seth hated me from the moment they set eyes on me," he tells me.

I'm shocked. "What? Why?"

"Oh, maybe because I was an arrogant, know-it-all, not good enough for their precious daughter? Or maybe because of the fact I was with their daughter at all." Joe's face takes on a resigned cast. "Mary wasn't naive. She saw how they treated me and was as upset by it as you are. She just chose to try to fix it differently." I'm not surprised he can tell how infuriated I am considering my fingers are clenched into fists at my side. "She believed Grace would bring out the best in them over time. Then the accident happened." Taking a deep breath, he admits, "It was never your brother-in-law they wanted to harm after Mary died; it was me. If it weren't for me, then Mary would never have been out in that car in the first place. She would never have been out with 'that child.' She would never have needed new clothes. She would have had it all." A lone tear slips down Joe's face.

I'm compelled to move toward him. Brushing it away, I whisper, "Did they say that to you?"

He nods. "In the middle of The Coffee Shop. Right in front of Matt. I mean, Hols—" He swipes at his own eyes. "Matt did everything he could to intervene. For years, I've scoured the accident reports. I know in my head it's an accident but..."

"No," I say firmly. I cup his cheek. "It's not your fault. It's the fault of the driver of that damned car. Where is he now?"

"Serving time for manslaughter, but she was out shopping because..."

"Because she wanted something nice for her family around the holidays, Joe. Millions of women everywhere were doing the same thing that day. Her parents have no right to blame you. You shouldn't be blaming yourself."

Shuddering, he lays his forehead against mine. "I was trying to protect you from them. They've made Grace cry before." Immediately, my body tenses. I want to go find these people and slap some sense into them.

Dropping my hand, I whisper, "What? Because of me?"

Joe quickly continues. "No. Sorry. Because Grace apparently wasn't missing Mary enough. Sick, right?" Heartbreakingly disturbed is more like it, but I stay silent so he can continue. "I wanted to protect you from having to deal with them, and all I did instead was push you away."

A sound tries to rip from me. I turn away to conceal it. When I finally have myself under control, I say flatly, "So, you weren't ready to trust me."

He spins me around. "No, it's me not trusting myself. Somewhere along the way you effortlessly became a part of my life. I'd come home and find myself thinking of you, not of the past. I don't know when you filled in the loneliness with laughter and the emptiness with smiles. I just know you did. And when it was gone because of my own damned mistake, I knew I had to fix it."

By the time he's done saying that to me, both of his hands are cupping my cheeks. Instinctively, we begin leaning toward each other when two things happen simultaneously: the phone rings and Grace yells, "Daddy! I'm getting hungry!"

Shakily, I pull back. "I'll go to Grace," I say before I dart for the open door.

Hearing a muted curse, Joe snaps up the receiver with a "This better be important," just as I reach Grace's room. I crouch down to her level where she's ensconced with Elmo in a bean bag chair. "Hey, baby, so what do you want for dinner?"

"Nubbets!" she shouts with abandon.

I smile at her fondly as I stroke the black curls that are haphazardly escaping the tiny bands I love watching Joe manipulate with his long fingers. "Is chicken what Daddy was going to give you?

"No, but it might be what she has to eat. Holly, can I speak with you for a moment?" Joe's voice is grim behind me.

Uh-oh. "Be right back, baby." Pushing into a standing position, I follow Joe out the door out of Grace's earshot. "What's wrong?"

"It's rare when it happens, but I was called into work." Frustration is warring with the need to race out the door.

"Then what are you still doing here?" His face blanks. "Come on, Joe. We're both frustrated with each other, but this is different. You need help and I'm offering it. At least if you want me to?" A hint of vulnerability enters my own voice.

"Want you to?" He yanks me so close, I crash hard against his chest. Clutching his biceps for support, my lips part in surprise. "Please, God, just be here when I get home so we can work the rest out." His lips are so close to mine, I can feel the air from his mouth pass into mine.

But now's not the time for the promise of what I know those lips can offer to me.

"I'll be here," I whisper.

Releasing me, his hands linger against my tattoo under which my pulse beats. "I've got to go," he says before he turns and heads out the door.

41

HOLLY

I startle awake feeling another presence in the room. Protectively, my arms curl tighter around Grace, who's snuggled asleep against my chest.

"If you knew how beautiful that looks after what I just endured..." Joe's voice comes from the darkness across the room. It's filling the room that held girlish giggles with an oppressive bleakness. In the dim light, I can just barely make him out when he stands to cross over to where we are. His clothes are immaculate, but his face bears the traces of blood he didn't quite manage to wash away.

It's his eyes, though, that force the question out of me.

"Do you want to talk about it?" I whisper, cognizant of the warm bundle I'm holding.

"Not with Grace around. Here." He leans over and slides his muscled arm beneath his little girl. My breath catches as the bare skin of his forearm brushes against my stomach where my shirt's ridden up. "Give her to me. I'll put her down and be right back."

Straightening, he lifts Grace out of my arms. I immediately scramble to right myself. He frowns down at me. "Holly, it's the middle of the night. There's no need to lock yourself in a suit of armor."

If you only knew, I think to myself, but before I can form a response, Joe strides out of the room with Grace. Spying my camera, I smile thinking of all the goofy pictures Grace and I took earlier tonight. "I wonder how many pictures of the TV I'll end up printing out?" I chuckle.

I wasn't aware of Joe returning to the room until I hear a clink hit the table. Turning, I see him remove his hand from the baby monitor. "You let her touch your camera?" His voice is appalled.

I shrug. "It's just a camera. All the files were already backed up, just in case."

"Well, that's a relief." A shadow crosses his face. "It's about the only thing that is."

I wait a few moments as anger and pain chase each other across his face. Before I can ask again if he wants to unload his burden, he bursts out with, "Right after I was called in, there was a callout. When we got there, there was a small chance we could have saved him."

My eyes wander over his dark features, realizing grief is starting to settle in. "Who, Joe?"

He gives me a name I don't recognize. I shake my head gently. "I'm sorry, I just don't..."

My words get caught in my throat when he grinds out, "He was fourteen years old."

I can't breathe. I barely manage to ask, "Was it an accident? A wreck?"

Joe runs his hands through his hair, yanking it in frustration. "No."

No. The word echoes through my brain. I brace for what he's about to say even though in my heart, I already know.

"It was suicide. The parents are devastated—just devastated. Their whole lives are shattered." His dark blue eyes snap toward mine. "What in the hell possesses a kid at that age to think the world is so bad that taking their life is the answer?"

And here it is. The reason why despite my burgeoning hope tonight this would never be able to work out between us. "Because when you know the breath you're taking right now is immeasurably better than the pain you'll endure by taking the next, suicide can seem like the only answer," I whisper. "That's when the pills don't seem so hard to swallow, the knife may not be as hard to handle, and the barrel isn't scary to look into."

The only sound in the room is the buzzing from Grace's monitor. Even as I know my judgment is coming, I still stand. Because after everything, I've learned something these last few months. I may always have my past, but I am no longer that woman. I am stronger than I gave myself credit for and have as much a right to be loved as anyone else.

"No," his voice rasps against my skin, almost grating against it.

"You don't know everything about me," I counter quietly.

He strides forward and yanks me into his body. "For God's sake, Holly..." I cut him off even as I struggle to pull away.

"It's mine to share when I wish to share it and who I wish to share it with," I snarl at him, breathing heavily because, despite everything, his nearness is drawing me in to want to burrow closer.

"Tonight, I saw a boy finish the job with a knife. I couldn't save Mary, I couldn't save him, but I sure as hell can protect..." His voice dies out.

"Who? Grace? Why did my wanting to kill myself after a lifetime of abuse mean I could suddenly harm your child?" The rasp of my words hangs in between us, leaving everything still.

I'm frozen where I stand, my lips parted. I hear a whispered "Shit," even as his arms loosen. The thoughts that have buried themselves into my soul rise to the surface, pounding one after the other as each chamber of my heart moves.

Tainted.

Blood.

Unwanted.

Alone.

Slowly, I break out of Joe's embrace and grab my bag from the floor. I scurry toward the door as quickly as I can. I can hear his footsteps behind me. Just a few more feet. I silently plead with any god or goddess listening to let me out before he can reach me—before I break down.

I'm denied.

Even as my eyes begin to flood with tears, Joe's whispering, "I didn't mean it to sound like that. God, I didn't... Please look at me."

I shake my head, unwilling to comply. But I'll give him the explanation he feels he deserves.

"I was fifteen. The night before I tried, I overheard my father tell my stepmother the next day he planned on using whatever he had to in order to make me take my first customer." My voice is dull, flat.

"What about the police? Couldn't you go to them?" Joe asks me quietly.

Turning my tear-streaked face up to him, I ask dully, "Who do you think my first customer was supposed to be? They were already clients of my stepmother's."

Joe's head whips to the side like I slapped him.

"I made my choice. I had the gun to my mouth when Maria intervened."

Joe interrupts, "Was she a friend?"

I shake my head. "She was my stepmother. She was tired of being the only breadwinner in the family." I take an enormous breath and continue whispering, "The gun went off."

"You're still here." He reaches out to touch my hair, but I step away.

"Maria isn't." I let that knowledge settle into his mind. When the shock and horror appear on his face, I shut down. Completely. "What happened next isn't just a story about me, and I won't share it. Not now. Maybe not ever. Don't ask me if I regret it. Looking back, the answer is simple. No."

Joe rears back. I've surprised him with my vehemence.

"I survived, Joe, and two monsters are dead—my stepmother and my father." At his confusion, I give in enough to explain, "My father went to prison and died there." I struggle to find the right words for what I'm about to say. "But I knew my price for my life would be high."

"What price is that?"

"The fact that for the rest of my life, someone will always look at me the way you're looking at me right now." Opening his front door, I slip out into the cold dark, feeling none of it because it can't be colder than what's permeating my soul.

Which is nothing.

42

JOSEPH

Horrified, I'm frozen in place as Holly races out to her car. "What have I done?" I whisper aloud. Cold air seeps through the thin shirt I'm wearing. I shiver as I stare at her her taillights disappearing down my driveway toward the street. She barely pauses. I'm sick, knowing it was my own stupidity, my own knee-jerk reaction, my past grief reflected on the faces of the family tonight that sent me over the edge of sanity at Holly's shocking news.

I wish I could go back in time as the man I am today and fight for the girl she was. She deserved someone to protect her from the mistreatment of heartache back then—hell, tonight, I think with a surge of anger at myself. Holly deserves to be worshiped for bringing so much joy to those around her, celebrated for capturing people's spirit and energy.

Holly's never questioned me once about my asshole behavior of late; she accepted it, me, my life, and became such an integral part of my world. My pain grows brutal as the lights of her car fade in the distance until I can no longer see them. "Fuck," I hiss. Closing the door softly so I don't wake my daughter, I turn and freeze.

Holly was in such a rush to get away from me, she left her camera. My heart cracks open a little more, and I didn't think it could do that tonight. Gently, I pick it up and press the button so I can see the pictures she took with Grace tonight. Expecting to find photos of my living room or the corner of my fireplace, I'm not prepared to have the slivers of my heart compressed back together so tightly it's as if they never shattered. I try not to cry as I flip through the photos slowly.

Grace and Holly are lying much as they were when I first walked in. Only they're blowing kisses at the camera. My fingers trace over each of their faces on the little 2x2 window, my throat closing around my heart which has lodged in it.

Moving to the sofa, I sink down to where Holly was lying earlier. I slowly scroll backward through the pictures. As I reach the ones of the corner of my television, I can't help but smile. There's my Grace's natural talent shining through, I think with some amusement. Thirty or so pictures later, I can see where Holly obviously has control of the camera once again, and my breath constricts.

Grace is sitting on the floor holding her mother's picture with a beaming smile on her face. In my absence, Holly obviously had no problem encouraging my daughter's curiosity about her mother. In fact, she's given her—me—this gift of beauty in the knowledge that while Mary won't be with us, being with Holly would never dim that for her.

Or for me.

Shuddering, the epic magnitude of my mistake tonight slams into me. Her voice, so hollow and empty, screams in my head. Maybe I'm overreacting because of what I saw tonight, but it feels like ignoring it is tantamount to a different kind of death—that of Holly and me.

But I can't leave and go after her. I hear the little rasps of breath through the monitor reminding me so clearly why I can't.

Shifting, I reach in my pocket to grab my phone to text her when something happens: the camera buttons start to flash. "Oh, God. Don't tell me I broke it," I plead aloud to the empty room.

Accidentally, I hit the shutter. The flash fixed on top engages like a crack of lightning in the darkened space. I jump backward, startled. "Jesus," I mutter. Then as the picture briefly appears on the back, I grin. My photo-taking ability is only slightly more elevated than that of my three-year-old's.

Sitting the camera on the table, I send a quick text to Holly. *You forgot something.* I wait for a response.

Long minutes later, I'm flipping back and forth trying to decide which photo is my favorite when I receive a response. *Keep it. I don't need anything to remember the look on your face.*

Even as I hold the camera in my hand, knowing there's no way she'd say that about something as crucial as this, a crazy idea begins to form. It'd be mad, I think to myself. It'd be opening myself up like I haven't been... My eyes dart up to the picture resting on my mantle.

Since the night I haphazardly proposed to Mary. The night I learned Grace was on her way.

Dazed, I realize I'm staring my past in the face and holding my future in my hands. But if I don't do something quickly, it's going to slip away out of my life as permanently as if it died.

I refuse to let that happen.

Turning away from Mary's glowing face, I stalk into my bedroom and close the door.

It's time to take the shot at my future I planned on doing earlier. Weeks ago. Before Eden and Seth confronted me at The Coffee Shop.

Only now, it looks like for now it's going to be a one-way conversation.

HOURS LATER, I think I've captured everything I want to on Holly's camera as the sun begins peeking its way above the clouds. I open a text and send a message to Holly. *It was your camera. If you want it, meet me at The Coffee Shop at ten.* When the message shows Delivered, I place my phone on the nightstand before rolling over to get a few hours of sleep.

Baring one's soul is a lot more exhausting than it looks.

And I might be blind from all the flashes that went off as I tried to capture what I needed to say without words.

43

HOLLY

Anxiously, I sip on a latte as I wait for Joe to come through The Coffee Shop door. This makes my second one since I arrived almost thirty minutes ago. I'm a mass of jitters and not just from the caffeine I'm mainlining.

If it wasn't my camera... If it was anything else, I'd have just forgotten about it. But I need my camera. I need to have the ability to focus, to see, to live even if the idea is nauseating right now. And taking aim with my camera's the only way I'll be able to do that.

It's not just any camera either. It's the one I was gifted by the siblings after I graduated UConn. That camera means more than just the photos on it; it's held the promise of my future for the last twelve years. It's tough and durable. It's been dropped and kicked. And even if it occasionally needs a little more TLC, it still—in my mind—takes the best shots out of my collection.

I'm sure he's just going to plop the camera on the table and leave. Whatever had the potential to grow between us was destroyed by my past. Even though I knew it would be, it's still painful. And it's going to leave a vicious scar on my heart.

Coming to the conclusion I might be worthy of love has been an epiphany I never expected. I thought I'd go through life having to compromise my dreams to pay the penance for my past when it's because of my history that I deserve this life and the chance to grab love with both hands. But I can't remain by Joe's side as only his friend when the depth of my emotions is so much more than that. Nor can I be judged for what I know to be a decision I had to make in a split second to live.

He deserves more, but as for me? I finally realize I deserve everything.

Just as I'm about to raise my cup to my lips, the bells tinkle over the door. Joe steps through, carefully holding my camera. My heart begins an irregular rhythm in my chest. I achingly admit I'm prepared to walk away from the man weaving in between the patrons who hasn't taken his eyes from me. Because I can't keep feeling pain on behalf of love.

And that's what happens every time Joe's dark blue eyes look at me and I remember I'm not who he wants to be with. Not because of who I really am.

Noelle Greene—for all intents and purposes—died when I became Holly Freeman. Her death gave me a life I may not deserve, but one I've earned through years of penance and contrition. I may not be worthy of this man, but that's not to say I'm not worthy of love.

I am loved. I just need to remember that to get through the next few minutes.

Sliding into the booth across from me, Joe doesn't say anything. Instead, he grips my camera tightly between his long fingers.

"Planning on letting that go?" I ask quietly, breaking the silence that stretches between us.

He opens his mouth to speak, but before he can, Ava steps up to our table with a steaming cup of coffee in her hand. "Here you go, Joe." She sets it next to his forearm before disappearing down the aisle, leaving us once again in our silence.

This time, I end it quicker. "You don't have to say anything. I... appreciate the fact you look at me differently since you now understand what it is I'm made of…" I don't get to finish before he interrupts.

"Shut up, Holly." My eyes widen when instead of handing over my camera, he reaches for my hand. Yanking me to the side, I'm pulled from the booth until we're face-to-face.

And he's still holding my hand.

My heart is pounding so hard I feel like he can feel it through our jackets. "What do you think you're doing?"

"I finally understand why you've never understood things are changing," he says strangely.

"Changing?" I struggle to pull my hand away. "I don't understand what you mean."

Lifting his other hand, he stills me merely by cupping my chin. His calm and steady breaths are in direct contrast to my own jagged attempts at air. "You will." Leaning forward, he brushes a soft, tender kiss against my flaming cheek. Before he pulls away, he whispers, "Look at the pictures on your camera, Hols."

Pulling back, I blink, "What did you do?"

He smiles as his thumb lazily brushes against the bone where his lips just branded me. "You won't listen to me if I try to talk to you right now. So, I decided to show you what I'm feeling in a way I knew you'd have no choice but to focus on." Pressing his lips against my forehead, he leaves his lips there to murmur, "I hope I'll see you later."

As he pulls away, I call out, "Joe?" I'm confused. I expected him to walk away, not stand here and encourage the heart I'm trying to numb against more pain.

"Just look at the pictures, Hols. Then come find me." Pulling away, he turns and walks down the aisle toward the front of The Coffee Shop. Even as confused as I am, I can't help but admire the confidence in his stride that accentuate the muscles that look like they were crafted by ancient Greek sculptors.

Sitting back down, I reach across the table for my camera. For long moments, I do nothing but absorb his essence, which has transferred itself through the pads of his fingers over the textured grip. Head bent, I'm cloaked in my own world. I tell myself if I can survive the hellaciousness of my past, I can survive anything. Even this. With that in the forefront of my mind, I turn the playback display on.

And immediately let out a gasp.

Joe has the camera extended from his left arm. He's lying in the middle of his bed with nothing on but a sheet. His right arm is tucked beneath him. The pose is sensual, but it's the look on his face that's captivating me. It's his lower lip that's being caught beneath his teeth, the hint of a blush riding his cheekbones, the worry in his eyes.

The picture is screaming at me wordlessly, asking me if after everything if the man in the image is enough.

For me.

"Oh, my God," I breathe.

Quickly, I scroll back through the photos to get to the beginning. Damn, it's like a reverse flip book where the character dances in the corner of the page. Only this is a reverse striptease or in my case a reverse open-heart surgery without any anesthetic.

When I reach the first shot Joe took, I zoom in as close as I can as on his face reflected in the mirror. There's nothing hidden from me. He's daring me to pretend I can't see everything he's feeling at that moment: anxious, afraid, terrified that he ruined our friendship, lust, and something else that has tears burning in the back of my eyes.

Lowering my camera onto the table, I put my head into my hands. Rubbing my head to ease the pain, I feel an ache in my chest. This wasn't supposed to happen. We were just supposed to be friends.

How did we both wind up getting lost in each other?

Now, what am I supposed to? Even though he knows some of everything, he doesn't know it all. After seeing the blooming love on his face for me—and God, I recognize it as often as I've taken photos of my in-laws staring at my siblings—how do I handle it when he turns away because of the rest of my past? Our past?

My chest heaves as I try to hold in the sobs desperate to break free. Blindly, I reach for my phone. Unlocking it with my thumb, I quickly pull up my Favorites.

One ring. Two.

Cassidy's sweet voice answers. "Hols? What's wrong?"

I get out a single word, "Amaryllis," before the tears start to leak from my eyes. I don't know that anyone in our family has ever said it —the one word to tell our family to stop whatever it is they're doing and come to wherever we are. It means the person who says it is essentially dying—emotionally or physically—the way Amaryllis did out of love for Alteo each time she pierced her heart with the golden arrow to give him that which he most desired.

Right now, I'm saying it because I'm the one broken and bleeding. I hurt so badly because I can't go any further with my life of lies on my conscience.

Not when I'm falling in love.

"Where are you?" she demands.

"The Coffee Shop," I whisper.

"I'll be right there," she says, right before she disconnects.

A few minutes later, Cassidy strides past the waning crowd. Ava opens her mouth to greet her but changes her mind at the frightened look on Cassidy's face. My knee is bouncing up and down under the table. I'm sick to my stomach.

Much like Joe did, Cassidy immediately reaches for my hand. "Who knows, Holly?"

My response comes out jumbled. "No one knows. It's who I want —no, need—no, want... God, I can't do this without him knowing everything." Even as I find a spot of ketchup on the wall immensely intriguing, I feel my sister's finger's tightening.

"Joe." It's not a question. My head snaps around, and my lips part. Her lips soften into a smile. "I think the only two people who didn't realize your relationship was becoming something more were the two of you."

I let out a small moan. If I'm this transparent to my family, what must I have said or done in front of Joe...

"Absolutely nothing," she tells me, mortifying me further when I realize I must have spoken out loud. "Holly, you—"

"Scoot over," Ali interrupts us.

Cassidy scowls. "What are you doing here? I told you I had this handled."

"And I told you there's no way in hell you'll be able to handle this on your own."

Despite my own heartache, I can't help the corners of my lips lifting. Automatically, I reach for my camera, but Ali presses my hand down gently.

"No, Hols. Not now." I blink uncomprehendingly.

"You're finally taking steps to stop hiding behind a past that held you back from living," Cassidy whispers. "Tell him whatever you need to, baby."

"But Phil, Em, Cori..." I rattle off my siblings' names even as Ali begins to shake her head.

"We're all in agreement, Hols. Nothing can hurt us now. Caleb and Keene have done everything possible to make it so our pasts ceased to exist."

Cassidy nods in agreement. "If this is the burden holding you back from a miracle, let us help you cut the straps to release it."

My hand begins to tremble beneath Ali's. "What if he walks away? I told him about some of it last night..."

"And where was he today, Hols?" Cassidy presses. Her fingers tap the now cold cup of coffee in front of her.

I shrug my shoulders weakly. "This—our story—we're so much more."

Ali leans her head on Cassidy's shoulder briefly. "Of course. Because together, we're everything."

With my sister's simple words, the panic begins to recede. "Yeah. We are."

Ali's fingers dance lightly over my amaryllis tattoo. "Strength, Hols. You have more than your fair share of it. And remember, you have all of ours if you need to lean on it."

"I don't think you're going to need much though," Cassidy interjects. "Joe's not a fool. He's had love and lost it. He already knows what the worst-case scenario is in this situation."

"What's that?" I whisper. For me, it's imagining the revulsion on Joe's face as I tell him our family history.

"Losing someone he loves. Again. Only this time, it will be his fault."

44

JOSEPH

I've been waiting at the house for hours since I left Holly at The Coffee Shop. There's been nothing from her—not a text or a call.

Pacing back and forth in the room where she bared so much of herself to me the night before, I groan aloud. What if I was wrong? What if she can't forgive me? *Then you find a way to break through*, I tell myself firmly. *You don't give up at the first challenge.* Like the love I had for Mary, the love I have for Grace, the feelings Holly generates in me are complex and endless. And I can't let them go.

Standing in front of the fireplace, I realize the pain I usually feel when I look at the picture of Mary and Grace isn't there, although the sadness will always linger at a beautiful life cut way too short. "I'll always miss you," I tell her honestly, my fingers gently tracing the edges of the frame. "There won't be a day some part of me won't. You gave me a miracle that kept me going in the long years it's taken me to recover from your death, but..." My voice gets thick. "But my feelings for Holly are different, Mar. Probably because I'm different. I'm not the same man you fell for. A part of me will always love you. But I have to move on, Mar. I've been fighting my feelings for Holly because..."

I'm so caught up in trying to vocalize my emotions to my dead fiancée that I never heard the storm door open. I jump, almost knocking the frame off the mantle when I hear Holly's voice complete my thought. "Because feeling leaves you vulnerable to everything you've managed to protect yourself against." Her golden eyes are damp as if she's been crying, but they're filled with an understanding that relaxes something deep inside of me.

My hand slides away from the frame, but I don't move toward her. I sense the distance is by her design. Cold whispers across my neck, not from any chill in the spring air. "Yes."

She swallows. Even from this distance, I can see her eyes begin to water. "Did I ruin everything?" I rasp. I'm tortured, tormented, to think between last night and right now I've hurt this woman who has made me realize that love is worth anything, even walking through fire.

Especially if she's standing through the wall of flames on the other side.

"No." Her head drops. I watch her rub her hand against her tattoo back and forth before her head snaps up with determination. "But I might."

My heart stops in my chest. "What do you mean?"

"I am so much more than what I told you last night. About who I am. No," she corrects herself. "We are. And before you become any more involved than you already are, you'll know it all."

I let out a deep breath. "Why do I have a feeling I should sit for this?"

Her golden eyes are dulled. "I'd recommend it."

I cross to the couch and drop down onto it, and Holly shifts so she's standing in front of me. She doesn't realize it, but with every-thing she's managed to instill in me about photography in the last few months, she's doesn't know she's standing in my ideal photo. Mary's picture is on the mantel, just far enough away to be out of focus over Holly's left shoulder. Holly's standing in front of me, vibrant and full of energy with her leg thrown out to the side in the final third of the "frame." My past, my present, and my future, all are coalescing together inside my heart. Something that had been tightening inside of me releases. No matter what she's about to tell me, I know it's going to be okay.

It has to be because it can't be any other way.

"Holly?" Startled, she jumps a bit. She's frightened, and I wish I could ease that fear with something other than words. "Talk to me."

"Before I begin, I need to ask you to promise me something." My eyes drop down to her full lips. If it involves my lips on hers, that will be an easy promise to make.

"Joe!" she snaps, but she can't prevent her lips twitching.

"Crap, I really need to learn to control that inside voice," I mutter.

"As Grace is getting older, it might help," she murmurs. "Otherwise you're going to be answering a whole host of...wait. Where is she, Joe?" Holly becomes agitated. "The things I need to tell you, she shouldn't overhear."

And just like that, my heart knows it's taken the fall into love for the second time in my life. "I dropped her off at school before I met up with you. I hoped, prayed actually, that you'd come to see me after looking at your camera," I admit.

Even though I showed a hell of a lot of my own vulnerability on that camera, Holly's face crumbles further. "Joe, last night you seemed so appalled..." Her voice trails off.

I surge to my feet. "I was—*am*—appalled," I correct myself. Grabbing her close, I don't let go when she half-heartedly tries to push me away. "I'm shocked at what you had to live through, and at the level of desperation you reached. I never saw it from the victim's side before," I admit painfully. She sags in my arms in relief. "What kind of pain did you live with day after day to reach that point?" I run one hand through her thick, burnished hair. I feel her body shudder against mine. I feel a desperate need to lay my lips upon hers, to seal what's building between us.

Her next words drive all thoughts of that out of my mind when I fully absorb the load she's been carrying.

"We all had some level of horror to that degree, Joe." She pulls back and her face is blank. "All of us. We're not a family through blood or through legal adoption. We're a family because we found one another through pain, through agony, and through a twisted fate that intersected our lives at just the right moment. And we fought to hold on when life wanted to tear us apart."

My head is spinning with what her words imply. "All..."

She pulls out of my arms and holds up her wrist. Her amaryllis tattoo is glorious in the rich red color against her pale skin. "All of us who bear this mark," she informs me quietly. "Every. Single. Freeman."

My head spins, and I'm nauseated at the implications. "How did a system fail so many children for so long?"

Her smile is sad. "Not everyone is a hero. Not everyone is even a human. Some people are just so horrific, they should be categorized as monsters and thrown into a cage." And with that extraordinarily sage statement, Holly launches into the Freeman family history.

Learning about Phil and Cassidy's history of abuse before they managed to escape only to be found by Em and her aunt in a park, bleeding and clinging to one another as the anchor in each other's world when Cassidy was just a few years older than Grace is soul crushing. I'm astounded to hear about how Emily's aunt raised all of them only to die suddenly and how the three of them fought to remain together before the older sisters declared themselves as emancipated minors. My knees lock so I can stay standing when I hear about Ali's father, the perpetrator of the most massive human trafficking ring in US history. Then Holly tells me about how she, Corinna, and Ali were each sold by their families for drug money, how they were locked into a shipping container for months before they were rescued.

I want to go to her, but Holly's wrapped her arms tight around herself as she talks about the days the three girls huddled together after their rescue and the additional worry she endured as she waited to find out whether she would be serving time for involuntary manslaughter. Her voice breaks as she tells me how she got her name —from a woman who finally fought for her in a world that never took a stand for her. For any of them.

My heart pounding hard in my chest, I realize Phil Freeman is more than just a brother; he's a goddamned miracle. He could have quickly fallen into the darkness of his own violent brutality, and what would have happened to any of them then? And as her voice begins to go hoarse, I realize the only reason she'd ever share this is because she's doing exactly what I did last night through the camera lens.

She's baring it all to me because her heart is in just as deep as mine. My own rolls over in my chest in reaction.

"Why?" I rasp after her voice finally goes quiet.

"Why what?" she responds.

"Why do you think it would matter?" I lift her wrist, covered in beautiful, glorious red ink more binding than any legal document, to my lips. Since the story of the amaryllis legend was part of her explanation, I completely agree with Phil's assessment of his family. Strength, beauty, and pride—each member of the Freeman family has it in spades.

None more so than my Holly.

She blinks up at me. "How could it not?"

I lay my thumb upon her lips. "Hols, what you just told me infuriates me." She stiffens in my arms. I shake her. "For you. For all of you. But there isn't a person alive who would blame any of you for what you had to endure to survive. Did you think I was going to turn you away?"

Her eyes slide away, giving me my answer. And not so slowly, my anger builds.

"For God's sake!" I explode, letting her go to begin pacing. Holly leans back against the arm of the chair as I let loose my temper. I barely take notice. "Not everyone who cares about you is going to let you down. Not everyone is going to hurt you."

"I know." Her voice is calm as the lake outside the Freeman farm.

"Then what kind of reaction were you expecting? For me to denounce you? To walk away?"

"Not after Cassidy and Ali talked some sense into me," she admits. "After they calmed my fears and reminded me I have the strength to stand on my own. It took me a bit, but I realized that a man who was willing to expose his own vulnerability needed to know I trusted him with my own." She pushes up from the arm of my couch to stand right in front of me. Her hand reaches up to touch my jaw. "I saw what was in your eyes, Joe," she whispers. "I saw the tenderness, the..."

"Fear that I fucked everything up after I was trying to fix it," I whisper, slowly sliding my hands around her back. "I think I'd rather face a fire burning out of control than ever see you walk out on me like that ever again."

A smile dances around her mouth. "Let's hope you don't have to do that anytime soon, okay? Even though I had Grace to distract me, it's still going to take a while to get used to you being called out and the worry."

I bow my head to rest on hers in reverence. A whoosh of breath leaves me. This woman will bring me to my knees by her fiery strength and devastating valor. If more men and women on this planet had it, then I'd worry less about the world I'm raising Grace in.

Slowly, I skim my hands up over her back, my hands large enough that my thumbs ripple over each of her ribs. As they graze the underside of her breasts, Holly's eyelids flutter at the sensation. Her reaction tells me this is going to be exquisitely beautiful. The fire we have growing between us isn't going to flicker out; it's going to dance and flash. But if I have the choice, I might never put it out.

"The first time I kissed you, you thought I was drunk," I murmur. Her breasts heave against my hands.

"I thought you figured it was a mistake," she whispers scant inches from my lips. I shake my head from side to side.

"Never that, Holly. I thought I ruined everything between us. On top of that, it was the first time in years..." I don't finish the thought. Mary has no place in what's about to occur between Holly and me. Besides, I made my peace with my past before Holly arrived earlier.

"And now?" Her bright gold eyes hold mine captive.

"Now, I'm not caught between the past and the present. I'm tied up in knots over the present and the future." I brush my lips along her jaw.

"Why?" Her voice is breathless.

I drop my head to the prominent blueish vein on her neck next and allow my lips to trace it. "It's hard enough for a man to admit he hasn't kissed a woman in so long. But—" I pull back and meet her dazed face head-on. "—it's next to impossible to admit the fact that..."

Holly slides her hands up my chest, distracting me. I swallow. Hard.

"I'm trying to explain—"

She interrupts me. "That what I'm about to feel in your arms is everything I saw in those pictures?" And just that simply, Holly erases all of my fears as quickly as I removed hers.

"Yeah," I growl right before I pull her body tightly into mine. My lips crush down on hers, and she responds instantly.

Instead of the olive-infused vodka that painted her lips the first night—the night we lost Justin to the mouth of the beast—all I taste is the pure sweetness of Holly and the remnants of the coffee she was drinking earlier. I sip from her lips slowly, my tongue tracing them lightly to gain entrance. As her lips part, I plunder in. Our tongues touch and retreat, igniting what we've held at bay for so long.

One of my hands finds purchase in her hair, holding her head steady as I slip a leg between hers. Rocking her hips into mine, I know there's been no moment in the last three years as perfect as this one.

45

HOLLY

J oe slides his hands from around my ribs to under my arms. Lifting me quickly, he fits me to his frame. Breaking the kiss, he walks us backward toward the couch a few feet, before dropping me down and covering my body with his own.

Feeling the weight of his lean muscle over my body sets my body trembling. From the tips of my fingers down to my toes, I can't control the emotion.

"What is it, Hols?" Joe's lips whisper across my cheek as they mark every inch of my face. They're just not where I want them—fully locked with mine.

"Joe..." My voice comes out as a breathless moan. His soft laugh is his gentle reply.

"This first time, I want to savor every inch of your skin. I need to make you tremble beneath me." Lifting his head, he then proceeds to wreck me. "I want to make sure you never again forget the beauty of this—" He touches my head. "—and what comes out of these." He brushes my lips. "You need to remember this is precious to me." He rests his hand in between my breasts on my heart. "The fact it beats against my hand is a miracle."

"I..." I'm at a loss for words. Then his hand shifts over my breast. I arc into him, moaning.

Leaning down, he presses his lips against the tip of my breast. "I knew you wouldn't have been here if you didn't forgive me, but I need to apologize. Forgive me for not opening up when I should have, for not admitting my feelings changed, and most importantly, for hurting you over and over again."

Lifting my hand to rest it in his thick dark hair, I tug him back up. Holding his face captive, I whisper out my own confession, "Only if you accept mine. My feelings changed so long ago, I can't remember when I wasn't holding back. And I know my pulling away..."

Joe rears his head out of my hands. "How long ago?"

My mind blanks. "How long ago, what?"

Leaning so close his nose brushes mine, he whispers, "How long ago did your feelings change?"

Without thinking, I blurt out, "Since the day we went to go see that god-awful movie together."

A slow smile tips his lips up at the corners. Laying them on top of mine, he whispers, "Then don't you think we should stop wasting time?"

Wrapping my arms around his neck, I open my mouth to answer but find my lips taken in a slow kiss. Shifting, I hitch my leg up alongside his leg. Joe shifts to align the rigid length of his cock in the notch of my legs.

I break the kiss to arch against him. "Ahh."

He trails kisses along my neck while grinding himself into me. "That can't possibly feel as good to you as it does to me."

I grab one of his hands and pull it to my breast where my nipples have tightened considerably. "Bet you're wrong," I tease gently. It's me who's left gasping when he rolls the hardened nub between his thumb and forefinger.

Moaning, I score my fingers down his back. Twisting in his hold, I expose the cord of my neck. Joe rakes his teeth down it gently, eliciting goose bumps all over my skin. "So good," I whisper.

"It's going to feel even better," he murmurs back. My lips are

captured in another long, drugging kiss. My mind clears of everything except for one thing: the man who's become my best friend is
about to become my lover. It sends a tidal wave of emotions surging
through me. I clutch Joe around the neck and bury my head in the
crook of his shoulder. I do something completely unexpected.

I start sobbing.

"Hols? Honey, tell me what's wrong?" Joe's body freezes above me.

I shake my head. "Nothing. That's just it. Absolutely nothing. I
just couldn't be more..." I search for the right word.

"What?" He resumes stroking my arms, my cheek, brushing away
the tears.

"Amazed. I never pictured you'd..." His soft laugh interrupts me.

"For someone who sees everything as clearly as you do, you
weren't looking." I blush to the roots of my hair. "Then again, neither
was I." Joe presses his lips against mine, separating mine with a brush
of his tongue.

For long minutes, our mouths speak for us. Without words, I tell
him of my disbelief and wonder. He tells me of his acceptance and
adoration. We sip each other's unspoken happiness from the other's
lips, feeling nothing but joy in each other. Finally, he tears his mouth
from mine.

"Holly, I want to take my time running my hands and my mouth
all over your body. Is that what you want too?" Husky, his voice still
holds a note of anxiety.

I slide my hands under his shirt. "Do I get to help you lose a few
clothes in the process?"

His dark blue eyes almost turn black they go so dark. His
fingers skim over my exposed skin above my jeans. "I want to touch
you."

My answer is to roll my hips up into his as I pull his head down
for another kiss. "You already are."

"More," he demands.

A teasing smile crosses my face. "Are you sure you're up for that?"

My laugh is pure joy when Joe pushes up off my body, yanking me
to my feet. "Is that a challenge, Ms. Freeman?" Even though he

sounds mortally offended, both of his dimples are out. His eyes are shining in the way I've only ever seen him look at Grace.

And now, he is smiling at me that way.

Please, God, let this work, I pray desperately. "It sure is, Mr. Bianco," I flirt back openly.

I have a half a heartbeat to prepare before I'm in a fireman's hold over Joe's shoulder. "Joe!" I screech. Laughing, I pummel his back as he makes his way down the hall.

"It's time for you to go to your room, young lady," he says sternly. But Joe can't quite keep the laughter out of his own voice.

"Have I been bad?" I ask cheekily as we pass through the doorway to the master, a room I became intimate with earlier when I was examining the dark gray and white motif on my camera as Joe lay exposed on the sheets.

Once I'm in front of him, my hair is brushed away from my face by his long fingers. There's a subtle tremble to them. "No," he whispers. Lowering his head, I rise up on my toes to meet his descending lips. "I never thought I'd ever find someone like you."

"But..." Joe lays a finger across my lips, preventing me from saying what we both already know: *You already had someone in your life to love.*

"I've loved and the part of me that did died." My heart deflates hearing those words. I can't hold my head up knowing that I'll never have all of him but knowing I'll accept it because even a part of this man is worth all of any of the others I've ever met. He catches my chin and forces my eyes back up to his. "I never thought I'd find someone who I wanted to live for, Holly."

My breath catches.

"Yeah." Joe runs his fingers through my hair, deliberately twisting his fingers in the length before letting it go. He skims his hands down my back and rests them on my hips. Catching my shirt under the hem, he begins to lift it. "You can imagine the shock I felt when I realized the feelings I had for my 'friend' weren't that friendly." His rough hands brush against each of my ribs, sending chills dancing along my skin. Within seconds, my shirt's whipped over my head and my hair floats back down to my shoulders.

Then I'm clutching against him as he takes my knees out with mere words. "Every second of agony it took us to get here? I'd do it all over again as long as I knew I'd get to hold you against my heart."

"Joe," I whisper. I'm unable to get words past the clogged feeling in my throat. I'm grateful he doesn't seem to need them.

Ripping off his long-sleeve white tee, he yanks me into his body before capturing my lips again. I wrap my arms around his neck, pressing my breasts against his hair-roughened chest. My nipples harden inside the cups of silk covering them as they rub against the rough abrasion of his chest hair. Breaking our kiss, my hair cascades down my back over his arms that band me against him.

"So beautiful," he whispers. "Never anything like you before. So delicate, strong, and..."

"What?" I whisper as I run my fingers through his hair. Tipping his head back, I lean down and kiss his brow, his eyes, his nose, before brushing my lips against his.

Joe reaches behind me for the clasp of my bra. "A miracle," he murmurs. "Every inch of you is a gift." He stands to his full height. "But the inches that are the most precious are those that sit right here." Pulling back slightly, he runs his fingers along my collarbone and then gently down between my breasts. He cups the weight gently in his hand.

My head falls forward and crashes into his chest. I hear the breath escape his mouth as I scrape my nails lightly down his chest. I open my mouth and press my lips over the part of him that blew past my defenses.

His heart.

"Holly." His tortured groan makes me bolder. My eyes flick upward. His head is bowed down toward mine, his fingers trailing up and down my arms. "I love how you feel against me."

"I want you to feel it all," I breathe against his skin. Seconds later, I'm airborne before landing against his firm bed. I barely have a chance to get my bearings when I feel him crawl up my body, his hard, warm body in direct contrast to the crisp sheets beneath me.

Our legs tangle together; our hands and lips are roaming on each other's bodies as we roll across his expansive bed. Joe pins me face-down and begins nuzzling the nape of my neck, sending chills down my spine. I arch my back, trying to push my shoulders tighter against his chest when suddenly, his control snaps.

Flipping me onto my back, he growls, "Lose your shoes," as he begins to attack my belt feverishly.

All too willing to comply, I pry off my flats, kicking them some-where. His hands slowly skim from my shoulders down gently over my breasts, my stomach, which quivers under his touch, until he reaches the snap of my jeans.

I might pass out from how hard I'm panting. The nights I dreamed of him touching me don't come close to the feel of his hands burning through my skin. The desperate longing in his eyes obliter-ates anything my imagination tried to conjure in my sleep. The heat of his mouth on my skin causes me to writhe against his sheets, help-less to anything but the feel of this man, this moment.

This love.

"Faster, baby," I whisper, encouraging him to pick up the pace. But my body reacts with a head-to-toe shiver beneath the slow perusal he gives me once he's stripped my jeans off and tossed them off to the side of the bed, leaving me in nothing but a pair of damp silk panties I would do just about anything to have melt away.

Joe trails his fingers lazily over the skin of my ankle, up and over my knee, until gravity forces him over me again. Now, the abrasion of his jeans against my inner thighs causes me to whimper.

It's not enough.

I rock my hips up against him. He thrusts me back into the bed. Lowering his head, he captures a beaded nipple into his mouth before flicking it with his tongue. Then he holds it to the roof of his mouth before rolling it with his tongue. Then, I groan aloud as he nips at it before sucking it deep. Soon, he switches to my other nipple to deliver the same delicious torment. I can't stand it.

I cry out, "Oh my God!" before my fingers holding his head in place tighten almost to the point of pain. My hips are furiously rolling into him, seeking relief.

He doesn't make me wait.

Joe lifts one hand up to my mouth, slipping his thumb between my lips. I suck on it greedily before he pulls it out and yanks at my panties. Without losing my gaze, he moves his fingers in, curling them against my front wall, his thumb brushing against my clit simultaneously.

I detonate.

My head flies forward against his shoulder, and I bite down. Hard. Laving my tongue against him, I mark him as surely as he's branding me.

Mine. It's all I can think as Joe's fingers prolong the waves of my orgasm with their slow thrust in and out of my body. His head turns from where it was buried in the pillow, and his lips find mine again. After our lips break away slightly, he whispers, "You're beautiful, sweetheart."

I blush. "I always wondered how far that blush went." His eyes travel the length of my body before they raise back up to mine. "And now I know." I shake my head.

"Is that all you want?" I lift my hips. His face darkens, and he swallows hard.

"No."

Sliding a hand over his flank, I pull him closer. "Do you want to know what I want to know?"

His breath wafts over my face as he leans in. "Yes."

My lips are touching his when I whisper, "If your body being connected to mine is going to feel as good as the nights I dreamed about it."

46

JOSEPH

I feel her hands run up my sides as I brace myself over her body. I'm panting as Holly reaches for the snap of my jeans and slowly lowers the zipper. Doing so, she frees more than just my cock. She releases me from the idea that I might fail her. I slide my arms beneath her as my cock falls into her waiting hands.

Almost greedily, her fingers reach beneath my boxers and begin stroking gently, learning every ridge, bump, and vein along the way. I push myself deeper into her grip, letting out a long growl.

Shoving against my shoulder, the woman who has become my heart rolls me to my back and begins pulling down my own jeans. Since I was barefoot waiting for her, it only takes lifting my hips slightly for her to yank my pants over my hips.

And suddenly I'm exposed, body and soul.

Yanking her on top of me, I ignore the stirrings of my body as I capture her lips in a searing kiss. Even as my hands roam her smooth skin, I feel hers run over mine. It seems everywhere I touch, she returns the favor. It's heightening my own arousal to the point I can barely contain myself from throwing her onto the bed and pounding into her. Instead, I roll her to her back and firmly kiss her, leaving us both breathless.

"Hols, sweetheart, I can't take much more of that," I gasp.

"Then take what we need," she pleads.

What we need. Her words settle the ball of anxiety warring with desire in my gut. I push up on my elbow, hovering over her and admiring the way her hair fans out on my pillow, and whisper, "I can't believe you're going to be mine."

Blinking rapidly, her hand comes up and cups my jaw. "I've been yours for a while, Joe. It's just neither of us was ready for it."

"I'm ready now." I nudge my hips against hers. "Are you?"

She nods. I slide one of my legs in between hers. My cock becomes coated with her as I glide it against her center over and over. Holly's eyes melt before they ignite, just like I've seen a fire do when it's about to explode into uncontrollable flames.

On an upward glide, the leaking from the tip of my cock brushes her inner thigh. She shudders in response, tiny little bumps raising all over her skin. I lean down and nip her shoulder. "How did I get so lucky?" I wonder aloud.

"I don't know, but if you don't come inside me soon, I might combust. I mean it."

I grin down at her before I become very serious. "Hols, I haven't... I mean, I know you have... Is it safe?" Shit. How am I supposed to ask her about this when I don't really want to know about any other man. "I don't have anything here to protect you," I finally blurt out.

I swear I can hear my heartbeat thud in my head as I wait for her response.

I don't have to wait long.

Holly pushes at my shoulder. "Sit up." When I'm sitting cross-legged on the bed, she straddles my legs. Gripping my shoulders tightly, she lowers herself down until her pussy hugs my cock. Rocking back and forth on me, her face tips up to mine. I let her take control of the kiss as I'm desperately clutching her hips so I don't lose her slick warmth.

"I have an IUD. And I haven't been with anyone in close to a year," she whispers against my lips. "We're protected if you're comfortable with..."

I nudge the head of my cock inside on the next glide. "Is this enough of a response?"

Her moan is my only answer. Slowly, I release the pressure on her slender hips. Soon, I'm buried deep inside Holly's warmth, and tears spring to my eyes.

"What is it?" she whispers. Her face is so close to mine, there's no way she didn't notice the moisture spilling down my cheeks.

"It...you...so damn right," I manage to choke out. I wrap my arms around her as tightly as I can. I'm not trying to thrust into her; I'm not even sure I can. I just want to absorb her into me so I can never let her go.

"I feel the same way." Our foreheads collide. Slowly, I rock her backward. Call it instinct, but the movement doesn't thrust into her hard. All it does is gently force me deeper into her already filled channel. But at the same time, it somehow manages to nudge her turgid clit. Holly gasps.

Wrapping her arms and legs tighter around me, she rocks back. Her body is flush against mine, our lips connected, and our hearts are touching.

Perfect.

Back and forth, just the way our relationship grew, we guide each other to a culmination that has me burying my head into the side of her neck, groaning with her head tossed back as her inner walls clamp down on me hard. Long moments later, still wrapped in each other's arms, I hear her whisper, "The world could end, and I'd finally be happy."

If it's possible, I tighten my arms around her even more as I slide out of her slowly before I fall back against the pillows with her clutched against my heart.

I'm never letting this woman go.

Never.

I'll do everything in my power to make sure she understands I plan on going to my grave with her name being the one that crosses my lips.

47

HOLLY

"What are you so nervous about?" Joe asks as he reaches for my hand. Hours later after he's explored every inch of my body, we're headed to pick Grace up at school. I can't stop my leg from bouncing in the seat next to him. "It's not like she's going to take one look at us and tell all her little friends, 'Daddy and my Holly were k-i-s-s-i-n-g,'" he mocks me slightly.

I glare at him, even if he doesn't get the full impact since his eyes are on the road. "No, but Ali might be there," I remind him. "And my sister is a hell of a lot more astute than you give her credit for."

"Hols, if it were up to me, I'd rent a billboard on Route 7 and announce that you're mine." I freeze at his words.

"Really?" I whisper. "What about..." My voice trails off.

"What about what?"

I hesitate to bring them up, but we were a little distracted earlier. "Seth and Eden?" I say hesitantly.

There's a heavy silence that descends in the cab of the Explorer. Joe's knuckles turn white on the steering wheel, he's gripping it so hard. Damn.

"They don't have a place in my life, Holly, nor in Grace's."

I'm confused. "Then why were you..."

"Because they threatened your family." I suck in a breath at the bitterness in Joe's words. "I couldn't let anything happen to you."

"Joe," I whisper achingly. "You were trying to protect me?"

He pulls up to a stoplight and faces me. "During lunch that day, I had it all planned out. I was going to see if you still were interested in perma-single status or if there was someone who might be able to change your mind."

My hand is shaking when I raise it to my mouth.

"But then I screwed up," he continues matter-of-factly.

"We both screwed up. I was so consumed with the fact you didn't want me," I say achingly.

He shakes his head. "Not want you." The light turns green. "At first I relished our friendship, Hols. It really was just that." Glancing over, he catches my nod. "But as I said, it began changing. How I began to feel was like there were no limits, no rules. I think for the first time in years, what I felt was hope."

My throat goes tight because what Joe's saying is exactly what I've been feeling. "Me too," I whisper.

"Were you going to say anything?"

And that's when I have to take a deep breath and possibly break his heart. "No."

He's silent until we pull into the parking lot of Grace's school. Putting the car in park, he turns to face me. "Why not?"

I tug my lip between my teeth. Just as quickly, his hand comes out and pulls it out. Quirking his lips in a half smile, he says, "I want to be able to kiss those lips later."

Shocked, I blurt out, "But Grace will be there!"

He leans forward and tugs the back of my neck, pulling me close so the only thing I see is his dark eyes. "Tell me why you weren't going to say anything," he demands.

"Because I was afraid of telling you what I was."

"Why?"

"I was afraid of exactly what happened last night. I knew I wasn't good enough—clean enough—for you, for Grace. Hope was all I had. As long as I kept it alive, then it was enough to live on. When that started to go away, I thought I was going to die from the pain," I whisper helplessly. "I never realized you could actually be alive and still be dying until I saw you with someone else."

His eyes close in pain. "I swear I never meant to hurt you..."

I lean until our foreheads are touching. "I know. Now."

"You went from being my friend to more. I didn't realize it was self-defense being unable to open myself up to being that vulnerable until I realized you were walking away last night and I thought it was for good."

"It almost was," I admit. "I finally realized I deserved love."

He shudders against me. "Thank God."

Pulling back, I meet resistance when his hand stops me. "What?"

"Thank God you realize you deserve love. Because I'm going to spend a hell of a long time making you understand this isn't a game I'm playing, Holly."

My heart thuds wildly in my chest.

"I don't know exactly how it happened, but I refuse to fight against these feelings anymore. I already know I've been blessed with finding three women in my life where the fall seems almost effortless."

"Three?" I choke out.

"Mary." His fingers move away from my neck, and I mourn the loss. "Grace." They cup my chin and pull my face closer than it already is. "And you," he says, right before he kisses me in full view of anyone passing by. My mind is so scrambled by his words and his lips on mine, I forget where we are until there's a tap on the window. It sounds like a woodpecker, but in my lifting daze, I realize woodpeckers don't peck against glass. Just wood.

Oh crap.

"What'cha doin', Aunt Howee?" Kalie yells, her voice muffled through the glass. Turning my head, I find Ali standing there holding my precious niece in her arms, a serene smile on her face. I can almost hear the "Told you so" transmitting from the broad smile on her face.

I guess I don't need to worry about her reaction. I smile shakily.

She shakes her head and motions for me to roll down the window. "Too bad Miss Tiffany is out sick. I'd pay money for you to repeat that kiss when you pick up Grace," my sister says mischievously.

Joe laughs while I flush to the roots of my hair. "You're such a brat," I grouse.

"No, I'm overwhelmingly happy. We'll see you both at family dinner tomorrow night, Joe?" Ali queries.

Oh shit. Family dinner. I throw myself back into my seat with a groan.

"What is it, sweetheart? I already know everyone. It can't be that bad."

Together Ali and I both say, "Yes, it can."

Joe pales a little. I regain a bit of my equilibrium and laugh. Turning to Ali, I ask, "I get camera rights."

"Hell no, you don't. Someone will be taking pictures, but it won't be you, baby girl."

I glare at her. "Go away. I'm not speaking to you."

"For now. Tomorrow, I'll be your best ally against Phil, and you know it." Unfortunately, I know Ali's right. I flap my hand at her, and she shoots us her dazzling smile before turning to put Kalie in her car seat.

I call out, "Ali?" She turns. "Thank you for everything. You know I love you, right?"

Her eyes well up. "I didn't have a doubt, baby." Before I start bawling, I quickly roll up the window.

Turning back to Joe, I'm not surprised when he reaches for my hand. I am surprised when he asks, "Why do they call you baby girl?" His thumb brushes across my knuckles.

Smiling, I return the gesture and explain our family pecking order conceding with, "As the youngest, I think they've always been protective of me."

Lifting my hand to his lips, he whispers his lips across my fingers. "I love you had that."

"Me too."

"I want that for Grace."

I rear back in shock. "What?"

"I want her to have brothers, sisters, cousins that she's close to like your family is. Sometimes it was lonely growing up an only child."

"What are you saying?" I whisper, exalted and terrified at the same time. I'm sure he sees both on my face because the intensity on his face gentles.

"Nothing more than I love where we're going, Holly. If I have to get through a family dinner of a different sort to do it, so be it." He opens his door. "Wait for me. One of the things you need to learn about me is that I help my girl out."

My heart melts as I see him stride around the front of his Explorer. *My girl.*

There's no way he didn't understand the way those words affected me as I was in his arms kissing him the minute the door opened.

God, let this be right. Let this be what you meant for me to deserve.

Pulling away, Joe brushes his nose against mine before he grips my hand and tugs me toward the entrance of the school. "Come on. If we have time, I want to add you to the list of people authorized to pick up Grace."

Right now, you couldn't break the smile on my face even if I was confronted with the censure of the entire town over my relationship with this man.

48

JOSEPH

"You weren't kidding when you said I'd be on the hot seat," I whisper to Holly the next night.

She shakes her head slowly, not taking her narrowed eyes away from her brother.

Phil has been nothing but an unmitigated ass to me since Holly, Grace, and I came in thirty minutes ago. Unfortunately, he's not alone. All of the Freeman spouses, fiancés, and Charlie—the man I met at the bar during the fund-raiser—are all engaged in a third degree that makes the exam I'm preparing for to make lieutenant a breeze.

There's one thing I know for sure: Holly is loved and well protected.

Curled into my side, she goes to open her mouth, but I jostle her. Shaking my head, I murmur, "Let me handle it, sweetheart."

"This is a bunch of macho bullshit crap," she declares loud enough for everyone in the room to hear.

Phil takes her to task. "Hols, the children. Such language."

She screams. Literally lets out a banshee cry and lurches from my arms to go after her brother. "You're going to end tonight thinking the best thing that ever happened to you is Em spitting in your face," she yells.

Phil laughs at her. "Please, like you didn't expect this?"

"Some hazing to welcome him into the fold, yes. The complete and utter crap you're throwing at him about why it took him so long to get his head out of his ass? No," she declares.

Colby holds up his hands in mock surrender. "I'm out. If I keep on giving her man grief, Holly's likely to withhold her banana pudding."

"Smart man, Colby," she returns. "You know I will."

Keene and Caleb just laugh. Caleb says, "I'm particular about my kind of sweet."

Keene gives him a look of disgust. "Seriously, that's my sister you're talking about."

Phil tacks on, "And mine. For Christ's sake."

I turn to Holly. "I think you missed something in your rundown of the family before we came over. You forgot to mention Phil and Keene are biological brothers."

There's a deadly silence across the great room. Suddenly, the whole place erupts with screeching laughter. Cassidy and Ali are holding each other up even as they have their daughters wrapped around their legs begging to be lifted. Corinna flings the knife she was wielding across the counter and lays her head down into whatever she was chopping. Emily spews her drink right into Phil's face—not that anyone but Phil seems to care. Caleb, Colby, and Jake are grinning while Keene shoots me a look filled with such filth I should need a shower to remove the dirt.

And Holly—my beautiful Holly—is doubled over with laughter.

It's Charlie and Jason who explain.

"Actually, Keene is Cassidy's biological brother," Jason calmly explains. "Not Phil and Keene."

"Not by a long shot," Phil interjects. Jason hushes his husband.

"They didn't know when Caleb and Cass first started dating," Charlie adds. "Keene was kind of..."

"Rude. The word is rude, Charlie," Cassidy chimes in. Keene

glares at his sister. Now that I'm aware, I see the resemblance in the shape of their eyes, their noses, and their smiles.

"It's their coloring that throws most people off, Joe," Holly explains once she's regained her breath. "Unlike this one who is basically a perfect clone of you and Mary—" She swings Grace up into her arms. "—Keene favors their mother whereas Cass has their father's coloring."

I want to ask how all of the atrocities happened to Cassidy when Keene is so obviously protective of those he cares about, but before I can, Charlie mutters, "It's a long story. One night over a glass of scotch we'll share it with you if Holly doesn't do it first."

"Here." Holly hands me Grace. "I have a banana pudding to make. Try not to get yourself eaten alive before you get a chance to taste it."

Charlie looks at Holly thoughtfully as she makes her way into the kitchen area with Corinna, who's picking lettuce out of her short hair. "I've known that girl since she was eighteen years old and I've never seen her as content as I do tonight."

I suck in my breath. Here it comes. Judgment.

Charlie lifts a massive paw of a hand and runs it over Grace's curls, which are in perfect pigtails since Holly did them earlier. He smiles. "Your daughter is beautiful."

"Thank you. For a long time, she's been the light of my life." Kissing Grace on the top of her head, I put her down so she can wander freely.

"For a long time, the six of them were the best part of mine." As I straighten, I look at Charlie with new eyes. "I met them when they first came to the investigator I worked for to hide their identities. Here they were, six kids who told me a story that was so heinous, it was almost unbelievable. And then as I began to research it to bury their lives, what I found was worse than what they told me. From then on, their well-being became my mission." With an odd smile, he adds, "Even lost my last wife over it when she tried to hurt them. Like I said then"—I'm gaping at him—"I can't find more kids to love, but I can always find another wife if I want one."

Scrubbing my hand down my face, I don't know whether to laugh or be scared at what I'm hearing.

Charlie takes the decision out of my hands simply by breaking my heart.

"Phil, well, he's going to bluster his way through this dinner making an ass out of himself and likely making Holly full of piss and vinegar. Let me reassure you that you wouldn't be here if he didn't accept you—if the family didn't. But Phil? He's going to give it to you worse than any of the others before you simply because you're the last one. The last man he'll get to give hell to because you're the last man he has to let go of one of his sisters to." Charlie shakes his head. I smile tenderly at Holly as she laughs at something Corrina says.

"As for me? She's been my baby girl for longer than she was theirs." His voice cracks. My head snaps around. "Don't know why God does what he sometimes does things—gives gifts like those kids to people who don't deserve them. Takes the good lives before the evil ones." His eyes drift toward the kitchen where peals of laughter can be heard. "She always been holding back her light, that part of her too scared to give in and let go to love because of knowin' how dark and twisted her path took her. She could have died a lonely girl if she kept on it. It's moments like that that make me believe there really is a God, even if we don't understand him, because my Holly's over there laughing with her sisters as she plots out revenge against her brother for making her man's life a living hell. Instead of a broken grave, she's got a whole heart." Charlie faces me. "Your own path hasn't been easy."

I close my eyes. "No, it hasn't." Flashes of the day Mary died intermix with the good. Finally, I open my eyes and my gaze lands on Holly as she snatches up Grace as my daughter runs past the kitchen island. Holding Grace aloft, she plants rapid kisses to her exposed belly, making Grace laugh.

"Memories, pain, they're offset by the passage of time. They're never diluted, but they're able to be looked at with less agony." I blink at the sage words. "I like to think of life as scales. And love is the thing that balances out all the crap we have to deal with."

I quietly absorb his words. "You're extremely wise."

"That's what happens when life hands you atrocities and you decide to shove justice back in its face. Now." He looks at me very seriously. "The most important question I have to ask you is this."

Warily, I take a step back. "What's that?"

"Are you a Yankees fan?"

I let a small smile cross my face. "Mets. Lifelong."

"And to think, I had just about given my blessing."

I laugh. "Charlie, you'll never get me to switch. My father tried for my entire childhood. I even admit to crying during the game when David Wright retired."

"And you were just about perfect for my girl."

Horror crosses my face. "She's a Yankees fan?"

"I took her to her first game at the stadium myself."

I groan. "This is going to get very bad, isn't it?"

Charlie slaps me on the shoulder guiding me toward the kitchen. "Batter up, Joe."

Finding Holly amid her sisters, I proclaim, "The Yankees? You like the Yankees?"

Her eyes narrow before she booms, "All Rise!" She belts out the announcer's proclamation used for right fielder Aaron Judge when he steps up to bat. "I even have the MLB Extra Innings package so I can keep up with the games. Just because my boy's on the injured list doesn't mean I don't try to catch every game in the Judge's Chambers!"

Without missing a beat, I say, "Good, then I'll bring Grace by your house so we won't miss watching the Mets."

Her lip curls into a sneer.

Charlie chuckles next to me. "That's my girl."

"Sorry, Charlie, but that's my girl," I correct him. "The fact she likes a team that's been bought and paid for is just a minor hiccup in our relationship."

As Holly sputters with indignation, I pull her into my arms. Lowering my head, I capture her lips midprotest. She wraps her arms around my neck, and her capitulation is the sweetest thing. By the time I let her up for air, I realize the true blessing of love is the power to exchange pain, joy, laughter, and strength as easily as you exchange kisses.

Because you need all of them to get through the rough roads ahead.

Even if it's just baseball season.

49

JOSEPH

I'm on a three-day rotation at the station. I miss sleeping with Holly in my arms. Grace is with my parents though Holly plans on picking her up after a wedding she's shooting this morning. All the girls, including my mother, plan on getting their hair cut at Shimmer before grabbing lunch.

It's been two months since Holly and I laid all our shit out. It's a beautiful summer, but it's also the busiest time of year for both of us. Not only is Holly working six out of seven days of the week, but summer also brings out all the mischief in Collyer. During lunch, I run into Mike Idrissi when I went to get takeout from Frances'. He said they had six college kids in lockup for drunk driving. I merely rolled my eyes knowing we'd cut that many out from their cars last week alone, and not just the drivers.

"Were we ever that stupid?" Brett gripes when I tell him about what Mike said when I get back to the station.

"Yes, but we were smart enough to call for a ride," I remind him. "Our fathers would have busted our asses. Hard."

"Ain't that the truth." He pauses before casually asking, "How's Holly?"

"Great. She had a wedding this morning, but she was going with my mom and Grace to get their hair done."

Brett's lips twitch. I shove him. "What?"

"Dude, you don't even hear yourself. Your world is back in a perfect orbit again—all domestic bliss and shit. You're so gone for her."

I shrug. He's not wrong. I am in love with Holly, though she and I haven't said the words to each other. We've danced around them. I don't know if she thinks it's too soon to say, but my heart knows. I'm just waiting for the right time to tell her. I mean, how do you not fall in love with a woman who's strong, yet vulnerable, who's been through hell and back, yet isn't afraid to open up her heart to the possibility of love?

It's just not possible.

"Is it hard?" Brett asks.

"What?" I furrow my brow at him.

"Being in love with Holly after Mary?"

I sigh. If it was anyone but Brett, I wouldn't bother trying to make them understand, but this is my oldest friend. "It's like there's two of me. It makes no sense, but I'm not the same person I was before the wreck. Mary—she loved this funny guy who was always telling jokes that made her laugh. Until the day she told me she was pregnant, I can't remember a day I was serious. About anything other than how much I loved her."

"Joe," Brett interrupts me, but I keep plowing through.

"It was all-consuming, what I felt for her. I couldn't imagine a day in my future without her. But that's not what was meant for us," I conclude quietly. "Holly? What I feel for her is different because I'm different. I'm not the same man I was then."

Behind me, I hear a door snap quietly closed. Whipping around, I listen to footsteps thunder down the stairs. With a few quick strides, I'm across the room. I see a flash of sunset hair dash out the door just as I reach the top of the stairs. "Fuck, Brett. Why didn't you tell me Holly was standing right behind me?" I snarl as he comes up behind me.

"I tried to interrupt." His face is sorrowful.

"How much did she overhear?"

"Almost everything."

Shit. Running my hands through my hair, I stalk back into the break room. Picking up my cell, I type out a quick message. *When I'm done with work, I need to see you. I've been too many days without you.* With a swoosh, it leaves. Anxiously, I wait for a response.

I don't know how many minutes later it is before I receive a luke-warm *Okay* in response.

Typing quickly, I ask, *Do you mind if I come over?* I don't want to be at my house when we settle this. I want Holly to be around her things so when the memories of when I tell her I love her are in her mind, they're not entangled with those of Mary.

Mary—and my love for her—has no place in my relationship with Holly.

It's scary to realize my hands are shaking while I wait for her to respond. *Sure. See you later.*

"Did you get a hold of her?" Brett comes up behind me while I'm still clutching my phone.

"I'm going over later." Frantically, I'm typing. Asking—no, pleading—with my mother to keep Grace for the night. Her text, *Of course, honey. Give Holly our best*, causes a gust of air to release from me. "Now I have to figure out how to get my girlfriend to forgive my stupidity long enough for me to tell her I'm completely in love with her. Not the memory of my deceased fiancée."

Brett opens his mouth, but nothing comes out. "Yeah, I got nothing for you, buddy."

"Thanks for your support, asshole."

50

JOSEPH

After some finagling with my mom to keep the girls out longer than initially intended, I beat Holly to her house. Letting myself in with the key she'd previously given to me, I search frantically for some inspiration. While I'm doing so, there's a firm knock at the door. Frustrated because I know I don't have a lot of time, I stalk over and fling it open.

I freeze temporarily in shock before anger surges through me.

"What the hell are you two doing here?" I growl at Eden and Seth.

"We followed you from the station. We want to talk with you." Eden sounds as broken as she has for the start of every conversation we've had last three and a half years.

"So you stalk me to my girlfriend's home?" I ask incredulously.

A flash of pain slashes across Seth's face at my words. "The last time we talked, you denied feelings for this woman."

"A lot has changed since then." I lean against the jamb, blocking their entrance into Holly's home.

"How can you just move on?" Eden whispers.

"Just? You stand there like you have any idea of what I've been through. You know who does? Holly."

"I bet," Seth sneers. And just like that, I snap and years of secrets come spilling out of my mouth.

"She does, because she was willing to let me go to see me happy, Seth, even if it meant my being with someone else. Something that not even your daughter was willing to do since she got pregnant on purpose."

There's a mew of a sound from Eden. Seth pulls himself up to his full height, still several inches shorter than me. "Excuse me? You dare to accuse my daughter..."

"I don't have to accuse her," I say flatly. "I loved Mary, and I was thrilled over the news of Grace. Maybe everything would have worked out the way she planned, but life happened." Shaking my head, I rub my hand over my forehead. "One night I had a little too much to drink after Mary's funeral. I went into her closet and found her journal. I started reading it to be closer to her. It was in there she admitted to..."

"Stop!" Seth roars. "Stop telling these lies to make yourself feel better about going around with a new woman."

I see an Infiniti come down the lane.

Holly's home.

"If you want, I'll show you the journal," I say wearily. "I just don't want Grace ever knowing anything beyond the fact she's the sun and moon in the sky."

"Seth, honey, let's go home and talk about this," Eden encourages him.

"No! I won't stand here and let my daughter be maligned by... by...."

"If you can't control yourselves, I'm going to have to ask you to leave," comes a cold voice from behind me. In unison, we turn to find Holly standing a few feet inside the door with her arms akimbo. Her eyes are narrowed on Seth like she wishes she could personally squash him with the leather riding boots she's wearing.

"We're having a private conversation," Just that quickly he dismisses her. Before he can open his mouth again, she stalks forward.

"This is private property. As the owner, I can assure you that I do not sanction this occurring on my property. You have one minute to leave before I contact the CPD to notify them of your disturbing the peace." Turning her head toward me slightly, she wonders aloud, "I wonder if you'd be able to get Detective Idrissi to include a stalking charge as well."

Eden tugs at Seth's arm. "Let's go, Seth."

Mary's father levels a narrow-eyed stare at me. "We're not done, you and I. I want to see that journal."

"I'll be all too pleased to let you see it," I assure him before I hustle Holly inside and close the door behind us.

Even as I try to get my bearings, it's her rasping breath that fills the room. "And at this juncture, I think you have a right to be upset," I try to joke to lighten the oppressive mood.

She turns incredulous eyes on me. "Are you kidding me right now?"

"Shit. I'm sorry, Hols. I'm sorry they came here..."

"Stop apologizing and talk to me! This isn't a joke, Joe," she snaps.

Pulling her into my arms, I lay my head against hers. "I know it's not." I feel the warm brush of air against my lips as her breath pushes out in a burst. "It wasn't too long before I met you for the first time," I admit.

She stiffens in my arms. I can tell she wants to put some distance between us, but I won't let her.

"I'd been working on the 5K on a day off while Grace was napping and I couldn't hack it anymore. So I went into her closet. I hadn't even begun to clear things out at that point." I rest my head on the crown of hers. "It was like it was waiting there for me, Hols. All this time, all the times I sought refuge in that closet to smell her scent one more time, and for some reason, I couldn't hack it. I don't know what made me reach for the bar to grab on to, but when I did, it couldn't support my weight." I laugh bitterly. "One of the home projects I never got around to. When the bar came down, a mess of things fell to the floor. Her journal must have fallen out of a bag. I can't imagine what would have happened if I didn't find it and Grace did." My body shudders in reaction.

Holly wraps her arms around my waist and squeezes me tightly. "I've got you."

I wrap mine over hers. "I know."

"So, that's when you moved into the anger stage of your healing," she surmises.

"I honestly don't know what I was," I admit. "I was pissed, but I loved her too, Hols. And I can't imagine a life without Grace in it any more than I can imagine one without you..." My voice trails off as Holly stills in my arms.

"Is that a good thing?" Her voice is subdued. In light of what we're talking about, I give her that play otherwise I know I'd be ranting at her for not appreciating her value to my life.

Which is everything,

"Yeah, sweetheart. It is." I bend over and brush my lips against hers. "So, this isn't quite the welcome home I wanted to give you."

Her lips quirk. "What were you going for?"

I brush my lips against hers. "Romantic." I kiss her again. "Tender." My third kiss lands on her neck. "Seductive. I wanted you in the right frame of mind to listen to me when I caught you up on the part of the conversation you didn't overhear earlier."

51

HOLLY

"What...what do you mean?" I knew Brett saw me, but I wasn't sure if Joe had. I'd dropped by the station because I'd missed him. Being without him for even a few days with only a few phone calls is an adjustment, but one I'm committed to making. I'd never ask him to change who he is; that's who I fell in love with. But when I walked into the break room, I overheard him discussing how he'd always be in love with Mary.

To say my mood plummeted from exuberant to devastated would be an understatement.

To help me understand the long-term ramifications of how to approach Joe's grief over losing Mary, I've been reading articles online about how soon is too soon for love to happen after someone becomes a widower. Although Joe and Mary weren't married, classifying their relationship as anything else doesn't seem to work. The answers are oblique at best; there's no definitive period for mourning. Some psychologists are clear this sense of duality Joe expressed to Brett is rational, that he feels like he's a different person due to the tragedy that affected his life.

I just wonder if this means I'm going to be competing silently in Mary's shadow forever for the heart of the man I love.

"I mean, you missed the part where Brett asked if I was in love with you."

"What?" The words come out as a choked whisper. Joe moves toward me, but I back away, my hand held up.

His face twists. "Was I completely wrong? Do you not feel the same way, sweetheart?"

Not feel the same way? "Tell me," I plead.

Stepping close, he brushes the hair clinging to my face free. "The first moment you walked into the conference room, it was a kick to my heart. When I saw you, I fought against myself; I was so drawn to you. Then I heard you laugh. Unknowingly, you began to crack a wall I didn't realize I had built around myself. But it wasn't until you became my friend that I saw your soul. How could I not fall in love with that?" Brushing his lips across mine, he leans forward until our foreheads are touching. "I'm just the lucky bastard who managed to get you to fall in love right back."

Tears are silently running down my face. His thumbs swipe them away. "I'd do it all again. Every moment of my life. Every ounce of pain just to have this single perfect moment."

Joe inhales sharply. His eyes close under the force of his emotions.

"I love you, Joseph Bianco. And you should also know I've fallen in love with your daughter." At his blinding smile, I reach up and cup his cheek. "It didn't happen right away, but somewhere between that first family dinner and feeling your hand in a bucket of popcorn, you managed to chip away years' worth of not believing I was worthy of love and instead gave me the greatest gift I've ever received."

"What's that, my love?" Just hearing those words from his lips makes me curl my body a little closer.

"Hope. Love gives you hope. Whether or not you ever were able to love me back, you gave me the hope that I was able to be loved."

He growls. "If it takes the rest of my life, I will make you understand this is more than right. You are burned in my heart and my soul, Holly."

Beseechingly, I tip my head back, pleading without words for him to kiss me.

He obliges.

For long moments, we're wrapped in each other's arms expressing our love with just our lips. It isn't long before that's not enough. Slowly, we stumble back toward the sofa. Piece by piece, we peel each other out of our clothes until there's nothing between us but air.

When Joe enters me, I gasp. Hitching one leg around his hip, I wrap the other around his back to take the full measure of his thrusts. "Look at me, sweetheart," he pants.

When my head tips down, I find his face a tender twist of love and need.

The way he's always looked at me when he's made love to me.

Tears spring to my eyes.

"Now you see it, don't you?" he murmurs, sliding his hand beneath my knee. His hips can push in deeper at this angle.

"Yes," I pant back. Sliding my hands into the hair at the nape of his neck, I ask, "Can you?"

He nods, too overcome to speak. Dropping his head down to my nipple, he suckles briefly before laying a kiss over my heart. His hips are still driving deeply into mine.

"God, Joe, I'm so..." And I barely get that out before I tighten around him. I moan my release softly in his ear.

I feel Joe lengthen a little inside me before he begins spurting hotly, his climax seconds behind my own. When he comes down from experiencing his own pleasure, his arms tremble before he relaxes some of his weight down on me.

We begin kissing again as soon as our mouths get close.

"I love you," I whisper, overjoyed at being able to say it.

"I love you, Hols. No matter what."

52

JOSEPH

Two weeks later, I stride into The Coffee Shop with Mary's journal clutched in my hand. I was surprised when I received the call last night from Seth asking to meet me so he could read it. He offered to come to the house, but I stopped that idea. Holly agreed to take Grace to the park with Ali, Cassidy, and their kids, but just in case they came back early, I didn't want Grace to walk into ugly vibes.

If I have my way, Grace will never believe my relationship with her mother was anything other than a fairy tale.

Seth readily agreed when I explained why I wanted to keep this out of the house, frankly surprising the hell out of me.

Holly's been nothing but supportive. It's been incredible having her know everything, being able to lay out all my reasons for preserving Mary's memory for Grace. I've been able to talk through the conflict of loving her and my anger at finding out she was so insecure over our relationship, she felt the needed to hold on to me by getting pregnant.

Not that Grace is a mistake. Never that.

"It's just, I trusted her, Hols." I was sitting at her bar while she made up a snack board when we finally got out of bed. Snagging a carrot, I chomped down. "There were reasons I wanted to wait. I wanted to get the house ready, be more comfortable at the job. Hell, I actually wanted to ask her to marry me."

Holly looked thoughtful, which I appreciated. I knew the conversation couldn't be an easy one. "Do you think she needed that acknowledgment of your relationship because of her parents? From what you've told me, they didn't approve back then. Maybe she needed a reason to not cave in under pressure, Joe." Shaking her head, she turned back to cubing some cheese. "I didn't know her or you, but if she was prone to giving in, it might explain things. It wasn't to undermine you; it was to shore herself up."

I was thunderstruck. Because in just a few words, Holly took away months of anger and bitterness, leaving me with a tremendous sadness for my deceased fiancée.

It's that sadness that carries me toward her father. I've moved on to a woman who not only ignites my soul, she also knows how to calm the out-of-control blazes.

What do he and Eden have except tragic memories? And here I'm about to add to them when I give him this? My hand clutches tighter around the soft pink leather journal I'd see Mary writing in.

Unlike the last time I saw him here, Seth isn't antagonistic when he stands to greet me. "Joe." His voice is weary and laced with latent pain. As a father, as someone who did love Mary, my heart aches for him.

But I have Holly. The warmth of her love fills me with the strength I know I'll need to get through this meeting.

"Seth." I hold out my hand to shake his. To my surprise, he takes it.

"I appreciate you agreeing to meet with me. Eden...I...we both know we've been less than supportive."

"Of all people, I think you know I mean it when I say I truly appreciate your pain."

"That's not what I'm talking about, son." For once the endearment doesn't grate like it normally does. Seth's eyes are red-rimmed. "You're a solid man, a good father. I used—no, abused—you when the reality was, I wasn't ready to let my baby go." Tears well up. "And now she's gone anyway."

Lifting the book to the table, Seth's eyes latch onto it. His face pales. He clearly recognizes it as well. He should as Mary wrote in it throughout her pregnancy. "She never meant to hurt any of us, Seth. Not by what's written in here nor by dying." I let out a sigh. "Mary was doing what she did best—trying to find a balance between the ones she loved. Trying to find the strength to do that."

"That's...wise." His voice is husky.

I don't mention it was Holly who gave me that insight. I slide the book across the table. I expect him to grab for it, but he doesn't. He just stares at it as if he wishes he could open it and hear his daughter's voice one last time other than in his head. Reaching out his hand, he pushes it back to me.

"I don't need to read it, Joe. Eden and I believe everything you said that day."

Speechless, I fall back against the booth in shock.

"It's going to take you a hell of a long time for you to forgive what we did to you...to Grace. But you deserve our apology. That's why I wanted to meet with you today. You're a fine man and a better father, Joe. Maybe when you find it in your heart, we can try again." His voice cracks. "Grace, she's all we've got left now." Quickly, he slides out of the booth to make his way out of the door.

Before he makes it past me, I grab his arm. "Tell Eden we'll figure something out soon. Grace misses you both."

He swallows, nods, and leaves without another word.

I sit and stare at the book. At my elbow appears a cup of coffee. Matt says, "A hell of a lot of people would be proud of what you just did," before he ambles off.

Lifting the hot coffee to my lips, I sit there sipping it thinking about the past, the present, and the future.

And it's with the future in mind, I turn to the pages in the journal where Mary talks about getting pregnant deliberately, and I tear them out and fold them up. I'll drop by Amaryllis Events to ask Holly to shred them.

If Grace wants to read her mother's words, she only needs to know how much she was wanted. Because she absolutely was from the moment I knew she was coming.

Accidents, even staged ones, can be miracles too.

53

HOLLY

I don't consider it lying, per se. I told Joe I'd be later than usual for dinner with him and Grace because I have to drop off photos to a client.

I am dropping off photos.

It's just the client part that's a bit iffy.

Driving down High Ridge Road in Ridgefield, I find the house I'm looking for. I'm not surprised to find there's a gate. At the box, I hit the buzzer. A woman's weary voice answers, "Yes?"

"This is Holly Freeman from Amaryllis Photography. I have a package to deliver for Mr. and Mrs. Seth Moss." There's an audible inhalation of breath on the other side before the gate opens.

Tapping the accelerator, I drive my Infiniti through the gates. I park at the apex of the circular drive just as the front door opens and Seth and Eden step out. Eden reaches for Seth's hand and clutches it.

My heart bleeds for the pain Mary's parents endure, and yet at the same time, I admire them. The events of the past few years rocked them to their core yet there they stand—right or wrong—holding each other as their anchors.

The photographer in me would love to capture that for them one day. The woman in me knows now is definitely not the time to mention it. I pull the acid-free black box on my passenger seat with me when I slide from the car.

My feet crunch on their gravel driveway as I make my approach. Climbing the front steps to the porch, I offer a simple "Hello. I'm Holly."

They both nod but don't speak. Eden's eyes are glued to the box in my hands while Seth's sad eyes are tracing every inch of my face before he offers me a wan smile.

Joe told me about his meeting with Seth a few days ago, how it didn't turn out at all what he was expecting. These people aren't evil; they're just broken. Even while Joe was talking, I thought it might help them to know their daughter would never be forgotten.

So it was then I decided to bring them the pictures I've had waiting in a box since Mother's Day. I'll tell Joe at some point when the wounds of the meeting aren't riding so close to the surface. Right or wrong, Grace is their grandchild. Maybe this will help get them to the place they need to be for her sake.

"Every day, I get to see your daughter through Grace. And through Joe. Sometimes it can be hard to be the woman who loves him first after that." They're surprised by what I'm saying, but it's the truth that I've only admitted to myself. "She gave him so many gifts, but the most important one is Grace."

"We know." Eden's voice is wobbly when she finally speaks.

"Most of the pictures in this box are professional ones I took around Mother's Day, but I printed out some others I took recently." I hold out the box. Their eyes widen, but they don't take it. "Please, this is a gift for you," I encourage them.

"Why would you do this?" Seth asks, releasing his wife's hand to reach for the box. His eyes widen a bit under the weight.

"Because you're good people who were hurt. Terribly. You're not monsters. You deserve to find your way back to happiness." With that, I turn on my booted heel. I leave them standing on the porch holding a myriad of photos of Grace and Joe.

Hopefully to start them on the right path to healing.

54

JOSEPH

I can't believe Grace is going to turn four in the fall. I'm sitting on the back porch of the Freeman farm watching her cavort around with Kalie, Laura, and Jonathan while Holly, the rest of the Freemans, Charlie, and my parents are littered around. Grace told me she didn't want to have a party unless she could swim. That gives me about two months to plan it—well before her actual birthday.

"The timing works out perfectly for that, Joe," Em calls out. "Cori will be back from her honeymoon…"

"What if I don't want to come back?" Corinna calls out. Colby curls her into his side with a grin.

Em ignores them and continues. "And it's before we head to Nantucket so Jake and I can do the deed."

Jake shakes his head. "The romance in that statement is overwhelming, Em."

I chuckle when Em just glares at him.

Holly drops down next to me. "Speaking of which, did you talk to your boss about getting time off to come with us?"

Shaking my head, I tell her, "Not yet." Putting down my beer, I call out. "Hey, Pop! Can I have a few days off to go to Em's wedding?"

He yells back, "Does this look like work?"

"No."

"Then ask me when I'm behind a desk and you might get the answer you want!"

I turn back to Holly and say, "I should be good."

The entire group laughs. Holly smooths her hand up and down my back. I relish the feeling, but I realize something is missing as I feel her fingers catch along my T-shirt.

A ring. My ring.

For all intents and purposes, we haven't spent a night apart since the first time we made love. Even if she's left to drive home, Holly's been at my place until well after Grace has gone to sleep. Many a night, we've all stayed at Holly's, so much that Holly has been making noises about redecorating her guest bedroom into a Pottery Barn Kids paradise for my daughter.

There's nothing in my heart, nothing in my soul, holding me back from asking the woman I love to become mine.

Except for one thing.

Leaning over, I kiss Holly deeply in front of her sisters and future brothers-in-law. "I want to talk with Jason and Phil for a few," I murmur against her lips.

Em hoots above us. "You *want* to talk with big brother?"

Corinna grins. "It could be Jason. Phil's just glommed onto him today since it's the first time Jason's wearing shorts all season." The group laughs. I push to my feet. Holding a hand down to Holly, she waves me off.

"I'm good down here. One of them will likely sit..." Corinna drops down in my spot faster than a game of duck, duck, goose. Holly shrugs good-naturedly.

Brushing a finger down her nose, I move away toward Phil, who really has been surgically attached to Jason. "Hey, guys."

Jason holds out a hand to shake mine. "Joe." His voice is warm.

Phil smiles but doesn't unwrap his arms from around his husband. I grin at him before saying, "They're saying you won't let go of Jason because of his shorts."

Jason bursts out laughing while Phil straightens and glares at his sisters, who are all waggling their fingers. When Phil admits, "Sadly, they're not wrong," I join Jason in his laughter.

Their love is so open and so beautiful. It's a union formed of trust, dedication, and family. Being accepted into this group and getting to know them so well, it's a model of everything I want with Holly.

I open my mouth, and it all comes out.

"I love her." Both of their heads swing toward mine. "Every moment I spend with her, I know the next is going to be better. I know together life can be anything with her."

"Joe..." Phil says slowly, but I keep going even as Jason wraps his arm tighter around him.

"I can't imagine a day in my life without her waking up by my side. I love her, and I want to marry her. I'm asking for your blessing, Phillip."

Phil swallows hard and looks over my shoulder. "You had it from the moment you told me you loved her."

I sag in relief inside, but my whole body locks up at his next words.

"Do you know you're the only one who ever asked me for permission? I am so. Fucking. Honored—" His voice goes hoarse before he continues. "—to say you absolutely have my blessing, Joe."

I hold out a hand to the man I pray will be my future brother-in-law. He looks down at it disdainfully. "You need to get with the program." He clasps my shoulder and pulls me in for a tight hug.

"Just keep making her as happy as she is today, Joe. That's all I ask," he mutters next to my ear before letting me go.

"I'll break my back every single day trying, Phil."

"Welcome to the family, Joe." Jason grabs me in his own hug. Tears burn in the back of my eyes. This man and I have come full circle, from tragedy to triumph.

"Thank you for accepting me," I choke out. "Then and now."

Jason's arms tighten just a bit before he lets me go.

Phil slings an arm over my shoulders. "Now I don't know about you two, but I could use a drink. And besides, we need to plan a shopping trip to pick out my baby girl's ring."

"Um, sweetheart? Do you think maybe Denise might want to help Joe with that?" Jason's voice is dripping pure sarcasm.

"She can come too." Scanning the crowd, he spots my mother. "Denise! Come inside for a second. We need your help."

My mother flits her fingers at Phil while she finishes a conversation with Charlie.

And I burst out laughing because I know this is what my future holds: family and laughter and love.

As I seek out Holly—who's still sitting next to Corinna, but now with Grace curled up on her lap—I realize there's going to be a whole lot of love.

I can hardly wait.

55

HOLLY

W hen Joe suggested we get away for the weekend, I thought it would be next to impossible. July is our busiest time of the year, and he's been pulling a couple of additional shifts at the station. But somehow, we managed to snag three nights and two days to get away about a week after our family barbecue.

A crazy quirk had me shooting a wedding an hour away from our destination of Westerly, Rhode Island — where Brett's parent's keep a summer rental cottage they're lending to us. Joe offered to head up early to lay in our supplies to give us more time before I got there so I could just drive in and we could permanently lock ourselves in for days once the wedding was over. While it kinda sucked we'd have two cars to bring back to Collyer, I was entirely on board with more together time while we were there.

My first impression of the house when I pull up just before sunset on Friday is that it's charming. Set in a small valley, the white Cape Cod is at the bottom of a long gravel driveway. I can make out an above-ground pool just off to the left. There's a small covered doorway with huge windows on either side. "I wonder what the back looks like," I muse aloud as I slide out of the car. Out of habit, I grab my camera backpack and head to the front door.

By the time I make it there, Joe's already leaning against the jamb. "What do you think?"

"It's great," I tell him honestly.

"Brett and his dad put in a lot of work over the years. Here, give me that." He takes my camera bag from me before leaning in to give me a lingering kiss. Soon, I've forgotten about the house, Brett, my bag, and the entire world with the fire generated between us. "How was the wedding?"

My mind is still fuzzy from his kiss. "Hmm?"

He grins.

"Oh! The wedding was fine. I'll show you pictures while we eat."

"Let me give you a quick tour and then you can get changed while I cook."

Lifting myself up on the balls of my feet, I press my lips against his before I move away. "Best offer I've had all day."

I swear I think I hear him mutter, "I hope not."

HOURS later after Joe managed almost to burn the siding off Brett's family cottage because he had the grill too close to the house and he had to call profusely apologizing while I laughed like a hyena in the background, we're sitting in the hot tub with glasses of prosecco. Joe simply smirked when I told him I didn't pack a suit.

Which is how I ended up naked on my boyfriend's lap sipping the bubbly wine.

I lean forward to put my glass down on the edge of the tub near the towels when Joe shifts. I smile at him before saying honestly, "This is a perfect night," over the frothing bubbles of the tub.

He reaches over and kills the pump. I frown, confused. "Are we getting out?"

"Not just yet." Adjusting me so I'm straddling his lap, he pulls my hips against his.

I arch a brow at him, and he flashes me a grin showing off both dimples I love so much.

"We're not doing that either."

"No?" I rock my lower body into his. Joe growls before capturing my lips in a passionate kiss.

"I want to talk with you about something." Something in his voice alerts me to the importance of what we're about to discuss. My heart begins beating hard, something Joe's got to feel as my breasts are pressed up against his chest.

"Okay," I whisper.

He pulls my hand from around his neck and kisses it while holding my gaze.

"The moment I saw you, my life began to change. Something in you called to me." Lifting my hand to his lips, he kisses it. "It was something deeper than how beautiful you are; it was that core of your soul that you reserve for those lucky few you allow inside. It pulled me from the abyss I was stranded in, and soon I was living in a world I never saw before."

Tears begin to trickle out of my eyes. I nod.

"You became my best friend, someone I cherished as much as I cherished my own family. You were someone I had to keep safe, to protect. And above all, you're the woman I love." His voice drops even deeper when he chokes out, "The woman I'll always love."

"Joe..." My voice cracks. He's simply killing me.

My hand is pressed against his chest. My left hand, I notice vaguely. "Marry me. Please. Spend the rest of your life with me, Hols. Love me, love my daughter, love any children we might have together." His voice breaks on the last. He raises my hand to his mouth, his eyes pleading.

I don't even need the nanosecond it takes for the word to fly out of my mouth that's going to change my life. "Yes."

His eyes flash before his lips part. "Really?"

"How could you doubt it? I love you so much," I sob, throwing myself into his arms.

Joe crushes me against him, pressing my spine so hard I swear there might be bruises. I don't care. I don't care about anything except for the fact I'm going to spend the rest of my life with the man I love.

The man who loves me enough to move beyond his past to ask.

The man I just said yes to.

"Shit! The ring." Joe releases me to fumble beneath the towels. I laugh, even as I wipe the tears from my eyes.

"I don't care. We can move straight to..." And then my breath falters.

The ring is a round diamond in rose gold surrounded by pavé diamonds. The overhead lights catch the facets, sending light dancing everywhere. It's absolutely stunning. "Oh my God," I gasp.

He slips the ring slowly over the third finger of the hand he's been holding against his heart. "It had to be perfect. So, I took my mother shopping."

I smile.

"And Phil."

"What?" My lips begin trembling again.

Once the ring is lodged at the base of my finger, he presses his lips to it. "Hols, you all didn't grow up in a traditional family, but that man has been serving two roles for so many years. He's not only been your brother, but he's also been your father raising you to be a strong, independent woman who found her happiness. And he succeeded beyond his—anyone's—wildest imagination. You're the last girl he has to let go. I wanted him to understand I appreciate the importance of that when I asked for his blessing to marry you."

I burst into loud tears. From the moment Phil took us in, he's been a royal pain in our collective asses. He's been alternately obnoxious, overly protective, and more loving than six men combined. He's also the worst secret keeper in a family that shares everything. "When... when did you ask?"

Smiling down at me tenderly, he pushes my damp hair off my face. "The night of the barbecue."

I wail harder. "And he kept a secret that long while he wasn't under a...an...NDA." Sobs rack my body as I wrap my arms around his neck. "Thank....thank you for...for being you. For including him. For loving me."

Standing with me in his arms, Joe sits on the ledge before sliding us out of the tub.

"The last part, my future wife, is my absolute pleasure."

56

HOLLY

Joe carries me through the house to a different door than the one he dropped my bags in earlier. "I wanted this to be a surprise." He leans down and nuzzles my nose. Reaching down with one hand, he pushes the door open.

My slightly swollen eyes bug open when I see the vases of amaryllises mixed with sunflowers. An unusual combination unless you have a brother who's a florist. "Adoration, loyalty, and longevity," I whisper the meaning of sunflowers.

Joe chimes in with, "It all started with your determination, pride, and beauty, my love." Laying me down on the bed, he lifts my wrist with my tattoo—which now also holds my engagement ring.

I'm drowning in the kind of romance I never expected from a man. Ever.

With a single finger, Joe electrifies my skin. He drags that finger from the tip of my damn hair over my cheek, down my chin, and across my nipple, which has pebbled up before he reaches it. Flicking it back and forth with that single finger for just a moment, he continues his descent, down over my ribs, my stomach, my folds until that finger just enters me.

I moan even as I tighten around him. "Joe," I beseech. I want him inside me now. I want to feel connected to the man I love, the only man I will ever love.

He joins me on the bed. Our skin is still damp from the hot tub, but as we roll with each other across the bed, the sheets begin to absorb the moisture from our skin. I'm on my back when Joe frames my face, his own awash in wonderment. "You said yes."

"Of course I did," I say simply. "I love you."

The pupils from his eyes obliterate the blue as our passion kicks up to a whole new level.

Joe's mouth becomes voracious everywhere: the curve of my shoulder, the bend of my elbow, the underside of my breast. He's making a feast of my body. My skin—as pale as it is—is sure to have abrasions on it tomorrow.

I don't give a shit.

I'm giving back as good as I'm getting with my mouth and my hands, finding every sensitive spot on his body. The underside of his bicep is a particularly sweet spot. I linger there for a few minutes before he pushes me away, panting.

I'm up on all fours crawling over him when he urges me, "Keep going, sweetheart," after I've straddled his hips.

Confused, I tilt my head, hair falling everywhere. "Up or..." My lids lower to half-mast. "Down."

With a growl, he pulls my hips over his stomach until the inside of my thighs have been abraded by the friction. "Up...for now."

Wow. I begin to pull my lip between my teeth, but Joe forestalls that by sticking a finger in my mouth for me to suck on instead. Holy hell.

"I might not make it," I admit after I release his finger. His smile is pure wickedness, but all he does is crook his finger at me, encouraging me higher as he slides down flat onto the bed.

"You'll make it. In fact—" He lifts my hips when they're in range to adjust them over his mouth. I grab ahold of the headboard for purchase. "You might 'make it' a couple of times before I let you go."

I whimper in response to his words and to the gentle feel of his tongue on the inside crease of my hip.

My head falls backward, and I grip the upholstered headboard tighter as Joe makes a meal of me. He parts my lips with his thumbs, trails his lips up to latch onto my clit.

I let out a long moan.

One, two fingers enter me so deeply that my insides begin to quiver. "Too quick," I gasp.

"Not quick enough," he snarls. His lips and chin are damp with me. He looks disheveled and delicious. He begins again and I know I'm going to fly over the edge but...

"I want my turn," I manage to gasp out.

Joe stills beneath me. Quickly, I swing a leg over him and reverse my position so I'm facing his legs. Sliding my body against his hair-roughened one sends shivers down me.

But now I can taste him.

"Have I mentioned I love your mind, Mrs. Soon-to-be-Bianco?" my future husband murmurs against the inside of my thigh.

I merely trail my lips up his shaft in response. Right before I swallow him deep.

For long moments, we're so consumed in devouring the other, we manage to hold off. But then Joe slides his mouth from my center and bites the inside of my quivering thigh. "Sweetheart, I need to be inside of you," he says hoarsely.

Giving his cock a final tug with my mouth, and eliciting a deep groan, I free him. I start to roll off him when he stills me.

"Sit up and ride me. Take me, baby."

Bracing my hands in between his spread legs, I balance myself, and then I feel the familiar nudge of his cock head against me. Pushing down slowly, so slowly, it isn't until I feel the dusting of hair against my ass do I feel complete. Whole in both my body and soul for the first time ever.

This man loves me—Holly. Every dark part of me, he accepted. And we're going to be married. It's no wonder I have tears streaming down my face when my head is turned to the side to accept his kiss.

"Why the tears?" he whispers.

"I'm so happy."

Even as one of his hands raises to cup my heart, he agrees, "Me too."

Joe begins to make love to me slowly, tenderly, despite our erotic position. His hands are free to roam my body, and they do. They never stop long enough in one place to make me fly over the edge but hover enough to keep me there.

We stay this way for a long time until my body is quivering from the slightest breath of air. I'm rocking myself forward and back to get the friction I need against his almost motionless cock when he whispers in my ear, "Take us over, my love." He pinches my clit and holds it.

His cock is barely moving, but between the pressure of his fingers and the pressure inside, my walls start shaking with the intensity of my orgasm. I cry out, clutching his upper thighs.

Joe is right behind me. His cock releases in spurts, warm and wet. He pulls his hands from me to brace them on the bed. Giving himself a little more purchase, he pushes inside me as hard as he can, grinding deep before wrapping me tightly in his arms.

Slowly, we collapse against the bed, Joe softening inside me. My eyelids are fluttering shut when I hear his drowsy "I love you. I'll always love you, Mary." Joe's arms loosen around me but don't completely let me go, as he drifts into sleep.

But I'm now wide-awake.

Mary? Oh my God.

My heart's pounding as I lie there until Joe's body relaxes enough so I can slip him from mine without pain. My lip begins trembling, but I bite down hard enough to draw blood.

I have to do anything to stop the horrible pain from bursting out of my mouth.

Long minutes later, illuminated by the clock on the side of the bed in glowing red lights, Joe feels for the ring on my hand, kisses my shoulder, and rolls over to get comfortable. All while sleeping.

Meanwhile, I slowly slide off the bed bleeding not just from my lip, but from my heart. I stand by the bed trembling. Suddenly, I'm embarrassed by what we did. Wildly, I look around for something to cover myself up with, but I don't see my bag.

Get it together, Holly. First things first, a bathroom. There's an attached master. Stepping through, I close the door behind me before turning on the lights. There! My bag is sitting next to the master tub. Walking directly to it, I grab out clothes willy-nilly and slide them on. My hands are shaking. I grab them and start wringing them together to calm myself down. My fingers, unaccustomed to wearing rings, catch on the engagement ring Joe slid on a few hours before.

My fingers hover over it.

I want to go home. I need to be at home while I try to make sense of all this.

And I can't be wearing the ring of a man who's still in love with his dead fiancée.

Tugging gently, I pull off the ring. Tears fall hot and fast on my burning cheeks. Spying the ring box on the corner of the vanity, I put the ring in safely before laying it on the counter. Digging in my purse, I jab myself with a pen while I'm searching for my keys.

I find them, and I'm about to turn out the light when I realize I can't leave like this. He has to know why. I grab the pen and a scrap of paper. After hastily scribbling a note, I slip it under the ring box before slinging my camera backpack and weekender over my shoulder.

Backlit by the bathroom light, Joe's still out. His cheeks still have little dimples marking them as if he's having dreams he never wants to be out of.

I wish I could be that person, I think achingly. On that thought, I blindly cross to the bedroom door.

And escape.

57

HOLLY

Stumbling out of Brett's family cottage, I'm unable to form a coherent thought. One thing ricochets through my mind over and over again.

It's not me who he loves. I'm just a substitute.

I wish I could go back to being the person I was before I met him. Someone who could deflect men as inconsequential and move on. Not now.

For the last seventeen years, I survived thinking maybe it was divine intervention I managed to survive. That my shot missed for a reason. I escaped dying then, but ultimately, I just put myself on a path where I decided to drag out my pain instead.

Back then, I had nothing to live for. Now, the blow is so severe I think death might be easier on my heart.

Reaching my car, I fumble with my key fob before managing to get the lock undone. Sliding behind the driver's seat, I roar out of the driveway, blinded by my tears.

Driving toward the highway, I feel the hole in my heart grow bigger with every tear that falls down my face. I have hours to go to make it home. I want to talk to someone about as much as I wanted to slide his ring off my finger, but I'd be an idiot not to tell someone I'm driving back to Collyer in the middle of the night.

No matter which of my family members I reach out to, the pain is going to suffocate me. Pulling to the side of the road, I say hoarsely, "Call-Ali-Home." As I wait for the call to connect, I lean my head on the steering wheel, taking in desperate breaths.

Her sleepy voice answers in confusion. "Holly? Is everything okay?"

I manage to get out a guttural "No," before racking sobs hit my body. I can hear her soothing voice in my ear while Keene starts snapping like a protective bear in the background. "I'm coming home, Ali."

"Tell me why, baby. Can you do at least do that?" Ali begs.

Wiping my eyes with the back of my hand, I whisper, "He asked me to marry him." Ali gasps, but before she can say a word, I continue. "We had just celebrated with... It was so beautiful..." My voice trails off.

"Then why are you coming home, Hols?"

Taking in an enormous gulp of air, I choke out, "Because after when he was holding me, he said, 'I'll always love you, Mary,' right before he passed out."

There's a deathly stillness on the line. "No..." Ali's voice is full of disbelief.

I laugh, but the sound is so sharp I'm surprised the windows of my car aren't shattering. "Yes. I stayed as long as I could before I left. I took the shot at love. I guess it just wasn't enough." And with this, my sobs come harder than before.

"Where are you?" Ali demands.

I pull myself together after a few minutes to tell her, "About an hour and a half out. We were at Brett's family cabin in Rhode Island."

"Keene's up. He's going to track your phone. I want you to call me every half hour until we know you're home. Do you hear me?"

I nod before I realize she can't hear me. "Yes," I whisper.

"Come home, baby. We're waiting for you."

I hang up without another word. I sit for a few minutes trying to get my bearings before I slowly ease my car back onto the road.

HOURS LATER, I'm standing in my bedroom, having made it home to Collyer, to the safety of the farm. My head is now aching as much as my heart. My home was lit, surprising me. All the timers must be malfunctioning. Still, it felt welcoming after feeling so cold and so alone.

Unfortunately, during the last thirty minutes of my drive, my phone rang almost incessantly with calls from Joe. I didn't answer. I won't. Not right now.

How do you recover from the humiliation of not being enough? When the man you love looks you in the eyes even as he's still connected to your body and whispers another woman's name? When he doesn't realize he's done it and just cuddles you closer as you try not to die in his arms?

I'm curled in the oversized chair in my bedroom—a room dominated with a bed I've shared with Joe. I realize right now I can't stay in here. Racing into my bathroom, I stare at my face in the mirror, I see a pale, skeleton of the woman who stood here yesterday, one who was excited to be heading off for the weekend with her man. One who was hopeful for the future. In the mirror's reflection, the sun begins to lighten the sky. I frown. I didn't realize it's that early—or late. Amazing how time flies when you don't give a damn whether it exists or not.

I stumble out of the bathroom, overly emotional, tired to the extreme, and already missing the most important organ in my body. My heart. That I left in a warm bed in Rhode Island.

Looking around the room wildly, I realize there's no way I can stay another minute in this room. Too many memories flood my mind— from the first night of Joe stepping into my bath the night Justin died to every night he's slept by my side since we became an us. I don't know what the hell I'm going to do. I have to find the courage to fix this head-on, but where is it going to come from? I feel as weak in my soul as when I was removed from the container. There's no fight left in me.

Sweat beads along my forehead and starts to trickle down my cheek. Raising a hand to my forehead, I realize I'm warm. Great, I think in disgust. All I need right now is to get sick. Rolling my eyes toward the ceiling, I mutter, "It's not enough I have a heart that's dying, you want to kill me off too?" Walking over to my dresser to find a hair tie, I lift up my mass of hair into a loose knot just when a horrific screeching sounds out around me.

The fire alarm!

Racing over to a window, I realize the glow of what I thought was the sunrise is actually fire from somewhere in the house.

Oh. My. God. I'm not sick. My house is on fire!

I have to call 9-1-1. I have to get out. I have to warn my family. Then, as if Joe's standing in the room next to me, I hear his deep voice telling me one of the biggest problems is people not thinking calmly to get out during a fire, something we talked about after he had a particularly bad day at work. The worst thing is when we go in blind, when we have no clue where to find the victims.

Right. *Calm down, Holly.* Taking a deep breath, I think about what I've seen on TV. *Get wet towels before you lose water pressure. Block as much smoke as possible if you can't get out.*

Racing into my adjoining bath, I soak some bath towels in water just before the water pressure goes off. I run back to my bedroom door. Testing the handle, I immediately yank my hand away. My hand is scorching from the metal. It feels like I just took off two layers of skin. Tears begin to flow down my cheeks. Refusing to give in, I wedge the towels under the gap between the hall where the smoke is beginning to seep under the door into my bedroom. *Now get as close as you can to the floor. Call 9-1-1.*

Beginning to cough from the smoke still winding its way past the towels, I drop to my knees and crawl over to my bedside. Crap, even the floor is hot. Both knees and hands hurting, I reach for my cell. I'm grateful it hasn't melted; it feels like it's been baking in the sun at the beach. Quickly pulling up the phone app, I dial. "9-1-1, what's your emergency?"

"Fire," I cough. "Freeman farm. Pine Lane."

"Copy. Sending units to your location immediately. Are you safely outside the building?"

I cough harder. "No. Master bedroom. Left side facing the drive." More coughing.

There's a half heartbeat of silence before the dispatcher asks, "How many people are in the home?"

"One. Me. Holly." Suddenly, it's too much. The events of what happened earlier and now this? I need them all to know. "If they don't make it in time..."

"They're on their way, Holly," the dispatcher says urgently.

The light from outside casts a beautiful glow against the black silk of my sleep shirt. I have no idea if they'll make it in time. I also know all 9-1-1 calls are recorded. Joe told me that. "Tell my family I'll always love them. Even Joe. Even though he doesn't love me the same way. I know—" I have to pause to cough again. The smoke is getting thicker. "—he loves Mary so much. I can't be her. I understand. But I'll always love him." The last words are almost incomprehensible.

Seconds later, the pressure, the stress, the smoke—it all overtakes me. I start to lose consciousness. I never hear the 9-1-1 dispatcher screaming in my ear. Nor do I hear minutes later the glass to my bedroom window being smashed as Brett makes his way in and carefully picks me up in his arms, cursing. "Get a bus! And find out where Joe is! Tell him to go directly to Greenwich Hospital!"

I don't hear any of it because I'm already in a place where I can't be hurt anymore.

JOSEPH

I wake up without Holly in my arms, but I'm not concerned.

Finally, she is mine. She is going to be my wife.

For the rest of our lives, we'll wake up together every morning.

Stretching in bed, I reach for my phone since it's flashing. There are new messages. Assuming Holly is in the bathroom since there's a light glowing under the door, the only person trying to reach me would be my mother.

I couldn't have been more wrong.

After listening to Ali Freeman's blistering message about not coming after her sister, I'm up and out of bed. Throwing open the bathroom door, I find the ring box with the engagement ring I spent an inordinate amount of time choosing for Holly nested inside.

Before listening to the next message, I sit down on the toilet and read the note aloud.

"I always thought there was room for both Mary and me in your heart. Tonight, you showed me I was wrong. I wish I could marry you knowing that, but I can't." I'm dumbfounded by the words.

What the fuck happened?

I storm back into the bedroom to get my clothes when the wreck of a bed gives me a moment's pause.

"Joe." Holly arched into me as I thrust into her body.

Emptying myself into her, I crushed my lips down hers. Burying my head into her neck, I toyed with the ring I'd slipped on her finger hours earlier. "I love you, Mary."

Mary?

Undiluted panic floods through me as I race around the room throwing on my clothes. *Fuck me, fuck me, fuck! What did I do?*

You just ruined your future, asshole, I think bitterly.

"Goddamnit!" I roar. Racing back into the bathroom, I grab the note and the ring, shoving both into my pocket, when my phone buzzes.

My mother.

"Mom, what's wrong?" I demand. I'm racing around the bedroom trying to find my wallet and keys when suddenly her next words freeze me in place.

"Honey, there's been a fire." She bursts into tears.

My mother doesn't cry. She's been the wife of a fireman for too long. This means only one thing.

It's someone we love who was bitten by the bitch.

"Who?"

"Joey..."

"What happened?"

"Baby, sit down," she whispers.

"Ma, just tell me who the fuck it was!" I roar.

"Holly." And my legs give out. "I don't know what happened, I thought she was with you. But she was at home and was trapped. Brett got her out, but she's at Greenwich Hospital."

"I'm heading straight to the hospital." I hang up on my mother without saying goodbye. Barely remembering to lock the door, I stumble like I'm drunk to the car. I can taste the freshness of the summer air in my lungs. Grasping the hood, one thought repeats over and over through my brain.

My fault.

My woman ran from me and right into hell because of me.

Swinging into driver's the seat, I set speeding records to get from the cottage to Greenwich, where based on Ali's voicemail, I know I'm likely to be met with a wall of Freemans ready to take me down.

I WAS RIGHT, and I was wrong.

I was met by Holly's entire family, but it was only Ali and Keene staring daggers at me across the room. The rest of the Freeman clan were awash with confusion but leaving me a wide berth as I sat with my head in my hands.

We've all been in the waiting room for hours while they stabilize Holly's oxygen levels. The doctor came out earlier to let us know she was suffering from smoke inhalation and some second-degree burns on her hands. Unconsciously, I clench my own in fists upon hearing that. She'll be unable to do much for herself until her hands heal. Even something as simple as brushing her own teeth will cause them to be more sensitive.

My heart is screaming. If I hadn't screwed up the most crucial moment of our time together... If I hadn't said just the wrong thing at the worst time... If...

I'm wrenched from my thoughts by Ali dropping into a chair next to me. "Do you even realize what you did tonight?" Her voice is a brittle rasp.

"I didn't," I admit. I lean back and close my eyes. "I got your voicemail and was livid. I found the ring and her note. Then..." My eyes open expecting to meet her infuriated ones. Instead, all I see are orbs of pain reflecting what my heart's feeling. "I was about to come back to Collyer to beg her to listen to me when I got the call."

The anger drains out of Ali's face, leaving nothing but sadness. "Joe..." she starts, but I interrupt.

"Ali, I don't know why it happened. I close my eyes and all I see are hers. I hear her laugh and the burden of the world falls away. She's with my daughter and all I imagine is the day Grace will call her

Mama." Ali's eyes flash at that. "I hold her and the sky never goes dark because all I'm surrounded in is the light of her. I love her. Just her." I hold her eyes for another half of a heartbeat before I close them again.

I hear Ali let out a breath. "Okay. Joe, if she..."

"When. She's going to be fine," I hiss.

I didn't realize Keene came up behind his wife until he growls, "Cool it, Bianco."

Taking a deep breath, I let it out. Getting myself in check, I say to Ali, who's now leaning against Keene, "You were saying?"

"If she wakes up and doesn't want to see you, I'm not pushing it, Joe." I go to argue, but she continues. "She's going to be vulnerable between the fire and what happened. Someone has to protect her." Keene leans down and kisses his wife's head.

"Why? Why won't you let me fix this?" I want to let all of my emotions out at the target in front of me. It'd be so much easier than turning them inward where they belong.

Ali's lips lift sadly. "Holly's so scarred by what's happened to her, she buried her emotions. She fought falling until she could work out the fear of loving someone, trusting them with all that she is. After tonight, she's going to dive back into her shell."

No. That can't happen. Ali must see something on my face because she goes on. "She's so wise about so many things except her own heart. And then she hands it over for the first time and tonight happens? She's going to seek out all of those hiding places again until she feels it's safe to come out again."

"I'll wait for her," I whisper hoarsely.

"Joe, you might be waiting a lifetime," Ali warns.

"You don't understand." I stand, unable to keep still. "The feelings I have for her mean I'll wait forever even if it means one more day of her loving me."

Turning, I walk up to the desk and ask the person behind the counter where the chapel is.

Even as I make my way there, I slowly begin to pray.

59

HOLLY

I'm suspended in the space between being fully awake and sleep. I drift between one and the other in what seems like one heartbeat and the next. But I hear the occasional bit of conversation when I slide into consciousness.

"She's damn lucky they got to her in time."

"Just a few more minutes and her family wouldn't still be in the waiting room."

Or another time.

"I wonder how long it will take for her hands to heal."

My hands would likely heal a lot faster than my heart.

"Hols, it's Cori and Ali. We're all here, baby. Come back to us."

Always there for me. From the moment we were in that damn container together.

Then my subconscious drags me under. Remembering the smells of the fire, the acrid smell of the smoke, Joe not being by my side to keep the demons away, my mind goes back to the night I pulled the trigger. I try to scream as my nightmares assail me, but the smoke I inhaled decimated my voice. Still, even in my sleep, something must have alerted someone because the next thing I know, my writhing body is weighted down with no help.

Shit, I've been drugged.

There's no escape now.

Joe. Even though his love for me isn't the same as mine for him, I can't help but wish he was next to me. My soul is screaming out for him.

As the drugs take away the pain of each breath, I'm dragged deep into my own subconscious to where I've hidden myself to face the most significant challenge yet.

My life.

"You're not supposed to be here."

"Why? Because I killed someone? I never meant to kill her."

"No, you meant to harm yourself. I'm so sorry, but it had to be that way. You'll understand. It's wasn't your time. You have to live first."

Sure, I do. "I don't have a life. I have a penance."

She tilts her head to the side. "Did you know your brother brings me flowers?"

I hesitate. It isn't my place to share this. "Jason..."

"Still feels guilt since he couldn't save me. I know."

My smile is filled with bitterness. "I guess you know it all, then."

"He's down there praying for your life—praying for your every breath. He's praying for love."

I turn my back to her. "Love is never a mistake." The pain I feel in my chest when those words leave my mind and enter hers are scorching.

"No, it isn't. But Holly, right now he's praying to die if you do."

I whirl around in shock. "What?"

"By the way, it's a beautiful ring."

My mouth falls open. "Jesus, I'm not having this conversation."

Mary shrugs. "Maybe, maybe not. Come visit me sometime and you'll know for sure."

"Isn't that what I'm doing now?" I drawl sarcastically.

"I mean at my grave, Holly. That means you have to fight to get there, don't you."

My lips tremble. "I hurt."

Her face softens. "It's going to get worse before it gets better."

"What happened tonight...I don't know that I'm ready to face it. Face him. Can't I stay here for a little while?"

Her eyes well with tears. "No. They might want you to stay if you do."

"Oh." I find I'm disappointed. It's so beautiful here.

"But can I ask a favor before you have to go? Can I give you a hug to give to my Grace? I know you're hurting and you must hate me..."

I cut her off. "How can I hate you when your heart is what made the two of theirs?" In this place, I can't be anything but brutally honest. "It's not your fault. He just can't love me the same way."

Wrapping her arms around me, Mary whispers, "I hope not, Holly. Because I know you're going to be surprised by the way he does love you."

～

"Doctor, I think she's waking up!"

I really wish everyone would stop yelling. I reach up to tug at the mask covering my face. "No, Holly. That's your oxygen mask. We really need you to keep that on."

Oxygen? What? The last thing I remember is...

Heat.

Smoke.

The fire!

My heart rate accelerates just as a doctor comes bursting into the room. Jason's in scrubs right behind him. The relief on his face is evident. "Hols." His voice breaks.

I try to talk, but I don't have a voice. The only sound is a squeak that's masked by the oxygen pumping through my mask. My brows lower in a V, and tears form in my eyes.

"Shh, sister. I've got you," Jason croons as the doctor examines me. He checks my eyes, reflexes, and mobility, and listens to my lungs. After urging me to cough—like that's difficult—he appears to be pleased. "You were very, very, lucky, Ms. Freeman. Another few minutes and I don't know what we'd have been looking at."

My face turns toward Jason. I'm surprised to see his cheeks wet. He reaches for a tissue to wipe his tears. "You scared us, baby girl. Other than checking on the kids, no one's left in two days."

Two days? I make a strange sound, but Jason hushes me. "No talking, Holly, and for damn sure no taking off that mask. You took in too much smoke. Your arterial blood gas levels were too low. The doctors have been pushing IV fluids and pumping magnesium sulfate through you to get your airways open and to get the swelling around your throat down. They're also pushing antibiotics in to keep any infection away."

Tears start to burn in the back of my eyes. He grabs another tissue and gently dabs at them. "You're going to be just fine. I swear it, baby girl. Just a few days of no talking. Then whispering. By that point, we'll have you home."

I make another choked sound. Do I even have a home? Jason lets out a curse. "Our home, Holly. They're not going to let you out of here unless it's with medical supervision. Right, Doctor?"

"That's correct, Ms. Freeman." I shake my head as frantically as I can without it hurting. He frowns. "It's in your best interest."

Jason lets loose a watery chuckle. "I think she's objecting to the 'Ms. Freeman.' All of my sisters-in-law are casual people. Just call her Holly."

My doctor looks at me for confirmation. I slowly nod. "Okay, Holly. We're going to get you well. Then we're going to get you out. Deal?" He touches my arm briefly.

It's then I glance down at my hands. They're wrapped up in gauze. My heart starts to pound in my chest uncontrollably. I begin to shake.

"Hols? Hols, it's not that bad. I swear to you. They're just a little burned," Jason promises me.

They? Both? I lift up my hands to find them both wrapped in

white gauze that reminds me of mittens. I don't know if the burning is so bad I can't feel pain or if it's the drugs. Either way, it doesn't matter.

They can't be as bad as the pain in my heart.

Lowering them carefully to my bed, I let out a weary sigh and close my eyes. Having lost my home, my love, and my future surrounding my heart like a shield, I'm not ready to face anything just yet.

60

JOSEPH

Holly's been conscious for a few days. Each morning, I drive down to Greenwich with a new drawing from Grace, a card, and a care package from me. Since they're so worried about infection, Jason's the only one allowed to see her now that she's been pulled back from the edge. He's texted me photos of Holly holding the pictures my little girl's drawn for her, her lips curved in a facsimile of a smile. I can see the oxygen cannula sitting to the side. I'm grateful she thinks to remove it before Jason takes the photo, but I want to yell at her to put it back on so she gets better.

Still, even I crop the photo so when I show it to Grace, she doesn't get scared. Instead, she just hugs me tighter.

Tonight I'm making her favorite dinner of grilled cheese and tater tots when she bursts out with, "Mommy talked to me last night, Daddy."

I freeze in place. I don't know how to handle this.

"Daddy! Don't burn my cheesy sammich!"

Shit. Quickly, I flip over the grilled cheese. "Sorry, honey."

"It's okay. Mommy said you're good at fixing things. You'll fix Holly," my three-year-old daughter says confidently.

Before I burn our dinner, I turn off the burner. I don't turn around. "What did you say, Gracie?"

"Mommy said you'll fix Holly, but it won't be quick. So, I shouldn't be sad I won't see her for a while."

I hope your mother really believes that because your old man screwed up huge. "Well, honey, your mommy would know."

"Daddy?"

"Yes, baby?"

"Why are you sad again?" Dark curls fall to her shoulders when she tips her head to the side. "Is it because of Holly?"

I nod. I'm suffering every moment I'm awake. It just gets worse when I'm lying alone in a bed I've shared with the woman I love. My heart is collapsing onto itself more and more every day. If it wasn't for Grace, I don't know what I would do.

The doorbell interrupts my thoughts.

"Be right back, honey," I mutter. "Stay away from the stove."

Striding down the hall, I check out the peephole and sigh harshly. Crap. Mine and Mary's parents. This is the absolute last thing I need right now. "Mom. Dad. Eden and Seth. Grace and I were just about to have dinner," I say with a slightly warning note in my voice.

Eden steps forward and wraps her arms around me. "Joe, we're so sorry." Her voice is muffled against my chest. I look over at Seth in confusion. His face is haggard.

"We're both sorry, son. Can we come in?"

"Grandma! Grandpa! Gram! Gramps! Are you having tots with us?" Grace runs down the hall and throws her arms around my father's legs. He lifts her up and buries his head in her neck. She giggles.

"What...?" I don't get to finish the question before this week's *Collyer Courant* is being slapped in my chest by my mother. Pulling it back, I want to hurl it across the room when I see the shell of Holly's home after the fire sank her teeth into it. Instead, I stare at it, absorbing even more pain into my soul.

Knowing I'm the reason she was even there.

"You almost lost them both," Eden whispers.

I give her a jerky nod.

"We're still so lost. Every day, I keep expecting Mary to open the door, but instead, we're trying to survive each moment without her." Swallowing, she shakes her head. Tears are glowing in eyes that haven't seen happiness in more than three years. "We're so sorry we never even gave Holly a chance. We didn't want to think you were moving on and forgetting her, Joe."

Her words lance through me. "How could I when I have Grace?" Holly's own words come out of my mouth.

"I know. And loving someone else doesn't mean you didn't love our daughter."

"No, it doesn't." And it doesn't. I did love Mary. I just stopped loving a ghost and fell in love with a woman who ignited a fire deep in my soul. I just don't know if Holly believes that anymore.

Surprising me, Eden says, "She brought us a gift."

"Holly did?" I'm dumbfounded. I had no idea.

Seth, who had taken Grace from my father, puts her down. She takes off to the next grandparent to do her bidding. Reaching into his back pocket, he pulls out his wallet. Flipping it open, I look down at a picture of Grace and myself. I'm holding her on my lap in a field of flowers in the botanical garden. We're laughing in each other's faces, and Grace's hand is reaching for something past my head. "She said every day she sees Mary through Grace, and she appreciated how terribly hurt we were."

I swallow the lump in my throat. As much as she was feeling insecure about my feelings, my Holly still took the time to reassure Mary's family about their pain. "I lost her," I admit. "I don't know what to do to get her back."

Grace takes that moment to run over to me. "Baby, can you go play in your room for a few? I need to talk to the grandparents."

"What about dinner?" she demands.

"I'll help Daddy make a new dinner in a few," my mother assures my daughter.

"Okay! I'll go draw a picture for Holly, Daddy!" My face tightens in pain, which doesn't go unnoticed by any of the adults. Her little feet make little sound as they prance down the hall.

"Come on in." Walking down the short hallway, I make our way down toward the great room. Dropping down into an oversized chair, I close my eyes.

"The fire's not your fault, Joe," Seth starts out.

"No, but her being there was," I tell them all baldly. The sharp intake of breath around the room causes me to open my eyes. "How about that for guilt? Mary's dead because I took an extra shift so someone could go with their family during the holidays, and Holly's in the hospital because I screwed up so badly and I have no idea how to fix it." Dropping my elbows to my knees, I hang my head.

"Define 'bad,' Joseph," my father snaps. I shake my head. I'm not going to be able to hold the tears back.

"What did you do? For the love of all that's holy, tell me it wasn't something I have to kill my own son for," my mother demands.

I bark out a short, bitter laugh. "I don't know, Mom. Does saying Mary's name when we were just intimately connected constitute murder-worthy? This being right after I proposed. If so, then yes. Get the knife out. I'm ready."

Eden gasps, "Oh, my word." Her face turns bright red, but she doesn't flutter away like she usually does.

"So, that's why she was at the house," my father surmises grimly.

I nod. "She'd met me at the cottage, so she had her own car. I woke up and found her gone. The next thing you know, Mom's calling me to tell me..." The tears flow down my cheeks. I brush them away impatiently. "She left my ring. She almost died thinking..." It's like a tidal wave coming over me. The dam inside bursts and hot tears streak down my face. "Now, I can't get in. I can't hold her. I can't apologize. I can't make it right when..."

"When you'd die just for another chance to talk with her again?" Seth sums up.

I nod. "I have no one to blame but myself, but..."

"But what, son?" my father asks somberly.

"I have no idea why!" I burst out. "Why? Holly and I have..."

My mother clears her throat. Loudly. I get the point.

"Why, then? Why?" Shoving to my feet, I begin to pace back and forth like a trapped cougar.

Seth glances at Eden before clearing his throat. "If I could offer an explanation..."

"Other than I'm a dick?" I bite out sarcastically.

His smile is small, but it's there. "There is that, of course. But there's actually a psychological explanation for it, Joe."

There is? I gape at him.

"There's been studies conducted about it. In fact, there was one conducted by Duke University in 2016." Even though I felt like Seth was psychoanalyzing me during my entire relationship with his daughter, I welcome his knowledge now.

I drop back into my chair. "Really?" I ask in disbelief.

He chuckles softly. He reaches for Eden's hand. "Really. Not for nothing, but I called Eden by Mary's name once and..."

"And let's not go there," Eden says tartly.

"Your father called me by the dog's name once," my mother pipes in. My eyes swing to the man I've wanted to be most of my life. I know I'm gaping especially when my mother adds on, "It doesn't help that we were in a certain position."

"Jesus, Ma. Stop. Just stop." But my heart feels moderately lighter that maybe my enormous faux pas might not be the end of the world.

"That being said, Joe"—my head swings back toward Seth—"you likely said..." He swallows hard. "Mary's name because you're classifying her and Holly in the same emotional place in your heart. You need to be one hundred percent certain of your feelings. Take the time to talk with someone now before anyone gets hurt."

The lightness evaporates. "You mean hurt worse," I say dully.

My father crosses the room in a few quick strides. "What happened wasn't your fault, Joe." I turn my head away. "Listen to me. I'm not talking to you as your father, I'm talking to you as your boss. It appears to be a problem with malfunctioning wiring in the timing device Holly used in the wall. Now, just imagine if she wasn't home.

It's possible the fire could have spread to the other homes on the farm."

My breath is coming in short, choppy jerks as I imagine the damage.

Fire breathes.

Fire lives.

Fire burns.

That goddamned bitch.

If Holly hadn't made that 9-1-1 call, how far would it have spread before it was stopped?

"Okay." I wipe the tears from my face. Taking a deep breath, I say to my father, "I need to make sure my head's on straight before I fight for her." Then I turn to Seth. "Who do you recommend I talk to?"

My father tugs me into his arms. "Nobody's going to let you down, son."

No, I don't think they would.

But I've already let Holly down. And now I have to fight so I won't do that again.

61

HOLLY

I've been out of the hospital for a few weeks. Living with Jason and Phil has been a massive comfort to both my mind and my soul.

I didn't realize how hard it would be to be back on the farm until Jason drove through the gates and I began to have a panic attack, which in turn set off a fit of coughing so hard, he had to stop the car to treat me. Shoving a rescue inhaler in my mouth, Jason calmed me even as Phil sat in the front seat, helpless and cursing.

Instead of the two of them taking me to the main barn—where our whole family was waiting to welcome me home—they drove me directly to their home. That's where my healing truly started to begin.

Jason's taken an unpaid leave of absence from work to care for me, something which I tried to protest and pay him for. Jason gave me a disdainful look and merely laid his finger across my lips to hush the protests coming from my ruined voice. "We're fine, Hols. They understand. I'll still have my job when I go back. Stop worrying and get well. That's the only thing you have to do."

I was too tired to protest then. Now, I'm grateful for the tender care they've administered while I try to get my emotional strength back to face what I've put off for so long—what happened the night of the fire.

I'm sitting on the grass at the back of Phil and Jason's property. The tulips Phil planted years ago are in full bloom and almost obscure me from view. My hands can feel the silkiness of the delicate petals, an improvement over yesterday and the day before. But they are still much too weak to hold on to the weight of my camera.

I'm desperate to look through the viewfinder and get some perspective.

Unconsciously, I begin to flex my fingers gently. The burns aren't terrible. Both my doctor at the hospital and Jason assure me there will be no permanent nerve damage nor will there be any scars, but I sustained burns likely by touching my metal doorknob and the scalding floor. They're going to be tender for a while. The best thing I can do for them is to continuously try to work out the stiffness using the discharge therapy exercises and apply the prescription pain-relieving cream. And not to strain them by doing anything more than eating and dressing in the loosest clothing imaginable.

Glancing down at Phil's oversized University of Charleston sweat-shirt and Em's leggings, I'm actually grateful for the first time I'm not as stacked as Corinna. Ruefully, I think I'd never be able to go without a bra for as long as I have without losing what's left of my mind.

"Whatever you're thinking of that put that smirk on your face, you'd better share, baby girl." Phil's voice intrudes my thoughts. Turning my face up to his, I see he's carrying a tray of coffee and something completely unexpected.

My first camera. My heart begins to pound hard in my chest aching to reach for it.

God, I need to gain some semblance of myself.

I'm so twisted up inside, I don't know what to feel anymore. I don't even know where to start.

"I hope one of those is for me," I say softly. My voice is still jagged. Even though I've been reassured countless times it will heal, it's still a painful reminder of everything that happened.

Joe's brought by cards from Grace every single day since I woke up. In the beginning, I also got cards and packages from him as well, but as time's passed, his messages to me have become more abrupt. Although they're still heartfelt, the notes are so brief, I can feel him pulling away.

I should be grateful he's holding on until I'm healed, but will my heart ever be strong enough for him to say goodbye? Maybe I should have just accepted his love for what it was—understanding he'll always love Mary more—and take any part of his heart as a gift.

Considering what I never thought I'd have, it's still more than what I ever thought I'd be blessed with.

I've turned away from Phil, so I don't realize how close he really is. It isn't until I feel the heat of his chest against my back that I understand my big brother is doing what he always does—shielding me from the world. Remembering Joe's words the night he proposed, I realize he's doing what every father does as well—protecting his little girl. Tears prick my eyes.

Stretching his long legs on either side of mine, he wraps an arm around my waist. "Want to share what's on your mind?"

I start to shake my head, but something stops me. I need to get this poison out of my system once and for all. "Do you love Cass more than the rest of us?"

Phil's arm tightens so hard around my waist, I can't breathe. I start coughing uncontrollably. "I can't breathe, Phil."

"What the hell, Hols? Where the fuck is this coming from?" Phil's voice is disturbed. He tries to turn me to face him, but I shrug his hand away. I need anonymity for this.

"You saved her life, Phillip. You met her first. You loved her first." The words are torn from me. "I don't begrudge that. None of us would." It's nothing but the truth.

Phil's arms loosen but don't let me go. Instead, he leans forward and rests his chin on my shoulder for a few moments before his murmured words suck every ounce of air from my body. I'm surprised I don't need my inhaler—another sign I'm starting to heal. "And you and I have both killed to survive, Hols. We both know we'd do it again in a heartbeat to protect those we love. We'd both bleed out and die to protect everything this family stands for—unconditional love." He gently kisses my hair as silent tears cascade down my face. "We've never talked about it, honey, but we're survivors of a different kind. We've survived the knowledge we've taken a life, and we'd do it again."

"Do you regret it?" I whisper. How much of the course of my life would have changed if I hadn't stood there watching Maria's life slip away?

"Do I regret it? Absolutely. Would I do it again? In a heartbeat. I saved myself. I saved Cass. You didn't mean to kill your stepmother— more the pity. You meant to hurt yourself which causes me no end of pain to think you didn't have one of us at your side to protect you." Sobs rack my body, and Phil just holds me tighter. Lowering his forehead into my shoulder for a few moments, he gathers his own thoughts before speaking.

"So, to answer your question, yes. I will always love Cassidy because we escaped our hell together. I will love her differently because our beginning was different. I will love Emily because she has this huge heart when she thought she was protecting it. The same for Ali for standing up for what is right in the face of any adversity. I will love Cori for her determination and courage. And you, Hols? I will love you because you're filled with wisdom and vision. You're the epitome of honor and vitality. You will never know what I went through when we realized you were in that house..." His voice locks and I feel the wetness of his tears against the side of my face. "Just as our love grew differently, I don't love you because I love all of the rest of our sisters. I love you for you. Each love is separate, and they all blend perfectly. They're like the flowers in this garden. Each one is damaged. Each one is perfect. Each one is beautiful. Each one is already leaving me."

Phil's so close I know he can feel my heart pounding through my back. "I always thought..."

"What? That you were loved because you came with the others?" Phil scoffs. "That's ridiculous. You're loved because you're you."

I'm outright sobbing. "Phil…"

"Ali already told us, sweetheart. The day you think you have secrets in this family is the day I'm dead and buried. Are you ready to talk about it?"

I shake my head, but then I nod. "He still loves her."

"He always will," Phil tells me firmly. "But you have to realize his mistake wasn't about you. His love is entirely for you. His heart is big enough for loving both of you."

"I…I don't know how to begin to fix this."

Phil shifts and reaches for my camera. "I think I do. Let's bring you back to where you belong, Hols." Looping the strap over his neck and loosening it, he slips it over mine as well. "You're not to hold the camera," he orders.

My heart skips a beat just before another sob wrenches from me.

God, I love my brother.

"We've got all day, baby girl. Find your focus. Hold on to me and tell me what buttons to push." Phil scoots closer and braces his elbows on his partially raised legs so the camera sits perfectly in front of my face.

Swiping at my tears, I lean forward. Through the viewfinder, I can see the remains of my home in the distance. If you'd have asked me an hour ago before I'd had this heart-to-heart with the man who gave up his whole life to raise five women who weren't related to him, I'd have said that resembled my heart. Instead, I catch a glimpse of Phil's flowers at the bottom of the frame. "Zoom out," I whisper.

My brother complies.

There at the water's edge are branches of Phil's dogwood tree dipping in, obscuring the charred ruins. Beauty and strength overpowering the pain. "Take the picture," I urge him.

He presses the shutter.

I watch the shutter blink through the viewfinder. Suddenly a bird lands on the branch. Hope. "Again," I whisper.

He presses it again.

The bird sits on the branch for a moment. Suddenly she takes off. "Again, please."

It flashes just as little heads pop up. "Beautiful," I murmur.

"I wasn't looking at that," Phil says casually. I turn my body to the side so I can see his face. "I was too busy watching my sister come back to me."

"Phil," I whisper brokenly, before throwing my arms around him and letting loose a torrent of sobs.

"You will never understand how grateful I am to sit here all day doing this." He brushes his lips against my forehead before they curve in a smile that I've been fortunate enough to get on film—when he's had all of us in his arms. "This is your chance to order me around, Hols. Use it wisely."

Turning around and settling back into his arms, I pull his wrists toward me so I can see. And for hours without complaint, my brother gave me back not only another piece of my life, but he also gave me back my perception.

Not just about what happened to me, but about so much more.

He gave me the ability to view myself with a little more pride. And he helped me understand that love is more than I'll ever comprehend. It isn't there just to cause your heart to flutter and dance. It's also there to accept and forgive.

I just hope forgiveness is something I'm worthy of once I've healed. I need Joe to forgive my leaving instead of staying to talk things out; my overthinking what was likely a mistake that could have ended in a tragedy for all of us. I need him to understand it wasn't a rejection of him or Grace; it was my fear of being worthless to a man like him.

I just have to figure out how.

62

JOSEPH

Holly's been out of the hospital for a few weeks. During that time, I've been in regular therapy sessions with a psychologist named Alice Cleary. Dad, not having a clue what to do, got a recommendation from Jason. Jason explained Alice was a bit unorthodox but had helped Corinna during a traumatic event in her life.

After our first session, I told Dad that if I wasn't in love with Holly, I might hit on the shrink, who must be in her late fifties.

He exploded with laughter.

Alice is a damn hoot. Whether you're one of her private patients or you see her through her association with Greenwich Hospital, she keeps a stash of chocolate so huge that I've had to run nightly to keep the pounds off. Especially since she's in cohorts with Corinna Freeman. I walked into our first session, saw there were orange-frosted cupcakes on the table, and muttered, "Fuck," loudly enough for Alice to scream with laughter.

Her response: "Obviously you've had baked goods from the Amaryllis Bakery before."

I cut my eyes to the side and said, "I'm in love with Holly Freeman. That's part of the reason I'm here."

"Well, it will be fun to catch up about my friends, then, Joseph. Have a favorite kind of music?"

"It's Joe," I corrected her. "Normally I just listen to my Spotify playlist."

She handed me her iPad. "Pull it up, and then get comfortable. Coke, Pepsi, coffee, or water?"

Within minutes, I was ensconced on Alice's couch at her home office with a Coke and a cupcake. "I'm going to have to take one of these home for my daughter."

"How old is she?"

"She going to turn four." I shook my head. "It's hard to imagine. It's flown by so quickly."

"What does she look like?"

I pulled my wallet from my pants and flipped it open to the picture that Holly took of us. I had no idea what was revealed in my expression as I looked at it—a mixture of love and pain. "Here you go."

Alice studied it, looked between it and me, before handing it back over. "She looks like you except for the eyes and smile."

My mouth quirked. "Grace got those from her mother."

Alice settled back in her chair with her coffee. "You love her mother still?"

I nodded. "Always." I swallowed. Even after all this time, it was difficult to say out loud. "Mary was killed by a hit-and-run driver a few days before Christmas when Grace was about eight-weeks-old."

"I remember reading about that." She leaned forward and pressed her hand against mine. "I'm so sorry for your loss."

"There are some days it feels like it was a different me..." My voice trailed off.

"And some days when it feels like it was yesterday," Alice concluded.

I nodded. "That's part of the reason I'm here." We talked for the majority of that time about how it felt to be thrown into single parenthood so unexpectedly at such a young age.

~

ANOTHER SESSION, Alice didn't waste much time when she asked me, "You mentioned you're in love with Holly."

My heart flipped in my chest. "I did something completely... I feel so much... God, how is she ever going to forgive me." Standing, I shoved my fingers through my hair before I started pacing back and forth.

"Here." Alice handed me a stress ball. "You look like you want to throw something."

I barked out a laugh, and though I didn't throw it, I squeezed the living hell out of it.

"What happened?"

"Oh, nothing major," I told her bitterly. "I only proposed, made love to her, and then called her Mary's name."

"Okay, so what did you do after?" Alice asked me calmly.

"What do you mean?" I hissed.

"Did you reassure Holly of how much you love her, not your dead fiancée? Did you show her how precious she is to you? That she's not some sort of substitute for what you lost?" Alice pushes me.

"No, because she ran from me. And by doing so, she was trapped in her house when it caught on fire!" I yelled at her.

Alice sat back in her chair, her expression one of shock. "So much makes sense now," she murmured.

"What?"

But Alice just shook her head.

"Joe, I want you to answer something for me. And take a deep breath before you do. If someone were to ask you to describe your love for Holly, could you do it?"

I collapsed down into my chair. "Yes, I could."

"Then do it," she challenged me.

"At first, I thought we were friends. It developed into so much more. I changed with a look, a touch. She ignited something inside of me I'd never felt before."

"And now?"

"Now, if I can't figure out how to get her to believe that it's her that I love, I feel like my soul that's going to extinguish."

Alice stood and reached for my hand. "You're a lucky man, Joe."

I laughed bitterly. "Why? Because I've lost two women I've loved?"

"No, because you have such a beautiful heart that can hold such love. Unfortunately for you, it also holds a tremendous amount of guilt, but we'll work through that."

"It was my fault she was there," I whispered.

"And what if she'd left to go get a celebratory bottle of champagne and was in a car wreck, Joe? Would it have been your fault for proposing?" Alice probed. At my startled jerk, she continued. "Life isn't about what happened, but about how we react to it."

What had I done since the night I proposed? I got angry, I was terrified, and I prayed. But what had I done to show Holly I was always going to be there for her other than send her a few cards and some pictures from Grace? How had I fought to show her she was special, knowing I had screwed up that night in such an enormous way?

"You've given me a lot to think about, Alice."

"Good. Then I'll see you soon, and we'll talk about it then."

I THOUGHT about everything Holly wouldn't be able to do without her hands in working order. I called Jason and asked what she was wearing around the house that was comfortable for her to get on and off with her hands. After he laughed in my ear asking if I was asking for practical or personal reasons—and I told him to kiss my ass—he said, "Mostly her sister's clothes. Everything's gone, Joe. We'll take her shopping when she feels up to it."

I volunteered to go instead. Taking my mother and daughter along with me, we made it our mission to max out my card. I found Holly the softest camis and lounging pants at Free People, her favorite store based on all the clothes I've peeled off her in the past. As soon as I touched the set that was called the "Yes, Yes, Yes" set, I immediately added it to the top of the pile. I asked for that to be gift wrapped with a special addition to it.

Then I arranged for Jason to meet with me to pick it all up during my next shift at the station.

Imagine my surprise when Phil walked in instead.

"Joe." Phil holds out his hand. I blink at him before holding out mine in return. "Finally got your head together?"

Immediately, my back goes up. "What do you mean?"

His eyes narrow on my face. "I mean, I want to know if you're going to make good on your promise to me about making my sister happy for the rest of her life. Holly needs to know she's loved for who she is. If that's not you, then we'll catch her during the final fall."

My chest expands before I let out the breath I was holding. "She is loved for exactly who she is."

"And who's that?" he challenges. "As a substitute for someone she'd wish back for you in a heartbeat if she could just to see you happy?"

"No, for being the person I'd die for right now, this very minute, if it meant that she'd live the rest of her life knowing she's loved for exactly who she is," I growl at him.

The antagonism drains from him. The fatigue of the last few weeks since the fire has taken its toll on him. None of us have escaped without suffering. "I know, Joe. I just had to be sure because when I bring whatever it is you're about to give to me to her, I want her to know what motivated it."

"She'll have no question about that after she opens the last box, Phil," I assure him. "She'll never doubt I love her ever again. It's her. Now. Forever."

His eyes flash before he smiles. "Then where are these boxes I'm bringing home?"

"Did you drive or did you walk?" I ask.

"I drove. I'm heading back to the house right after this."

"Bring your car around back. I'll load them into yours."

~

"I GOT IT, Joe. This box is last," Phil says impatiently.

I'm nervous. I'm going for broke with what's in this box. I hate that I'm asking her brother to deliver it, but until she's ready for me to be there, this is the best I can do.

"They're all numbered," I remind him again.

"You know, I was going to avoid hitting you. You're coming close to getting a punch to the stomach just on principle," Phil grumbles as he slams his trunk closed. A trunk filled to capacity with gifts for the woman I love.

I can't help what I do next. I kiss the tips of my fingers and lay them on the back of Phil's car. "That's from Grace, baby."

"Jesus, if I didn't know you loved her before that, I'd know then." He pauses in his act of mocking me to ask, "How is Grace handling things?"

"Okay. Things are better with Mary's parents, so that's helping. I know she's loving being able to send cards to Holly and knowing they're helping her heal. She's getting impatient to see her, but I keep reminding her that little girls have germs we have to be careful of."

Phil's lips quirk. "You never know. Girls have a mysterious way of healing themselves."

My eyes narrow. "What aren't you telling me?"

He claps me on the shoulder. "Just that the strength of women will surprise you, Joe. I'll be in touch."

63

HOLLY

I'm restless. I take it as a good sign that I'm healing. I need to be doing something, but I can't because my hands aren't quite ready for me to tackle more than pulling on or taking off clothes. Jason predicts I should be back at work—at least editing—within another week.

Phil and I made him go back to work. After making sure I'd be okay alone for a few hours, Phil's taken off on a mysterious errand saying he'd be back soon.

It's time to face what I had been avoiding up close. The shadows of what was my home.

Slipping into a pair of shoes, I begin to walk down the lane toward the back of the farm. Hopefully, Phil won't freak when he sees the note I wrote in Sharpie on his kitchen island if he gets back before I do. Somehow, I doubt it, but this is something I need to do on my own.

Going for broke, I turn down the fork which leads toward my house versus Ali and Corinna's homes.

It's the deep ruts in the road I notice first. I squat next to one of them. The gravel road which handles our vehicles so easily must have been a challenge for the emergency responders. The depth tells me how long the weight of those red engines sat here, the men and women inside them using every bit of their strength and determination to put out the flames before they could jump into the tree line and threaten Ali or Corinna. I walk farther. Even from this vantage point, I can see some blackening behind the house where my porch used to be.

The fire started in a malfunctioning timer. It isn't anyone's fault. Standing here in the ruins of my home, I can only be grateful I was even home. "What would have happened to my family if I wasn't here to call 9-1-1?" I wonder aloud.

"I don't know for sure. We don't like for people who have been rescued to think about what-ifs in our business," a voice I know well comes from behind me. Spinning in surprise, I'm confronted with misty eyes in a face that's seen too many fires. Joe's father.

Tears begin to track down my face. "I'm so sorry. I made a mistake. I was..." Helplessly, I spin around. "I don't know how to apologize for everything I've done."

"What? For being human? For having a heart that was hurt? You sure as hell had better not be apologizing for being trapped in a fire that you were a victim of."

"I'm sorry for pushing everyone away," I get out. "I just...I just..."

"You needed to heal from too many blows," Joe's father tells me wisely. I nod.

"Yes."

"You've got what it takes to go the distance, Holly." I twist around to look at him, confused.

"What do you mean?"

"Even though you were hurt by my son, you still stepped out on the ledge and were willing to risk your heart to be loved. That's the kind of woman a fireman needs at his side. This isn't a career where the people we love don't stumble. But the most important thing to know is that they'll pick us up when they do." Chief comes directly over to me and cups my chin in his hands. "Are you ready for him to help you up now?"

I take a deep breath and look over at the remains of my house.

They're just things. Every photo that was hanging in there is backed up about six different ways from Sunday. And the memories, well, those are all in my head. I'll never forget the first time Joe made love to me in my bed. I'll always remember Grace crawling between us because she got scared sleeping in a new house.

Those are the things you take with you wherever you go. All that matters is the people you're with.

"I've been ready," I admit. "I just didn't know how to reach out."

"How about we start with my walking you around here explaining what happened? Then I'll drive you back to your brother's before he has a meltdown."

"That's not exactly a perfect date, Chief. Maybe you can tell your wife to get you to work on that?" I sass with just a hint of a smile ghosting my lips.

His eyes probe mine for another minute. He swallows. Hard. "I've never been so glad to know someone got out in time, Holly."

My chest heaving, I fight the tears. And lose.

"He can barely function now without you. And I would give anything to see my boy smile again." Pulling me into his arms, Joe's father both shreds and heals my already battered heart. Because I know it's up to me to make the first move toward reconciliation.

We stand in the ghostly remains of my house for a few minutes before he pulls back. "Come on. Let's walk the perimeter."

And slowly, I begin to pick my way around the remains of one life before I figure out how to grab hold of the one waiting for me.

The one I should never have let go to begin with.

By the time Chief drops me at Phil's, I have an idea. "Can you wait ten minutes, Chief?"

"Take what time you need, Holly," He shoves his truck in park, leaving the engine running.

I need my phone.

I race inside to hear Phil yell out, "Where in the hell have you been, missy! I have a bunch of stuff with your name on it!"

"Not now, brother. Chief's outside waiting for me." I dash past him and into the room I've been using. Spying my phone, I grab it and the homemade invitation that's been sitting on my bedside.

"What the hell, Hols?" Phil comes charging out after me. He's got a determined look on his face.

Spotting Phil, Chief cuts the engine and slides out from behind the wheel. "Phil." He holds out a hand.

"Any idea what this is about, Chief?"

Joe's father runs his fingers along his chin in a way so reminiscent of his son, I just grin. "Looks like your sister's healing" is all he says.

Phil rolls his eyes. I shove my phone in his hands.

"Is Joe working today?" I demand. Both men's eyes get large, but it's his father who responds.

"He's at the station, yes."

I turn to my brother. "FaceTime him. Now."

"Uhh, Holly. I don't want to spoil anything..."

"Now, Phillip. Before I tell Joe that you put your cat in that tree your damn self to get the fire department here in T-shirts last summer."

Chief chokes on his laughter.

"Jesus, you must be feeling better," my brother mutters. Unlocking my phone—which reminds me I need to change the password once my hands can navigate the small buttons easier—he pulls up the FaceTime app. "Hey, Joe."

"Phil? Why are you calling from Holly's phone?" His confusion is evident.

"I just got back to the house from an errand I was running." A look crosses Phil's face I can't decipher. "Anyway, Holly wanted me to call you, so here she is." My brother lifts the phone until it's facing me.

"Hey." I wave anxiously.

"Hols, baby." Joe's voice comes through my phone like he's about to dive through it.

"I just wanted to let you know I'll see you and Grace soon. I promise by then, I'll have my head all sorted out."

"Baby, there's nothing for you to sort out," Joe starts, but I interrupt him.

"Yeah, there is. It was my fear that made me leave the night you proposed. I was too afraid of what I was being compared against when everything happened. What I should have realized is that our love can't be compared. Not to anything or anyone. I forgot in all those years of trying to feel nothing, what feeling everything felt like. If I lost you..." I shake my head. "I don't know how I'd go on because I love you more than the next breath in my body."

"Tell me we are not having this conversation over FaceTime with your brother standing right there," Joe demands.

That's when I admit, "And your father."

"Pop's there too?" I nod. And what does my man do?

He bursts out laughing. Slowly, I begin to smile.

"You do realize I'm on shift for the next two days, Holly. Your timing is complete shit."

I shake my head. "No, it's not. See, there's this hot fireman who told me it's not finishing first that's important."

"I didn't need to hear that," Phil mutters to Chief.

"Neither did I, son. Neither did I."

Joe and I both laugh.

"I can't believe you remember that."

"I remember everything." There's a long silence between us before I hold up the invitation and continue. "I'll see you at Gracie's party in three days. But before that, I have to go see someone first."

"Who's that, baby?"

"I'm going to see Mary." There's a sharp inhale of breath from everyone. "I have a lot to thank her for."

"God, Hols." Joe's voice is broken. "You don't have to..."

"Yes, I do. There's so much I owe to her."

"Like what?" This from my brother.

"Like giving life to a little girl I'm going to love forever. Like getting the man I love on a path of righteousness. Like being an amazing person who inspires loyalty and devotion long after she's gone. Those things shouldn't be forgotten."

"I said it earlier, you got what it takes, girl," Chief tells me, pride dripping from his voice.

"Holly?" I still can't see Joe's face, but his voice is sending shivers up and down my spine. "That errand your brother ran was to come to see me."

I turn accusing eyes to Phil, who just shrugs and grins.

"I love you too. Now, go wrap yourself in my gifts until I can do it." Joe's voice has that husky note that drives me wild.

"I feel like I'm watching live porn," Phil comments drolly. I roll my eyes at him.

"And on that note, I'm out. Son, your mother and I will drop off Grace at Eden and Seth's."

"Later, Chief," I wave.

"Later, Pop," Joe calls out.

"Holly, come take your phone and let me go inside to get your surprises ready," Phil grumbles, but I know him better than that. Above my phone, his eyes are shining with such pride. I almost drop the phone during the handoff. "Love you, baby girl." He turns to walk away.

"Thank you, brother."

"For what?" he asks over his shoulder.

"For giving me the best perspective I've had since you first handed it to me." Phil stops dead in his tracks. Shaking his head, he makes his way inside the house before I lift the phone, and there he is.

The man who made me realize that life wasn't worth living unless it had love.

"You look beautiful." His voice is a rasp. "All those pictures of you in the hospital told me that you were alive. This tells me you're healed."

"Not entirely, but I'm getting there," I whisper. His face looks concerned. "I'll be better once my heart is back in its right place."

A slow smile causes his dimples to come out. "Then what I gave to Phil might help with that."

"You didn't have to do anything," I protest. He shakes his head.

"You said yes, Hols. I'm holding you to that." I hear him being paged over the speaker. "Now go. Get what I gave to Phil for you. Tonight, I want a new picture."

"Deal. Stay safe," I whisper.

"I have too many reasons not to stay safe." Joe disconnects the call. I stand there for a moment with my phone pressed to my chest.

The next minute, I'm sprinting up the front walk. "Phil, what did Joe give you for me?"

"And I see your patience is now at an end," comes his drawled reply.

I laugh because it is.

I'm suddenly impatient for everything. I want my life back.

I want to wrap my arms around Joe and tell him I love him for the man he is: the kind of man who'd give his heart to two women blessed to receive it in one lifetime.

64

JOSEPH

It's hours later when I get the picture of Holly holding the letter I'd had wrapped with the "Yes, Yes, Yes," pajamas from Free People clutched against her stomach.

And around her neck she's wearing her diamond engagement ring on the chain I hung it on before I slipped it into the box the salesperson wrapped.

For the first time since she left that night, I took a breath that didn't feel like I was choking because I knew my prayers had been answered.

She still loved me.

Unashamedly, I bowed my head and cried.

When Grace walked up and asked, "What's wrong, Daddy?"

I told her, "Nothing, baby. These are happy tears."

And they are. They might be some of the happiest I've ever shed.

Because I know in my dreams tonight, I'll see her beautiful face.

Smiling.

Alive.

And healing.

I send a prayer of thanks up to whomever wants to accept my gratitude.

65

HOLLY

T wo days later, I'm wearing one of the outfits Joe sent to the house for me. It's an adorable linen berry shirt dress with the most perfect name of any Free People design. Ever. In fact, it's so perfect, I made Phil go online and order it for me in two other colors since using a computer is still a bit of a challenge.

The style is called Italian Love Story.

I don't know if Joe bought it for me because of the design or the name, but as I cradle a large bouquet of white roses and forget-me-nots toward Mary's grave, with my engagement ring bouncing against my chest on the chain Joe boxed with my new lounging pajamas, I feel serene. Because I get it now.

Love is the strength of two people who live through the trials and tribulations of everyday life and still want to hold on to each other when the sun goes down every night. Hardship and pain are going to happen, but through forgiveness, mistakes have the chance to be corrected. Hearts can be mended. Together, you can move on.

That kind of love is what I've built with Joe. And in the ashes of my house fire, what we'll rebuild.

Approaching Mary's grave, I know what I'm going to say to the woman whose life had to be cut short for me to find mine.

And it starts with two simple words.

"Thank you." My voice is still rough and scratchy. Jason and the doctors assure me it will be back to normal with care and not abusing it. "For so much. First, for Grace. All she will ever know is that she was loved and wanted because she was—*is*," I amend. I feel a slight breeze waft over my skin. I lift my face to it and smile.

"As for Joe, we're so blessed to be loved by him, Mary. Both of us. You were so young, yet you recognized that his heart was worth any fight. It almost cost me my life, but I can't say I wouldn't go through it again so long as it led me to now." Reaching up, I clasp my engagement ring in my hand. "I swear to you I will make them both happy for as long as I live."

"Why don't you turn around and tell me that so we can get started?" a rough voice says behind me. Spinning, I drop Mary's bouquet at my feet.

"Joe." Within seconds, his strong arms are wrapped around me like he's never going to let me go. I inhale his scent, so fresh and clean in comparison to the acrid smell of smoke that's been seared in my brain no matter how hard I try to get rid of it. I feel his hair against my fingers, the silky smoothness so gentle against my still-tender skin. His heart is pounding against mine. I realize how close I came to losing him not only because of my fear but because of chance.

"I'm so sorry," I manage to get out before burying my head against his shoulder to let the torrent of tears fall. He doesn't say anything; he just holds me tighter. For right now, that's all I need.

We stand there for long minutes, not moving as the wind blows gently around us in harmony with the rustling leaves in the trees shadowing Mary's grave. Pulling back slightly, I use my damaged hands to trace the worry lines away from his face. Each millimeter I trace smooths out, returning his distressed features to the handsome man I left behind in Rhode Island.

He continues to regard me solemnly throughout my tactile perusal. "What would I have done if you were lying right here next to her because of me?"

"This isn't your fault." My denial, swift though the shaft of pain from his quiet words, is deep.

"Everyone keeps trying to tell me you saved your family, that the fire would have spread to Ali and Corinna's homes." Joe slides a hand into my hair. "I'm not in love with them. I'm in love with you. And you were supposed to be lying beside me wearing nothing but my ring, Hols. Instead, because of my carelessness, I almost lost you." His hand slides out of my hair to cup my jaw. "I swear to God, I will never be that insensitive again."

"You weren't. Not intentionally. I overreacted." But he needs to understand something that's been on my mind. "Do you think I could have lived with the knowledge something happened to my family?"

His brow lowers. "Of course not."

"Do you believe things happen for a reason?" When his look changes to one of confusion, I press him harder. "Do you think maybe—just maybe—everything happened the way it did because it needed to? I wouldn't have been able to have lived with myself if my family was harmed, but what if I always wondered about you and Mary? Instead, everyone is safe and I know, I *know*, down to my soul how much you love me. Regardless of what I was, did, done, will do." My voice cracks between the overuse and the power of the emotions I'm feeling. "You love me."

"Forever," he growls. "Never doubt that no matter what stupid things I may do over the years, sweetheart."

Running my hand over his cheek, I whisper the words that have been ready to burst from my heart since I saw his face on my phone just days ago. "I promise to love you, I promise to honor you, and I promise always to fight to live. That's all I can do."

Slowly he smiles, both of his perfect dimples appearing. Staring down into my eyes, he murmurs, "I love those words. How about we work them into our wedding vows?"

I nod even as his head lowers. Just a quick graze of his lips against mine, a vow of its own kind.

A promise of more.

Later.

"Right now, sweetheart, we have a delayed-early birthday party to get to. Grace is anxious to see you." Joe tugs my arm.

"Is that what you're calling it now? She doesn't turn four until October, Joe." It's just barely August.

"Listen, this party was supposed to be weeks ago. Dealing with her almost four-year-old's patience lately has not been fun." Joe begins to guide me away from Mary's grave.

"Wait!" I cry out. Squatting, I gather the bouquet I dropped. Carefully, I lay it at the foot of her tombstone. I touch my fingers to the cold granite and whisper something meant just for the woman who will always hold a piece of Joseph Bianco's heart. As she rightfully should.

"Thank you for making sure I stayed safe. I'll be sure to give everyone your love." Standing, I don't feel the breeze lifting the ends of my hair. I remain still until Joe wraps his arm around me from behind. He quietly addresses his lost love.

"Hey, babe. I'll bring Grace by soon." Joe lays his own hand on Mary's stone before he gently guides me away.

"Are you ready to go?" His soft look tells me he didn't miss a thing. I lean into him. "I am."

Together we walk to his car, not saying anything. We let our love fill the silence, knowing it won't last once we get to a party riddled with curious adults and rambunctious four-year-olds.

But that's life.

Our lives.

Thank God.

EPILOGUE

"Mama! I can't find the shoes Aunt Em brought over earlier. Where are they?"

"I ate them," I yell back up the stairs to where Grace is getting ready for her senior prom with Kalie.

"That's not funny." There's a long pause. "Are they with you?"

Running my fingertip over the top of the dark blue box holding Grace's Stuart Weitzman crystal-encrusted heels, I feel the first prick of tears in my eyes. My voice is only slightly huskier when I yell back, "Yes!"

"Bring them up?" Grace's shrieking order is oblivious to my emotional overload. Grace became mine in my heart since that moment in the cemetery when Joe and I left to go to her delayed almost-four-year-old birthday party. She was my stepdaughter for a short time after we got married a year later. And when we felt comfortable Eden and Seth understood they would always be her grandparents, I legally adopted her.

It was a packed courtroom that day with Freemans, Biancos, and Mosses. And none of us had a dry eye by the time the judge proclaimed Grace to be my adopted daughter.

Grace still visits Mary's grave as often as she can. But it's lacrosse season, and since she's the team captain, time is something she doesn't have a lot of. So, Joe and I still make sure there are fresh flowers every month at the base of her tombstone.

She hasn't been forgotten.

"Could you not call me from your cell versus bellowing down the stairs?" I yell back. Picking up my wineglass, I take a long drink while Corinna laughs uproariously. "Keep laughing, sister. Your turn is coming."

Corinna shrugs. "I'm not that worried."

"That's because you plan on sending Nicole with Em to shop for prom dresses!" I declare. Nicole is Colby and Corinna's youngest child and the only daughter of their three children.

"Of course I do. I mean, really, has anything changed over the years?"

Ali walks in from the back deck where the rest of our family is waiting for the big prom dress reveal to pour herself some more wine. "Do you mean in terms of our lives or your fashion sense? Those are very different answers."

The three of us laugh because she is totally right.

Our lives are insane, but we wouldn't have it any other way.

Cassidy and Caleb's oldest, Jonathan and Laura, are due home from their first years at Harvard and Skidmore, respectively, any day now. I should know when, but trying to keep up with Joe, Grace, Joey, and Lily's schedules—not to mention my own—well, I just hope Cassidy programmed in an alert so I don't miss the welcome home barbecue. Their youngest just finished his freshman year of high school.

Ali and Keene's have been dealing with the trauma of girl teen years right alongside Joe and me as Kalie and Grace have remained thick as thieves. Keene swears all the women in his life were put on this planet to turn him gray well before his time. The silver in his hair these days looks good on him. So does being surrounded by all of his women: Ali, Kalie, and their twins, Regina and Valerie.

Jenna, Jake's daughter from his first marriage, heads downstairs from where she's been helping the girls. Her own slightly rounded belly sticks out in front of her. "Holly, I swear to God, if Grace didn't look just like Joe and Mary, I'd swear she was Em's. Talk about a budding fashionista."

Holding my glass away so I don't drop an ounce of my wine, I bang my head against my marble kitchen island. "Just what every mother wants to hear," I joke.

"Em would," Corinna declares.

"Em would what?" She's being tugged into the kitchen by her seventeen-year-old adopted daughter, Talia, whose prom was last weekend since she attends high school in Ridgefield where Jake was recently promoted to the instrumental director of their music department. Their son, Jonah, is coming home tomorrow from his junior year at UConn, following in Ali, Corinna's, Jenna's, and my footsteps.

Go Huskies.

"You want to raise a little fashionista," Ali teases.

"I've helped to raise several of them," she retorts. "Starting with you and Holly."

"I'm just devastated you're not including me on your list," Corinna deadpans.

Em opens and closes her mouth before she simply holds her hand out at Corinna and turns toward the mostly empty bottle of wine for fortification. This is an argument they've had over and over the years, primarily for fun. "We're almost out," she calls out.

"Check the wine fridge," I tell her. "There's more Sancerre in there. It will go great with the chicken."

"We'll be out of it long before then. I'm going to need someone to put a straw in a bottle for me, or I'm killing someone," Cassidy announces as she storms through the door with her youngest son behind her. "Charles Phillip, Go sit in Aunt Holly's living room. Do not turn on the television. Do not use your phone. In fact, hand me your phone right now."

"Mama," Chuck whines.

"Do not push it, young man. Just be glad your father didn't hear what I did." The room goes static at Cassidy's pronouncement. "Now, go. Think about what you said, how it makes me feel, how it would make your father feel, and I will call you when it's time to eat."

"Yes, ma'am," he says meekly, slinking off toward my family room where black-and-white photos of our enormous family cover every available surface.

After Chuck makes it out of earshot, we fall on her like a pack of lemmings. "What did he say?" Em hisses.

Cassidy's ocean-blue eyes narrow in the direction of her fourteen-year-old son. With the mean mug she's sporting and the silver beginning to lighten her dark hair, she looks so much like Keene, there's no way anyone could miss the fact they're biologically related. "I over-heard him ask your boys"—Cassidy nods at Corinna—"to get him condoms since 'his dad hasn't had the talk with him, but there's an older babe at school that he wants to bang.'" Cassidy air quotes.

Corinna sucks in a deep breath and pushes away from the counter. "To which Peter and Michael said?"

"'Dude, you'd better talk with your dad.'"

Corinna relaxes and picks up her glass. "Good. They can live."

Cassidy grins at her. "It's also why they're still outside and only mine was dragged in here. Caleb is going to flip that first, Chuck was so damn disrespectful, and second, he didn't go to him."

We all hear Chuck groan from the couch.

I pitch my voice a little higher. "I wonder if it's one of Grace's friends. I should run upstairs and ask her."

A panicked sound escapes from the vicinity of the couch.

"Hmm. You know, you might be right, Hols. I'm sure Kalie knows her. Let's go ask," Ali agrees, placing her glass on the counter with a clink.

"No, Aunt Holly, Aunt Ali! Mama, I swear, I just wanted to be cool and show off. Pete and Mike were talking shit..." Chuck jumps out of his seat.

"Watch your mouth," Cassidy snaps at her son. He looks properly contrite.

"Sorry, Mama. Pete and Mike were talking about how Uncle

Colby had the talk with them and..." Chuck isn't given a chance to finish as Corinna loses her mind.

"He what? Oh no he didn't. They're barely thirteen!" Stomping over to the doors that lead to my back deck, Corinna storms out in search of her husband and twin sons.

Pursing my lips, I check my watch. Now I'm the one who's yelling upstairs. "Grace? How much more time do you need?"

"Another twenty minutes!"

Kalie's voice comes right after hers. "Thirty tops!"

Ali and I exchange glances before we race for the door, the rest of our sisters close on our heels. Cassidy's the last as she's still scolding Chuck, but she's still not far behind.

She's such an amazing mother. Then again, all my sisters are.

Two hours later, after taking at least two hundred pictures of Grace, Kalie, their dates, and their friends, the kids climbed into a limousine and headed toward Stamford where prom is being held. The remainder of our children—those not at college or living with their own families—are off to sleepovers. Finally, the adults are sitting down for an intimate family dinner for twelve.

Considering there usually are twenty-eight of us when you count Jenna, her husband, and Charlie—who has long since retired from Hudson—it's a riot.

And we love every second of it.

Because we were at our house due to prom instead of the farm, we're gathered around a long picnic table that Joe and his dad made partially from the remnant boards of my original house that stood here fourteen years ago after the fire that almost took my life and ended my future before it truly began.

The sun's just dipped down low enough to cast an orange glow over every inch of the sky it touches. There's raucous laughter around the table. All of our men are still bitching about the pain of their tattoos they got last weekend, with Keene leading the charge. He's appalled he's still having to wear flip-flops. "Suck it up, baby." Ali feels no sympathy. She went through that exact pain when we were eighteen.

It was a shock when Jason announced all our men were going to get tattoos a few weeks ago during a family dinner, "You should know all of us"—he motioned to Caleb, Keene, Colby, Jake, and my husband—"decided we're going to get tatted."

"*What*?" we'd all shouted simultaneously.

"You all bled to become the people you are. To become the people we love, so..." I spun in my arms to face Joe, who at forty-two is still the most gorgeous man I've ever seen. "We had a tattoo artist draw up the arrow Amaryllis used to pierce the flower. We're going to get them in exactly the same places you all have them."

All our men did it too—except one. Charlie. He destroyed all of us when he announced, "I'm going to get a white amaryllis with a golden arrow piercing it. After all, I have to represent both sides of my family. This way I can do it exactly where they intersect, at the single moment where a selfless act turned into love."

Now, I go to reach for my camera, but Joe stays my hand. He nods toward Phil, who's standing next to Jason, holding a drink in his hand. He looks unusually serious.

I kick someone under the table. Ali yelps, gives me a glare, and is about to blast me before she follows my line of sight. She digs her fingers into Keene's arm, who stops talking to Caleb midsentence. Cassidy takes notice and nudges Em. Em swallows her drink before leaning over to whisper in Corinna's ear. Corinna stops Colby's conversation with Charlie by placing her hand over his mouth.

Phil smiles, even as he reaches for Jason's hand.

"We've been living in Collyer for thirty years this summer. In the early days, we scraped every dime together to be able to afford the mansion, the start-up capital for the business, but I knew we'd never give up, and that's because we had each other."

Damn. I reach for my napkin to start mopping the tears from my eyes. Phil continues.

"We're in such a better position now than we were then, but that

has nothing to do with the fact we've met our goals, professionally."
His bright blue eyes take in all of the men who came into our lives
starting with Charlie, moving to Jason, Caleb, Keene, Colby, Jake,
Joe, and then back to Jason again. "There will always be a small part
of us that remains broken; nothing can change that. But that path
led us to this family and to this life which is so much more than so
many have." Taking a deep breath, he continues. "I made you all a
promise in a little trailer years ago, that we would be a family no
matter what happened. A family based on respect, strength, heart,
pride, and beauty. I just wanted to say I'm so proud that not only did
we accomplish that together, but each of you've found your perfect
half who you built your own families on with those same
principles."

Joe's arm slides around my shoulders to support me as Phil's
words cause sobs to rack my body. The glint of the gold arrow from
the tattoo on his wrist winks at me. Every time I see it, I'm struck
dumb.

My eyes are torn from my husband when I hear the cacophony of
tears around me.

All of my sisters are being held by their spouses, and Charlie has
risen to stand by Jason, his arm thrown around my brother-in-law's
shoulders.

"I'd do it all again just to be your brother," Phil whispers. "Every
second of it. Just to be right where I am right now seeing the joy on
your faces."

And that does it.

I jump up out of my seat and fly around the table to wrap my
arms around Phil right about the same time as my sisters. We're a
sobbing huddle as we hold on to the man who could have walked
away from any of us at any time. He had no obligation morally or
legally to bind himself to us. Only we know the real sacrifices he
made for our family. As exasperating as he can be, he's the most loyal,
devoted brother anyone could ever wish for.

Then, now, or ever.

And the only thing that holds him to us is a heart so strong that

bleeds because of love and a tattoo of a flower on his wrist that repre-
sents that.

"I love you, Phil," I whisper.

"Love you, Phil," Ali murmurs.

"Always," Corinna adds.

"There aren't enough words," Cassidy chokes out.

Em says, "Yes there are. Phil taught us the right ones. We're
family."

We stand in our huddle for a few minutes before the air changes.
A male hand slides over Phil's shoulder. "Thank you, brother," Keene
says hoarsely. "You didn't just save them, you saved me too." Cassidy
and Ali start sobbing uncontrollably. From bitter rivals trying to find
their way in a complicated family dynamic, the two men have
become so close throughout the years as the wounds of Keene's past
healed.

Caleb comes up behind Cassidy. "That's true of all of us."

I feel Joe's warmth behind me even though he doesn't say
anything. He nods his head against my shoulder in assent.

Tears are falling down Phil's face hard and fast. Jason pushes in
between him and Cassidy. "I've been in love with you since the
moment Corinna pulled you into the lake on top of me."

Watery laughs break out around our huddle. Jason continues. "I'd
do it all over again right alongside you."

Phil's face contorts, and he shoves his face against Jason's
shoulder.

Then Charlie pushes in on Phil's other side. He tugs him into his
arms tightly. We all hear him whisper, "Love you, son. Proud of the
man you became and the family you raised."

It takes hours for us to recover from Phil breaking down in Charlie's arms.

LATER THAT NIGHT, I'm tracing my fingers around the tattoo on Joe's
wrist where the arrow rests. His tattoo was difficult because of the

scars he sustained from being burned a few years back while rescuing a resident from Collyer's local nursing home. It's what took both him and Brett out of the field and put them both permanently on desk duty. Joe sustained burns to 15 percent of his body, Brett 20.

They both recovered, but it wasn't easy.

We had to endure painful skin grafts. There were physical therapy sessions which put Joe into a deep depression that affected our kids. And finally, I put my foot down and demanded he get help from psychologists brought in by Victims Assistance, Alice, even Seth. Joe was infuriated, saying he was handling it.

"You're not!" I remember screaming at him. "I'm so afraid I'm going to lose you the way you lost Mary, and I'll be the one broken." I tore out of our house and jumped in the car to just get away from his bitterness, his frustration—all being taken out on me because I loved him through the anger, pain, and fear.

By the time I got home six hours later, having forgotten my cell on the kitchen charger, Joe was frantic. When I walked in, eyes swollen from crying my frustration out at Candlewood Lake, he'd been running his good hand over his closely shorn hair in aggravation.

"Don't you ever go driving off when you're that upset!" he'd roared the minute I'd walked in the door. "Do you know how out of my mind I've been trying to reach you? And where's your phone?" He'd picked it up and threw it across the room. It shattered the screen.

It was the first emotion he'd shown since he realized he was going to be benched after the fire.

I burst into tears.

It wasn't the first time over the next several weeks either of us would, but God, were they healing.

Joe's mental and physical recovery made him realize the criticality of the Victims Assistance program more than ever. When his father offered him the chief role, deciding it was time to turn over the reins to a new generation and spend more time with Denise, he turned it down. Instead, Joe went before Collyer's Town Council to ask for funding for an assistant chief position to be created with that role directly in charge of a more formalized Victims Assistance Program for both the CFD and CPD. He was eloquent when he stated, "We're losing too many of our brothers and sisters to the aftereffects of their jobs. We ask them to be our heroes, but we don't give them the tools to regain their superpowers."

It was a unanimous vote of approval.

As for me, Amaryllis Photography doubled in work with the marketing Jenna put out there. I still focus on my first love, weddings, but I finally found a full-time photography hire who is more than able to handle all other special occasion events—things like graduations and family reunions. It was a good thing Ali never quite got around to teaching Megan Murphy how to write her resume all those years ago, I think a little smugly. Otherwise, she might not be happily engaged to a certain police detective and planning her wedding for the late fall.

Feeling blessed, I close my eyes and let out a soft sigh before I kiss Joe on the most cherished part of his body.

His heart.

"What's going through your head, Hols?" My head is tipped back so I'm looking into the dark blue eyes that breed true in the Bianco men.

But Lily? She has my eyes. They light up even the worst of our days.

"I still wonder how I deserve this life—the family, you, the kids." Joe frowns. I quickly continue. "Every day, I'm given more blessings, Joe. So many. Tonight was another one."

Joe slides down so his face is next to mine. "Because you have a heart that's as gold as your eyes, as gold as the arrow I have put on my skin as a reminder of you? Because not once, but twice, you reminded me why it was so important to live?"

"Joe..." I protest, but not for long as he rolls me onto my back.

"Love has a way of obliterating pain. Haven't we learned that?" I still as he continues to whisper, "But trust me, we earned this life. And sweetheart, we'll continue to earn more of it. But there will be times when it gets dark. Just keep holding on to me with all the love you've got, and we can make it through anything together."

In my heart, I know he's right. I also know every hurt, every scar, every bruise that's been heaped upon us and the ones we inadvertently laid upon each other have just made us stronger.

The way it has with all of my family.

Because if love has a way of obliterating pain, it also gives you the strength to live fully. And live free.

"I love you," I whisper, my lips grazing his.

"And I, you."

Those are the last words we say for quite a while.

THE END

COMING SOON

I've experienced the ways love can change a poor man into a rich one, a sinner to a saint, and make people beg for redemption.

Yet nothing I'd ever done was as profound as marrying the woman I love.

Every mission I took was a risk worth taking knowing I'd go home to her loving arms.

What I didn't know was in my quest to right all the wrongs of the world, I was destroying the only part of it I'd die for - my marriage.

The ripple effect of miscommunication and the sin of my omissions would change all of our lives.

And it would be my wife who would pay the price.

Ripple Effect by Tracey Jerald
February 3, 2020

Amazon/Kindle Unlimited
Add to your Goodreads TBR
Sign up for Go Live Notice

ALSO BY TRACEY JERALD

Standalones

Close Match

Ripple Effect

The Amaryllis Series

Free to Dream

Free to Run

Free to Rejoice

Free to Breathe

Free to Believe

Free to Live

Coming Soon

Return By Air - June 2020

Also coming soon, keep a close eye on the Lady Boss Press site! Tracey is honored to be writing as part of the Kristen Proby's Boudreaux universe!

Title and release date to be announced very soon!

WHERE TO GET HELP

On average in the United States they estimate every 28 seconds someone attempts suicide. In 2017, 47,123 across the nation were tragically successful. That's 129 people per day or approximately one person every eleven minutes. (American Association of Suicidology) In addition, they estimate there were an additional 1,179,325 attempts that weren't fatal. No matter how you look at those numbers, there are too many lives affected.

It is important to shine a light on topics like this with the hope that it will provide people the opportunity to ask for help, to seek intervention, and to try to heal.

There is no shame in asking for help. If you need assistance or someone to talk to the National Suicide Prevention Lifeline can connect you to a local crisis line 24 hours a day, 7 days a week. Call 1-800-273-TALK (8255), or go to Directory of AAS Accredited Crisis Centers / www.suicidepreventionlifeline.org.

ACKNOWLEDGEMENTS

I was on an airplane when I typed "The End" on Holly's story. So first, to all of my fellow passengers who gave me strange looks as I sobbed, I'm sorry. I hope I didn't scare you too much. It really was an emotional moment for me.

To Nathan, my heart, my soul, my beloved. Really, that says it all, but thank you for supporting the need inside of me to write in so many big and small ways. I love you forever.

To my son, I love you beyond the words I'm typing right now. In the time since I first started the Amaryllis Series, your curiosity about what Mommy has been doing behind her computer has grown. Maybe someday you can read these books. Like in about twenty years, okay?

Mom, thank you for all the little ways you support me. You intuitively know when I'm about to rip out all my hair and say or do something to keep my spirits up. I love you.

Jen, if you're reading this before the book, you should know better by now. Stop and go back to the Legend. There are not enough ways to thank you for being everything to my heart and my life. Oh, but I can thank you for making me watch The Mummy.

My Meows, now that we've solved the world's problems with the revelation of home training, we're all set, right? Like we've said before, there's nothing we can't do as long as we're together. I love you all so much.

To the Bacon and Bingo Brunch Brigade. I'm still holding my side laughing from that night. BTW, who's responsible for collecting the money?

To Jennifer Wolfel. You must know I love you if I dissed my beloved Yankees. Enough said. Thank you for your honesty and wisdom.

To Sandra Depukat from One Love Editing. Yes, I will give you a cookbook. But it will be just for you. And no, you will not need to edit it! Either that or we will just have to go shopping at Free People. You make me shine. I love you so hard.

To Holly Malgeri. My twin, I am so blessed to have you back! It's a circle; starting and ending the series with you by my side. Having you in my life makes every day better because you're you.

My cover designer, Amy Queue of QDesigns, it took one shot! Your brilliance continues to astound me. Love you!

To the team at Foreword PR, I know there is so much that happens behind the scenes that I can't begin to comprehend. Alissa Marino, you are my hero!

Linda Russell, yeah, you're getting your own line. Deal with it. How do I thank you for everything you've given to me? For the wisdom I needed? For the faith I lacked? For the kick in the ass when I needed it. You are truly family; tribe. And oh, so much more.

For my Facebook group — Tracey's Tribe. You are my home. I'm sending my love to you always. Did you find all your call-outs in the book? XOXO

To all of the bloggers who read and take the time to review my books, thank you from the bottom of my heart. It is not an easy job, and I appreciate every word you write.

And finally, to my readers. I am overwhelmed by your emails, your comments, and reviews. I love hearing from each and every one of you. Thank you for your support and for choosing to read my words.

ABOUT THE AUTHOR

Tracey Jerald knew she was meant to be a writer when she would re-write the ending of books in her head when she was a young girl growing up in southern Connecticut. It wasn't long before she was typing alternate endings and extended epilogues "just for fun".

After college in Florida, where she obtained a degree in Criminal Justice, Tracey traded the world of law and order for IT. Her work for a world-wide internet startup transferred her to Northern Virginia where she met her husband in what many call their own happily ever after. They have one son.

When she's not busy with her family or writing, Tracey can be found in her home in north Florida drinking coffee, reading, training for a runDisney event, or feeding her addiction to HGTV.

Made in the USA
Columbia, SC
09 March 2020